Cathy Williams can remember [...] Mills & Boon books as a teenage[...] she's writing them she remains a[...] her, there is nothing like creating romantic stories and engaging plots, and each and every book is a new adventure. Cathy lives in London. Her three daughters—Charlotte, Olivia and Emma—have always been, and continue to be, the greatest inspirations in her life.

Lorraine Hall is a part-time hermit and full-time writer. She was born with an old soul and her head in the clouds—which, it turns out, is the perfect combination for spending her days creating thunderous alpha heroes and the fierce, determined heroines who win their hearts. She lives in a potentially haunted house with her soulmate and a rumbustious band of hermits in training. When she's not writing romance, she's reading it.

SECRETS BEHIND HIS RING

CATHY WILLIAMS

LORRAINE HALL

MILLS & BOON

First published in Great Britain 2024
by Mills & Boon, an imprint of HarperCollins*Publishers* Ltd,
1 London Bridge Street, London, SE1 9GF

www.harpercollins.co.uk

HarperCollins*Publishers*, Macken House, 39/40 Mayor Street Upper, Dublin 1, D01 C9W8, Ireland

ISBN: 978-0-263-32024-4

09/24

MIX
Paper | Supporting
responsible forestry
FSC™ C007454

This book contains FSC™ certified paper and other controlled sources to ensure responsible forest management.

For more information visit www.harpercollins.co.uk/green.

Printed and Bound in the UK using 100% Renewable Electricity at CPI Group (UK) Ltd, Croydon, CR0 4YY

EMERGENCY ENGAGEMENT

CATHY WILLIAMS

MILLS & BOON

To my wonderful daughter Emma
and the inspiration that she is

CHAPTER ONE

AND...BREATHE... YOU'RE here now, so just...breathe.

Unlike the brash glass towers everywhere, the Moreno HQ was housed in an anonymous grey, five-storey, brutalist slab that felt threatening in its lack of pretentiousness. Inside, however, was an eye-watering marvel of pale marble, glass and concrete. Sammy, head down and walking at speed towards the reception area, cut a slight and unimposing figure: five-foot-three, close-cropped dark hair with skin as pale as milk and huge, cut-glass green eyes. Under one arm was her portfolio: five years of hopes, dreams and ambitions were contained within, not to mention blood, sweat and tears.

Most businesses in the heart of London would have been bustling with people. At least, that was what Sammy had vaguely assumed. Here, however, it was an oasis of deathly calm—very unnerving, to say the least. She wished that she'd made a stand and insisted on Rafael Moreno travelling to Yorkshire to see *her,* instead of her having to make her way to London, at great personal expense. He was the one who was in the process of ruining her life, after all.

Fat chance of that happening, though.

Phil, the assistant bank manager at the local building

society, had been brilliant over the months and years with all her financial stuff. She had gone to school with him, and had been in his class right the way through, and he had suggested to Clifford that he could do her a favour and get her a meeting with Rafael. It was the way it worked in a small place where everyone knew everyone else.

So travelling to London? It was a small price to pay to see the Big Man, Sammy thought without an ounce of gratitude.

She padded her way to the ice-cold, smoothly polished concrete desk behind which two incredibly beautiful girls sat in front of a bank of wafer-thin laptops.

'I have an appointment with Mr Moreno.'

'Name, please?'

'Samantha Payne.' She waited while an impeccably groomed blonde took a rudely long time scrolling through her screen before nodding, without bothering to look at her at all.

'You can go up—top floor. You'll be met there. I've been advised to tell you that Mr Moreno works to a tight schedule. He can't spare you more than half an hour.'

'I'll make sure to be grateful for small mercies,' Sammy muttered under her breath, turning towards the small bank of discreet chrome lifts that blended seamlessly into the pale-grey walls.

Her heart was pounding as the lift purred its way up four floors. She could have taken the stairs—she would have welcomed the exercise as a little extra thinking time—but the business of asking where they were seemed more trouble than it was worth. Besides, there was such a thing as too much thinking time. Too much thinking time risked teetering into unhelpful panic.

Rafael Moreno: the self-made billionaire whose face seemed to be relentlessly plastered on the cover of every tabloid gossip magazine month after month, although he was so much more than just a sexy guy with an army of women swooning over him. He was also the golden boy who had made a fortune before he'd turned twenty-five—a tech genius who had refused to be limited to just tech and had moved some of his considerable fortune into other, equally profitable areas that included commercial developments, boutique hotels across the world and, most recently, his own wine label.

He was the guy who couldn't be stopped when it came to climbing the ladder. In fact, Sammy reckoned that, when it came to Rafael Moreno, there were no more rungs left. He'd climbed all of them and was aiming for whatever there was beyond ladders.

Crazy, when she looked back and remembered the boy he used to be. She didn't think Rafael Moreno did much looking back, though, but who knew?

Suddenly, the lift doors opened and, sure enough, there was another stunning woman waiting to escort her through to wherever Rafael had his office.

Here, at least, there was the quiet hum of vast sums of money being made. Sammy had no idea who occupied the other floors of the building but the men and women here, all decked out in snappy clothes, were serious and focused, and barely glanced in her direction as she walked by the open space with its clever glass partitions and luscious plants. How many screens did one person need, anyway? Everyone seemed to be facing an army of them on their chrome-and-glass desks. There were more computers here than people.

'I should advise you that Mr Moreno...'

'Yes.' Sammy pre-empted what was coming. 'Is a very busy man who only has half an hour to spare for me. I was already warned by the girl downstairs. Don't worry, I don't plan on locking the door and keeping him prisoner until he hears what I have to say.'

This was met with stony silence that lasted until an imposing door was pushed open...and then, on the threshold of his office, nerves really kicked in. Yes, she'd seen his picture here and there in grainy print; and yes, she'd often glanced at reports of his meteoric progress in the financial jungle, where he took no prisoners; but was she ready to meet this guy? Maybe not...

She disapproved of him on every level. She'd disapproved of him fifteen years ago when he'd entered their small, comfortably cushioned world in the back of beyond like something from another planet, disrupting routines and flouting conventions. And she disapproved of him now because, from every report she'd ever seen, he'd become just what she'd expected—a guy who played by his own rules and didn't give a damn about anybody else. A man who didn't glance over his shoulder to see what havoc he might have left in his wake.

He had his back to her and was staring out of the window but then he turned round slowly, giving her plenty of time to realise that he was still as sinfully sexy as he had been as a sixteen-year-old—with his raven-black hair, dark, dark eyes with eyelashes any girl would kill for, his features chiselled to perfection.

The only difference was this was no boy. This was a man: tougher, harder, colder...the sharp contours of his face betraying experiences learned over the years in a ruthless climb to the top.

She'd wondered whether he would recognise her. Fifteen years was a long time; she'd been a kid of just twelve, invisible behind her shyness and early adolescence.

He didn't have a clue who she was. She could see it in his cool, closed expression as he looked at her in silence for a few seconds.

'Sit.'

Noticeably, he remained lounging by the window as she shuffled to the chair in front of his desk and rested her portfolio on the ground next to her.

'You're here about the hotel.'

Rafael strolled towards his desk, dark eyes pinned to the elfin girl in front of him whose face looked vaguely familiar, although he was damned if he could put his finger on it.

He knew what she was here about: some nonsense about the hotel he had bought. Of course, the deed was done; the hotel up in Yorkshire, along with the various outbuildings on either side of it, belonged to him. He had bought the lot and he had no intention of yielding to any bleeding-heart sob stories about slicing up his acquisition to share with anyone else.

But he had some experience of people from that part of the world. It was a closed community, suspicious of outsiders and happy to close ranks to make life difficult for them. He didn't fancy a difficult life, so he'd agreed to this meeting—but it was going to be a waste of time for both of them.

He glanced at his watch and, when he looked back at

her, her eyes were cool and scornful. They were green eyes, clear as glass, framed by thick, dark lashes and set against smooth, pale skin. Under the heavy jumper and thick, dark skirt, which he suspected had been worn in a token gesture to the fact that this was a meeting of sorts, she was slight. Her dark hair was very short, but it suited her, emphasising the delicacy of her heart-shaped face and the hugeness of those green eyes.

Right now, however, there was nothing fragile about either her posture or her expression.

'I'm here about the outbuilding attached to the hotel, to be precise.'

'This is hardly orthodox,' Rafael drawled, moving to sit behind the desk so that she now felt in the position of someone being interviewed for a job she wasn't going to get. 'Cutting to the chase, I've bought the hotel, just as I've bought the places alongside it. As you'll probably know, I have every intention of developing the lot into a niche boutique hotel, and taking those acres of tumbleweed and overgrown fields and doing something creative with them. A mower might prove to be a good start on that. I've cast an eye over your objections and it would seem that…' he scrolled through his computer, then looked at her '…your plans were to buy one of the outbuildings for yourself?'

'Correct.'

'That's unfortunate for you. You have my heartfelt sympathy but business, as you know, is business.'

'This is more than just *about business* for me,' Sammy said through gritted teeth. 'I've spent *years* putting money aside so that I can accumulate a deposit to buy somewhere suitable for my venture. That outbuilding was my dream come true because I had also got someone in to look at converting the upstairs into a place for me to live.'

'And that's a shame,' Rafael said politely. 'You might have something to say about Clifford selling the hotel to me, when he'd presumably already accepted an offer from you for the building attached to it, but...' He shrugged—as if, "what do you expect me to do?"—and kept his eyes pinned to her face.

'I have, as it happens! You offered him a stupid amount of money. His daughter is ill and that sort of money would mean that he'd be able to give her private medical treatment. He was in a no-win position.'

'Hardly my fault.'

'The hotel was doing fine, Mr Moreno! It was making sufficient money with the regulars, and in the summer months it was holding its own. It's part of the community. It's been there for over eighty years—and you want to bulldoze it!'

'It's decrepit and in need of some serious money spending on it. Plus, it's heading in the wrong direction when it comes to making a profit. Trust me on this, Miss Payne. This is my business—I can spot something living on borrowed time from a mile away. There was no way Clifford was going to be able to keep on top of the repairs. He knew that. I did him a favour. If your little concern happened to fall by the wayside, then you need to step back and look at the bigger picture.'

'The bigger picture being the usual situation of a large, faceless conglomerate consuming the small, family business? Clifford and I had agreed that the money he made from selling that side-building to me would have gone towards upgrading the hotel!'

'I know how much he offered you the place for. It would have been a drop in the ocean when it comes to making a dent in the work needed to haul that decaying old place into the twenty-first century.'

Sammy swallowed and tried to control her temper which was threatening to break its leash and run haywire. She dropped her eyes and clasped her fingers on her lap.

'Why did you come here?' Rafael asked softly. 'Was it to try and get me to change my mind—even though the machinery has already started rolling for completion on the new hotel within the next couple of weeks?'

'I've worked my fingers to the bone for the past five years.' She did her best not to sound self-pitying, because by the looks of it this wasn't a guy who empathised with anyone's plight. 'Worked to get myself into a place where I could actually buy somewhere to open my patisserie and café. I've sorted out all the equipment and it hasn't been cheap. I've done the maths and worked out how to make a living doing what I love and what I'm good at. Clifford felt awful about selling to you. I was the first person he told. He suggested...'

'What did he suggest?'

'He suggested that you sell the outbuilding to me. If you want to somehow modernise it to fit in with your plans for the hotel, then maybe we could work out a re-payment plan. I know it'll make money—with its location, and it being attached to the hotel, there's footfall. I would be willing to pay the mortgage even if I couldn't set up business immediately, even if I had to wait for work to be done...'

Rafael burst out laughing.

'My apologies,' he said, without a trace of apology in his voice. 'But let me show you something.'

He fiddled on the keyboard and then swivelled the screen round so that she was looking at it, then he vaulted upright, his body long, lean and fluid, and swerved to stand behind her. He leant down, his hand resting on the arm of the leather chair in which she was sitting, and pointed to the screen.

Sammy's vision blurred. She could make out something impressive and fancy, spinning round on the screen to afford a view from several angles, but it was hard to focus on anything because every nerve in her body was quivering at his sudden proximity.

'So, you understand why that would be impossible?'

'Sorry?'

Rafael stood up and then perched on the edge of his desk so that now she had nowhere to look but at him... and the the brown column of his neck where the white shirt was unbuttoned, cuffed to the elbows, the way the dark whorls of hair curled around the metal strap of his watch and the tight pull of his trousers over muscular thighs. Memories of her fourteen-year-old self gazing at him from the side-lines in those long summer months before he and his father had upped sticks and left now accosted her, making her thinking sluggish and woolly.

'Clifford owned a hotel rooted in the past,' Rafael said. He was talking slowly and gently, the voice of someone trying to explain the obvious to a halfwit. 'The entire lay-out of the place left a lot to be desired. Some of the bedrooms actually shared a bathroom! Others had fireplaces that were so blocked, it's a wonder they weren't a registered fire hazard. It might have been languishing in its faded glory as a traditional timepiece, ticking along like an ancient grandfather clock, but that formula no longer works in this day and age. Those outbuildings? Falling apart at the seams. Destined for landfill, I'm afraid. The beautiful countryside in that part of the world demands something that people actually want to pay money to stay in, and that hotel and everything alongside it stopped fitting the bill fifty years ago.'

'Clifford's great-grandfather...'

'Look, don't get me wrong, I sympathise with you and I admire you for having the guts to come here and make your case. But the truth is, I'm doing you a favour. If you'd bought that outbuilding, you would have found yourself lumbered with a liability in five years' time when the main hotel started to fall apart.'

Rafael swept aside any further pointless objections with a wave of his hand. 'As a gesture of goodwill, I will reimburse you for any money you might have spent in the expectation of getting the place, although I'm assuming you will be able to make use of whatever equipment you may have bought wherever you end up?'

He paused, allowing an uncomfortable silence to gather between them before continuing with an elegant shrug, 'I'll admit that the prospect of a patisserie would have held considerable appeal, especially with the upstairs done up as a place of residence, but I have no intention of keeping that building. It would require too much work, given the state that it's in, and besides, there's no place for it, as you've seen for yourself from what I've just shown you. My team of architects lean more towards a minimalist look than shambolic clutter.'

He stood up, looked down at her for a few seconds and frowned.

'Do I know you from somewhere?'

Sammy gazed back at him with a sinking heart.

'So, there's nothing I can do to persuade you to…?'

'Completely reconfigure the design of the hotel so that I can incorporate your plans through sheer goodness of heart? No. I'm afraid not. And, like I said…' his voice grew more gentle '…you're better off finding somewhere that wouldn't end up on the scrap heap anyway in a few years' time. Surely there are other premises you could look at?'

'My heart was set on Rafter's Hotel. Like I said, it's a really important part of the community, and it fitted the bill in so many ways. I'm sure whatever problems there were with the building's age could have been handled.' She raised her eyes to look him directly in the eye. 'If you had no intention of doing anything about the situation, why did you bother seeing me in the first place?'

'Good question, and deserving of an answer. Truth is, I like to do my due diligence when it comes to my hotels.'

'Your due diligence?'

'Make sure I'm not going to be treading on anyone's toes. You'd be surprised how tedious it can be dealing with a cohort of people who decide to make a stand against something they don't want.'

'And the general consensus was…?'

'That a renovation would do a lot to revive the community. My hotels come with a solid reputation and the year-round tourist influx would benefit a host of small businesses. Naturally, if Clifford had chosen not to sell, I would have shrugged and moved on, but I managed to make him see sense. I can assure you that I was extremely generous in my offer. He got a hell of a lot more from me than he would have from anyone else. Aside from that, I agreed to meet with you because, like I said, you deserved to be told first-hand why your deal went belly-up. I may be a businessman but I'm not without some sympathy for what you're going through.'

'You over-paid for the hotel?'

'I'm a generous guy.'

'I didn't realise billionaires made their money by feeling sorry for people.'

'I have a personal tie to that part of the world, if you really want to know.'

'Royal Stanton Grammar.'

She knew the school he'd attended for the two years he'd been living in the village adjacent to the one in which the hotel was located. Their eyes met and he held her gaze as he rooted through his memories, trying to dredge up any recollection of her.

His dark eyes narrowed and she fidgeted.

'So I *do* know you...'

'You were in Stanton for two years,' Sammy confirmed.

'So I was. I don't recall your name...'

'It was a long time ago and you've turned into a billionaire since then. No surprise you haven't got a clue who I am. Making billions must have taken quite a bit of your time.'

'Payne... Payne...' he said softly, frowning. He sat back and stared out through the window before looking at her once again. 'Did you plan on using your familiarity with me to your advantage?'

'No. I hadn't planned on telling you that I knew who you were at all.'

'Samantha Payne.' His eyes stayed fixed on her pale face and he tilted his head to one side and stared. Of course, he recognised her now, and was surprised he hadn't sooner—but then he hadn't been expecting someone from his past to show up in his present.

He'd been truthful when he'd told her he'd wanted to do the decent thing and explain the situation first-hand—while still, of course, making sure to impress on her that he was intransigent in his decision. Now, he felt a reluctant admiration for her tenacity in not backing down, even though she must have remembered that, well, even as a teenager, backing down had never been his thing.

'I should go.'

Rafael didn't say anything. He wasn't about to embark on a voyage down memory lane. Yet, against his better judgement, he remembered those strange, unsettling days when he and his father had gone to the very village she had mentioned because his father had managed to land himself a two-year stint working on a building site eight miles away. It had been a basic job but anything had been better than staying put in the East End of London with his father buried in misery and depression because he'd found that his wife hadn't just been unfaithful once, or twice, but too many times to count...

Theirs had been a volatile, disintegrating marriage to which his father had desperately clung even when the arguments had come on a daily basis—a marriage that should never have happened. It had been washed up in a series of confessions that Isabella Moreno hadn't bothered to hide from her only son, sixteen years old and growing

harder and tougher with each shouted, gloating, embit-
tered revelation. Yes, he had loved his father, but he had
also pitied him for not having the strength to walk away
from what had been bad for him.

Accusations had been hurled and tears had been shed.
If Rafael hadn't grown up by then, he'd certainly grown
up afterwards, when the dust had settled and his mother
had left arm in arm with her new, rich lover and no for-
warding address.

'You're a big boy now,' had been her parting words to
Rafael. 'You don't need me here any longer.'

'Did I ever?' he had returned, before leaving the house
for a welcome dose of fresh air.

His father had lost the plot. At the time, Rafael had had
no idea why. It wasn't as though theirs had ever been a
marriage made in heaven. To a child, it had been black
and white: it was teenage lust that had propelled his parents into an unwanted pregnancy. Juan Miguel Moreno,
aged just eighteen, had walked a very pregnant Isabella
Gutierrez up the aisle, she too only just eighteen, only
for her to give birth a fortnight later.

From memory, things hadn't been bad to start with, but
time had put paid to any notion of their marriage working. Rafael had grown up knowing just how frustrated his
mother felt at being with a guy who adored her but was
never going to make enough money to keep her satisfied.

She'd been the opposite of a domestic goddess. She'd
worked shifts, although afterwards Rafael reckoned she'd
been doing a whole lot more than working. She'd gone
out without saying where to, and she'd left her husband
to pick up the slack on the home front.

Why she hadn't left sooner was a mystery—perhaps

the habit of her marriage and the predictability of a husband she no longer loved but still relied upon had kept
her rooted until someone rich had come along to rescue
her. After she'd left, his father had taken to the bottle
to cope. If the job offer many miles away in some nice,
healthy countryside hadn't come along, Lord only knew
where things would have ended up. But they had gone
to that little village with its little village school and…

'Colin Payne.' He looked at the elfin figure in front
of him with her defiance and her angry green eyes and
made the connection.

Before she could say anything, his intercom buzzed
and his PA reminded him of the meeting he had at the
Shard.

Without taking his eyes from her face, Rafael told his
PA that he wouldn't make it and, before she could recover
from her astonishment, he surprised her further by telling her to cancel whatever remained on his calendar for
the rest of the day.

'I thought you could only spare me half an hour,'
Sammy said coolly.

'Things change.'

'Nothing's changed. You can't or won't do anything
to help me, and I get it. It was stupid of me to think otherwise.'

'Colin Payne was your brother. *Is* your brother.'

Sammy shrugged.

'He was in my form for the two years we were at
school together,' Rafael recalled.

'I didn't realise that you were ever *at* school. I thought
school was just somewhere you visited now and again
when it took your fancy.'

'Good times, bad times,' he murmured with a sudden grin. 'I admit, I didn't set a good example when it came to behaviour back in those days.'

'Actually, that's the understatement of the decade. But that was a long time ago and I haven't come here to reminisce.'

'I remember your brother and...now that I think about it... I remember *you*. You were very shy, always peeping from under that fringe of yours. Your hair was long back then—probably why I didn't recognise you immediately. I have a keen eye for faces.'

'Like I said, Mr Moreno, I didn't come here to talk about the past.'

Rafael watched the rise of delicate colour in her cheeks, shaken out of his usual steely self-control and aware of her—not just as someone to whom he conceded he owed an explanation, but as someone who...belonged to memories he had put away in a box, hidden and never to be aired. He was surprised that he hadn't remembered sooner because she did, in fact, have quite a distinctive face. Those eyes...

'You must have been...what...thirteen, fourteen when I had called it a day with A Levels and was packing my bags to leave? You weren't like the other girls, that's for sure.'

'You mean the other girls who kept begging for your attention?'

'Adolescence can be a heady time for some.'

'Not you, though. You ignored all of them. You missed the backstage tears.'

'I was more fascinated by the older women back then.'

'Good to know. Thank you for your time.'

She began to gather her things to leave, but Rafael

stopped her by asking, 'What's your brother doing now? He wanted to go into medicine, if I remember.'

'He's a nurse now. He ended up having to repeat a year after you disappeared. He'd always been a model student until you came along.'

Rafael didn't say anything. He remembered what life had been like back then, with his father a mess and him having to pick up the pieces. Rafael had had to make sure he got himself off to work and not back on the bottle because they'd needed the money to survive. He remembered himself as an angry, disillusioned, confused teenaged boy raging against the world, loving his fragile father but hating him at the same time.

There had been a lot of truancy back then but he'd been so bright that he'd never fallen behind. He hadn't asked anyone to copy him, but some of the other boys in his class had followed his lead. He'd been too wrapped up in his own anger to give much of a damn about how skipping classes might affect them.

That said, he wasn't in the business of apologising to anyone for anything. Besides, tough times made for tough people, and tough people did well in life. They knew how to handle its obstacles. He was a fine example of that.

'I never encouraged anyone to follow me.'

'But you never did anything to discourage them, either!'

'I did my own thing. I wasn't in the business of setting examples to anyone. At the time, there were more interesting things to do than listening to teachers who really didn't know as much as me and, if there were kids who wanted to fall in with that, then who was I to start preaching to them?'

'That's incredibly arrogant!'

'Maybe, or maybe I'm just being honest. I'm sorry if you feel that your brother went off the rails because of me, although it's probably healthier to think that everyone is responsible for the decisions they make. It's counter-productive to blame other people for their own poor choices. Send him my regards and, like I said, I would be happy to compensate you for any loss on whatever equipment you may have bought. I mean that. It took guts coming here and I admire you for that.'

She was already rising to her feet and heading to the door. He didn't try to stop her. He wasn't going to change his plans just because they happened to share a tenuous connection.

But he had to force himself not to follow her. Instead, he remained where he was, watching the angry sway of her slender hips as she stormed out of the door.

Lord only knew what his PA in the adjoining office made of the fuming slip of a thing who had just slammed a door behind her. Generally speaking, no one slammed doors behind them when they left his office, not even ex-girlfriends, which was a good thing; there had been enough angry exes to make the building rattle if they ever decided to join forces and slam doors.

Rafael enjoyed a colourful love life. He enjoyed women and, when he was dating, he was one hundred percent attentive and faithful. He just wasn't into staying the course. He didn't have the appetite for the disillusioning business of marriage and the pointless hope that fuelled it. He was always honest about that—some might say to a fault—but still, many an angry ex who had expected the unattainable would have slammed doors had they not feared his disapproval.

This woman, though... She hadn't thought twice. He rose to his feet, suddenly edgy. When he glanced down, it was to find that she had forgotten the folder she had brought with her and dumped on the ground by the chair.

It was too late to chase her down the road waving a folder...not his style anyway. He would have a look to see if a contact number was anywhere inside, or at the very least her email address. He would get his PA to do the honours and return it.

He settled into his leather chair, kept all calls on hold and flipped open the portfolio she had managed to forget in her furious haste.

Halfway to Harrogate on the train, Sammy belatedly remembered the damned portfolio. It had taken her days to meticulously prepare her business plan, but no way was she going to turn around and go back for it. Nor was she going to phone and ask for it to be sent.

Frankly, after the reception she'd been given, it was probably winging its way to the dump by now. She hadn't given it a passing thought because she'd been so worked up when she'd stormed out of his office, slamming the door behind her, aware of his glamorous PA half-rising to her feet in shock as she'd swept by. All those uninterested people who hadn't noticed when she'd arrived had sat up and taken stock when she'd left—which had almost made her smile, except the last thing she'd been in the mood to do had been to crack a smile at anything.

Of course, it was the mention of her brother that had been her undoing. She had been shocked that he'd recognised her and then to remember Colin…and, to top it off, to remember her as the shy thing peeping at him while all the bolder girls had flaunted themselves in the smallest outfits they could get away with.

She stared through the window at scenery flashing past.

Rafael and Colin had been in the same form. Who could ever have predicted that Colin, always so quiet and studious, would have become a dedicated member of Rafael's fan club? He'd gone off the rails, in true Rafael Moreno style and had dumped the school books for skipping class, as if he'd been making up for all that lost time when he'd been so diligent. Then, Rafael had disappeared in a puff of smoke, and her brother had discovered how woefully behind he had fallen. He'd failed four of the eight exams he'd taken. Rafael Moreno might have been capable of attending one class and still getting straight As, but no one else had been, including her brother. Everything had been delayed a year and her mother, fragile after the divorce, had become a bag of nerves all over again.

Sammy simmered and fumed and wondered what the hell happened now. She would have to start looking into things in the coming week. She rented somewhere at the moment, but she'd blithely given in her notice because she'd anticipated the fun of living above her café and doing the place up, somewhere that would be all hers. The thought of getting back in the rental market yet again made her feel sick. Her mum lived ten miles away in the nearest town. Should she migrate there for a while?

Sammy knew that she should feel angry and betrayed, because she had set her hopes high, had had it all just within her grasp... But how on earth could she be angry with Clifford when concerns for his ill daughter had driven his decision?

It was quite a lot to think about and yet, with all those pressing worries on her mind, she found herself drifting off to sleep, thinking of something else of a very different nature.

Or rather, *someone* else.

Rafael, with his darkly forbidding good looks and eyes that seemed to bore straight into her. He'd looked at her and she'd felt herself go hot and cold and then hot all over again. All she could hope was that he hadn't noticed.

He'd made her relive a youthful infatuation and she hated that. She might not have openly flung herself into his path like some of the other girls but, as twelve had turned to fourteen, she had done her fair share of daydreaming. She'd been no different from everyone else. Like them, she had never met anyone as fascinating or as good-looking as Rafael Moreno.

She'd been smart enough not to show it, but it seemed that he'd noticed her looking from the side-lines anyway: a thin, boyish, self-conscious adolescent without any of the generous assets all the other girls had seemed to have.

Memories floated in and out as she fell asleep, and they didn't have the decency to leave her alone even then; when the train pulled into the station, she woke to realise that she'd been dreaming of the damned man.

CHAPTER TWO

RAFAEL LOOKED AT Sammy's unprepossessing house from behind the wheel of his sleek, black BMW. The house was nestled in a row of similarly plain houses and was a pointed reminder of what he had escaped. The claustrophobia which had engulfed him for the two years he and his father had put down roots in a town very close to this one swirled around him. There was so much love for and impatience with his dad wrapped up in a small village where everybody knew everybody else—not to mention hope and despair.

He knew that this was a sweeping and unfair judgement of the place, but it was one that came from his gut. He had paid a fleeting visit back to the area when he had decided to build his hotel because, aside from his own personal experiences, the place was one of tremendous natural beauty, more than capable of holding its own against the saturated Cotswolds countryside or Cornish coastline, and it was ripe for just the sort of development he had in mind. If this worked out, he would consider something commercial in the area. It would be perfect for the sort of business development that wasn't reliant on access to London and he had a number of companies that would thrive in the wild Yorkshire Dales.

Coming here now felt more personal because he was back to see someone who had been a part of his life all those years ago. She'd lodged in his head since she'd showed up at this office the day before. He'd pictured her fierce, determined face, relived the shock of seeing her in the first place and had known that, thanks to her, a Pandora's box of memories had been opened that he hadn't been able to squash since she'd stormed out. He wasn't the sort who had much time for a past that couldn't be changed, but it seemed that the past didn't have much respect for that, and had decided to reassert itself after over a decade of conveniently hibernating.

Rafael could have simply posted the portfolio back to her, or emailed her to arrange a drop-off, but in the end he had decided on the spur of the moment to hand-deliver it. He could use the opportunity to visit the land agent and have another look around the hotel and the properties so that he could determine what he wanted to do before delegating his instructions.

He'd debated whether to phone ahead first, but in the end had decided to simply swing by. The fact that the first page of her portfolio was generous with information about where she lived and the various ways in which she could be contacted seemed to be fate inviting him to pay her visit.

And, in truth, reading through the pack she had prepared for him had opened his eyes to a guilty conscience he hadn't thought he possessed: guilt that he could have been more sympathetic to his father; guilt that his antics must have meant yet more worries for him at the time. He had since set up his dad in style, and always made sure to keep in touch, but nothing could ever make up for lost time.

Sammy's portfolio had also managed to make him feel guilty about *her*. He'd sent her packing without a backward glance. Was he so ensconced in his ivory tower that the pleas of someone whose future he had irrevocably altered should fall on deaf ears—even when he shared a past with that person?

Of course, he wasn't going to redesign his hotel to accommodate her, which would be utter madness, but he had a couple of ideas. There was room for manoeuvre. Anybody else and he wouldn't be sitting here now, that was for sure. But memories had a funny way of finding cracks in what he'd thought was rock-solid—such as his immunity to the weakness of any emotion.

Around him, the weak winter sun was already beginning to show signs of fading away, even though it wasn't much after three in the afternoon. He half-expected no one to be in so, when he rang the bell, he was disconcerted to hear footsteps approaching. Then the door was opened just a crack, with a chain separating him from green eyes peering suspiciously at him.

'I have something you forgot.' He waved the portfolio at the four-inch crack in the door. 'Just in case you're wondering why I've shown up on your doorstep.'

'I no longer need that, so you can go away. I have nothing to say to you.'

'Look…' He raked his fingers through his hair. 'I've read your proposal—'

'And you're going to change your mind and let me buy the place so that I can open my café and develop upstairs for myself?'

'Unfortunately not.'

'Then goodbye.'

Sammy pushed the door shut and he rang the doorbell again. There was no reply. Rafael kept ringing. When she opened it yet again, he was still there, six-foot-four inches of implacable alpha male in no particular rush to leave.

She glared at him.

Rafael Moreno was the last person on the planet Sammy had expected to see standing outside her front door at three-thirty on a wintry Saturday afternoon.

She was just back from visiting her mother. She had planned to tell her everything about the hotel, and the abrupt end to all her plans for opening her patisserie, but the minute she had sat down she had looked at her mother's thin, anxious face and had immediately decided that this was a bridge she would cross at a later date.

Caroline Payne hadn't had the easiest of lives. She'd lost her husband and the father to both her children over two decades ago, and Sammy often wondered whether she had ever recovered from the loss. Seven at the time, all Sammy could remember was her mother's quiet tears as she'd gone through the motions of living, but she'd really only existed, biding her time until grief would leave her alone. Sammy and her brother had hovered like ghosts in a void. Sammy could remember a sense that she'd been waiting until things returned to normal and would be less sad and confusing.

Unfortunately, it had taken a long time for things to return to normal. Her mother had met and married someone else with undue haste, desperate to be rescued from her inability to cope. John Deeley, the manager at the factory where her mother had worked, had entered their lives with an arrogant determination to take charge. Meek and mild-mannered on the outside, he had soon proved himself to be a bully who made up for his inadequacies by throwing his weight around within the four walls of the house. Shouting and belittling her hadn't been enough to make their mother leave him; it was only when he'd raised a hand to strike Colin that she had finally snapped.

Even then, it had taken ages before he had finally disappeared from their lives and only after the police had become involved. When Sammy recalled that period in their lives, she still felt the grip of childish fear suffocate her.

Her mother had pulled herself together since those days. She'd got herself a decent job, studied in the evenings and worked her fingers to the bone to make sure she was never late with a mortgage payment. She had instilled in her only daughter the idea that men weren't the be all and end all, and that independence counted for everything.

Sammy had known as she'd matured that her mother was devoting herself to making up for those lost years when she had been wrapped up in her misery, and then later, those years when she had subjected Sammy and Colin to the horror of a stepfather like John Deeley.

Sammy had done her best to reassure her mother that time had moved on since then. It was true that Colin had gone off the rails, which her mother had taken as her fault; but he was on the straight and narrow now. Sammy repeatedly told her mother that she was happy, was fulfilled, had found her calling, but guilt and worry had taken up residence in her mother's heart and refused to budge. But, amidst all this, Caroline Payne had done her utmost financially and emotionally to support both of her children.

Working in various kitchens, training finally to branch out and do her own thing, had come at a cost to Sammy. There had been arduous hours and not much of a pay cheque. She had been grateful to her mother for the hand-outs she had given her over the years. She'd promised herself that she would get where she wanted to be and would repay her mum for everything she'd done for Colin and her.

So to break the news that the whole thing was off thanks to Rafael…no chance.

Which brought her right back to the man plonked out-side her house, refusing to move.

'People are going to start wondering what's going on,' he had the nerve to say with a glimmer of a smile. 'If memory serves me, it's the sort of place where curtains have a habit of twitching, and the neighbours' curtains are remarkably close to yours…they've probably got their ears pressed to their front doors, even as I stand here try-ing to have a conversation.'

'I'm not interested in a conversation.'

'Let me in, Sammy. I may not have any intention of re-arranging my entire project to accommodate you, but I'm willing to consider other options that could be of interest.'

'What other options?'

'Let me in and you'll find out. Slam the door and I walk away, and you won't hear from me again.'

'You can come in, Rafael, but I'm warning you that, if you don't have anything to say that I want to hear, then you won't be hanging around for longer than five seconds.'

'Consider it a deal. I've always been averse to making a nuisance of myself.' He smiled as she unhooked the chain and pulled open the front door.

That smile knocked Sammy for six. It was something that hadn't changed. It was the same smile that had had every girl in school round-eyed and mesmerised. It was a slow smile of utter self-assurance. She could see the boy he'd been very clearly.

She sighed and stood back, allowing him to sweep past her. She was only doing this because he'd held out a thread of hope when he told her that he had an idea… If not for that, naturally she would have sent him on his way, smile or no smile. She had zero interest in taking a trip down memory lane with the man.

'Do you want something to drink?'

'Graciously offered, I must say. What's on offer?'

'Tea or coffee. The coffee's instant.'

'I must say I've never had to work so hard for a drink before.'

'You can go into the sitting room—' she nodded to a door that was slightly ajar '—and I'll bring you…?'

'Tea…one sugar. That would be very nice.'

Rafael watched for a couple of seconds as she disappeared into the kitchen, kicking the door shut behind her.

Maybe she thought he might make a nuisance of himself by following her into the kitchen to talk when her mission was to get rid of him as fast as she could. No problem. As things stood, he was very happy to take his time looking round him. The unprepossessing façade outside hadn't concealed anything surprising or wonderful. The place was certainly no Tardis; it was just as small on the inside as it promised on the outside. If he stood with his arms outstretched, he would be able brush his fingers against the walls. A small staircase led upstairs. He noted the neutral paint, the faded rug on the flagstone floor and the single utilitarian light illuminating the space.

He nudged open the door to the sitting room. This was obviously where the magic happened. The bookshelves groaned under the weight of cookery books. The pictures on the walls were cute, little surrealistic depictions of food; peering closer, he could see that some were hand-painted. The furniture was old but invitingly homely and the little oval table in the middle, along with a couple of other bits and pieces, was the genuine article—antique, polished so that the patina of the wood gleamed. The room was an intriguing mix of old and new.

He was studying one of the hand-painted pictures on the wall when he heard her enter the room and turned to look at her without moving.

'Yours?'

'I beg your pardon?'

'The paintings. Did you do them?'

'You should be sitting and waiting for me, not nosing around.'

'The temptation to inspect was too great. So, do you paint as well as cook?'

'When I get the time,' Sammy confirmed, nodding to a chair and pointedly placing his mug on the table next to it.

Rafael ignored her direction and took his time examining the cookery books. Some were huge; most looked very well worn.

He'd come to…what…assuage his guilt by offering her something to hang onto? Satisfy some never-before-suspected curiosity about the life he and his father had left behind all those years ago? Rafael didn't know. His entire life had been devoted to ascent. Ascent to a place where he would be untouchable. He had built a fortress around himself and that was just how he liked it. Yet here he was, with a woman who felt free to say whatever she wanted, to hell with what he thought—and, yes, he was perversely enjoying the experience. He reckoned that there was clearly more to be said for novelty than he'd ever thought possible.

'Are you going to sit or are you going to go through everything in the room with a fine-tooth comb?'

'You haven't changed. There was always a quiet determination about you, even when you were younger. Your face is the same as well. You haven't aged at all. When you left my office—or maybe it would be more accurate of me to say when you *stormed out of* my office—I began casting my mind back to those two years my father and I spent in these parts and I was surprised at what I could recall after all these years.'

'Really? How interesting...'

Her outfit the day before hadn't done her justice, he decided.

What she wore now suited her: faded skinny jeans, an old rugby shirt, likewise faded, some soft sneakers with the laces undone as though he'd caught her in the act of kicking them off. She had the smoothest skin he'd ever seen and the boyish haircut somehow managed to make her look ultra-feminine and very delicate.

'When we were at school, I remember other girls tossing their long hair over their shoulders and batting their eyelids, even though they were only about fourteen or fifteen. They were already learning the tricks of the trade.'

'The tricks of the trade?'

'How to flirt. You never did that.'

'I've never seen the point of flirting.'

'Never?'

'Can we just move things along, Rafael? Maybe get to the point? You said that there was something you want to run past me?'

'You told me that I led your brother astray—that he was the model student before I came along and decided to show him that there was more to life than burying himself in books.'

'It was okay for you! You never had to work hard! Everything came naturally to you. You could bunk off class for days on end and then show up and know exactly what the lessons were about, exactly how to get straight As without trying.'

Sammy dropped onto the sofa facing him and looked at him with open hostility.

'I've thought about that since I saw you. I hadn't thought about it for years but it all came back to me.'

'I don't see the point of this.'

'He was very unhappy. He used to talk about it. Not a huge amount, but enough.'

'He talked to you?'

'Why is that so surprising?'

'Because...because...'

'I can be an attentive listener.'

'And you were, back then? Would that be in between taking the day off to explore the great outdoors and smoking behind the bike sheds at school?' She arched her eyebrows with incredulity and Rafael burst out laughing.

His dark eyes gleamed as he tilted his head to the side and stared at her until she blushed.

'They were tough times for you and your brother. He used to talk about a stepfather...the name escapes me.'

Sammy's mouth dropped open.

'Colin talked about Deeley...our stepfather? That all happened before you showed up!'

'I think he was still in the process of getting over it,' Rafael said quietly. 'Whatever *it* was. He was never that expansive on the subject although, in fairness, I wasn't always one hundred percent on the ball. Which brings me back to the accusation that I was a bad influence—I wasn't. I was just a catalyst for his anxieties to come out into the open. Just in case some of your annoyance that things haven't panned out the way you wanted them to might have to do with the fact that I am the Big Bad Wolf in your eyes, from a historic point of view.'

The tea had gone cold and Sammy's thoughts were all over the place.

Colin, who was three years older than her, had seemed so contained; he had seemed just to get lost in his schoolwork while everything had swirled chaotically around him. But was Rafael right? Had he just been there... clever, wild, non-conformist, expecting nothing...allowing Colin to get rid of things buried deep inside? He'd been pretty rebellious after Rafael had left, but then he'd settled down. Now that she looked back on it, something had changed—he'd mellowed.

She heard him ask very softly, into the silence, 'And what about you?'

'What about *me*?'

'It was a long time ago, but whatever disruption your stepfather caused must have affected you as well...'

And just like that Sammy was thrown back to the past—to how devastated her mother had been after Oliver Payne's death and then how hurt and disillusioned by the mess that had come of her second marriage to John Deeley.

If Rafael had developed a talent for recall, then he wasn't the only one. She could remember how she had scorned those girls who had tried so hard to get his attention and, worse, how she had hated herself for secretly being as fascinated by him as everyone else seemed to be.

He had cast a spell over them. Reluctantly, she was forced to concede that her anger at finding out who had bought the hotel and pulled the rug from under her feet was partly fuelled by him being who he was—when really he'd just been a boy who had become an incredibly successful man and now wanted to invest in a community he had once been a part of. He hadn't been personally spiteful towards *her* in buying the place she had saved up for. It had just been business for him—as he'd said.

She forced herself to meet his piercing stare with a bland expression. In the very short space of time that she had been in his company, he was already getting under her skin. She wasn't going to start spilling her heart out to him and tell him all about her miserable time when Deeley had been around. She wasn't going to revert to being the shy fourteen-year-old peering at the cute boy who could have any girl he wanted.

'We all have things in the past that have affected us one way or another,' she said politely. 'You must have stuff you'd rather not talk about, and fortunately...' she paused for dramatic effect '... I won't be asking you to tell me all about it because I'm not interested.'

'That's very, very...' Rafael's lips twitched with suppressed amusement '...reassuring.'

'So maybe we could get back to the reason you're here?'

Their eyes locked.

'What else do you do aside from baking and cooking?' he asked.

'Sorry?' Sammy was confused. Why was he avoiding getting down to the business of why he had come here in the first place?

'I read in your spiel that you trained under some big names. I take it you have experience across the board when it comes to your culinary skills? I could have looked you up online but I wanted to ask you face to face.'

'Of course. I work twice a week at a restaurant close by. It has a Michelin star and it's excellent for keeping my hand in with the basics of French and Mediterranean cooking. I also advertise my services as a personal chef, which can be extremely challenging. My heart lies in the intricacies of baking, though, which is why I've decided to start with a café that does light food and specialises in pastries. You'll appreciate that I have to make ends meet somehow. I've sacrificed quite a bit to get experience over the years. I had to work extremely long hours. Putting aside enough money for the deposit on the café has been a labour of—'

'I've got that message loud and clear. Here's the

thing… I'm hosting an important series of meetings on a tiny island in the Caribbean in two weeks' time. It's a deal that involves the CEOs all coming together to dove-tail the sale of several of their companies to me. But it's important that the deal is done smoothly and, most im-portantly, in the space of a week. I'm hosting them at one of my new hotels—it's not officially open to the pub-lic yet. There's a new restaurant in the hotel that I'm on the verge of opening. I'm willing to try you out as Head Chef while we're out there. You'll be able to show me a variety of skills.'

'Head Chef…? Small island…? Caribbean…?' She found it difficult to keep up with what Rafael was saying. The words were coming fast at her and she barely had time to pin them down. What on earth was he saying?

'Excellent weather this time of year.'

'But… I'm confused.'

'Impress me.' He leaned forward, arms resting on his thighs, giving her his undivided attention. 'And I'll hire you to steer the restaurant. You can have free rein to come up with whatever menus you like, just so long as there's an emphasis on local produce. It won't be a per-manent situation—six months, the first of which will be the week of the meetings. Of course, I'll stay on after my clients have left to oversee the final touches, but I'll be out of your hair. After those six months are up, you'll be free to return here and open whatever kind of restaurant you want. You'll be paid enough so that buying a place of your own will be more than affordable. You'll also have me on your CV.'

'I'll have *you* on my CV?'

'You successfully run my restaurant in a start-up hotel,

and your database of clients will be guaranteed. You just have to let it be known that you impressed me.'

They looked at one another and Sammy eventually rolled her eyes.

'You are an *extremely* arrogant human being, Rafael Moreno.'

Rafael grinned. 'I know. I'm working on it.'

'So,' she said, swiftly bringing the conversation back to logistics, because she'd been tempted to laugh. 'If the restaurant is only now in the process of…of being operational, then how is it going to be possible for me to cook anything? What's the equipment like? And how many… er…people are going to be there?'

'Twelve, including partners.'

'Okay.'

'The equipment has been ordered. You can oversee what's coming. Consider it the start of your new, exciting career.'

'And until the stuff arrives—sandwiches and barbecues on a beach?'

'That does sound reasonably relaxed,' Rafael mused. 'And relaxed is the aim of the game for the week. But, no. No sandwiches or barbecues on the beach. High-end fine dining, champagne and caviar, and interesting excursions for the other halves during the day when business is being done. I have a local guy already in place for that. You look a little bewildered.'

'Should I go along with this…? I can't just stay put over there when you and everyone else has left after the meetings are over.'

'You'll have a fortnight to return here so that you can sort out your affairs before you return. Six months isn't very long. You might think that I would want you to stay put for longer, to prove your worth before I make a decision, but...'

'But?' Sammy echoed coolly.

'But, if I'm honest, the fact that I know you in a manner of speaking changes the picture.'

'You knew me yesterday and the picture didn't seem to be changing then. If I recall, you sent me on my way because there was nothing you were willing to do for me.'

'Maybe,' Rafael admitted truthfully. 'That was an instinctive reaction. I'm not a man who is sentimental when it comes to the past, but in this instance...' He shrugged, but his eyes were serious and thoughtful. His voice became rough. 'Let's just say that I read what you'd written in your proposal and maybe I'm more sentimental than I thought. I also think you have the sort of personality to get the hotel moving in the right direction quickly.'

'And what sort of personality is that, if I could ask?'

'Argumentative and determined not to take no for an answer.'

His voice was matter of fact. There was no criticism intended, but somewhere deep inside Sammy felt a sudden stab of hurt because...were those feminine traits? She was twenty-seven, and yes she had had boyfriends, but had any of them come to anything? No. Her last boyfriend, a guy she'd been dating for seven months, had told her, by way of an excuse for breaking up with her by text, that she was a little *difficult*.

She'd taken that to mean that her independence had ended up getting on his nerves, but what was so wrong with being independent? She had learned valuable lessons from her mother whose helplessness had been her undoing until she'd found the strength and courage to realise that going it alone was no bad thing. Worse would be to feel that she had to rely on some guy to make decisions that affected her life.

She looked at the drop-dead gorgeous man who was looking back at her with a shuttered expression and she thought of the women he was routinely pictured with. None of them looked the *difficult* type.

'I wish you'd just tell me what's missing from this picture,' Sammy said sharply, shaking her head clear of those silly, thorny thoughts. This all felt too good to be true—there had to be a catch.

'We won't be staying at the hotel,' Rafael revealed. 'It isn't due to formally open until the end of the month, which will give my managers plenty of time to ensure there are no glitches.'

'Where will we be staying? Where is this cooking going to take place?'

'At my house there. I hope you don't have a problem with that...'

CHAPTER THREE

HOPE YOU DON'T have a problem with that…?

Have a problem with vanishing off to a place she'd never heard of in a part of the world she'd never visited to cook for a man she barely knew and had contrived to forget how much she didn't like? All in an attempt to prove herself worthy of being given an opportunity to find a foothold in the culinary world, because he'd thoroughly trashed her chances there when he'd gazumped her on the deal she'd made to buy the place adjoining the hotel.

Why on earth would she have a problem with that? That was what she sarcastically asked herself on a loop over the course of the following two weeks as she got herself prepared for the shake-up in her life she'd been cornered into accepting.

Bitter though she was at the olive branch that had been handed to her—because she should never have been put in the position of having to have an olive branch waved in front of her in the first place—she had to admit that he was being generous. His PA emailed her with the contract outlining what was expected of her, the duration of her employment—one week on probation followed by the six-month contract—and of course her remuneration, which was more than generous.

At the end of her stint, she would easily have sufficient capital to find herself a suitable outlet for her business and buy herself somewhere decent enough to put
down roots. Those months away would be challenging, of
course, because she would know no one at all and would
be going it alone, in charge and without a familiar face to
guide her. The fact that she could fail to make the grade
after all that cast a long shadow but she had no choice to
speak of and would go with the flow.

For such a hard-headed businessman, guilt certainly
seemed to have sunk its teeth into Rafael; but she still
couldn't manage to get herself to any place of gratitude
because, generous offer or no generous offer, he was still
as arrogant as he'd been as a teenager.

She was forced to confess to her mother that the deal
with the hotel had fallen through and had plastered a
smile on her face as she'd put as good a spin on the situation as she possibly could.

'But…you're going to…*where*—to be a personal chef because you can't get the place at Clifford's hotel? I'm just not
following you. It all sounds very sketchy… I thought you
wanted to have your own place. It's what you've spent years
working towards! I just don't understand what's going on.'

Sitting across the kitchen table at her mother's house,
Sammy breathed in deeply and tapped into a reservoir
of phony optimism she'd never thought she possessed.

'It's a thrilling opportunity!' she trilled through gritted teeth. 'In fact, I'll bet not getting that silly place will
end up being the best thing that's ever happened to me!'

'But all your plans to move upstairs so that you could
own your own place as well as the bakery…'

'Oh, Mr Moreno—or *Rafael* as I call him, seeing that

we know one another—will be paying me sufficiently over the six-month period at his hotel for me to have quite some choice when it comes to another venue!' She swept that observation aside, making sure not to mention the little technicality of a probationary period. Why muddy the water when her mother was actually buying into the whole change of plan?

Sammy would do anything to spare her mum needless worry and so a little finger-crossing was perfectly acceptable if it made her happy.

Oddly, having tentatively mentioned Rafael's name to find that her mother had instantly remembered who he was, the fact that *he* was the billionaire who was now giving her this so-called chance of a lifetime somehow ended up reassuring her mother that all would be okay. This, despite the fact that the odious man had been responsible for ruining her future in the first place. Sometimes Sammy just didn't understand her mother, but still, she was at least relieved that she seemed to have stopped worrying.

She got hold of as much information as she could about the Caribbean island where she might just end up spending a few months. It was small—a dot in the middle of the ocean—but with a good infrastructure and a thriving economy based on the export of sugar cane, cocoa and tourism. There were strict controls in place when it came to the number of hotels allowed, and the size of them, and there were draconian hoops to jump through for anyone not of local ancestry to get permission to own land and build on it.

Rafael's name was mentioned as being one of the lucky ones. From the write up, the journalist in question obviously loved him, and Sammy abandoned reading about all the things he had done for the islanders after the first page. He obviously had a sprawling fan club, but thankfully she had no intention ever of signing up to become a member.

She knew that he would be travelling ahead of her, which was blessed relief. But, at dawn on the day that he had arranged for the chauffeur to collect her, she was suddenly floored by an attack of nerves and almost wished that he was going to meet her at Gatwick after all.

The bravado she had nurtured over the past fortnight, when she had been busy planning what to take and preparing detailed lists of what she would need on the catering front, seemed to have deserted her. At six in the morning, with wintry dark skies outside, she scrutinised her reflection in the mirror in her bedroom and tried not to feel sick with nerves.

It was going to be hot when she got there. She would be leaving horrible weather and stepping out into hot sun— at least, according to everything she had read. When she looked at herself, what she saw was a confusing sight: light jeans and a white tee-shirt underneath a thick cardigan with a duffel coat and a woolly hat. She looked like someone who hadn't a clue where she was heading or what to expect, and so had dressed for all eventualities.

The time had come—no backing out now. Her phone buzzed: a text message from Rafael's driver, which had been the agreed communication when Rafael had arranged for her to be collected. Her lift was here. She gave one last look but, as she pulled her cases out to the front door, she wondered whether her jumbled sartorial choices reflected the jumble of emotions running through her and the confusion of not knowing what to expect when she got to the other side.

* * *

The sun had just about set as Rafael approached the airport terminal. It was easy finding a spot to park because the terminal was tiny and the car park, for reasons that escaped him, was unnecessarily large. The sky was indigo and, even though he was at an airport, he could still hear the sounds peculiar to tropical nights: the clicking of crickets blending into the background noises of frogs and toads and all the other small creatures that emerged at night.

Planes were not on a loop here. The sky was empty but, as he parked the small four-by-four, he could hear the distant roar of one swerving towards the little island, so perfectly positioned that it always escaped the annual round of hurricanes that cut a swathe through some of the other islands further north towards Puerto Rico.

He'd had minimal contact with Sammy since they'd parted company a couple of weeks ago. A contract had been emailed, conditions laid down and signatures received. He had instructed his PA to email her with some information about where she would be going, and he had personally emailed her confirming numbers and telling her that she would have to be equipped to cater for two vegetarians. In return, she had sent him a list of basics she would need including an assortment of meats, fish and prawns, which could be frozen and used as appropriate. She would get fresh stuff when she arrived. They'd been business-like communications.

He'd felt the need to put some distance between them, although he couldn't quite understand why. This was about business, and it should have been clear cut, but she'd somehow got under his skin and he hadn't been able to get her out of his head for the past couple of weeks. He'd thought of her, angrily jabbing her finger at his audacity. He'd married it to memories of her as a teenager, and had been unnerved by how much air time she'd taken in his mind.

Rafael sighed and vaulted out of the car. Perhaps he should have taken a slightly more personal approach, especially given the situation in which he had recently found himself, which had turned out to be rather delicate, to say the very least. He needed Sammy on side rather than glaring at him from under her lashes.

The airport was busy. People were coming to collect friends or relatives, others arriving to drop off. It was still very warm, even though the sun was setting, and despite a light breeze. He was half-enjoying the sing-song lilt of the voices around him as he strolled towards the pick-up point outside the little terminal. Mostly, though, he was thinking about how he was going to play this one out.

He almost missed her as she appeared through the open side of the terminal where a stream of arrivals was making its way out, pulling bags, or else with bags loaded onto trolleys being pulled by the guys who worked at the airport.

Sammy was gazing around her with a lost expression, a chunky cardigan loosely knotted around her waist, in pale-blue baggy jeans and trainers and with a couple of pull-along cases with a coat draped over the handle of one. She looked very young and very wide-eyed, the breeze riffling her short dark hair, blowing it this way and that. Their eyes met and, even in the semi-darkness, he could make out her sudden stiffening as he walked towards her.

'Sammy.'

Sammy blinked. Eight and a half hours had taken her from a cold and bleak England to…somewhere that felt like another planet. The sky was clear and the heat was seeping through her clothes, making her perspire, and the noises were ones with which she was utterly unfamiliar.

She'd been abroad, but never anywhere tropical and, the minute she'd stepped out of the plane onto the stunted ladder that led down to the tarmac, she'd been confronted with the reality of just how much was about to change for her.

Frankly, *everything*—which had fired up another flare of resentment towards Rafael, the employer she hadn't asked for and certainly didn't want. But, now that she was here and he was towering over her, he seemed like an anchor in these unfamiliar waters.

'Let me take your bags. Is this all you brought with you? Tell me how your flight was—was it okay? I find first class always makes the most of a tedious experience.'

'I didn't expect you to come and meet me.'

'That wasn't the original plan,' Rafael murmured soothingly. 'But then I thought that here you were…a stranger in a strange land and you might find it helpful to see a face you recognise.'

They were heading towards the car park. The horizon fading away into a darkening sky looked limitless…a stretch of colour uninterrupted by buildings, housing, factories or even the usual network of busy roads that led out of airport terminals.

Sammy breathed in a heady aroma of exotic trees and plants and then eyed Rafael suspiciously out of the corner of her eye.

'You're being very nice to me, Rafael.'

'I didn't realise that was a crime. Here we are. The cars here are usually driven for their usefulness, hence this four-by-four pick-up. It can tackle all manner of poor roads.'

'You mentioned that you weren't going to meet me because your contingent of guests would be at the villa. Won't they be missing you?'

'They'll all big boys and girls. They can cope for a couple of hours.'

'Is that how long it's going to take to get to your villa?' Sammy frowned and clambered into the passenger seat. 'I didn't think that the island was that big...'

'It's not. Ready?'

He swivelled so that he was facing her. Their eyes met in the darkness of the pick-up and Sammy blushed. Her comfort zone was several thousand miles and over eight hours away. She shivered, and for a few seconds her brain went completely blank because, up close and personal like this, the sheer power of his presence and the force of his incredible, suffocating masculinity hit her like a sledgehammer.

She'd spent the intervening time reminding herself that she disliked him...but now the past and the present rushed at her, giving him form and shape, and making him more than just a convenient cardboard cut-out of a bad guy.

It took her a couple of moments before her brain re-engaged and, just as he turned the engine into life and began reversing out of the space, she said, 'So why is it going to take so long?'

'Thought it might be an idea to take you somewhere... so I could brief you on what to expect.'

Sammy relaxed against the head rest and smiled.

'I think I have a pretty good idea of what to expect.'

'You do?'

'Thirteen people...'

'Fourteen, as it happens,' Rafael corrected.

'I thought you said that there were going to be six couples and a singleton.'

'My apologies. There was a last-minute addition. Clement Hewell was always scheduled to come—he's frankly the overriding lynchpin in this deal—but originally he was coming solo. As it turns out, he's accompanied by his recently acquired girlfriend, Victoria.'

'Okay. Seven couples. It shouldn't make a difference to the catering.'

'You were saying that you know what to expect. Is this on the food front or on the people front?'

'Both, as it happens,' Sammy said. She shifted so that she was leaning against the door and looking at his sharp profile. She was too tired to argue, and besides, the conversation felt soothing and non-confrontational.

She might not enjoy the reasons that had brought her here but there was something oddly invigorating about being in this man's presence. Maybe it was the challenge of proving to him how good she was at what she did—that the gauche teenager he vaguely remembered had turned out into a capable woman with a career path ahead of her. Maybe there was something gnawing away inside, something that wanted to show him that he hadn't left a bunch of country bumpkins behind in his headlong rush to become a billionaire.

The silence thickened as the pick-up gathered pace, clearing the confines of the airport and heading out into quiet, dark roads, sporadically lit and interrupted by a lazy stream of cars and vans. She realised that he was waiting for her to continue.

'On the food front, I always tend to over-cater, but from experience when it comes to... I'm not sure how to put this...'

'Don't mind me,' Rafael murmured with amusement in his voice. 'You have to remember that I wasn't always loaded. My sensibilities are a lot less delicate than you could ever imagine.'

Sammy relaxed, something she hadn't expected to do. 'Okay. From my experience, rich people don't tend to eat a huge amount, and definitely not the wives and partners of rich men. They fiddle with their food and pick at it because they're always watching their weight.'

Rafael chuckled.

'Isn't that a generalisation?'

'Maybe,' Sammy admitted. 'But I'm just saying what I've observed over the years. So I've planned great food, keeping it nice and tasty, using local ingredients, which I've looked up, and I intend to make sure that I don't have much wastage. By the way, thanks for getting the basics in place for me. I really believe in not throwing anything out and it upsets me when I have to.'

'Very good.'

'Is that what you wanted to brief me on—picky eaters? Can I ask if everyone has arrived?'

'Two days ago.'

The darkness had gathered around them. Sammy could feel it pressing against the window of the air conditioned four-by-four. She was drawn to stare out at the passing scenery: the outcrops of houses against hills; the empty vegetable and fruit stalls by the side of the road; the sudden bursts of lively bars and rum shops with people congregated outside, drinking and laughing.

She was also driven to look at the man behind the wheel. The longer she looked at him, the harder it was to think straight, so she dragged her eyes away and stared ahead. That was much easier.

'How's it going? Or is that none of my business?'

Rafael didn't answer.

She'd relaxed, which was good. It was difficult *not* to relax over here. There was something about the heat and the techni-colour natural beauty of the place...

Rafael made a right, heading towards the small, bustling town which struck a nice balance between being authentic and serving up some great restaurants and cafés frequented by tourists for the most part. He personally preferred the out of the way places where the locals gathered, but then he knew the place like the back of his hand, and was well known in the community.

'I know you've been up and moving for quite some time, and you're probably in need of a shower and sleep, but, like I said, er...' He fished around for the right tone of voice and the correct choice of words.

'I don't need a lesson on how to behave around your guests, Rafael. I can handle myself around people—even rich and important people, believe it or not. Experience as a personal chef is great when it comes to teaching you how to socialise, even with people you may not have much in common with and might actually dislike.'

'There's a way of doing that?' He slid dark eyes across to her.

'It involves a lot of smiling.'

'You'll have to teach me some time,' he murmured. 'I've always had a problem with that.'

'I know.' Sammy laughed. 'I remember once seeing you outside the principal's office. I have no idea what you'd done but you must have done something.'

'I was always doing *something*. Looking back, the guy had the patience of a saint...'

'Anyway, you were chewing gum and had your legs stretched out and you were playing something on your phone. You didn't look as though you were going to be smiling your way through whatever punishment was in store for you. At any rate, I'll be perfectly fine finding my feet.'

'I'm not doubting that for a second.'

'Aren't you?'

'No.' He turned to her and their eyes met briefly. 'You don't strike me as being afraid of much. You *did* show up at my office and yell at me because I'd bought the hotel from under your feet. I've probably been scarred for life.'

He grinned. 'So, no need to become defensive. I have every confidence in your culinary capabilities as well as your social *savoir faire*. I had a look at your social media profile. You've had a convincing amount of experience working in different milieu—different restaurants with different chefs, and also catering for the rich and famous. It might have been a slow climb for you but not because you haven't excelled along the way.'

'No need to over-egg the pudding,' Sammy muttered, burning with a mixture of pleasure and embarrassment.

'I'm being truthful.' The main road, such as it was, had been left behind and they were now in the capital. It was a charming mix of restaurants, bars and shops, from the sophisticated, catering for wealthy tourists, to the authentic, where the locals tended to hang out. Rafael eased the pick-up into a spare bay along a buzzing little street that was bustling with people. 'Are you always this prickly when you're paid a compliment?'

His dark eyes roved over her flushed face. 'Look,' he said softly, raking his fingers through his hair. 'What I want to talk to you about has nothing to do with...your abilities to cook or mix or anything like that. Not at all. You couldn't be further from the truth.'

'Then what?' She hesitated. 'Have you...have you decided that I won't be suitable for the...for the...?'

'Let's go inside.' He nodded to the bar directly opposite them but his eyes remained pinned to her face.

He climbed out of the pick-up, hit the passenger side before she could even open her door and rested his hand on hers to help her down because it was a crazily high vehicle.

His fingers were cool against hers and sent a tingle through her as he touched her. *What was going on...?*

Sammy had expected a number of things, starting with sickening nerves, disorientation and borderline panic, all mingled with a healthy dose of sourness and resentment. She hadn't expected to feel at all relaxed, not at any point; nor had she expected to see any funny side to Rafael and she certainly hadn't expected him to be...*hesitant* with her about anything.

And yet, she had *sensed* his hesitancy when he had brought her here and suddenly she realised that she wanted this job a lot more than she had told herself. She'd worked and worked and worked to get this far and she couldn't face any more setbacks in her quest to forge her own path. She didn't *want* to have to start thinking about

putting aside more money so that she could find somewhere else, somewhere that wouldn't be half as suitable
as the hotel, which was no longer even a possibility.

She'd subconsciously started making plans with the
money he had dangled in front of her, even though she
had fought against the temptation; she had hung onto
the reality that there would still be a probationary period
to climb over, not to mention the sickening prospect of
being on this island on her own, making decisions that
would affect her future. Bracing lectures to herself could
only go so far.

She nervously detached from him as soon as her feet
hit the ground. 'So, want to tell me what's going on?'
she asked.

Silhouettes of palm trees swayed all around them, a
thick, dense forest leading to the sea; it wasn't visible
yet, but she could tell it was there from the salty aroma
in the air. The stars were tiny, glittering diamonds in a
velvety black sky and the warmth penetrated even her
thin tee-shirt and the loose jeans. Even the fact that they
were in a bar couldn't detract from the dramatic splen-
dour of their surroundings. In the darkness, all she could
make out was Rafael's powerful build and his chiselled
facial features.

'What's going on is that there's a slight spanner in the
works.' Rafael cleared his throat.

'Meaning? Look, if you're having second thoughts
about taking me on after this stint, then that's fine.
There's no need to think that I'm going to take you to
court because of a stupid contract.'

'Point of order—you couldn't. The contract stipulates
complete freedom for me to release you without obliga-

tion should I no longer think that you can handle the six-month part of the job at my hotel. Didn't you read the fine print, Sammy?' He shook his head. 'Anyway. This isn't to do with that. It's to do with…how can I put this?…a certain delicate situation that's, er, arisen concerning one of the guests at my villa…'

'I beg your pardon?'

'Let me get you something to drink. They do an excellent rum punch here.'

He ordered drinks and nibbles while Sammy looked at him in utter bewilderment. She was barely aware of a cocktail being put in front of her or of the plate of nibbles. He'd told her that whatever he had to say had nothing to do with her contract but, in that case, for the life of her she couldn't work out where this was going.

'The couple I mentioned… Clement Hewell and the woman he's brought with him…'

'Yes…?'

'He's an important player in this particular game. He needs to be persuaded into parting with the company because, without him, the various other IT and software companies would find it hard to amalgamate. His company has certain software programmes that are vital for the whole tie-up to be possible, and that means a lot, because a lot of jobs depend on this deal. Without his contribution, the deal falls apart, and with it two of the companies, which will splinter, and that will affect a lot of people's livelihoods. The climate's not great for job hunting, and I personally know of the dozens that will be let go if this doesn't go through; most are nearing retirement age and would struggle to find anything else.'

'That's just awful, Rafael, but I honestly don't know where you're going with this.'

'The woman hanging on Clement's arm? As luck would have it, I actually know her.'

'Which is a good thing?'

'Which is very much *not* a good thing.'

'But surely catching up…?'

'Clement is a decent, honourable guy in his seventies. I've met him over the years at social events. He's well known in financial circles as a mover and shaker, who's also honest, fair and extremely generous when it comes to giving to charity.'

'That's really good to hear…but I'm really not sure where you're going with this.'

'Victoria,' Rafael expanded, 'is a twenty-nine-year-old ex-catwalk model.'

There was a moment of puzzlement, then Sammy relaxed and grinned. Then she burst out laughing, her green eyes lighting up with genuine mirth.

'I get it.'

'Tell me.'

'She's an ex-girlfriend of yours.'

'From four years ago.' Rafael shifted uncomfortably. 'A brief liaison.'

'No need for details.' She was still grinning. 'That's not the end of the world, though, is it? Haven't you been out with lots of catwalk models in the past?'

'What makes you say that?'

'I've caught the occasional article.'

'You mean you've been stalking me?'

'Don't flatter yourself,' she said drily. 'I read the occasional tabloid and I've seen the occasional picture. Not my fault there are reporters around who can't think of anything better to do with their time than take photos of you and whatever woman you happen to be going out with.'

'Ouch.'

'What I'm saying is,' she said loftily, 'is it's hardly a crime for an ex to go out with someone else and for you to bump into them later on as a couple—although the age difference *is* a little concerning.'

'If only it was that easy,' Rafael said, the grin fading, his voice quiet and deadly serious. 'The first day was okay, but last night there was a knock on my door. I opened it to find her standing outside in a bathrobe with nothing on underneath. I managed to get rid of her, but this could prove to be a very worrying situation. It's not just the nightmare of having to be on the alert twenty-four-seven, and it's not even the inconvenience of a situation arising that might be seen as compromising through no fault of my own...'

'Meaning?'

'Meaning,' Rafael said wryly, 'she's caught flinging herself at me and whoever happens to be around leaps to an incorrect conclusion. I can't say I care what people think of me but, like I said, this is a very big deal and a lot is riding on it. I'd rather not risk Victoria getting it into her head to scupper it if she can through sheer malice. Clement is in a fragile place at the moment, recovering from the death of his wife a year ago, and old men in fragile places can sometimes be foolish. From the looks of it, he's in the foolish phase, besotted with the damn woman. He'll come to his senses, but this couldn't be a worse time for this to be happening. What I'm saying is, if Victoria gets it into her head to use her influence to spite me because I've rejected her, well, let's just say there will be some very desperate casualties looking for jobs they probably won't easily find.'

'Why don't you just tell her that you're not interested? Why would she be spiteful? Surely if you explain...?'

'It was something of a messy break up.'

'Are you saying that she wanted to hang on in there after you'd given her her marching orders?'

'That's quite a colourful way of putting it, but essentially, yes.'

'So she's still got feelings for you.'

'So it would appear.'

'I get your point. People do crazy things when they're vulnerable and your friend...well, you say he's vulnerable, but still, I'm not sure why you're telling me this when it doesn't involve me. Unless you want me to take her under my wing in the kitchen and teach her how to make puff pastry to take her mind off vengeful thoughts? Puff pastry will do that to a person.'

The joke fell flat.

'Actually.' Rafael suddenly looked uncomfortable, uncomfortable enough for Sammy to feel a shiver of apprehension thread through her. 'This concerns you a little more than you might expect.'

'How so?'

'Because you and I are an item...'

'I beg your pardon?'

'Practically engaged, as it happens. Just for the week, you and I are very much in love. It was the only way I could get her off my back...'

CHAPTER FOUR

FOR A FEW seconds Sammy thought she must have missed a crucial link somewhere. How had Rafael's dilemma suddenly become *her* problem? Her mouth dropped open and she stared at him, oblivious to a smiling waiter with a jug of punch topping up their glasses.

'Hence my reason for waylaying you,' Rafael volunteered into the yawning silence.

'Rafael,' Sammy was constrained to enquire, 'How has *your* problem become *my* problem?'

'I'm not proud that I've dragged you into this but on the spur of the moment, and with that woman standing in front of me at two in the morning, my options seemed limited. I told her to get lost or I'd see what Clement makes of her after-hours escapades and she immediately warned me not to try reporting back—said all she was looking for was a bit of closure for herself. Like I said, Sammy, Victoria has a vindictive streak and if she wants to cause chaos she'll make sure to do so—she would try and spin some fairy story to Clement and, trust me, the story would not be in my favour. But if I have a serious girlfriend in tow? She wouldn't dare try and there would be no risk to the deal being done.'

'But…'

'Hear me out.' He pushed the half-empty plate of nibbles to one side and leaned towards her, his fingers linked on the table, his whole presence swamping her.

'Do I have a choice?'

'I realise that this was possibly not what you were expecting...'

'*Possibly not what I was expecting?* Rafael, that's the understatement of the decade! I was expecting an oven, a hob and a non-stop round of food preparation!'

'So, it might be a brief with a slight difference, but I'll make it more than worth your while.'

'Really. And how exactly are you going to achieve that?'

'I'm prepared to...er...alter the terms and conditions of the agreement we had in place.'

'You're losing me.'

'No working here for six months, no probationary period. I know you were probably a little apprehensive about having to prove yourself in unfamiliar surroundings... were you? Maybe you were excited at the opportunity...'

'No probationary period? What does that mean? No working here for six months? And, just for the record, more apprehensive than excited, as it happens. Six months on an island where I don't know anyone...'

'Naturally, you would have been introduced to the various people at the hotel.'

'Like I was saying...where I don't know anyone, at the end of which I could have been found wanting, didn't exactly make for a relaxing prospect.'

'Look, it's a big ask. I know that. Work with me here and I'm prepared to release you from any commitment to prove your worth to me. When this stint is over, you leave here with a cheque in your hand and the wherewithal to advance your career however you want to.' He reached for his mobile, typed something in and pushed the phone towards her.

Sammy's mouth, already open, opened a lot wider. In fact, her jaw hit the ground. The figure he had typed in was eye-watering and she wondered whether he had accidentally hit too many noughts by mistake.

'You're buying me.'

'In a manner of speaking. But look at it this way: what I'm buying is just a week of make-believe from you. You're my personal chef, an old friend who's now my lover... You'll still do the catering, and you can mingle on the side-lines as befits the working woman that you are. We really won't be spending much time in one another's company. You'll be preparing food and I'll be working to get this deal done before it can be scuppered. I refuse to let malice destroy the lives of innocent people who are depending on this.'

Sammy's brain had got stuck on the word 'lover' and she felt slow heat crawl into her cheeks. She tried to think of herself in that role; her mouth went dry and her thoughts became a big, scrambled mess.

'I get it that you're horrified.'

'This is not what I was expecting. Like I said...'

'In the big scheme of things, a week is neither here nor there. I won't expect anything from you but a bit of acting and, like I just said, you'll probably be busy preparing food so the acting will be limited—a smile here, a fond glance there. I'm not a touchy-feely person at the best of times.'

'And your important business colleagues are going to buy into you falling madly in love with an impoverished

chef you happened to know when you were a kid?' She
shot him a look of blazing disbelief. 'They surely must
know that you date models and...gorgeous blonde women
with big hair and long legs?'

'Well if *they* don't, then you certainly seem to.'

'No one will believe you for a second, Rafael.'

'I'll say straight away that Victoria did.'

'Well...'

'In a lot of ways, it's far more convincing that, after
a string of unsuitable beauties, I've lost my heart to...'

'The girl next door? Or should I say *the girl who used
to be next door*? Thanks for the compliment.'

'To a girl who's the complete opposite of what I've always gone for—to a proud and ambitious working woman
who isn't interested in living a life of leisure, whiling
away her time doing her nails and shopping for designer
clothes.'

'Which is what the women you date enjoy doing?'

'I've never had a problem with that. At any rate, being
a full-time model involves more than nail-doing and de-
signer-clothes shopping.'

'Of course,' Sammy agreed dutifully. 'Who could disagree with that?' She was half-thinking about the temptation of taking him up on an offer that could open a million
doors for her and would certainly solve all her financial
problems for the foreseeable future, if not for ever. If she
did agree to his crazy scheme, would that make her easily bought or incredibly canny?

'It's an impossibly tall story to pull off, Rafael. What
does this ex of yours look like?'

'Six foot one, blonde hair, long legs.'

'Exactly! Now look at *me*.'

'I'm looking.' He paused just long enough for her to blush. 'Why are you so touchy?'

'I'm not touchy! I'm being realistic.'

'Look,' Rafael said gravely. 'For the reasons I've outlined to you, I really would like you to play along with me for the next few days. Like I said, once it's under our belt, you will walk away a wealthy woman with the career opportunities you dreamed of within your reach *immediately*—no need to spend six months on an unfamiliar island.'

The carrot dangled tantalisingly. It was a truly astronomical amount of money on offer. Maybe to him it was less than a drop in the ocean, but to her? Yes, all those career opportunities would be firmly within her reach, and more besides. She would be able to treat her mother to all the things she deserved after a lifetime of scrimping and saving for her kids.

Rafael was right. What were a few days in the grand scheme of things? It would all be just a game, and one rooted in good intentions at that. Rafael would be spared the inconvenience of an ex-lover making a play at him behind her husband's back, and Sammy would get to skip the six-month stay and head straight home to Yorkshire to achieve her dream of starting her own restaurant.

'I'm tired,' she said truthfully. 'It's been a long day.'

'Let's go.' He stood up immediately and she followed suit.

The utter madness of this man being her lover flashed through her head. But then, her mind veered off on a tangent and began playing with all sorts of inappropriate images that made her burn up inside. Images of him touching her...looking at her with those clever, dark eyes…seeing more than just a nuisance who had shown up at his office clutching her portfolio and calling his conscience into question.

It was madness, of course. Rafael Moreno would never see her in that light. Men tended to go for women who were clones of one another. He went for catwalk models, or at least women who *could be* catwalk models. He was the guy who could have anyone.

'How long do I have to think about this?'

'The duration of the car ride back to my villa.'

'And if I say no?'

'Then you say no.'

'What would you tell your ex, after you've said that we're an item?'

They were walking towards his car, a warm breeze rustling her hair. She's spent hours travelling and yet she couldn't have felt more alert.

Alongside her, Rafael's towering presence made her shiver. She threw a sideways glance at him and all she could take in was formidable, sexy masculinity which made her think back to the fascination that had held her in its grip all those years ago. Thank God times had changed and she had grown up.

He helped her into the pick-up, swerved round to the driver's side and, as soon as he was next to her, she repeated her question, curious to hear his answer.

Rafael murmured with a shrug, 'I'd tell her that we had an argument and were no longer an item. Then I'd just have to take my chances and work things out another way, if such a way exists. And, if old guys get laid off in the process, that would be something my conscience would have to come to terms with.'

He angled his body back against the door, one arm resting lightly on the steering wheel, so that he could look at her.

'Wow,' Sammy said. 'That would be a speedy break-up. One minute you've told her that we're all loved up, and the next minute, it's all over?'

'Not that unusual.'

'I always thought that things just drifted along until one day it all fizzled out...'

'Maybe for you. Is that how it's worked for you, Sammy? On the relationship front?'

'I didn't think we were talking about me.'

It suddenly felt hot and stifling in the car. Her heart picked up pace as their eyes remained locked. He'd started the engine but rolled the windows down so that fresh air blew through but, even so, she could feel her clothes tight and prickly against her skin.

'For me,' Rafael drawled, 'break-ups tend to be a little more abrupt. I'm not a great believer in the gradual fizzling out of a situation. I'm inclined to restlessness before the boredom sets in.' He waited a few seconds and then said matter-of-factly, 'Victoria would have no trouble believing that what was working one minute suddenly failed to work the next.'

He began reversing out of the space. Outside, people were coming and going, walking slowly, laughing loudly and having fun.

'And the reason for that speed-of-light change of direction?'

'You suddenly started trying to pin me down,' Rafael said without batting an eye.

'Wait. Me—try to pin *you* down? Just for the record,

that may pass muster with your ex as a reason for a swift break-up, but I can't think of a single one of my friends who would ever fall for that as an excuse for this unlikely relationship coming to an end!'

'So isn't it a good thing that we don't have to convince your friends?'

'I mean,' she continued, 'does that happen often with you, Rafael? Women trying to *pin you down*?'

'It's been known to happen.' Rafael looked at her, head tilted to one side. 'Women not understanding that I'm a free agent, utterly uninterested in settling down, even though that's something I always make clear at the start of any relationship. I don't do commitment. So, trying to pin me down? Always a reason for me to walk away. Never tried to pin a guy down, Sammy?'

'No,' she scoffed.

'Then what a good match we are.'

'You say you don't *do* commitment. Don't you believe in love?'

'I don't believe that this conversation is going anywhere. Have you decided?'

Sammy blinked and grounded herself back in the here and now.

'What if something goes wrong with this so-called failsafe plan?'

'Nothing will go wrong. You and I are going out and it's the only way she'll get the message that she needs to keep out of my way.' His voice became husky, the only real indication that the favour he was asking meant more to him than he had volunteered. 'A handful of days, Sammy, and then your life changes for ever...'

'Okay.' She breathed in deeply. 'I'll do it.'

* * *

Rafael hadn't been lying when he'd told Sammy that he'd suddenly found himself in a place from where, faced with an ex naked under a bathrobe with a crazy desire for *closure* via a bit of sex behind her husband's back, the only exit strategy he could think of was to involve her.

The arrival of Victoria, latched onto her much shorter and much, much older new love interest, had sent a shiver of apprehension through him. Even so, he'd greeted them both warmly and ushered them into his villa to meet the other assembled guests without a flicker of concern on his face. At his most optimistic, he'd hoped that she wouldn't be a nuisance. At his least, he'd wondered just how destructive she might turn out to be.

Truth was, theirs had been a messy break-up. Very quickly into their relationship he had discovered that she was a fragile and vulnerable woman who needed therapy a lot more than she needed him. He had done his best to encourage her into getting help but, the harder he'd tried, the more clingy she'd become and in the end, when her calls had come in every five minutes, he'd had no choice but to begin the process of detangling himself from her.

She hadn't forgiven him but she *had* eventually disappeared from his life and he had breathed a sigh of relief. To be confronted with her now was a nightmare.

He glanced sideways at Sammy who was beginning to nod off against the door. If he could have waited until she was rested in the morning to have the conversation, he would have.

As things stood… Yes, in a sense he'd bought her, as she'd said, but not just because of the reasons he'd given her, although those were all valid. He'd offered her everything he knew she wouldn't be able to resist because, after all, he was the root cause of all her problems. It seemed that, when it came to guilty consciences, she was very good at making him rediscover the one he'd assumed he'd buried. Something about her reminded him of a time when he hadn't yet become the hard, invincible guy he was now. She was a memory of days spent raging against the world whereas now, as an adult, he no longer raged against what he had learned to control.

He half-smiled as he heard the soft sound of her breathing and, when he looked at her, it was to see that she was fast asleep.

Sammy surfaced as the pick-up slowed and then stopped. For a few seconds she was disoriented, without a clue where she was, but she remembered fast enough as she straightened and glanced sideways at Rafael's profile.

A trip that hadn't been straightforward to start with had morphed into something she couldn't have anticipated in a million years.

He killed the engine and turned to her.

'We're here, Sleeping Beauty.'

'I didn't intend to fall asleep.'

'Travel has a way of catching up with a person. Still on board for…?'

'For pretending to be the couple we aren't? I suppose so.' She heaved a heartfelt sigh. 'It would be great to leave here with a plan going forward. Is there…anything I should know before we begin this charade, aside from the fact that your ex has suddenly appeared on the scene? Should we agree on where we met? How we've ended up here in this unlikely position?'

'That's the beauty of this plan,' Rafael assured her. 'We have history. There's no need to make anything up. We met accidentally after years apart, discovered a connection as we travelled down memory lane and, hey presto.'

'It all sounds so easy if you ignore the glaring holes in the story.'

'Let's not focus on the glaring holes. I find it pays to think positive.'

'So we meet, chat about old times and suddenly it's love at first sight and marriage on the cards?'

'Crazy love. Isn't it what the world wants to believe?'

'I'm thinking only an idiot would believe that a guy like you would be a victim of *crazy love.*'

'That's because you probably know me better than anyone who's here. After all, we *do* go back a way, and you *do* have fond memories of me as a teenager to fall back on. Crazy love was definitely not my motto for the day.'

'Yes, but…'

'Don't dwell on the details. Leave it to me to do the convincing.'

Sammy couldn't tear her eyes away from his darkly handsome face. She vaguely thought that stuff that seemed too easy to be true always turned out a mess, but that thought didn't have time to grow legs before he broke eye contact and pushed open his door.

Sammy blinked and actually began to pay attention to her surroundings. She'd slept her way through a drive up a hill and emerged from sleep to an avenue of coconut trees behind her and a courtyard fringed with trees and bushes ahead. Everything was lit with the same beautiful fairy lights that had lit up the terrace where they had earlier sat with their rum punches.

His villa sat squarely off the courtyard. She had envisaged something with a sprawling wooden veranda and a hammock or two, but she couldn't have been more wrong. Instead, it was a solid white house, very, very large, set on two floors, the entrance guarded by two columns that spiralled up both floors to the terracotta roof. It nestled amidst the trees and was uber-modern in its sharp angles and uncompromising lack of frilliness. This was the villa of a guy who didn't have a romantic bone in his body.

Nerves kicked in fast and she was almost glad of the steadying hand that reached to usher her out of the pick-up, then stayed on her arm as they made their way to the front door.

'Don't stress,' Rafael murmured, flipping a key from his pocket and sliding it into the door. 'It's going to be just fine, trust me. The partners will be out during the day doing things on the island; I got my PA to arrange a series of activities to keep them busy. The business associates will be locked away discussing all the complexities of the deal I'm trying to navigate. Dovetailing several companies so that they become one takes a lot of time and patience, hence the fact that we're all here instead of in a hotel somewhere. We need to focus and relax at the same time. You'll be in a pretty amazing kitchen, working some magic with food while everyone else is busy elsewhere. Couldn't be an easier scenario.'

'Let's agree to disagree on that.'

Before she could continue, he'd pushed open the door and, on cue, someone appeared to fetch her bags from the pick-up and bring them through.

It was after eight in the evening and she could hear the rumble of noise coming from somewhere towards the back of the villa beyond the hall in which they were now standing.

He'd released her but now it was her turn to grip his arm. She was aware of magnificent furnishings as they made their way through the villa, all white. It should have looked sterile but the white was interrupted by flamboyant tropical paintings on the walls and the rich lustre of expensive rugs on the marble floor. It seemed to go on for ever as they passed various rooms, again all white, all housing local paintings and sculptures. There were various rooms for various purposes. She felt she'd stepped between the covers of a very high-end interior design magazine.

'Where's everyone?'

'Outside—dinner is served poolside. The plan is for you to briefly meet everyone and then retire: jet lag, et cetera et cetera. I expect after the day you've had you won't be arguing with that.'

'After the past few weeks I've had,' Sammy said, 'I could sleep for the next hundred years.'

'Sammy.' Rafael stopped dead in his tracks and turned, stilling her with his hand on her arm. 'The Yorkshire hotel...that was business.'

'I get that, but you must have known that I had made an offer on the side building?'

'I knew, but it wasn't a consideration when I decided to outbid you. Business is business, after all. Besides, I had no idea who had offered on the outbuilding. It wasn't my concern.'

'Would it have made you stop and think if you'd known that it was me?'

'No.'

'When did you get so hard, Rafael?'

'That's a big question for eight-thirty on a Thursday evening.'

'Does that mean that you don't want to answer?'

'It means that, whatever our game entails, questions about my personal life are off-limits.'

Sammy shrugged, but her green eyes were still curious and steady as they collided with his.

'Okay. And, just for the record, questions about mine are off-limits as well.'

'Good. Glad that's settled. Great match, like I've said. Is it any wonder we're rushing recklessly into marriage when we get one another so well? Now, shall we meet the assembled party?'

But, as they strolled through the villa, heading out towards the massive infinity pool that was perched on manicured grounds leading down to a private cove, Rafael could feel his curiosity about her pique. He'd warned her off thinking that, because they were in this unusual situation, she was somehow owed access to his private thoughts or to the things that had made him the man he was: the hurt, anger and disillusionment that had struck during his formative years, emotions never to be forgotten. No one would ever have access to that part of him.

It was fair enough that she had laid down the same ground rules for him as he'd laid down for her, and really, since when had he ever been curious about any woman's back story? So he was surprised to find himself wondering about the woman by his side with her chin held high and grim determination plastered on her face.

The sound of laughter was getting louder the nearer

they got to the sprawling French doors that led out to the terrace and pool area at the back of the villa. The nights drew in early here but it remained warm enough for people to swim at night if they cared to. He never did.

He could feel her stiffen next to him. Good Lord, could she look more as though she were being dragged to face a hangman's noose?

Some nerves were understandable. He'd understand a shy smile, perhaps, as he introduced her to people she didn't know...and maybe, just maybe, an adoring look up at him... Was that asking too much?

When he glanced down, it was to see the last thing she seemed likely to give would either be adoration or a shy smile. Her mouth was pursed, her eyes were narrowed and her posture was rigid. This wasn't a woman in love with him. This was a woman who wanted to hit him over the head with a rolling pin.

He sighed to himself. There was only one thing for it. He turned to her and called her name in a low whisper. As she looked up at him, he cupped the nape of her neck with his hand, tangled his fingers into her short, dark hair and kissed her.

That kiss...

It was the last thing Sammy had been expecting. The mouth that covered hers was cool, the tongue that probed was moist and the reaction she had was devastatingly powerful. She was so surprised that she didn't pull back; so stunned that she lost herself in it and yielded to a drowning sensation quite unlike anything she had ever felt before in her life.

She tiptoed to return the kiss and her hand crept along

his neck and curved the shape of his jaw just as he pulled away and murmured with husky amusement, 'Thank you.'

In a heartbeat, she realised what had just happened. About to introduce the love of his life, and fearing that *love* was probably the last thing on her face, he had pulled her to him and kissed her...kissed her until she'd been soft, compliant and rosy-cheeked...*kissed her senseless*... until she'd displayed all the classic signs of a woman in love: pink cheeks, parted lips and dazed eyes.

Blinking like an owl, she turned to a collection of very appreciative faces. Some people were standing, some were lounging on recliners and a couple was actually in the pool. The backdrop of a starry night, the dark shadows of swaying coconut trees and in the distance the even darker strip of ocean made the scene look almost staged—especially as everyone seemed to have stopped whatever they'd been doing.

'Let me introduce you to Sammy.'

Rafael's voice snapped her out of her stupor and she duly plastered a smile on her face. Her eyes were adjusting to the darkness, the lights mounted on the wall behind them picking out over-sized planters with bamboo bursting up, several sun loungers with canopies that were the size of single beds and a shaded area, beneath which was a long table and chairs and a bar area. The pool itself was absolutely enormous, flat, shiny and still.

It could only have been a matter of seconds, but it felt as though it took for ever before the silence was broken by a woman slow-clapping and stepping out of the pool.

'I never thought I'd see the day when the inveterate bachelor decided to join the ranks of us in love...' came a low, amused, husky female drawl with just the tiniest thread of bitter rage detectable, Sammy was sure, only to Rafael and her. Because of course the woman in question emerging out of the water could only be his ex.

She was an Amazonian beauty with long, long blonde hair piled on her head in an artfully tousled bun and with a figure made for wearing very, very little. That was precisely what she happened to have on: a tiny bikini that left precious little to the imagination.

She took her time wading up the shallow steps and moved to stand behind a plump, elderly man sitting at a table with a couple of other, slightly younger, guys.

'Happens to all of us in the end,' Rafael said politely.

Sammy felt the weight of his arm slung over her shoulders and, because she'd taken an instant dislike to the woman, she linked her fingers through Rafael's and smiled, her smile as polite as Rafael's response had been.

He raised her hand to his mouth and grazed her knuckles with his lips. Sammy thought that it was a tremendous performance for the guy who didn't do touchy-feely. Her brain said that. Her body, however, blazed in instant response and she knew that colour was again crawling into her cheeks.

On wicked impulse, she slid her hand along his back and then dipped her finger beneath the waistband of his jeans and got a kick when she felt his body stiffen. She smiled and wriggled her wandering finger under the shirt to feel hard, muscled skin before slowly removing her hand.

Then she was being introduced to everyone.

'I told her that there was no need for her to sweat over a stove, cooking for us all when she got here,' he crooned, arm still firmly in place, this time with his hand just below the small swell of her breast. 'But...' He turned to her and kissed the tip of her nose. 'You insisted, didn't you, my darling?'

'I did, indeed... I plan on setting up my own restaurant, and practice is always going to make perfect. Practising on a captive audience for a few days couldn't suit me better!'

For fifteen minutes, doing the rounds, she was able to make some judgements on the group of people she would be deceiving for the next few days. There were seven men, aged between about forty to the oldest, Clement, who was in his seventies. The seven women were mostly in their forties and fifties, with the exception of Victoria, who was a mere year or two older than her.

Rafael still had his arm slung over her shoulders. He was still fully playing to the audience, and it was wreaking havoc with her composure.

She yawned and edged away just a little. There was only so much her blood pressure could take with this game of make-believe.

'Come along, darling, time for bed,' Rafael crooned and Sammy looked up at him with a suitably adoring expression. She batted her lashes; he grinned and in return dipped his head to kiss her again. This time his tongue flicked between her parted lips and her breathing hitched. He pulled back with a convincing sigh of regret.

Just as soon as they hit the stairs, she pulled away from him and glared, because he was grinning.

'Convincing acting,' he murmured, leading the way.

'I thought you weren't the touchy-feely sort. What choice did I have but to respond in kind?'

'Very true.'

'It's why you're paying me so much money, isn't it?'

'I don't like it when you put it like that.' Rafael frowned.

'Too bad. It's all just an act and I'm fine playing make-believe when we have to.' Her body was trying hard to agree with that infuriated statement but, when their eyes met, hers were cool and composed.

He nudged open one of the doors at the very end of the landing, outside which was a seating area complete with plants and a window overlooking the back.

Sammy stopped dead in her tracks. In the middle of the room were soft chairs and a sofa interrupted by a low, square coffee table in the middle. There was a sideboard, a bar and a business-like desk that drew the eye to French doors opening out to a warmly lit veranda. Through another door to the side, she could glimpse the bedroom.

'We're sharing a bedroom,' she said flatly, folding her arms and gazing at her luggage waiting for her just outside the bedroom door. The door was ajar, and she couldn't see the bed through it, but she was guessing that there weren't conveniently going to be two singles.

'It's a thing in this day and age when two people are going out and in love.'

'We're neither.'

'Sammy, perhaps I should have warned you, but I thought you'd probably work that one out without any help from me.' He turned round, shoved his hands in his pockets and looked at her. Just those dark eyes resting on her reminded her of the kiss that had shaken her to the core and then, hard on the heels of *that* memory, *why* he had kissed her in the first place.

'Don't worry,' he said wryly. 'You can have the bed. I'm happy to take the sofa out here. As you can see, it's plenty big enough for me, even though I'm not small.'

'You could have said that from the start.'

'I know, but it's fun watching you blush.'

'This isn't about *fun*.'

'I know.' He raised his eyebrows and stared at her with his head tilted to one side, still half-smiling. 'On a practical note, I think we managed to pull off the business of you working your fingers to the bone while you're here instead of relaxing and enjoying time out with the others…or with me…even though we're crazy about one another and can't bear to be apart.'

'Being a personal chef doesn't allow for much free time.'

'So you made clear to everyone there. Who'd have thought that making puff pastry could consume half a day? Well played, though, I must admit. No one will question you, although you might find that you have visitors popping in now and again. Perhaps you shouldn't have made it sound quite so interesting.'

'As long as Victoria isn't one of the visitors, then that's fine.'

'Who knows? You might find that I make an appearance just to catch up on how a roux gets made…'

'Ha ha.'

'Seriously, though, Sammy—thank you for this evening. Only a few more days left and life can get back to normal.'

She heaved a heartfelt sigh. 'I can't wait.'

CHAPTER FIVE

THE SUITE TURNED out fine. Sammy stepped into a bedroom the size of a football field with an adjoining bathroom. True to his word, Rafael decamped outside, taking whatever clothes he wanted with him and telling her that there was another bathroom off the sitting area which he would be more than happy to use.

'Where would I have stayed if this situation hadn't arisen?' Sammy had asked with genuine curiosity.

'The place has six bedroom suites, and four more in an annex beyond the pool, which is actually where Clement and Victoria are staying, as well as two other couples. You would have stayed in one of the suites in the main house here, simply because access to the kitchen would have been more convenient.

'Don't feel you have to rush to prepare anything for breakfast, by the way. I think that would be beyond the call of duty, considering you're supposed to actually want to lie in with me every morning rather than hurtling out of bed at six to bake bread. Might raise a few eyebrows if you really *are* buried in the kitchen twenty-four-seven when we should, theoretically, be enjoying some down time together—lazy mornings before the day has had time to kick off. Not my thing, but expectations might be high from our assembled guests, especially after last night's performance.'

'Shame. Early starts baking would have worked. My bread skills are second to none.'

'I'm sure I'll get to sample some of your creations at some point. Right now, though…no need to rush downstairs. I'll stay in the suite as well, although I'll be up and working by seven.'

Rafael lowered his eyes but he was alert to her graceful movements as she strolled towards one of the two cases she had brought, flipping it open and rifling through the contents before stepping back, folding her arms and looking at him pointedly.

'Don't worry, I'm on my way out.' He yanked back from the brink his thoughts of those casual touches earlier on. 'I think it might be a good idea if you join me for breakfast tomorrow.'

'Why?'

'Because for starters I'll have to make sure evidence of my overnight stay on the sofa is well and truly out of sight. Housekeepers can sometimes have loose tongues, and there are currently four of them doing the rounds. Might be a headache if it gets out that the lovebirds aren't sharing the bedroom. Besides, I'll drive you into town. You'll need to pick up provisions, and there's an excellent food market in the centre of the capital. I made sure the basics are all in place but you might want to see what fresh produce is out there. You'll find it all quite different from what you're used to, I'm guessing.'

'I'm excited to see what's available,' Sammy admitted. 'I spent some time looking up what I might expect and I've got a couple of ideas up my sleeve.'

'Nothing too elaborate, I hope.'

'Why?'

'I wouldn't want to have to hunt you down behind a pile of recipe books…'

'You could always avoid that by joining me behind them,' Sammy said sweetly, but then reddened when his eyebrows shot up at the unintended innuendo behind her perfectly innocent, perfectly sarcastic remark. 'What I *meant* was, I expect there's no chance of that when you've probably never cooked a home-made meal in your life.'

'Tut-tut. That's what I'd call a sweeping generalisation.' He grinned. 'You'd be surprised how many I've cooked, actually, but that's a conversation for another day. For the moment, time for us both to retire to our respective sleeping quarters. And Sammy?'

'Yes?'

'I just want to make sure that you're entirely comfortable with what we're doing.'

'In what way?'

'A fake relationship. It comes with certain strings…'

'Strings?'

'Being touched…it's expected. Were you uncomfortable with that earlier?'

His voice swirled round her like honey and she felt herself begin to burn from the inside out. When she thought of the heavy warmth of his arm draped over her…and, worse, the feel of his cool lips on hers…her pulse went into overdrive and she wanted to pass out. She didn't have his level of experience, which was something she hadn't taken into account.

Mouth dry, she managed to croak, 'No. Why should I?'

'Good. Just wanted to ask, but actually, I didn't think you were.'

'How so?'

'If you were, let's just say you wouldn't have got into the rhythm so effortlessly.'

'Yes…yes, I did do that. Get into the rhythm…effortlessly.'

'You certainly did.' His voice was approving. 'No one could have doubted our relationship when you slipped two of your fingers under the waistband of my trousers.' He grinned. 'Even *I* was a little shocked at just how much we were in love at that point.'

'Like I said, all part of the deal we made. You can rest assured that I'm fine with what has to be done. It's for an audience and, like you say, that audience isn't going to be watching twenty-four-seven.'

'Ample time to recharge your batteries in between sets,' he murmured with amusement.

He was so cool about it, so matter of fact. He'd touched her and she'd gone up in flames. She'd touched him and he'd been startled at her audacity. She wondered whether he thought that, in the back of beyond, all she got up to were barn dances, holding hands, and kissing under the mistletoe at Christmas.

'Ample time,' she agreed crisply. 'And now, if you don't mind…? I'd really like to get some sleep.'

Sammy tried to kill all wayward thoughts, but her sleep was broken by them nonetheless. She awoke early the following morning to find that she was still thinking about him and the effect he had had on her.

She'd had a crush on him a million years ago. Was

there a reluctant attraction still there? Some kind of hang-over from back in the day when she had looked at him with her adolescent crush carefully hidden?

Beyond that, was there something about him, some-thing compelling, that she still found vaguely irresistible? She'd made it her mission to be strong and independent—to turn her back on the path her mother had taken, when she'd collapsed after her husband had died and then had foolishly and weakly turned to a guy for support when she should have looked inwards for her own inner strength.

She'd carved her own niche, relied on her own resil-ience, and had always assumed that a guy would come in due course—someone decent and reliable who shared her dreams and would never let her down. Out there, there was paragon of virtue waiting for her.

So was she angry with herself because an attraction that belonged in the past had decided to resurface? Be-cause she should feel nothing for a guy who was literally draped in red flags? And yet she did. It felt pathetic to tingle like a teenager when he'd touched her for no bet-ter reason than a performance.

When she looked at the Amazonian blonde, she could see the sort of woman he was attracted to. He was in-different to *her* but it seemed she wasn't indifferent to *him*. She would have to start blotting out whatever fool-ish recollection of a crush had come along to ambush her common sense. She would have to match adult behaviour with adult behaviour.

She had a shower, dressed quickly in casual clothes and tentatively opened the bedroom door to see what awaited her outside. It was a little after seven and Rafael was at a desk by the window in front of his computer, working.

Every item of whatever he had used on the bed had been neatly tidied away and was folded on the coffee table in front of the television. Cushions were back in place. No one would guess that they had spent the night apart.

'I never saw you as a neat freak, Rafael.' She glanced at the folded clothes and then looked at him with her eyebrows raised.

'Isn't it great that you're discovering exciting, new stuff about the guy you're in love with?'

'Oh, yes, I can barely contain my excitement.'

'How did you sleep?'

'Terrific. Great bed; very comfortable. And you?'

'As well as can be expected on a sofa. Coffee?'

Rafael sat back and stretched, flexing his muscles, before standing up and strolling towards a coffee machine on a gleaming walnut sideboard which she only now noticed. The doors had been flung open to allow the balmy tropical air inside and, through them, she could glimpse a vista that could have been lifted straight from a magazine.

There was a distant view of bright-blue ocean, a stretch of greenery broken by swaying coconut trees—the very ones that surrounded the infinity pool—and bushes and foliage bursting with the bright colours of exotic flowers. All the familiar sounds were missing: the intrusive sounds of beeping horns, foot traffic outside her front door and the clatter of voices. It was peaceful and quiet, aside from birds, bees and the distant sound of a lawn mower doing something on the manicured grounds.

Determined not to let turbulent emotions get the better of her, Sammy smiled politely, nodded at his offer of coffee and strolled towards the open French doors.

He was barefoot in a loose white linen shirt and a pair of khaki shorts. He was so sinfully, spectacularly good-looking that it briefly took her breath away.

'It's okay to sit down, Sammy. We can go down in a while. No rush; breakfast is informal here. People grab what they want and at ten-thirty the day's work begins. We retire to one of the sitting rooms downstairs which is equipped with a conference table and all the gizmos to make transatlantic communication a breeze. Everybody else does whatever they want, although as I said today the partners will be on a day trip out and I'll take some time out to come with you to the market.'

'I'll see if I can get hold of some fresh fish and prawns. It wasn't the original plan for today, which was chicken, but ...seafood would be nice.'

'There's an excellent fish market. Opens every day bar Monday.'

'When was the last time you were here, just out of curiosity?'

'Sorry?'

'When were you here last? I know it's not part of my brief to ask personal questions, but it might help if I know just a tiny bit about you, seeing as you're the love of my life.'

Their eyes met and Sammy held his dark gaze.

Rafael hesitated. He had got her to this place, and it made sense for them to have some background information about one another, but intense privacy was so embedded in his DNA that he honestly didn't know where to begin when it came to sharing anything about himself.

Her clear green eyes were only mildly curious.

She was so slight, and her dark hair was so short, that she should have looked boyish—but she didn't. She was all soft femininity underneath the tough, prickly exterior, a contradiction, and all the more unsettling and fascinating for it.

He poured them both a cup of coffee and nodded to the sofa, encouraging her to sit and then sitting next to her, inclining his body to face her and extending his long, muscular legs.

'Okay, you're right. I suppose it makes sense for us to find out a bit more about one another. I don't come here often, as it happens. Not as often as I'd like. Of course it gets used: my father comes on a reasonably regular basis, and brings friends sometimes. And I open it up to my employees on a regular basis—a kind of bonus if they've done a particularly good job. For me, though, time is money.'

'How did you get to that place?'

'Come again?'

'The place where time is money. I don't remember you being particularly impressed by money or material stuff when you were young. Old jeans...old rugby shirt... You always looked like you couldn't care less about fancy clothes.'

'I didn't then,' Rafael said gently, lowering his lashes. 'And I still don't, but I found that what I do care about—which is making the sort of money that gives me freedom—comes with the fancy clothes and the material stuff.'

'It's a tough life.'

Rafael burst out laughing and, when he looked at her, his dark eyes were warm and appreciative.

'Never thought about making lots of money, Sammy? Buying freedom from small-town living?'

'No,' she said politely. 'And frankly I'm shocked that, having met me, anyone out there is actually falling for this act of ours. Two minutes of questioning and they'd know what I thought of people who put money ahead of everything. I hope you don't think I'm rude in saying that.'

'Borderline rude, now that you mention it, but I'm getting used to that side of you.' His dark eyes were amused. 'I should point out, though, that I don't think anyone will be asking for your definition of what you look for in a soul mate. You're over-thinking conversations that won't take place. Between work, being a tour guide for the other halves and you buried in the kitchen, long, meaningful conversations are going to be few and far between. If the going gets tough, I'll rescue you.' He paused and then, to his surprise, said, 'Anyway, everyone cares about money.'

'Yes, well, maybe in your world.'

'Money is freedom. Who doesn't want to be free?' He reached for his phone and ordered up some breakfast, courtesy of one of the assistant chefs on call: local coconut bread with scrambled eggs and fresh juice. His eyes didn't leave her face. 'But, getting out of the realms of abstract thinking and returning to your original question, I've had the place for years. It was...'

'It was...?'

'A celebration of making my first million, as it happens.' He looked at her, but her returning gaze was bland

and matter of fact. She was listening, but she wasn't hanging onto what he had to say. Something stirred inside him, something darkly tempting, a sensation that was as fleeting as quicksilver, gone before he could recognise it. Somewhere inside, a spark had been lit, and it left him with an uneasy feeling, one he dismissed as soon as it surfaced.

What was the big deal in sharing perfectly straightforward information because they happened to be in a situation that demanded it?

'My ancestry on my father's side harks from this island, as it happens. It was briefly colonised by the Spanish, hence the connection. My parents came here on a belated honeymoon when I was three.' He flushed darkly because *that* bit had slipped out before he could edit it.

'Okay, makes sense—I've read that it's tough buying land or property here without connections. How is your dad, by the way? I remember him…a bit.'

'Is that it? No more probing questions about my past in a quest for background information to add authenticity?'

'I can ask some if you like.' Sammy shrugged and then smiled. 'I thought we'd stick to the basics.'

'Excellent idea,' Rafael concurred a little tetchily. 'So, on the subject of the basics, my father is fine and living a splendid life in Valencia, which is where he comes from. After we left Yorkshire, he did a stint back in London, but then once I'd made my first million he expressed a desire to return to Spain after…after everything. It was well within my remit to give him what he wanted, so I did.'

'He must be very proud of you,' Sammy said thoughtfully. 'And honestly, Rafael, there's absolutely no need for you to come with me to get provisions. In fact, you'd be more of a hindrance than a help. I can dither a lot when it comes to buying fresh ingredients. I'll check out the kitchen before I go, and see what I need to prep and when, and if there's transport available…?'

'On tap.'

'Good.' She smiled briskly. 'If I'm to cook the meal I want to cook, then I'm going to have to leave very soon to go do my shopping.'

'No time? You're hurrying along the "getting to know me" business.'

'You enjoy. If I see anyone downstairs, I'll lay it on thick about the duties of a personal chef, and no time to waste. Between the roux and puff pastry, a girl could be tied up all day.'

Sammy leapt to her feet.

The market was an adventure. One of Rafael's dedicated drivers gave her a little tour around the town, pointing out where the various beaches were, telling her that she couldn't leave without visiting one of them. She had begun to feel two things for the first time in her life: on top of the world and in control.

They rolled down the windows and she let the breeze whip through her hair as she stared out at verdant roadside and bright-blue skies. Up ahead, telephone wires were covered in vines and ivy. The trees were bigger and lusher than any she'd ever seen before, and vegetation crowded the sides of the roads, as if in a hurry to stage a takeover. It was busy at ten in the morning with vans and scooters on the roads, and shops on the sides of the humming roads were open for business here and there with vivid fruit and vegetables spilling out from them.

They drove along the main road, zig-zagging, so that every now and then she would peer out and catch a glimpse of the ocean, which glittered a deeper blue than the sky and was as calm as a lake. Coconut trees were everywhere, springing up in unusual places, tangling with towering bamboo trees, the perfect playground for birds and butterflies.

Sammy was dropped in the square, on the fringe of the bustling market. Stepping out of the car, she took a few seconds to breathe in deeply, eyes half-closed, really loving the fragrant scent of flowers, sun and spices being sold, and enjoying the rich lilt of foreign voices that laughed and bartered.

She wasn't the only tourist enjoying the town although, thankfully, none of them were any of the women from the villa. The last thing she needed was to see a six-foot blonde swooping down on her.

She took her time shopping and let her mind drift from the food she was going to prepare to Rafael and some of the things he had let slip that had set the cogs in her brain whirring. She had a future that now seemed secure, a very happy trade-off for a few days of inconvenience.

Then she thought of the kiss that still lingered on her lips and was uneasily aware of the truth of the saying that there was no such thing as a free lunch. Would she face consequences of this decision that she couldn't foresee? Nope. She pushed that unease away, and was in high spirits by the time she made it back to the villa at a little after two, having grabbed something to eat at one of the local cafés.

The villa was quiet. Business was being done in one wing of the mansion and the partners were lazing on a beach somewhere, enjoying whatever five-star picnic had been prepared for them. Sammy got on with the business of preparing food with the radio on low, with the occasional sound of one of the housekeepers cleaning and a nice warm breeze rustling through the open doors.

Peace.

Sammy was most lost to the world when she was cooking. The kitchen was fragrant with the smells of herbs and spices and, before long, her bouillabaisse was done and dusted and absolutely perfect. She had got hold of three plump kingfish and was busy preparing them when she was aware of the soft pad of footsteps pausing at the door.

Victoria. She turned around with a sinking heart to see the other woman lounging against the door frame. Did the woman have *nothing* else to wear apart from items of clothing that could fit into matchboxes? The sarong draped loosely round her slim hips barely skimmed her thighs, and matched the pale-yellow shades of her bikini top. Her gold sandals were flat, but even so she towered over Sammy as she quietly shut the door behind her. She strolled to the centre of the kitchen before striking a dramatic pose as she half-perched on the ten-seater kitchen table. Her blonde hair was loose. It was very long, nearly to her waist, and hung attractively in damp strands over her shoulder.

'How was the beach?' Sammy eventually asked, because *someone* had to break the stretching silence, and Victoria seemed to have no interest in being the first to speak.

Sammy washed her hands and made an effort to smile, but was conscious of her food-splattered apron, lack of make-up and casual clothing that was great when behind a stove but less great when confronted by a woman whose job was to strut runways and dazzle.

'The beach was like any other beach.' Victoria shrugged one shoulder, but her bright-blue eyes were pinned to Sammy's flushed face with the coldness of diamonds. 'We really didn't get to know one another last night, did we?'

'It was a brief encounter,' Sammy agreed. 'Long-haul flying takes a toll.'

'Do you do much of that?'

'Very little. Is there something I can get for you? I ask because I'm in the middle of...' She made a vague expansive gesture towards the dishes still to be prepped and smiled ruefully without bothering to try to look sincere.

'Of course you are. A chef...fascinating. Rafael's managed to do a good job of keeping you under wraps! The last I heard, wasn't he dating that model who stole the Paris show a few months ago?'

'Was he? I wouldn't know. Not my world, I'm afraid.'

'I know! Adorable. So...remind me how you two met?'

'Perhaps another time, Victoria. I really would love nothing more than to sit and have a girlie chat about our relationship with you, but sadly I can't. So, if you don't mind...and I hate to be rude...?'

'Rafael never talked about his past when we were together. You *did* know that we were once very much *an item,* didn't you? Yes? So you can imagine my surprise when he produced you from the closet and told me that you were serious about one another!'

She wafted towards Sammy and stared down at her from her imposing height. Having just returned from a day at the beach, she smelled of sun and sand without looking as though either had got the better of her.

'I've been naughty and done a little detective work, and, wow! Fabulous CV—and lucky you, living in that super-peaceful part of the world! Crazy that you and Rafael should end up together when he's just completely the opposite of you! I guess meeting up again after all those years… Memories, yeah? Powerful, amazing, *adorable*. Your mum lives up there in Yorkshire, doesn't she? I believe that's in the blurb I read about you. She must be thrilled that you two are together!'

'Over the moon. Now, please…'

'It's not going to last—you know that, don't you?'

'Because what *you* had with him didn't?' Sammy retorted through gritted teeth.

'Because *nothing lasts* with Rafe on the woman front. And face it—look at the women he's dated! If *they* couldn't tame him, if *I* couldn't, then do *you* really think you can?'

This temporarily rendered Sammy mute because she'd been thinking pretty much the same thing since she'd laid eyes on Victoria. Why would anyone seriously believe that the guy who went for statuesque blondes would ever suddenly be bowled over by a five-foot-three brunette with cropped hair? On the looks front alone, there was a glaring disparity there.

'So…' Victoria pouted, stepping back just as the door was pushed open behind them. 'I'm just being kind because I *care*.'

She was smiling as she turned to the kitchen door where Rafael was now standing, his posture mirroring

Victoria's of only minutes before as he lounged against the door frame, his dark eyes cold and watchful.

'Looking for something, Victoria?'

'A bottle of water...'

She sashayed across the tiled floor, a picture of impossible physical perfection, and paused next to Rafael just close enough and long enough for Sammy to get the picture that *she* was what a guy like Rafael Moreno would always and inevitably be attracted to.

'But...' she laughed huskily and glanced over her shoulder at Sammy '...then I remembered that there are bottles in the mini-fridge in the bedroom.'

Rafael watched her march past him, then looked back at Sammy. 'What was that all about?' He moved towards her as she was turning away and spun her gently round so that she had no option but to look at him.

'Nothing.'

'Sammy, I can see that you're upset.'

'I can handle something like that. I can handle *someone* like that. You try working as a sous chef! You'd soon find out that it pays to be as tough as nails.'

'Why am I not convinced?'

'Because...because...'

'What did she say to you? If she's put a foot out of place, trust me, I won't hesitate to remind her of the mistake.'

'You don't need to defend me!' But her voice was a whisper and tears weren't too far away. Why—because she'd been taken down a peg or two? Made to see just how unsuitable she was for a guy like Rafael? *Because she'd been put in her place? Pathetic.* She'd surely been through enough not to let someone like Victoria get to her?

'You're my better half—at least for a week.' He pulled her gently towards him and as Sammy rested her head against his chest, she could hear the crooked smile in his voice.

'That doesn't count.'

'Ignore her, Sammy. You're a million times more of a woman than she could ever be.'

Sammy tilted her head to look at him. She had to crane her neck. 'That's not what the mirror's saying. Rafael, she just pointed out the obvious—why would a guy like you be attracted to someone like me? She just reminded me of how beautiful she was and how ordinary I am in comparison.' Self-pity clogged her throat. *Crazy. Stupid.*

'If you think you're ordinary, Sammy, then maybe you and the mirror need to get to know one another better. You're cute and feisty and sexy as hell, and truth is, I don't think I've ever met any woman quite like you.'

Sammy's mouth fell open.

Their eyes collided and in that split second she knew what Rafael was going to do. He was going to kiss her—a *real* kiss, with no audience in need of convincing.

Never had she wanted anything more badly in her life.

She gasped as his mouth descended, as his tongue plunged into the moistness of her mouth. She arched up to him, her body contouring his, slight and small against big and muscular.

She moaned in a hitched way as he swept her off her feet, their mouths still devouring one another's, and rested her on the table. He supported himself, hands flattened against the smooth, cool concrete surface of the table, and she wrapped her arms around his neck and didn't surface for air until the kiss slowed.

They were breathing heavily as they broke apart.

'Well...' Sammy broke the silence but then stuttered to a stop because she had no idea what to say, nor why her fingers were still sifting through his hair.

'Well.' Rafael smiled slowly. His hands on the table were still caging her but then he raised one to delicately trail a finger along her cheek. 'What are we going to do about this?'

'Nothing,' Sammy said quickly. 'We... I... This shouldn't have happened. We can just forget about it and carry on as though...as though...' She yanked her disobedient hand away and sat on it.

'Or...?'

'Rafael, don't...'

'Up to you,' he murmured, contouring her mouth in a sinfully erotic gesture. 'I'll sleep on the sofa until you command me to join you in bed. A gentleman couldn't say fairer than that, could he?'

That damned smile! That unfair way he roused her, so that her nipples pinched and the wetness between her legs made her want to fidget and squirm!

She didn't want the complication of this attraction! She *appreciated* that he was being a gentleman. She just wasn't sure that a gentleman was what she wanted...

CHAPTER SIX

OUT OF THE corner of his eye, Rafael was aware of Victoria holding court with a couple of the partners. The partners looked a little alarmed. In a minute, he would think about rescuing them, because Victoria had obviously had a little too much to drink and the canapés had not even made their appearance. By the time dinner was served, who knew where she would be on the inebriation scale?

Clement was saying something about business and Rafael dragged his thoughts back in line. It was a little before seven and they were all milling around in the sitting room, which was spacious and kitted out with an assortment of chairs and sofas all in shades of creams and pale-gold. Everything was artfully arranged so that no one would be left out of any group conversations. Unless anyone wanted to lurk in a corner, they were compelled to sit in a sociable arrangement and chat. Excellent for fostering a cordial atmosphere amongst people who might not know one another that well. Staff had been hired for the week and champagne flutes were being refilled.

Clement had turned to Geoffrey, a dapper middle-aged guy who was desperate for his small company to be amalgamated under a bigger umbrella so that their software could expand. Clement was musing about the stock market and what might prove a good investment. Rafael wondered if he was aware of his girlfriend over-gesticulating in the background. It didn't seem so. He was a talented businessman whose ability to focus was legendary. Victoria could have been doing cartwheels on the ceiling.

Rafael glanced at his watch and drained his glass—whisky, not champagne.

Where was Sammy?

She'd disappeared to the market first thing and since then he had only clapped eyes on her once, in the kitchen, where she'd been surrounded by mountains of fresh fruit and vegetables, and had shooed him out before he'd had a chance to remind her that she had to make an appearance in time for drinks.

Hell, was she even thinking of that kiss they'd shared? Because he couldn't get it out of his mind. He could still taste it on his mouth!

Let the two sous chefs he had hired get on with the nitty-gritty, he had told her. They needed the practice before they took up their positions at his hotel, and he and Sammy had to keep up their charade.

'I'll be there, don't worry.' She had pushed him firmly in the direction of the door. 'I haven't forgotten our deal!'

He breathed in deeply and remembered those big, green eyes staring up at him with amusement, and those soft lips that had done too good a job of reminding him what they'd felt like against his.

Rafael wasn't sure whether it was the novelty of their situation or the fact that there was history between them, but he was drawn to Sammy in a way that was confusing and a little unsettling. Where did that pull come from which made his mind wander off in the middle of back-to-back meetings; and which made him lose concentration until the only thing he could think of was seeing what she was up to? It had driven him to seek her out in the kitchen...because he just couldn't put that kiss to the back of his mind.

He wondered whether maybe the stark contrast between Victoria and Sammy was somehow messing with his head even though it shouldn't have, of course, because Victoria was an ex and Sammy was... Sammy wasn't even *current* in the truest sense of the word.

Victoria was a reminder of his greatest screw-up when it came to any relationship he had ever had with a woman. He hadn't so much as taken his eye off the ball as never had his eye on it in the first place. In the dying throes of their relationship, clinging and sobbing had alternated with threats of revenge, followed swiftly by tearful apologies and yet more clinging. It had been a mess.

Was his mind doing some kind of foxtrot between what Victoria represented and what Sammy represented, coerced into a phony relationship? Whereas Victoria had been an uncontrolled mess, Sammy couldn't be more controlled. She was as cool as a cucumber. She had no idea how those passing, dutiful touches had turned him on the evening before, whether he liked to admit it or not. She was playing a game for his benefit, and only because the carrot he had dangled in front of her had been too tempting to resist.

For the first time in his life, he was with a woman who wasn't chasing behind him and wasn't after more than he was willing to give. She didn't want to hear his back story so that she could get closer. In fact, she wasn't that interested in his back story at all. Their paths had crossed briefly when they'd been teenagers, and the experience had left a sour taste in her mouth. Left to her own devices, there was no way she would ever have sought him out because she just didn't like him very much. She wasn't impressed by his money, even though it was thanks to his millions that she was being given a passport to everything she had ever wanted for herself.

Although, he grudgingly had to admit, it was also thanks to his money that she'd lost the space she'd banked on having for herself in the first place—swings and roundabouts.

Whatever was going on, he was still trying to make sense of it. Victoria and Sammy side by side... Was Sammy somehow benefiting from the comparison—was that it? He was always in control when it came to women, so what was happening here? It was puzzling but it was also...exciting...even though he knew that this kind of excitement wasn't something he should be indulging.

His last brief fling had ended four months ago, with a striking model who had told him that he needed to grow up—by which she'd meant start committing to more than whatever lay a day or two ahead. He'd politely turned down the suggestion.

Maybe he was sick of models and was now vulnerable to falling for a feisty, down-to-earth girl from his past who didn't think twice about laughing at him and couldn't care less about commitment—at least, not with him. Was that it? He felt that, if he couldn't make sense of what he was feeling, he couldn't control it, which obviously wouldn't do.

He was in the process of trying to juggle his thoughts with whatever conversation was going on with the two guys standing by him when he glanced towards the door and...there she was.

For a few seconds, all the background noise faded and Rafael drew in a sharp breath as he stared at her over the rim of his glass with dark, brooding intensity. Every muscle in his body had tightened and the thud of a powerful sexual awareness hit him like a sledgehammer.

She was wearing the simplest of summer dresses, something straight and flowery, with tiny pearl buttons all the way down the front and thin spaghetti straps. She wore flat sandals, no jewellery except for some stud earrings and next to no make-up. She looked young, fresh, wholesome and incredibly sexy.

He cleared his throat and managed to propel himself towards her, dumping his empty glass en route and grabbing a replacement in the process.

'Sammy, my darling, you're here.' He managed to sound hearty yet caressingly intimate at the same time.

'Rafael, my love. Where else would I be?'

Sammy felt her heart pick up speed. She'd almost completely managed to avoid him during the course of the day. First, she'd been at the market, and then later she'd made sure that one of her young helpers, Jemima, had done the honours serving a casual picnic lunch at the pool house where the workers had been taking a break to eat.

He'd shown up at the kitchen at some point, purely to chat to her about her duties. She'd glanced at him leaning indolently against the door frame and had gone hot and cold with sudden, dramatic awareness. God knew, she'd tried to put that kiss they'd shared into perspective, but she hadn't been able to. It had detonated like a hand grenade tossed into her calm, ordered life.

She didn't get it. How could he manage to get under

her skin the way he did? He shouldn't be able to bring a smile to her lips, and he certainly shouldn't be able to ratchet up her curiosity about him until her head ached, but he did both. She'd kept telling herself that this was just a job, and that just about seemed to work until she laid eyes on him.

Such as now. He was in black: black jeans and a black figure-hugging tee-shirt, tan loafers and no socks. Nothing about him screamed 'wealth' and yet he still managed to look incredibly rich, laid back and sophisticated. Just behind him, she caught a glimpse of Victoria narrowly watching their interaction with a champagne flute half-raised, as though she'd been on the verge of gulping down the contents.

'You didn't expect me to still be shackled to the oven, did you?' she purred, conscious of Victoria's eyes on them. She was also aware of *his* eyes on her, a little amused and a little surprised. He'd obviously thought that getting her to pretend to respond to him convincingly would be as difficult as pulling teeth.

She looked up at him, placed her hand flat on his chest and stood on tiptoe, half-closing her eyes, mouth pursed for the kiss everyone would be expecting—something light and brief, in keeping with the fact that he wasn't the touchy-feely sort and public displays of affection weren't really his thing.

His mouth was cool and she started as he nudged his tongue between her lips, teasing a response from her and getting just the response she knew she definitely shouldn't give. Her hand curled into a fist, clasping the soft cotton of his tee-shirt. Her eyelids fluttered as she unconsciously gravitated towards him until their bodies were pressed together.

Sammy was drowning in that kiss. Her breathing slowed and, when he eventually made to pull away, she found that she was trembling.

'Now, *there's* a surprise,' he murmured softly into her ear.

She cupped the side of his cheek with her hand, still on tiptoe to reach him, but pulling him down slightly so that, as softly as he'd whispered into her ear, she could whisper back, 'Why? I do know the rules of the game, Rafael. Besides, your ex is all eyes. You don't want her to start getting suspicious, do you? I thought that was the whole point of the game.'

'So it is, my darling, so it is.'

Sammy pulled back, tore her gaze away from his and then peered around him to the assembled crowd. She smiled.

'Young love!' One of the older women raised her champagne flute with a broad, approving smile. Sammy laughed and pretend-punched Rafael in the stomach. She said something about maybe young love for *her,* but slightly less young for Rafael, who was a few years older.

She avoided Victoria. She mingled and chatted but was doubly aware of the other woman's shrewd eyes on her, and of Rafael always nearby, probably making sure she didn't put her foot in it somehow by saying the wrong thing.

He gently tugged her back as everyone began making their way to the dining room where dinner was being served. Ahead of them, Victoria had fallen into step with Clement. His arm was around her waist but he was talking to one of the other men. If he was even aware of the towering blonde at his side, then he gave very little evidence of it.

'Just look at that,' Sammy muttered to Rafael as they trailed behind them.

'Look at what?'

'Victoria and Clement.'

'What about them?'

'He's barely paying her a scrap of attention.'

'Not sure what you'd like him to be doing right now. He's pushing eighty. I don't think hijinks on the dance floor are going to work for him.'

Sammy glanced up to find Rafael grinning broadly. He looked down at her. Their eyes met and her heart sped up.

'Why on earth would he go out with her if he wasn't interested in her?'

'Of course he's interested in her, although, in fairness, possibly not for her mind.'

'He's a really nice guy, but I suppose when you've got tons of money, and you can have whatever toy you want, you're always going to pick the one that's the shiniest.'

'He *is* getting over his wife's death,' Rafael said gently. 'Maybe the shiniest toy in the toy box is just what he needs for his recovery. Besides, it's a symbiotic relationship.'

'Meaning?'

'Victoria likes his money and he likes being seen with her on his arm.'

'Rich men—they're all the same.'

'Tut-tut, Sammy. That sounds a lot like a generalisation.'

'Does it?' She stopped dead in her tracks and looked at

him. 'I'm thinking that *your* track record is along those lines!—beautiful women hanging onto you and you having fun with them even though you're not in it for their minds? Honestly, I just don't get women sometimes.'

Rafael was still grinning. 'You're very fetching when you're standing on your soap box. Has anyone ever told you that?'

'Actually, no.' But she could feel herself tumbling into his dark gaze. She drew in a sharp breath when he raised one finger to trail it along her cheek, finally outlining her mouth and letting his finger linger there for a few seconds. Her eyes widened and everything in her body suddenly began to disobey the rules. Her nipples tightened against the thin cotton of her dress. She was so flat that she could easily do without a bra, and she wasn't wearing one now. A spreading dampness between her legs made her want to rub them together. Her pulse was racing.

'There's no need for that,' she managed to say breathlessly as his finger continued to linger on her face.

'Oh, yes,' Rafael apologised in a voice that sounded far from apologetic. 'I didn't realise that there's just two of us here. Everyone else has made it to the dining room. We'd better race there or else they'll be wondering where we are—maybe thinking that the love birds decided to dump the dinner and just do the sex.'

'Don't say that!'

'Just a little joke, Sammy. No need to get ruffled about it. You're as red as a beetroot.'

'Yes, well, it pays to remember that this is…is *a charade*. It's not real! We just do…that kind of stuff when other people are around.'

Rafael had obediently lowered his hand but there was

coolness where his finger had been and Sammy hated herself for wishing that it was still caressing her cheek and setting her body aflame in the process.

Dump the dinner and just do the sex...

The throwaway remark sent her imagination whirling into frantic overdrive. She spun round on her heels and began walking briskly towards the dining room.

She just *knew* that he was still grinning as he followed her. Could the man see what was going through her head? Did he know the effect he had on her with those casual, meaningless touches?

She sincerely hoped not. Sammy knew the kind of guy he was. He was a rich man who snapped his fingers and had any woman he wanted come running at speed to do his bidding until he got bored with them. He would call that a generalisation but there was more than just a grain of truth in it—more than several *thousand* grains of truth in it. The last thing she wanted was for him to think that she was anything like all those other women—floored by his charm, bewitched by his wit and intelligence and turned on by his stupid good looks.

She forced herself to remember him as a teenager, bunking off school and leading her brother astray—much safer. But as they hit the dining room, which was abuzz with everyone peering at the seating plan, laughing and chatting, he caught up with her. She felt the weight of his arm around her waist as he pulled her back against him and lowered his head to breathe in her newly washed hair.

'This is one of those times, Sammy,' he murmured, and she twisted so that she was looking up at him with a puzzled frown.

'One of *what* times?'

'I can't have my beautiful partner looking as though we've just had an argument. We need to be married at least a year for that. So, my darling...' He kissed her softly, sweetly and briefly, and that soft, sweet, brief kiss knocked her senseless.

Her head was all over the place as they drew apart but it was ages before she could really focus on what was going on around her: the praise for the food she'd made; the questions about the market and what the fresh produce had been like; her plans for the place she wanted to open when she and Rafael returned to England. The champagne continued to flow, and she knew that she was smiling and chatting and answering questions, but all she could think of was Rafael: the way he made her feel and the stupidity of *feeling* the way he made her feel.

She even forgot about Victoria, though her not-so-dulcet tones seemed to dominate whatever conversation was happening at the other end of the long, rectangular table.

Between courses, Sammy excused herself so that she could supervise the next array of dishes to be served. She'd had just two glasses of champagne, and her head was in a very sober place when she re-entered the dining room to announce her dessert, only to be pre-empted by Victoria; she had gone from tipsy to word-slurring over the course of the evening.

Sammy shot Rafael a panicked glance as the towering blonde rose unsteadily to her feet and tapped her spoon on her champagne flute until everyone fell into bemused silence.

He gestured to Sammy to come and take her empty seat, and Sammy duly went to sit next to him. She was immediately reassured by the mere fact of him sitting next to her. Something about the warmth and rock-solid self-assurance he emanated made her feel as though, whatever happened, he would be able to sort it out.

Desserts were now being served as the room waited for Victoria to speak with Jemima and another assistant, Trisha, placing delicate bowls of tropical fruit salad and soursop ice-cream in front of everyone.

Victoria looked around imperiously, swaying slightly. Next to her, Clement was frowning with a hint of disapproving impatience.

'What's going on, Rafael?' Sammy snapped under her breath.

'I feel this is a "wait and see" situation,' he murmured in return but then he clasped her hand under the table, resting it on his thigh. Sammy felt herself relax just a little.

'To the love birds!' Victoria pinned her eyes on them and raised her glass. Everyone else duly raised theirs too and Sammy decided that she could deal with a drunken toast to love birds.

'Who would have thought? What a shock for the man who lives in the gossip columns to have finally found true love, and so *quickly*!'

Sammy's smile froze and her fingers curled a little more tightly with Rafael's.

'I just hope it's the real deal!' Victoria waggled her finger in a reproving manner while everyone began to look just a tiny bit uncomfortable. 'Because this is one very special lady!'

'That's enough, Victoria.' Clement's voice was mild but sufficiently commanding for her to hesitate and glance down at him.

'I just want to wish the happy couple my congratulations!' Victoria pouted. She stroked Clement's head and swigged some champagne for good measure. Then she looked back at them and flashed her eyes with teasing intent. 'So, can you tell us if we all need to start looking for wedding hats...?'

Sammy froze. She felt Rafael tense next to her. He rose to his feet, coolly thanked Victoria for her good wishes and then looked at Clement. 'I think,' he murmured, 'that girlfriend of yours needs to get some beauty sleep just as soon as dessert is done and dusted. A little too much champagne can sometimes be a very bad idea.'

It wrapped up the moment of awkwardness, but twenty minutes later, with everyone tired and yawning and the conversation back to less fraught topics, Clement paused by Rafael. He looked at him, then at Sammy, with a smile.

'Well, my boy.' He leant towards them, his eyes sharp and as bright as a sparrow's. 'You've found yourself a good one here.'

Sammy blushed. Her gut feeling was that Rafael might perhaps disagree with that statement, considering they'd only been thrown into this situation by a series of unfortunate events.

'Victoria may have had a little too much of the fine stuff for her own good, but she was spot-on when she said that this is a very special lady.' He tapped the side of his nose and smiled. 'Love at first sight—although it's not quite that in your case—is certainly to be recommended. My Gail and I fell in love and within minutes I knew that I was going to marry her.'

His voice was wistful. 'I thoroughly approve. So, if a proposal is on the cards, then you truly have my congratulations. It certainly is a fine thought to know that the company my dear wife and I built together will be under the auspices of a family man whose heart is in the right place.'

He straightened and nodded to Victoria, who was fidgeting in the background. She followed him out of the room along with everyone else, leaving Sammy and Rafael in the dining room on their own.

Rafael rose and immediately went to a sideboard and helped himself to some whisky, grabbing a glass of wine for Sammy. He shut the door to the dining room and slanted a glance at the remains of the day: plates, glasses and yet more glasses and bottles, all to be cleared later. Right now, he was busy wondering what the hell had just happened.

'So…' He sat, manoeuvring his chair so that he was facing her and leaned his long legs to one side.

'So…' Sammy parroted dubiously.

'Victoria was just mischief-making.'

'She implied that we were about to get married. We've gone from being an item to being practically engaged. I'm not sure I'm that comfortable with that.'

'Why? One remark about wedding hats from someone who'd had too much to drink does not an impending marriage make.'

'Why? *Why?* Engagements and weddings are serious business! At least, they are to people like me who live in the real world.'

'My world's very real.'

Sammy swept aside that interruption and fixed him

with a baleful stare. 'Plus, poor Clement seems to now think that wedding rings are going to be exchanged.'

'Yes, that's a little unfortunate,' Rafael admitted. 'He may have gone off the rails with Victoria in an attempt to distract himself from his grief, but he's always been a family guy, and the fact that he now assumes that I'm a reformed character might ease any lingering doubts he might have about this deal.'

'Is that likely? I thought it was all but done and dusted.'

'To quote that well-worn saying, "there's many a slip twixt cup and lip"… I wouldn't want him to start suspecting that there's anything fishy going on.' He raised his eyebrows. 'You shouldn't have been so charming.'

Rafael sipped his drink and looked at her. She was blushing. He'd never met any woman who blushed as much as she did, but then, she had none of the hard edges of the women he dated. She was basically a country girl with wide-eyed dreams who believed in love and romance. As she'd just said, engagements and weddings were a serious business. She'd been his fake girlfriend and now practically his fake fiancée—at least while they were out here—and he definitely shouldn't look at her the way he was doing now. He lowered his eyes even though he could still see her image printed on his retina.

'Nothing changes,' he said gruffly. 'Victoria knows where her bread is temporarily buttered and, as you can see, she may tower over Clement but he's still the guy in charge.'

'It just feels as though we're on a slippery slope…'

'Same slope, different wording. 'Fiancée' implies commitment, a bond that goes beyond two people in it for a bit of fun. We could start launching into disclaimer speeches but my feeling is that that would just end up muddying the waters. This deal is hugely important and not just to me. The ripples of its outcome will be felt by many. There's nothing to worry about—after all, what's a fiancée but a partner with a ring on her finger?'

Even so, Rafael agreed with her. It *did* feel as though they were on a slippery slope, but what confused him was that the slippery slope wasn't the result of this small complication. An inebriated, vengeful ex-girlfriend could say what she liked. Neither he nor Sammy had admitted anything about heading down the aisle any time soon, and if anyone else mentioned that at any point he knew that he could always laugh it off.

No, the slippery slope was what was happening inside him: the wild excitement he was getting from Sammy playing the part of his devoted girlfriend; the sneaky enjoyment he got from the blurring of those lines between reality and fantasy. It surprised him, but when he thought about it stopping some crazy desire in him refused to see common sense.

Even now, discussing Victoria and her malicious interjection with no one around to witness anything, he still wanted to reach out and brush his hand against her cheek to feel the cool smoothness of her skin against his palm.

He balled his fists and gulped down some whisky.

Sammy didn't seem to notice his turmoil; in fact, she seemed to be deep in thought. 'You're right,' she said eventually.

'So we're good?' Rafael asked, snapping back to the present.

'It's just a week.'

'I could have a quiet word with Clement as a precau-

tion…mention that we're both very private people who
would rather our relationship remain private before any
official announcements are made.'

'What about everyone else?'

'I very much doubt any of them has any interest in
broadcasting anything. Victoria is the loose cannon but
if Clement passes on my words of caution, then have no
fear, she'll listen to him.'

Strip away any media coverage a vindictive ex might
spread, pretend that was never going to happen, and
things still seemed to have shifted. The game felt a whole
lot more serious now. The physical contact…the urge to
touch… It felt as though there might be quicksand under
his feet…

'What do you see in them, Rafael?'

'Come again?'

'Victoria…all those models you go out with…what do
you see in them? I mean, Victoria might have been a little screwed up and got hold of the wrong end of the stick
with you, but those are the sort of women you date, aren't
they? Models—a rich man with no other wish than to
have a shiny bauble on his arm, like Clement. Although,
I feel that Clement will soon tire of his shiny bauble because he knows what it's like to have the real deal at his
side. But you, Rafael… I just don't get it.'

Rafael shook his head in a cobweb-clearing kind of
way, but her eyes remained steady when he finally looked
at her.

'You don't have to answer that,' she said abruptly. 'This
is a pretend relationship, and in pretend relationships two
people don't have to do anything but pretend to be at-

tracted to one another and pretend to know each other's history.'

She began rising to her feet and he impulsively reached out to stay her. Why? He was as surprised by the gesture as she seemed to be, although she slowly sat back down and stared at him. Those amazing eyes, he thought distractedly. How could green, calm, slightly curious eyes be so distracting?

'It's complicated,' he heard himself mutter.

'Life's complicated,' Sammy returned. 'Look at where the pair of us are right now! Two people who couldn't be at further ends of the pole when it comes to…just about everything.' She paused. 'What's complicated?'

'I didn't want to end up like my dad.'

'What on earth do you mean?'

'He sold his soul to a woman and that woman took him for a ride. The woman was my mother. When my dad and I moved to your part of the world, I was in a pretty rough place. My mother had dumped the marriage in favour of a guy with a lot more money and my father fell apart at the seams—as if someone had pulled a vital piece of thread that had made the whole shoddy garment unravel. I picked up the pieces, and realised that it was no good handing over your soul to any woman, because the end of that road might not be what you had in mind. So, yes, I date models because I like knowing what I'm getting into. I enjoy the fact that they like my money. I can handle that.'

'Your poor dad. I wish I'd known him a little better. He always seemed so polite and quiet.'

'He was a broken man. I prefer to go through life in one piece. Don't get me wrong—I love my father very much—but that never made me blind to his faults.'

'He was just someone who trusted,' Sammy said gently. 'Which isn't a crime. What's love but a leap of faith?'

'Which,' Rafael drawled, rising to his feet and shoving his hands in the pockets of his black jeans, 'makes me realise just how perfect this arrangement between us is. No leap of faith, and we both know exactly where we stand.'

Sammy smiled back at him and stood up, brushing away some non-existent crumbs from her dress.

'I should stay down here for a bit and supervise what to do with the leftover food. I don't want anything to go to waste.'

Rafael nodded. 'Up to you,' he said gruffly. He raked his fingers through his hair and shifted. Yes, she should stay down here...but he didn't want her to. He wanted her right by him, near him. Was he feeding this attraction? It was a disturbing thought and one he wanted to dismiss straight away. Boundaries were needed, and distance—none of this unholy want that overtook all his common sense.

'Yes, it is. So, I'll be up when I'm up, and Rafael...? You're right. Nothing to see here, as far as Victoria and her mischief-making goes, but it would be a good idea to say something to Clement just in case. And as for this *thing* between us, this arrangement? It works well because we know the boundary lines between us and there are no leaps of faith to be made.'

She laughed. 'I would say, as *understandings* go, as a win-win situation, it couldn't be more perfect.'

CHAPTER SEVEN

DID SHE KNOW exactly where they stood? She should do. She and Rafael were business associates who had temporarily joined forces to conclude a deal that would be beneficial to both of them. That was what she thought every time he wasn't around. It was a very reassuring approach to the situation.

For the past three days, ever since he had reinstalled those boundary lines between them, Sammy had done her best to take refuge in the kitchen. So long as she was there, hiding away with her two assistants behind pots, pans, hobs and ovens, she could just about manage to get her brain to do its thing and sternly repeat the mantra about them just being business associates.

Unfortunately, the minute she was in his presence, the last thing she felt like was a business associate. He was just sticking to the brief, playing the perfect partner, sending her hot sidelong glances when eyes were on them, and holding her lightly but intimately in a way that conformed to the image of the possessive guy who just couldn't keep his hands off his woman.

And, however cool and composed she tried to be, her body went up in flames at the slightest touch. The key thing was to make sure he didn't see the effect he had on her, but it was hard, because she had to respond in kind, which only turned whatever fire she was trying to control into a full-blown combustion.

The evening before, he had dipped a kiss on the side of her neck, a perfunctory piece of terrific acting, and she'd wanted to pass out. So for the past two nights she'd lurked in the kitchen until everyone had headed up, taking her time prepping for meals the following day and doing all sorts of unnecessarily complicated recipes that required far more attention than the end result probably warranted. And it had worked because, by the time she'd headed up to their suite, he'd been at the desk working and she'd been way too tired to do anything but yawn and then vanish into the safety of her bedroom. And she was up with the larks in the morning to finish the dishes she had spent the night before prepping.

They only really went into their acting roles at dinner but, even so, Sammy knew that she was going to be a wreck by the time the end of the week arrived.

On the bright side, however, whatever chat Rafael had had with Clement had succeeded because Victoria had backed off. If Sammy could have kept a level head, things would have been easier. Actually, if she could have stuck to the routine she had established—fragile though the routine was, because he could still manage to get to her with a sidelong look or a hint of a smile—she could just about have managed.

But tonight…no cooking. She had a night off.

Sammy stared at her reflection in the full-length mirror in the bedroom. It was a little after six-thirty. She had the windows open and she could hear the orchestra of music from all the insects, frogs and toads in the tropical foliage outside. She could also hear the sound of voices and laughter, because everyone was by the pool, gathering for a night on the town.

'I should really hang back,' she had said to Rafael the day before when the plan had been announced. 'Food to prep...'

'There's no dinner to prepare.'

'Lunch.'

'The other halves will be out again, exploring one of the more remote beaches. They'll be very happy with some local fare. I've made sure that my driver has sorted that out.'

'Yes but...'

'You're fishing for excuses not to come,' he had said irritably, his dark eyes cool. 'And it's not going to work. You clearly don't like this situation any more than I do, but we both signed up to it, so you're just going to have to factor in a night of relaxation.'

That sudden coolness in his voice had been a stark reminder of just how detached he was from the effects of the game they were playing. While she was a bag of nerves, he was as cool as a cucumber. He could kiss her and look at her with such heat that she could feel herself burning up, but none of it was real, and it was a real headache trying to deal with that.

'And this is a club,' he'd added for good measure. 'There'll be dancing and drinking so feel free to wear... whatever sexy little number you've brought with you.'

He'd grinned then, all coldness gone, and she'd wondered whether he was teasing her. Did he think that she was as wholesome as apple pie so couldn't possibly dress like...all those other women he was accustomed to dating?

Still, staring at her reflection now, Sammy thought about the outfits Victoria had showed up in for the past few nights: small and tight and leaving very little to the imagination. She was eye candy on a major scale. All the other women, who were much older, dressed expensively and sensibly: cotton and silk in neutral shades; elegant and timeless. Sammy had pictured the much younger versions of them dressed in exactly the same way—pearls and diamonds, nothing too short and nothing too tight; nothing tasteless.

Just the sort that Rafael would never be drawn to in a million years. She wondered whether Victoria secretly sneered at her. Of course, that didn't matter, but still... Summer sundresses and flat shoes worked well enough; and of course loose, workmanlike clothes worked for the kitchen because comfort was everything. But in a revelatory flash she'd seen herself from the outside and hadn't been overjoyed with the image.

So tonight...something different. Having brought nothing *sexy* with her to wear—not that she actually *owned* anything that could be called sexy—Sammy had sneaked in a couple of hours shopping on her own while everyone had been occupied, the partners hiding under hats on whatever beach they'd gone to, their other halves poring over documents ready for signing off.

She'd had fun. Shopping wasn't usually her thing, but this was different because she was shopping for a reason: to shock. Nothing too dramatic, because she wasn't dramatic by nature, but she wanted to assert herself as someone other than the hard-working, talented chef Rafael had been drawn to in some unlikely turn of events.

Now she slipped on her shoes, took a deep breath and

headed downstairs to the join the party. Several cars were laid on for all of them and, if she hadn't got her skates on, Rafael would have been up in a minute, knocking on the bedroom door and asking whether she'd decided to find some other half-baked excuse for getting out of the evening.

Rafael glanced at his watch.

He always seemed to be glancing at his watch when it came to 'the love of his life'. It had occurred to him only the evening before that no woman had ever kept him waiting as much as this particular one did.

And, sure enough, he was waiting now. She should have been here fifteen minutes ago. He could see Victoria surreptitiously looking at him out of the corner of her eye.

Thank God he'd had a word with with Clement and her—a gentle reminder to Clement that Victoria might want to take a more subdued approach to his very private relationship with Sammy.

'We're both very private people,' he had confided, whilst wondering how he had got to the point where this felt so much more dangerous than the harmless game of make-believe they had initiated a million years ago. 'The last thing either of us want or need is for our…er…situation to be discussed on an hourly basis.'

To Victoria, he had simply said, 'Any more toasts to the happy couple, and I'll make sure that Clement knows just how unwelcome we both find the attention. You wouldn't want him to disappoint him, would you?'

He hadn't bothered to explain why he didn't want the attention. He didn't bother to paper over the fact that she might have been a little perplexed at this from a guy who had never cared about anyone having an opinion on the love interests he had never sought to hide from public view. He knew that his peculiar change of stance would denote the seriousness of his relationship with Sammy.

He knew how Victoria's mind worked. The very fact that he wanted privacy would signify the importance of the relationship. Add to that the fact that he'd gone for a woman so completely different from any other woman he'd ever been involved with.

Deep in his thoughts, it took him a couple of seconds to register Sammy's arrival. Or maybe he'd just not been expecting the woman standing framed in the sliding panels of glass that led out to the back gardens. The lights from behind silhouetted her slender frame, the slim arms, the next-to-nothing waist, the delicate column of her neck and the short, short hair that emphasised the elfin prettiness of her face.

She was in some kind of wraparound sarong. It was gossamer-flimsy and fell to mid-thigh in a riot of orange, russet and blue. The vest top she was wearing revealed the small roundness of her breasts and the toned slenderness of her arms. The practical sandals, which had been a staple of her wardrobe for the past few days, had been replaced by some silver sandals with thin straps that crisscrossed her ankles in a vaguely gladiatrix style.

One hand was on her hip, the other holding a little bag that matched the sandals. Very, very slowly Rafael began walking towards her. She didn't move a muscle as he approached.

'You...' He raked his fingers through his hair when he was finally standing in front of her. 'You...you've dressed for the occasion.'

'I thought I would.'

'Good. Good.'

He was struggling to recapture his self-control. He reminded himself, as he had reminded her only a couple of days ago, that their relationship was nothing more than a business arrangement. He'd got caught up in a lapse of concentration at the time and had told her about his father, about the problems he had faced as a teenager when she'd known him all those years ago.

Of course, he'd immediately regretted confiding in her and had made sure to swiftly remind her that any momentary sharing of personal information wasn't a gateway to...to *anything*...just in case she'd got it into her head that it might be. As it turned out, he shouldn't have bothered, because she hadn't mentioned a word about it since. In fact, she had reverted to type, only showing up on a need-to-show-up basis.

Such as now, dressed in something soft, small and revealing. His eyes dipped and he sucked in his breath at the realisation that she wasn't wearing a bra.

'Are you okay?'

'What's that?' Rafael belatedly pulled himself together, but he could feel the thrust of an erection bulging against his grey linen trousers and he had to look away fast. ''Course I'm okay,' he ground out. 'I was just... I suppose...wondering whether you were going to show up.'

'I told you that I would. Isn't this the part where we should be falling into one another's arms so that we can convince everyone that this is the real thing?' She shot him a disarming, coy smile.

He was floored. Where was the blushing girl he had grown accustomed to over the past few days?

She reached up and ran her hand gently along his neck, curving the strong jaw, which he clenched in response.

'What are you doing?' he demanded huskily.

'I'm playing to the audience. Isn't that what we're supposed to do?' She made a show of peering around him slightly. 'I can actually see the malevolent ex glaring in our direction.'

'Sammy...'

'Yes?'

'What you're doing isn't so much playing to the audience as playing with fire.'

Sammy could feel her heart picking up speed. She could see from the look on Rafael's face that she had shocked him with her outfit.

How on earth could something as superficial as an *outfit* shock a guy like him? And yet, as he had walked towards her, she had seen the darkening in his eyes. He was taking her in, every inch of her, and she had been thrilled at his reaction.

Which, of course, was also superficial.

'What do you mean, *playing with fire*?' she asked demurely.

'You know exactly what I mean.'

A sense of heady power surged through her. Whatever ups and downs she had survived in her life, she had always lived within a comfort zone of her own making. She had formed an image in her head of the sort of guy she would eventually meet and had carved out a future based on that image: a nice guy, supportive, safe...the opposite of her appalling stepfather. She had known what she'd wanted to do with her life and had applied all her determination to succeed in her field to the exclusion of anything that might remotely have resembled taking a big risk. So yes, for the first time in her life, she was playing with fire.

Giddy with excitement, Sammy gazed up at Rafael and parted her lips. Her nostrils flared, breathing in whatever woody scent he was wearing, something earthy that went straight to her head.

'You want me to kiss you?' Rafael ground out. 'Because, if I do, it won't be because I'm playing to an audience.'

He kissed her. The world disappeared. She felt her whole body slacken as she melted into the kiss, into his arms, her hands weaving into his hair, completely lost in the moment. She was dazed when he pulled back and, when their eyes met, she knew that he wasn't in control either.

But people were watching, and she adjusted her skirt sheepishly as they both turned to face all the eyes that were glued to their moment of passion.

'Now, that's a couple who mean business,' Robert Kendrick said with a smile as he raised his glass.

Rafael had his arm around her shoulders but this time it was different. She could feel the tension of his hold and she knew he didn't want to let her go.

'Not like me,' Rafael said gruffly.

'That's what love can do to a guy,' Kendrick said, still grinning broadly.

'Almost makes a guy forget,' Rafael returned, 'that there's a certain booking at a club for us! We'd better get going.'

The kiss stayed with Sammy. It was like a bee sting

on her lips as the evening progressed. All the common sense she had invoked to prevent this rush of desire had been thrown through the window.

This evening, she was all about Rafael. The music was sensual and loud, and she let herself go to it, swaying and seducing on the dance floor and loving the way he couldn't take his eyes off her.

She forgot all about Victoria, barely glancing in her direction, but, with female instinct, she still knew that the other woman would not like what she saw. For the first time, someone else was competing for attention. She wasn't the only young, strutting beauty in between the staid, impeccably dressed older women. Sammy discovered that she relished the sensation.

'Let's get you home,' Rafael whispered into her ear as the evening drew to a close. The music had slowed and he was pressed against her, his hard body moving rhythmically to the music, his thigh pushing between hers and his hand on her waist, guiding her to his beat.

'I can't wait.'

'Are you saying what I think you're saying?'

'Depends what you think I'm saying.'

'Sammy...'

'I know. You don't have to spell it out, Rafael. This isn't about two people who plan on having a relationship. This is about the here and now, and I don't understand it any better than you probably do.'

She moaned softly as his hand dipped lower, nestling just above her buttocks. Through the flimsy fabric of her shirt, she could feel its heat burning into her.

'You're not wearing a bra,' he murmured. 'I like that.'

'Do you, now?'

'My imagination has been freewheeling ever since we got here.'

'So has mine.' Sammy couldn't believe she'd actually said that. She felt a rush of daring recklessness.

'I want to get you into bed.'

The music stopped, and they reluctantly pulled apart, but remained close enough for him to say shakily to her, 'But I'll ask that question again when the bed is within sight, because when the music is blaring and drinks have been had words can sometimes be rashly spoken.'

'Maybe I'll be saying the same thing to you,' Sammy murmured, casting a lingering look at his darkly handsome face.

Piled into a car with another of the couples on the way back, Sammy sat in a state of simmering excitement. In her head, she replayed the evening, from standing in front of that mirror and looking at herself in clothes she usually would never have dreamt of wearing in a million years. Tonight had been the culmination of what she had felt the second she had walked into Rafael's office, all guns blazing, to confront him about the hotel.

She had felt the breath catch in her throat then when she'd seen him and, even though she'd tried her best to stifle that wild, crazy physical response to him, she hadn't been able to. It had grown under tropical skies and this game they were playing had nurtured it into a full-blown, irresistible craving.

He was forbidden, for all sorts of reasons, and she knew that. He was a guy whose goals in life were so different from hers, a complex guy who didn't want to settle down and who scorned the straightforward path she had always envisaged for herself. Yet this was the first time she had discovered how alluring the forbidden fruit could be.

She rested her head against his shoulder in the back of the car and gazed out at the scenery flashing past. The windows were rolled down and the breeze blowing through the car was warm. The foliage at the side of the road was dense with huge, flowering bushes and tall, thin coconut trees. Rising up the side of the hills were bright squares of light where wooden houses nestled into the forest.

Looking up, Sammy could make out the pinpricks of stars against the velvety black sky. There was no light pollution at all here.

She sighed and vaguely thought about what waited for her back in England. Her career would begin to take off. Looking for somewhere to buy would be hectic yet enjoyable, because there would be no concerns about money. She should have been thinking about that, and making plans, but it all felt very far away. The only thing in her head right now was the man against whom she was resting.

The cars all arrived at the villa at the same time and there were sleepy goodnights from everyone. Victoria was there, sulky and lurking slightly behind Clement. Sammy ignored her, and she noticed Rafael did as well, confining his brief conversation to Clement while his ex glared and fulminated. Somewhere during the course of the evening, Victoria had seemed to stop trying to dazzle. Now she looked a little sad in her drooping silver sequinned dress that barely skirted her thighs and the high heels that made her tower over everyone in the party.

Sammy and Rafael headed up to their suite and Sammy felt the thud of anticipation like a drumbeat inside her. He was holding her hand and, as he pushed open the door, he turned to her.

'Okay—question time.'

'I'll go first.' She leaned against the wall and gazed up at him with a sexy half-smile. 'Sure you're going to be all right with this?'

'Let me think about that,' Rafael murmured, flattening his hands on either side of her so that she was deliciously caged in.

'I mean,' Sammy elaborated huskily, 'I wouldn't want you to get all upset because you think I've taken advantage of you after all that dancing and drinking...' She walked her fingers over his chest and then stroked the side of his face. Her heart skipped a beat as his eyes darkened with desire.

He held her hand and grazed his mouth against her knuckles.

'I'll do my best to keep regrets to the minimum...'

'Good, and so will I. Because we're here, Rafael, and I don't think I've ever wanted anyone in my life as much as I want you right now. I don't understand it, and believe me I know it's not going anywhere—which is a very good thing—but I can't seem to help myself.'

'Ditto.'

And then he kissed her, one hand still propped against the wall, the other teasing the underside of her breast through the stretchy material of the vest.

Sammy groaned. The wetness between her legs was driving her crazy. She wanted to guide his hand there, wanted to pull aside her panties so that he could touch her and drive her even more crazy. He lifted her as though she weighed nothing and she wrapped her legs around him as they managed to make it to the bedroom.

'I think your place rather than mine,' he teased, nuzzling her ear. 'Somehow, a bed is a lot more appealing than a sofa.'

'I don't care where we go.' Sammy groaned truthfully. 'Just as long as we get there quickly.'

'You won't be getting anywhere quickly,' he murmured huskily in return. 'At least, not if I have my wicked way.'

He was true to his word. He took his time, leaving the lights off so that the only light came from the moon casting shadows and angles though the shutters into the bedroom. The fan overhead was a pleasing background whirr, picking up from where the night sounds outside left off.

He deposited her gently on the bed and she immediately wriggled up against the pillows so that she could look at him in open appreciation as he got undressed. He was magnificent. Her mouth fell open as he stripped off his tee-shirt, revealing a tightly muscled torso and powerful arms, his chest darkened with hair. Her breathing was uneven as he continued the striptease without an ounce of embarrassment. His boxers were black and she could see the very visible outline of his erection. She held her breath as the boxers came down and he casually touched himself, stroking himself as he lazily strolled towards her.

'Enjoying the view?' he ground out, settling on the mattress but, rather than lying next to her, he knelt over her.

'V-very much so,' Sammy managed to stutter, eyes glued to the mesmerising sight of him stroking himself. 'If only I had a camera.'

'What a wicked thought...'

* * *

Rafael smiled. This level of intensity and excitement felt like something he'd been waiting for all his life, freed from all the restrictions he was so accustomed to laying down in his relationships. She was the one laying down the rules, and the rules were *his* rules. How much more perfect could a situation get?

Gazing at him with green, slumberous eyes, she was the epitome of everything desirable and, with a groan of abandon, he pushed up the flimsy wraparound skirt. She had satin-soft thighs and a flat stomach. He gently eased off her underwear, but he didn't have the patience to take off the rest of her clothes. Instead, he bent to bury his head between her thighs, and the first taste of her was as sweet as nectar. He flicked his tongue along her wet slit and found the bud of her clitoris. He teased it until she was panting and writhing against his mouth.

Taking it slowly, something he excelled at, was beyond his reach. He'd never wanted anyone as badly as he wanted her and the fact that she felt the same way about him was even more of a turn-on. He couldn't get her clothes off fast enough and neither could she. Together they flung her stuff over the side of the bed, and he had one moment of excruciating pleasure as he reared up to look at her naked body.

She was so slight, so smooth. Her breasts were small and perfectly shaped, barely a handful, and he could practically span her waist with his hands; yet there was a well-toned strength to her ballerina-like body that spoke of the physically testing career she had made her own, always on her feet and seldom slowing down.

Everything about her struck him as perfect. He tasted

her everywhere. He licked her breasts and suckled on her ripe, pink nipples until she was begging him to take her. He stroked her belly and kissed her so that she was senseless with desire. Every second of touching was agony because all he wanted to do was be inside her.

When he could stand it no longer, he reached for protection. His fingers were so shaky that he could barely rip open the foil packet. Sinking into her was bliss. He'd died and gone to heaven. She was tight around him, and her body moved in sync with his so that, as he arched back to orgasm, she too tightened and stiffened, moving in unison with him.

Rafael came on a shudder that forced out a groan of satisfaction and then, sated, he rolled off her and lay beside her.

'No regrets?' he murmured, stroking her hair from her damp forehead, and she drowsily smiled back at him.

'None at all. I never thought I could do this…never thought I could sleep with a guy I don't plan on having any kind of relationship with. But… I just did…and I've never felt so liberated. So, regrets? None…'

CHAPTER EIGHT

RAFAEL LOOKED AT Sammy from under his lashes as she unpacked the picnic he had had prepared for them. He was playing truant from real life and enjoying it. His guests had left the day before. Everything had been signed, sealed and delivered and he had breathed a sigh of relief. Victoria might have fumed and simmered in the background, but she had heeded his thinly veiled words of warning, and had decided to take on board where her bread was buttered.

Rock the boat, he had implied, *and say goodbye to the lifestyle you've got with Clement.*

He hadn't worked out what he was going to do about Sammy but, the minute she had become his lover, the rules of the game had drastically changed. There was no longer pretend-touching for the sake of their captive audience—it was real touching, and the real touching was mind blowing.

He hadn't worked out why she felt so addictive but he guessed that it was because there was no pressure on him to do anything but live in the moment. She made no demands. She never mentioned anything about a future, and never uttered those terminal words: *where do we go from here...?*

She hadn't dropped a single hint that she wanted to carry on seeing him once they returned to England. Had she wondered? He had no idea. She was so unashamedly open with him about everything, so unimpressed by his wealth and his status, so sexually curious and enthusiastic...and yet something about her remained carefully concealed.

He would have suggested continuing what they had, but in fact remaining on the island after everyone left had been suggested by Clement, thereby putting him in the fortunate position of just having to go along with it.

'You've worked to produce great food,' Clement had said the evening before over their last supper. 'Now you two need to take a little time to yourselves without having to think about us all. You should stay on here for a few days. I'm sure—' he had winked at Rafael '—the world can spare you for a week or so.'

Rafael had laughed and slapped Clement on the back. Sammy, though, had remained silent for a few seconds, seeming to mull over the suggestion. He'd had to damp down his initial irritation at her response, and had had to laugh at his ego, which was telling him that any other woman would have bitten his hand off to stay on for another week.

Since when had his own invincibility gone to his head? he had asked himself. Since when had he had the expectation that any woman would want to put herself out for him? Was he really that arrogant?

So he'd impatiently laughed at himself, even though he'd been stupidly piqued by her deliberation. Then, when she'd smiled, nodded and glanced at him sideways with that sexy little look of hers, he'd wanted to punch the air with satisfaction.

'Do my humble picnic offerings meet your high standards?' he asked now, his dark gaze lingering on her face. He was stretched out on the oversized towel they had brought, hands folded behind his head.

He couldn't have picked a better spot. The cove was a fifteen-minute boat ride away and was completely private. Now that it was just the two of them and his time wasn't committed to other people, he wanted to show her the best the island could offer, and it didn't come better than this.

Coconut trees sat against a backdrop of lush, tropical mountains. It was just a tiny inlet but the turquoise water was very calm, like a pool, and the sand was like caster sugar. The boat he had driven was anchored to the left and bobbing gently on the water.

She had oohed and aahed when they'd arrived, and he'd felt a real kick of pleasure, a desire to take her to more places just so that he could see that smile on her face as she looked around.

She was rummaging in the picnic basket and wearing a very similar expression of wonderment. Rafael smiled and propped himself up on one elbow to watch her.

'It's perfect. I like the champagne. Can you be done for being drunk and disorderly behind the wheel of a boat?'

She glanced at him and Rafael felt that familiar tug in his groin as his libido kicked into gear. *Those eyes... that perfect mouth...* Just thinking about how she could turn him on made him horny. He thought about her kisses and how she could lick him in ways that made him lose control within seconds.

'Thankfully, there's no traffic in this particular part of the Atlantic. Stop fussing there and come and sit by me. You're beginning to go pink. I want to rub some sun cream on you—make sure you don't get burnt.'

'That's very considerate of you.'

'I'm an extremely considerate person.'

'It's so beautiful here, Rafael. I don't know how you can resist coming as often as you can.'

'Time is money.'

'And doing nothing is good for the soul. Especially if you're doing nothing in a place like this.'

'Are you beginning to think that you might want to stay on and do the six months here after all?' he teased, eyes darkening as she sashayed towards him.

He intended to have that prissy black one-piece off her before too long, but right now it was pleasant playing with images of what was underneath it: those pale, small breasts; those perfect rosy nipples that he couldn't get enough of; her flat, smooth stomach.

'Maybe!' She laughed back at him.

Rafael watched as she settled on the towel next to him and shoved on her sunglasses so that, when their eyes met, he couldn't see what she was thinking.

'Maybe? You're not being serious, are you?'

'Why not? Before I came here, I had no idea what it was going to be like, but everyone is so friendly, and honestly...? Who in their right mind could resist the temptation to spend a little time out here? It's not as though I'd get the chance to come back here any time soon.'

Sammy lay down on the towel and closed her eyes but she knew that Rafael had sat up and was staring down at her.

When Clement had said that they should take a few days' break on the island to enjoy themselves, having spent the week catering to the needs of clients in their various ways, she had waited to take the lead from Rafael. She'd wondered how he would react to that suggestion. He hadn't said a word about what would happen next with them and their situation. They'd been ensconced in a bubble, in which the sizzling excitement of touching one another for show had exploded into the real thing, and she'd been carried away to cloud nine.

But she wasn't an idiot. He was only in it for a bit of passing fun. He wasn't going to take things any further, and over her dead body was she going to give any hint that the thought of walking away from this fantastic experience made her feel sick. It wasn't as though she'd invested feelings in him, was it? She'd known the rules of the game from day one and she wasn't stupid.

If she wanted more of him than a few days out here, then it was just because he'd opened a door in her and she was enjoying the experience. She'd committed to having fun with her eyes wide open, and she wasn't going to suddenly turn into a martyr and start feeling angst about her decision. He might not fit the bill of her 'for ever' guy, but he was making her see that there was no crime when it came to having a bit of fun.

So she'd made a show of thinking carefully when that suggestion had been made before slowly nodding and agreeing, yes, why not stay on a while longer? She wasn't playing hard to get because there was nothing to get. She was looking after herself because she knew what he was like, and she wasn't going to end up as another of his casualties.

'You have things to do in England.'

'I know.' She opened her eyes and peered at him from

behind the safety of her sunglasses. 'But you've shown me that taking a walk on the wild side can be a good thing.'

'How so?'

'Well…' Sammy sat up so that they were at eye level with each other, and she tilted the sunglasses on her forehead to meet his gaze squarely. 'When I first saw you again, you were the sort of guy I instantly disliked.'

'Thank you straight away for the compliment.'

'You can't blame me. You'd swiped the rug from under my feet.'

'Not to mention having spent some of my youth making sure your brother hopped on the bandwagon.'

'Actually,' Sammy mused, briefly shading her eyes and staring off at the ocean, 'I thought about what you said and I think you're right. You didn't so much lead Colin astray as allowed his rebellion to find a voice, which was probably a good thing for him in the end.' She sighed. 'He may have skipped a year, but it was the best thing that could have happened, because he returned in a better place.'

'That's a generous admission from you,' Rafael said truthfully.

'You're a considerate person offering to rub sunblock on my back, and I'm a generous person admitting that you were right about Colin. What saints the pair of us are.'

Rafael grinned, then looked at her in a slightly different way, his eyes lazy and appreciative.

His hands were nowhere near her but her whole body shivered, as though he'd physically touched her. Her nipples tightened and there was a wave of intense sensation that washed through her, making her mouth dry and her pupils dilate. She felt hot and sluggish.

The pull of lust was something she had massively underestimated—that was something she was very quickly realising. Right now, she just wanted to dump the serious conversation, lean into him, feel the coolness of his mouth against hers and put his hands where she wanted them to be. But she could feel the urge to say something that would paper over that cracks of apprehension that he was beginning to *matter*. Not just as a guy she was having fun with, but as a guy who was complex and three-dimensional, demanding more than just a romp in the sack.

'You were telling me how much you disliked me at first sight.' Rafael returned her to the present and to what she wanted to get across to him—that she was as casual about what was happening between them as he was. 'Or maybe I should say *second* sight, because you weren't exactly a member of my fan club back in the day.'

'The waiting list was long for that particular role,' Sammy said drily. 'From what I remember.'

'And would you have joined the waiting list if it hadn't been as long?'

'No.'

He burst out laughing. 'I like the way you tell it like it is without any consideration for a man's fragile ego.'

'You have the ego of a steel vault.'

'But moving on from the compliments…'

'I learnt a lot from what my mother went through,' Sammy told him thoughtfully. 'She had such a rough ride of it after Dad died and after she married that awful man. She married in haste and repented at leisure. It gave me time to work out that love was something you should never rush into. That you might think a guy is going to be good for you but, unless you really know what you're looking for, you can so easily end up making a big mistake.'

'You're going round the houses here, Sammy.'

He reached forward to stroke a lazy finger over her mouth and then along her shoulders, taking his time. 'You have amazing shoulders.'

'Stop distracting me, Rafael.'

'Why? I like distracting you. In fact, I think I could make a career choice out of doing that.'

'I'm trying to explain…'

'Tell me.'

His voice was husky and seductive and didn't give the impression that he was hanging onto her every word. It gave the impression that the only thing he wanted to do was tug off her swimsuit and make love to her.

Sammy shuddered because she wanted that badly herself. It was unsettling to realise how much of a hold her body had over her brain and how vulnerable that made her feel. She frowned, trying to connect disparate threads of thought, but her head seemed to be all over the place.

He just had to touch her or even look at her with those dark, sexy eyes and all of a sudden she couldn't think straight. That was a dangerous place to be and the feel of that danger was like a feathery touch against her skin.

'I've been very careful when it comes to guys.' She cleared her throat and propped her sunglasses back on because it felt safer. 'I mean, I've gone through life not wanting to make any mistakes.'

'But you had boyfriends…yet you're not married. So doesn't that imply that mistakes were made along the way?' Thankfully he stopped the tactile exploration and looked at her with his head tilted to one side and his expression serious.

'One serious boyfriend,' Sammy admitted. 'I thought

it was going somewhere. We both did, but in the end it fizzled out. There were no hard feelings and we're still friends on social media. I'll always have a soft spot for him in my heart but he wasn't the one for me.'

'It all sounds very flat.'

'What do you mean?'

'Two earnest people trying to make something work… holding hands, gazing into each other's eyes and waiting for the spark and then nothing…but good friends still, like brother and sister.'

'It was nothing like that!' Sammy protested vehemently, thinking that that was exactly what it had been like.

'Sure about that?' He raised his eyebrows and grinned. 'I'm guessing this is where I come in?'

'As a matter of fact, it is. You showed me that I could have a fling without it meaning anything at all and enjoy myself.' He was still grinning, which got on her nerves, but at least he'd stopped touching her so that she could get her thoughts in order. 'You didn't tick any of the boxes—you still don't.'

'The boxes being…? No, let me guess—is reliable one of them? Diligent, hard-working? If you say "considerate", then you'd have to admit that I happen to tick at least one of those boxes…'

Sammy ignored that interjection. Those boxes were indeed the very ones she had but, said aloud, they seemed dull and boring.

'You don't tick any of the boxes,' she returned, ignoring the grin as she'd ignored the interjection. 'You're pure fun that's not going anywhere, and you've done me a favour by making me see that a situation without a future doesn't necessarily mean that it's a situation I shouldn't have.'

'Glad to be of service.'

'It's good to be getting that out of my system.'

'Having fun?'

'Being reckless.'

'Am I as reckless as it gets for you?'

'You are, as a matter of fact.'

'Good. I like that and, now that you've got that out of your system, shall we get down and dirty with the reck-lessness?'

'It's so hot. We could go swim, I suppose—not that I'm much of a swimmer.'

'I swim like a fish. You just have to hang on to me. We need to get in the right mood for swimming, though. Maybe a little bit of that recklessness you were describing a minute ago? If I'm to be your teacher in all things rash and daring, then I think it's only fair that I do a thorough job of it before you return to the safety of your comfort zone and Mr Dull waiting on the horizon.'

He tugged down the sensible strap of her swimsuit, traced where the strap had been, and the little inden-tation it had made in her shoulder, and then let his fin-gers drift down to circle the jut of her nipple against the stretchy material.

Sammy surrendered.

She opened herself up to him, arm flung over her face as he took his time disposing of the swimsuit. She had to do her fair share of wriggling out of it to help things along, but she did, because need was getting the better of her.

The way he touched her made her feel as though she were being touched for the first time, as though his clever fingers and his questing mouth had managed to access parts of her she'd never known existed. He nuzzled the softness between her small breasts before settling on an engorged nipple and tugging at it so that sighs turned to little cries and whimpers.

'You're beautiful; you really are,' he murmured huskily.

'You're just saying that.'

'I never say stuff I don't mean. I can't tell you how much you turn me on. Just thinking of you gives me an erection.'

Sammy sighed happily and let him explore her. He touched her everywhere. In the space of a few days, he seemed to have familiarised himself with every inch of her body. Yes, she knew what to expect, and yet every flick of his tongue on her skin was a revelation.

He held her hips as he contoured her belly button with delicate licks. Sammy groaned and pushed her fingers through his thick, dark hair. She was barely aware of him reaching for protection. He never failed to use it. She could have told him that she was on the pill and he would still have protected himself. He was very, very careful about making sure that no one could pin him down for any reason whatsoever.

She welcomed him in. Her whole body sank into the utter pleasure of feeling his bigness fill her up, and when he came it was with a convulsive shudder. He took her with him, took her to the same soaring heights and left her weak as a kitten afterwards.

When he rolled off her, he lay there for a few seconds and linked his fingers with hers in a gesture that was very intimate and casual at the same time. Sammy stared up at the sky, in tune with him and loving the way he was absently holding her hand.

Thinking that...thinking what?...that this was really paradise? And not just because of the blue sea, the white sand and the swaying coconut trees. She could get picture-postcard stuff all over the world. What made *this* picture-postcard special was the man lying next to her, seeing the same sky as she but probably thinking very different thoughts.

She looked sideways and her heart constricted. The mantra she had been repeating to herself suddenly felt hollow and different thoughts began creeping in—a different view of what had been happening inside her over the past few days. She thought of the way this man made her laugh. Even before they'd become lovers, when they'd been playing the game in front of his clients, her skin had tingled where he had touched it and her heart had raced when he'd glanced at her.

She didn't believe in this kind of love, she frantically told herself. She had her checklist—the very checklist she'd only just finished telling him all about! Except... had she done that for his benefit or for her own?

She stood up suddenly and began putting on the swimsuit.

'Where are you going?'

'For a swim.'

'I thought you weren't a strong swimmer?'

'I'm going to paddle. I won't get into any trouble if I paddle.'

'Wait, Sammy.'

Rafael leapt up behind her and stuck on his trunks as she made her way to the edge of the sea. He circled her arm, tugging her back.

'What's wrong?'

'Sorry?' Sammy shielded her eyes and looked up at him. The water swirling round her ankles was warm and clear. Her pulse was racing, and her head had suddenly started spinning stories about involvement with the last guy on the planet she should be involved with. She resisted reaching out to touch his face.

'Have I said something to…upset you?' Rafael raked his fingers through his hair and shifted awkwardly, his other hand still circling her arm.

He looked touchingly concerned but Sammy knew better than to feed into something that wasn't there.

'No. Just…phew…it's baking hot.'

She flapped her hand in a fan-like motion and smiled. Should she start making noises about returning to England? He'd mentioned staying on for a few days, and she'd been happy to go along with that vague timeline, but should she now put a number on those days and take control of the situation instead of drifting?

'You swim out, Rafael. I'll sit on the edge here. It's nice. I can watch you swim and show off how fit you are.'

He relaxed and grinned. 'Well now, I admit I can rise to that challenge.'

'I'm warning you, though, that if you start floundering out there you're on your own.' He was so beautiful, so smart…so damned irresistible. Was this just fun or was it something else?

'Understood, but that's never going to happen. I'm not a guy who flounders.'

'But you *are* a guy who brags.'

He was still grinning, all trace of concern at her change of mood gone. 'If you must know, and to brag a little bit more, I forced myself to learn how to swim as soon as we moved to Yorkshire. I decided that there were no hurdles I wasn't capable of overcoming, so I went to the pool a few times, listened in on a swimming coach giving lessons to a couple of old ladies and then went to that lake in the woods—you know the one? I jumped in and hoped that I'd remember the instructions from that coach.'

'You're kidding.'

'It was a lot more educational than school. Besides, what was the worst that could happen?'

'Death by drowning?'

'Yet here I am.' He burst out laughing and dipped to kiss her on the mouth until her head was reeling. 'But just in case I do flounder,' he murmured, 'you'd better make sure you don't take your eyes off me.'

Sammy retreated back to the beach, sat on the towel and watched him. He struck out, lean body cutting through the blue, blue water with powerful, even strokes. Surely he hadn't learned to swim like that from eavesdropping on a swimming coach at the age of fifteen and then jumping in a lake? But then, he was the guy who would never allow himself to fail. He would never *flounder*.

And that included floundering in his private life. She knew his back story, and knew how it had impacted on him and how it channelled all his decisions about relationships. There was no weakness inside him when it came to women. He wouldn't have any thoughts about this situation between them that had started as a charade and was now…whatever it was. A pleasant distraction for him…and for her, something that was beginning to feel a lot more than that.

She didn't want to keep thinking about that.

Instead, she got her phone and was playing on it when

it buzzed. Sammy was so surprised that she almost didn't pick up, but her mother's name flashed on the screen. Why was her mother calling her? She and her mother messaged daily, but phone calls were usually reserved for birthdays and *situations*. Situations that often involved her brother and whatever news her mother felt she had to convey *urgently*—usually, Colin would later tell Sammy nothing had been truly urgent at all—or else to pass on some gossip about a neighbour that likewise 'couldn't wait'.

So she picked up the call with some hesitation. She sat up and gazed blankly out to the horizon, into which Rafael seemed to have vanished in record time. He was now making back for land, swimming back as rhythmically as he had swum out. Her mind was drifting but the minute she heard her mother's voice she sat up straighter.

'Sammy, darling, I'm so glad I got hold of you.'

She sat up straighter still, then stood up, because she knew from the tone of her mother's voice that whatever conversation was about to take place wasn't going to be a good one.

Rafael was heading back, having resisted the temptation to disappear into the great blue yonder. He hadn't been exaggerating when he'd told Sammy that he'd learnt to swim by literally throwing himself in at the deep end. It had all been part of his anger at life all those years ago. He'd loved to push the boundaries, never more so than when it came to swimming; he'd bunked off school too many times to count so that he could go down to that lake and freeze his butt off swimming as though his life depended on it.

He'd never stopped enjoying the freedom it afforded him. He had a magnificent indoor swimming pool in the basement of his mansion in London and swimming in it was the best therapy anyone could have. So it had been tempting to push the boat out today, but he knew that Sammy would end up getting worried about him if she lost sight of him.

He didn't know *how* he knew that. He just did, and it gave him a warm feeling inside that was pleasurable, if a little confusing. He'd dated women in the past, and spent months with the same woman, and yet had never felt this weird thing he felt with Sammy.

He *knew* her. At least, it felt like that to him. It was unsettling but he liked it, even though there was just the merest hint of alarm bells ringing in the distance somewhere.

Now, as he glimpsed her in between strokes, he got the feeling that something was up. For starters, she was on the phone. Who was calling her? He knew that she'd told her mother something vague about staying out on the island for a bit longer, but that everything had been sorted with the work placement. He'd been in the bedroom when she'd made the call. She'd strolled through the room, completely naked, idly pausing to look at something or other and talking in a low, soft, reassuring voice while he'd lain on the bed watching her and making suggestive expressions while she tried not to laugh.

He reached shore just as she was ending the call and the minute he saw her face he knew something was off.

'Talk to me,' he said urgently, reaching for a towel and, after a quick dry, slinging it over his shoulders as he walked towards her.

'I was just on the phone to my mother, Rafael.'

'And you look as though you need something forti-fying. Go sit under that tree in the shade. I'll bring you some champagne. You're white as a sheet.'

He felt a sickening jolt of panic as he busied himself with the champagne, which was ice-cold in its frozen sleeve. Whatever was going on, he was going to make sure she knew that she could count on him.

Hell, what if there had been a death in the family? He felt nauseous just thinking about it but, as he approached her with the two glasses and the champagne bottle, his expression was inscrutable.

She was sitting on one of the over-sized towels they had brought with them and had drawn her knees up to her chest. Her short hair was ruffled by the breeze and still dry because she hadn't actually dived into the water at all. He'd noticed that from the distance, looking back at her when he'd paused for breath, and had absently thought that it might be fun to teach her how to swim. Everyone should know how to swim, and he did have his own private pool, after all.

'Okay, Sammy. Drink this and then tell me what's going on with your mother. Is she okay? Colin…is he okay? Has something happened to either of them?'

Sammy leaned towards him, as if sensing his strength and wanting to be supported by it.

'She's found out.'

'Found out what?'

'About us. Victoria got in touch with her. She phoned really upset because she was told that we're engaged and that you're not the kind of guy I should be getting en-gaged to.'

'How the hell did Victoria find your mother?'

'I guess it was just a case of following the clues. In the spiel on my website, I reference my mum quite a bit—that she's my inspiration. I suppose she got hold of my mum's name and then just did a little detective work.'

'So she got to screw me over after all,' he said grimly. 'She might not have gone public but going private was just as destructive.'

'She gave Mum a rundown of your history and the fact that you've never committed to anyone, and of course my mother is super-protective when it comes to me. She kind of made it her mission to instil common sense in me when it came to guys. So for her to find out that I'm apparently engaged after five seconds, and to a man who plays the field and is proud of it… She's devastated.'

'Jesus, Sammy.' He held her gaze. 'What did you tell her?'

Rafael stiffened, every damning word driving a knife deep into a part of him he hadn't known existed. A part of him that wasn't as invincible as he had always cared to think. He was that man: the man who had never committed; the man who played the field and had always done so without a conscience. The guy who had figured that to be upfront from the start was to deliver immunity from the consequences of broken relationships. To hear those words delivered casually by the woman now speaking them was to be judged and found wanting in a way that cut to the core.

'I told her that I could take care of myself and that she wasn't to worry.' Sammy drank what was left of the champagne in one long swallow that made her splutter. 'And when it ends,' she continued in a rush, 'I can tell her that it was a learning curve and that I'll never rush into anything ever again, but that I have no regrets.'

'No fizzling out? I thought you were a fan of the gradual tapering off when a relationship starts going pear-shaped,' Rafael said.

'No—no fizzling anything. I'll tell her that I discovered, once we left this paradise, that you were someone I couldn't live with in the real world. I'll tell her that you were my adventure.'

Rafael gazed at her long and hard. What was really going through her head? What was going through his was terrifying because he knew that more than his body was involved in this dangerous game. His heart had become involved as well. But did she feel the same? It was impossible to tell.

'We should give her time to digest everything.' He lowered his eyes.

'What are you saying?'

'We stay here for a little longer. I can oversee the hotel and work remotely. We can let the dust settle so that when we return to England your mother is less…devastated and more philosophical about what you…*we*… might have to tell her. I won't let you break that kind of news on your own.'

'We stay here?'

'And you …' he smiled crookedly but his dark eyes remained serious '…you might find that I really am the kind of guy you could never live with in the real world…'

CHAPTER NINE

SAMMY WANTED TO return to Yorkshire immediately. She could easily imagine her mother worried and fretful and wondering what the hell was going on.

There was no way she could ever think that a sudden engagement was ever going to be anything but trouble. Even if there'd been no engagement—if Sammy had said in passing that she and Rafael were going out, maybe casually dating, or had been out for a cup of coffee together—her mother would still have had her antennae quivering with suspicion. Rich guy and speedy attraction...add those two things together and what she'd get was *trouble*.

Her mother's past had taught her enough about chancers for her to be instinctively wary of someone like Rafael. Frankly, to be wary of any guy showing up and suddenly becoming an item in her daughter's life after five minutes. Victoria's call would have set the wheels in motion, and mention of an engagement would have been the icing on a very bad-tasting cake.

Rafael, though, calmly talked her out of it as they sat on that beach towel, each staring out at the blue ocean whilst working their way to a solution to the sudden complication that had arisen.

'We can easily stay here for another couple of weeks, by which time your mother will have calmed down,' he said.

'You don't know my mother.'

'No one can stay anxious for weeks on end. After a while, it dulls.'

'Again, you don't know my mother. After our step-father disappeared from the scene, Mum suddenly took on a ton of guilt for the massive wrong decision she had made in marrying him in the first place. She made it her mission to make sure that I, in particular, didn't do any-thing rash when it came to my emotions.'

'What about Colin?'

'She automatically assumed that Colin would be able to look after himself.' Sammy half-smiled. 'Don't ask. At any rate, she drummed it into me that I should always be careful never to be taken advantage of.'

'Is that why you developed that checklist for boring men?'

'"Kind, thoughtful and reliable" doesn't automatically mean boring.'

'If you say so.'

'Anyway, I could stay away for a week or a month or a year and my mother would still be worried sick that I was making a mistake. I think we should go back to Eng-land and tell her immediately that the whole engagement thing was a fabrication.'

'We could do that.'

But then he turned to look at her, reached and touched her, just a light, feathery touch that had made her melt.

'But Sammy, let's be honest with one another. The engagement might have been a fabrication but what we have together—this thing between us—that's real.' He paused, frowned and took a sudden step back. 'The passion, I mean. The flame that can't be put out. Don't tell me that *that's* not real.'

'Yes, well...'

'Sure, we could go back over there, and we could go into a lengthy explanation about Victoria and Clement and pretending to be the couple we weren't at the time. Shall I tell you what your mother would think of that?'

'Can I stop you?'

'Any time you like.'

'Tell me. What would Mum think if we showed up and told her the truth, now that you seem to have a crystal ball?'

'She'd think that after everything she's told you, after every word of warning she's issued over the years, you've let yourself be seduced into a lie by a guy who messes women around.'

'I've told her that you're not the man Victoria described.' Sammy broke eye contact, but he'd made a point, and it was one she hadn't considered. Of course her mother would be disappointed, and would think that she had rushed headlong into lust with the wrong guy. She'd remember Rafael the youthful rebel, the boy who had led Colin astray, and all her defences would shoot into position.

Sammy had truthfully told her mother that Rafael wasn't the guy Victoria had made him out to be; that he wasn't the guy the tabloid papers portrayed who moved from woman to woman, picking up and putting down like a spoilt kid in a toy shop.

She uneasily ran through the sincerity in her voice as

she'd waxed lyrical about Rafael to her mother, persuading her out of her anxiety and persuading herself into the dawning realisation of something she must have known for a while. The realisation that she had fallen for a guy who hadn't returned the favour—not when it came to love, which was so very different from passion—and that she'd gone and done the very thing she'd always told herself she would never do.

A sick feeling swirled inside her.

Forget about her mother and her disappointment if they rushed back to England so that they could spill the beans on the little game they had set in motion—one look at her and Caroline Payne would know that her daughter had fallen for Rafael. So much for all her teachings.

'What did you tell her?' Rafael asked her curiously.

'That Victoria was a woman with an axe to grind and that she would do anything to make sure you paid the price for dumping her—woman scorned and all that stuff.'

'Hmm.'

'But I see what you mean.'

'That it's better for us to stay here for a bit until things flatten out?'

'It would be an opportunity for me to slowly begin to tell Mum that perhaps I got carried away by being out here…that lust got the better of me, but that everything she'd ever said about using my head when choosing a guy was right, because bit by bit I could see that you weren't the one for me.'

'Not dull enough,' Rafael murmured in agreement.

'In the end, common sense would win through and

by the time I return to Yorkshire Mum would be fine with it all.'

'And you haven't thought of the other upside to us remaining out here.'

'Which is what?'

In her head, she had been dealing with the rollercoaster ride of emotions that had swamped her without even really realising: *she was in love with Rafael.*

She loved everything about him, from the way he laughed to the way he touched her, to the things he said that made her think and the way he teased her until she was laughing at herself with him.

'That we exhaust this,' he said.

'This?'

'This crazy passion we have for one another. It'll subside. Crazy passion always comes with a sell-by date. But, if we were to walk away from it before it naturally goes, then both of us would always be left with a want that hadn't had a chance to be satisfied, an itch still waiting to be scratched. We stay here two weeks, perhaps even a bit longer, and we see this through to the end. No dissatisfaction left because that itch hasn't been scratched.'

Sammy nodded, lost in her own thoughts and sadly thinking that, whereas her feelings for him ran too deep to quantify, his feelings for her were best summed up as an itch to be scratched.

But she needed time, and a couple more weeks here would give her the time she needed.

Rafael strolled through the glass sliding doors of the villa that gave out to the landscaped gardens at the back. To the right the swimming pool was lit up with lights that were cleverly strung between swaying palm trees and threaded through some of the dense foliage. The blue of the pool was very dark, a dappled swirl of shadows casting stripes across the flat, still surface.

The veranda here was very wide and circled the entirety of the back, wide enough for clusters of chairs, tables and potted plants. Beyond the lit section the landscape disappeared into tropical darkness, which was dense, and pierced here and there with fireflies and the gentle swoop of bats diving in search of food.

Sammy was in the kitchen. Standing out here with a glass of wine in his hand, he smiled to himself at the thought of her shooing him away, telling him that she wanted to surprise him with a special dinner. He liked the way she'd been pink from the heat of the kitchen, her whole body radiating satisfaction at doing something she enjoyed.

The plan to remain on the island had been a good one. They'd been here for ten days in total, and he knew from the conversations they'd had that her mother had come down from the sharp anxiety she had felt when she'd first found out about their so-called engagement.

For a brief second, he frowned because something else occurred to him: where was the boredom? When was that due to set in—shouldn't it be round about now?

Sure, he had had longer-lasting women in his life in the past but, thinking about it, he'd never spent so much undiluted time with any of them. He and Sammy were practically together on a twenty-four-seven basis. They'd fallen into a routine of going to the hotel, doing all the due diligence together before it opened. She practised cooking, and the same sous chefs he had hired when his business associates had been there worked alongside her in the hotel restaurant, getting familiar with the appliances. They cooked together for the team in place at the hotel for when it opened and, lately, for some VIP families on the island.

While she did her thing, he did his, working remotely from the conference room at the hotel, on call for anyone who might require his input. So it was a little bit puzzling that he was in her company for so much of the time and yet still got a kick from looking at her. He was still so horny for her that he couldn't get enough of her. She could have been wearing sackcloth and ashes with a side order of hobnail boots and he would still have wanted her.

She had set a wonderful table on the veranda. They would be dining al fresco, she'd told him, and it was going to be a very special meal because he had yet to see what she'd been getting up to in the kitchen. All the stuff she'd made so far had been relatively casual and light.

He looked round as he heard her approach from behind. Rafael stared. The light from the conservatory behind illuminated her. She had dressed for the occasion in a frothy lilac dress that he hadn't seen before that skirted her slender thighs and was belted at the waist with a thin, golden cord, and wore flat, strappy sandals and a little necklace with a shell that he had bought for her on impulse at a market they had gone to a few days ago.

She looked like a figure from Greek mythology—a very sexy one.

He slowly walked towards her, smiling as he neared her. 'I like the outfit.'

'Thank you. I got it yesterday at that shop—the one by the boutique that sells those paintings.'

'I didn't see you escape to do that.'

'Because you were working at the hotel and I went to get some stuff from the supermarket. I thought…'

'That you would try and distract me from eating whatever delicacies you've prepared because all I'd be thinking is how much I wanted to eat *you*?'

'That's a very corny line, Rafael.'

But Sammy was smiling as he drew her against him, one hand behind her neck, the other curved possessively over her bottom. Her body curved against him in a way that was exciting and familiar at the same time. She felt the tell-tale dampness spread between her thighs and the sensitivity of her breasts brushing against the silky material. She wasn't wearing a bra; she'd stopped that ages ago. He'd told her that he liked to be able to touch her, lift her top as she walked past in the villa, suckle against her nipple and enjoy her without the faff of having to unclasp bra straps. Since she liked that situation as much as he did, she'd been more than happy to comply.

'I know,' he agreed, grinning. 'I'll try and think of a few better ones. I like the table. You know, there was no need—nothing wrong with us eating in the kitchen.'

'You need to see my talents as a chef!' Sammy smiled. 'Now, if you sit, I'm going to bring our starters out and also the wine.'

'Yes, ma'am.' He was grinning. 'I never knew how much I would enjoy taking orders until you came along.'

Sammy smiled and held back as he strolled towards the table and sat, eyes still on her, hungry and hot. She was surprised and relieved that he hadn't asked her what this special meal was all about. She'd glibly told him that she just wanted to prove her skills, which was true enough, although only part of the story.

Truth was that time was flying by. One week was turning into two. They'd set a time limit but it had been a vague one—two weeks or thereabouts. *Thereabouts*, however, didn't stretch into 'for ever' land. *Thereabouts* meant that they would probably have roughly another week left before he started making noises about returning to the fast lane in London.

When Sammy thought about that, her blood ran cold. Should she wait until he said something—maybe told her that they needed to talk? Was there any way she could brace herself for that kind of conversation? What would she say? Would she just nod, shrug, laugh a bit and then say something vague about it being good while it had lasted?

If she were true to herself, then would that be her response? She had spent the past ten days making sure to hide her growing feelings from Rafael, needing to think things through without him suspecting anything. But now, with their timeline drawing to a close, thinking things through had to come to an end. She would have to take the bull by the horns, do what she had to do and then stand back and see where the cards fell.

She'd chosen the wine, and he rose to relieve her of it as she headed to the table, doing a balancing act with the wine cooler and two bowls of prawns in a spicy pepper sauce. The prawns on the island were the size of lobsters, and just as delicious.

'So, chef, will you tell me about this dish?'

'Try it and you can tell me what you think is in it. It's a game I sometimes play with some of the families I've cooked for in the past. Occasionally service is formal, but a lot of the time I've cooked for stressed out working couples and served up in the kitchens. 'Course, the kitchens aren't quite the sort of kitchens most people are used to—they're kitchens fit for kings and queens.'

'You like that—cooking privately as opposed to in a restaurant?'

'It's a lot more personal, but there's also a lot more resting on what you produce, and sometimes people can be quite difficult. If they're paying, they think they own you.'

'It's like that in any job,' Rafael mused quietly. 'You get paid to do a service and the person paying is always aware of that. You're working for them and they own you. I saw that with my dad. When we moved to Yorkshire, he got a job, but he was still pretty fragile. There were days when he could barely make it out of bed, but he forced himself, because he knew that he was on a payroll and the minute he stopped doing as he was told the pay would stop.'

'Whenever you talk about your dad, your tone of voice changes.'

'Does it?'

'Hardens.'

Rafael thoughtfully tilted his head to one side. 'I guess it does.' He sighed. 'Not that I talk about this at all, but yes. Growing up, it was hard not to pity my father. Survival and resilience deserted him and the worst of it was that the marriage, as I think I've told you, wasn't a good one. It definitely wasn't made in heaven. But…'

'But? No, wait—don't say a thing. Give me your plate and I'll see to the main meal. I think you're going to love it. It's a very special dish.'

'Need a hand?'

'I've got this.'

Her heart was beating like a sledgehammer as she prepared their mains. She made sure that every garnish was in place and every bit of food on the plate was positioned just so, from the fondant potatoes to the exquisite lobster and the tiny carrots and fresh peas.

He was confiding in her. Was he even aware of that? She didn't think so. She'd barely been aware of it herself until she'd woken up to her own feelings and had begun to take note of the things that were said between them, the little intimacies spoken in passing.

He shared things with her: titbits about his past. He laughed and told her funny stuff that had happened with clients over the years. A couple of days ago, he'd told her of the effort he'd put in to make sure he succeeded because success was everything.

She lapped up those confidences, lashes lowered, hardly breathing, never daring to encourage in case he backed off and turned away.

'Ta-da!' She laughed and flamboyantly laid his plate in front of him. He laughed back and looked at her admiringly.

'A picture should be taken.'

'Already did that.' Sammy slipped into her seat and glanced at him across the flickering candles. 'Can't have a website without lots of images, and I'm doing a lot of work on my website while I'm here. You were saying… about your dad and the way he was after your mother left…?'

'So I was,' Rafael continued absently. 'I was saying that it's partly thanks to you that I've squared off some of my disillusionment with my dad—a hangover from the way I felt all those years ago.'

'How so?'

'You had a rough ride as well and yet you haven't become bitter or cynical. You still believe in love, and you still believe that Mr Right is out there, waiting like a knight in shining armour to marry you and give you the happy-ever-after life you want. You could say I've softened my stance on my father and his life choices. I always loved him but I can see how he could end up a broken guy.'

'I'm really pleased about that although, you know, it's not *quite* as straightforward as Mr Right galloping on his horse towards me.'

'You're not kidding.'

'Although, it's not as impossible as you've come to think.' She felt a fine film of perspiration break out as she wondered where to go from here. Somewhere in the course of the past few days, as she'd untangled her feelings about this man, she'd realised that telling him the truth was going to be the best thing for her. The best way to be her own authentic self.

And she even dared to hope that it would not be in vain. They'd shared a lot. He'd talked to her in a way that she knew, in her gut, he'd never talked to another woman before. He'd told her stuff and, because he wasn't a guy who shared, she'd known that that *stuff* represented true confidences.

He hadn't even been aware of those moments. Like just then, when he'd spoken about his father. Could he see that behind those words lay a world of hurt that he was exposing for her to see? Surely that meant *something*? Sammy knew that he was right when he'd said that, despite what she'd gone through, she still held on to her optimism. She still believed in love. Was she being an idiot to think that he might love her without realising it? That she could tell him how she felt and that he might think about it and realise that he felt the same way? That his heart had been ambushed without him realising, just as hers had?

'What are you thinking?' Rafael looked at the distant expression on Sammy's face. 'That was stupendous, by the way.'

'I know.' She grinned. 'I'm not a bad chef. Maybe one day I'll have a Michelin star.'

'Don't do that. Michelin-starred restaurants can be very overrated, especially for a man who grew up on the wrong side of the tracks.'

'I'll bear that in mind.'

'I was going to ask you what's for dessert, but I've just decided that *you're* going to be my dessert. Come sit on my lap. I want to make love to you right here, right now. Then we can go swim in the pool to cool off. And when we go upstairs we can do it all again.'

'Is sex all you think about, Rafael Moreno?' Sammy laughed but she shuffled off her chair and he adjusted his so that she could straddle him. She linked her fingers behind his head, kissed him slowly and tenderly and then sighed with pleasure when he undid the corded belt from her waist and chucked it on the ground.

She shifted this way and that as he raised the dress, pushing it up to her neck where it gathered in soft folds so that he could lick her swollen nipples. She moaned when he pulled away, looked at them and murmured how beautiful her breasts were.

'Small and perfectly formed,' he observed. 'Touch me, Sammy.'

She laughed huskily and, when she stood up to yank the dress off, followed by her underwear, he did the same with his trousers and tee-shirt until they were both naked and feverish with the excitement that had exploded from nowhere.

He kissed her, pressing her against him. She felt his hardness against her and nearly swooned. Love, passion and desire all merged into something that was overwhelming. She gently pushed him so that he was back in the chair. Then she knelt between his legs and took him into her mouth, touching his thighs and his rigid shaft the way she knew he loved.

His groans of pleasure were such a turn-on, it was an effort to remain there when all she wanted was to straddle him and feel him deep inside her. She raised her eyes to see him arched back in the chair, his big body swamping it, his eyes closed, and she nimbly mounted him and felt the soft, silky slide of his bigness in her with a powerful surge of satisfaction.

She moved on him, slowly then a little faster, and then, as she felt their bodies reaching the same point of no return, she flung her arms around his neck and buried her head against his shoulders as the wonder of her orgasm swept her away.

She was as weak as a kitten when finally the pleasure subsided, and she opened her eyes and sat back, still feeling him in her.

'Rafael,' she murmured huskily.

'Jesus, that was amazing.'

'You mean that?'

'Of course I do.' He smiled. 'The ground moves every time…incredible. If I were ever to be caught up in an actual earthquake, no one would be able to say that I wouldn't know what it felt like.'

'It's the same for me.'

'Glad to hear it.' He stroked his fingers through her hair and their eyes tangled in a lengthening silence. Sammy could feel the pulse in her temple beating steadily as she continued to look at him and this time there was no hiding what she was feeling. She'd spent enough time covering up her feelings for this guy. Now was the time for truth or else they would part company and the moment would be lost.

'Sammy…'

'You know what I want to say, don't you?' she murmured gruffly.

'No, I don't. Don't say it, Sammy.'

'I'm in love with you, Rafael.'

'You're not.'

He fidgeted and she eased off him to stand back, valiantly looking at him, proud of her nudity and wanting him to see the woman who wanted to live her life uninhibited with the man she loved.

He didn't meet her eyes and she swallowed and slowly put the dress back on. Her body was still hot and sticky from love-making, although somewhere inside her something was shutting down. But she wasn't going to give this up without a fight.

'Don't tell me what I am, Rafael.'

'This wasn't part of the plan.'

'Plans don't always work out the way you think they're going to. I didn't even like you when I first met you, and

I fooled myself for ages that you weren't the sort of guy for me, even though I was attracted to you.'

'I need to get dressed.'

Sammy looked away, for the first time feeling the space between them and holding on to her pride with difficulty, but determined to speak her mind and to heck with it.

When she next looked at him, they were no longer lovers but uncertain strangers staring across a divide. At least that was what it felt like to her. She saw the way he had shut down. His expression was shuttered and defensive.

'Rafael, I know how you feel about love and commitment and marriage and all that stuff...'

'I honestly don't know where you're going with this, and it's not something I want to talk about.'

'You're afraid of involvement and afraid of being open to your emotions. But look at us for the past few weeks, Rafael: we've been brilliant together. We've shared things, we've talked...and I mean *really* talked. You don't want to admit it but you're like me. I didn't want to fall in love with you because you didn't make any sense for me and my life, but I did. Sometimes you just can't help what happens to your heart. Maybe it was the same for you.'

Sammy looked at him hopelessly. She breathed in deeply but already her mind was running ahead, predicting the inevitable outcome. She would have to leave. She was speaking her mind and everything she was saying was falling on barren ground because the signs hadn't been there—not for him. It really had just been a physical attraction for him and, even if it hadn't, even if he felt something for her, his beliefs were too ingrained for him ever to change them.

Mentally, she was packing her suitcase. The soft sounds of insects, the warm, still tropical air, the darkness of the pool and the optimistically laid out table now seemed horribly mocking, so she tried not to look at any of it but to keep her eyes firmly focused on the man gazing at her with cool, unreadable eyes.

'I'm sorry to disappoint you, Sammy, but no. It wasn't the same for me. I am not a man who's in search of love. I never have been and I never will be. I thought we were on the same page. If I'd had the slightest idea that you might begin thinking that this charade we've been playing was the real thing, then there's no way I would ever have involved you in it in the first place.'

'No,' she agreed dully.

'I like you, Sammy.' His voice gentled. 'But liking isn't loving. Liking is enjoying someone's company.'

'Okay.' She looked up at him. He was being kind and she couldn't stand it. 'I think I'm going to pack and get back home.'

'I think that's a good idea. I can arrange a flight back for you tomorrow.'

'Sure. Thank you.'

'In the meantime, I'll go to the hotel. Everything's ready for the opening in a month's time. There's no harm in sampling the product.'

'Quite.'

'And Sammy…?'

She was beginning to turn away. She twisted to look at him over her shoulder, one last glance at the guy who had turned her world upside down.

'Yes?'

'I'm sorry I couldn't give you what you wanted. But, trust me, one day you'll look back at what we had and you'll thank me, because you'll know that I would never have been good for you. You deserve the guy who meets your checklist.'

She nodded and turned away.

Rafael felt as though time had suddenly slowed down. His brain was sluggishly receiving information but processing it was painful—painful but necessary.

He watched as she walked away from him into the house without bothering to slide the glass doors shut behind her. For a while he was frozen, staring at nothing in particular, then he moved to one of the chairs by the pool and sat staring at the glassy water.

He should have known. He should have read the signs. She was romantic. She believed in love and she wanted the happy-ever-after. The second they had embarked on their charade, he should have known that there was a chance that sooner or later what was false had a chance of merging into something real.

For her. For him, it was all just the physical stuff. Okay, so they'd talked, they got along. But he was standing firm by what he'd said, that *getting along* wasn't the same as *falling in love* and surrendering his soul into the safekeeping of someone else. There was no leap of faith involved in *getting along* with someone.

This hadn't been about drifting into coupledom for him. He had vivid memories of the amount of time his father had wasted on love. He had drowned trying to resuscitate it when it was well and truly dead, and where had that got him? Rafael had been left picking up too many pieces not to have learnt valuable lessons from the experience. Lessons that had protected him from the very thing that had happened to Sammy!

He had sworn never to put himself in a position of vulnerability, open to hurt and pain, and in a place where others might suffer because of his choices. She would be better off without him. She was a special person who needed to find her soul mate.

Uneasy with his introspection, Rafael glanced up at the bank of bedroom windows. He couldn't see her, because the shutters were closed, but he knew that she would be packing. He texted his PA and told her immediately to book a flight out of the country for Sammy and that her details would be on file. It was done. Half an hour later, his phone pinged with the message that the relevant information had been sent to Sammy.

Making up his mind, Rafael stood up and headed indoors, already on his phone telling the guys at the hotel that he would be testing the sleeping quarters for the next couple of nights.

'Make sure the mattresses are comfortable,' he said, heading to his office to complete the call and gather up the work-related stuff which he would do once he was at the hotel. 'We don't want any guests deciding that they're too hard, too soft, too lumpy or just not up to scratch. Wealthy guests always expect the best.' As an afterthought, he phoned through to the hotel again and asked for a team to be sent to clean the villa as soon as possible.

He knew Sammy. He knew that she would be packing and probably apprehensive about bumping into him.

He scowled as it struck him that he was reluctant to bump into her as well. Everything that had just happened in the past half hour should have turned him off big time but when he thought of her, as he was thinking of her now, his body reacted in unpredictable ways.

He still wanted her. Still craved her.

He would wait an hour then he would go pack a bag and head to the hotel. She would be gone the following morning and…life would return to normal. He might have shared more with Sammy than he had with any other woman but, in the end, he was insulated against the very thing she had wanted. She would ease out of his life just like every other woman had, barely leaving a ripple behind her.

CHAPTER TEN

RAFAEL KNEW JUST when Sammy left the island.

In fact, he was in the hotel when he heard the sound of the aeroplane that would deliver her back to England; that was how small the island was. It had roared overhead, and he'd gritted his teeth and tried not to think of her staring out of the window, her heart hardening in the face of his rejection.

Within the week, he too would return to England, and henceforth business dealings with her would be done via his PA. There was no need for him to know anything about what she did with the considerable amount of money he would be handing over to her.

And, as for their fake engagement, it might have been whispered to Sammy's mother but it had not ignited in the press, so when he returned, there would be no public curiosity to douse.

As for Caroline Payne, he was sure that Sammy would retreat from the make-believe fantasy with no harm done to her relationship with her mother. She would be the decisive one who had cut the ties, having realised the error of her headlong rush into infatuation. She had poured her heart out to him in a no-holds-barred performance that he could only admire, and she would surely be bitter at the way he had reacted—coolly, firmly, with no way back for discussion.

Of course, she would tell whatever story she wished to tell to her mother, and he couldn't fault that approach. Bitterness would fuel her. He would be in the lead role as Big Bad Wolf, knocked back for the first time in his life, dismissed to lick his wounds in a dark cave somewhere, and he was happy with that. He couldn't be happier.

A woman in love with him? No way. He blamed himself because he had been swept away by the sex. The truth was that love had never been a complication he would take on board—*could* take on board—however convenient the situation was and however hot the sex.

And however warm the laughter, stimulating the conversation, tender the touches...

He closed his eyes and breathed heavily. She'd left yesterday and it felt like a lifetime ago.

The conference room at the hotel should have been his sanctuary. Work had always been his go-to, but now, with his laptop in front of him and a string of emails to deal with, he just couldn't focus. His chest hurt. His eyes hurt. His *brain* hurt. In his mind's eye, he saw her thinking, reflecting, remembering. She would remember everything—the way she had walked into love and the way she had proudly told him how she felt, even though it must have been daunting for her, given everything he had said in the past about not believing in love.

Would she already have been to see her mum? Or would she be bracing herself, buying some time before she launched into a smiling, self-deprecating, eye-rolling speech about what an idiot she'd been, and thank God she'd seen the light before it was too late?

And in her heart? In her heart, she would remember the good things they'd had, but in her head, he would crystallise into the sort of guy she knew she should have stayed away from. If she forgot the way she'd confessed her love, then she would never forget the way he'd rejected her.

How fast could love harden, only to be replaced by hate and then eventually indifference? She would look back over her shoulder and curse herself for her foolishness in falling for him.

Rafael surrendered to his thoughts and snapped shut the laptop. Through the bank of windows, he could see the endless stretch of blue sky, and in the distance the streak of turquoise ocean turning dark as it meshed with the horizon. It was not yet four in the afternoon. He felt he could keep sitting right here, staring through the window, until that blue sky turned violet and orange and then finally inky black. The swirl of his thoughts paralysed him. He'd led a nomadic life when it came to the opposite sex. But Sammy...

He pressed his thumbs against his eyes and felt sick. Always able to see problems clearly, Rafael was caught in the unusual place of not knowing what to think or what was really going on. He had a pounding headache.

He poured himself a glass of whisky. It wasn't going to help, but he downed it anyway. He scowled at the empty glass in his hand and all over again succumbed to the second-guessing he'd been trying to keep at bay.

In love with him... She'd told him that he was the last person she could ever fall for. She'd said that she went for a type and he wasn't that type. She had her checklist! Had he been at fault for taking her at her word and believing what she had said? Or had he been so busy enjoying her that he'd steered clear of asking questions to which the answers might have proven unpalatable?

But she was gone, and she would thank him for turning her away; would thank him for putting her back on the path to finding the sort of guy she deserved. He wasn't that guy. He wasn't a guy who did love. How many times had he made that clear? A thousand! Yet she had defiantly ploughed ahead, ignoring what he had told her. She was someone who forged forward. That was just her trademark. She braced herself and fearlessly went where angels feared to tread. He should have taken that into account! Sammy was a law unto herself.

His stomach tightened again and he felt a stab of pain deep inside.

Well, as it stood, whatever love she had would sour quickly...but again that thought twisted something inside him. Looking at the bigger picture, though, it would still be for her own good! He would end up being the fall guy in a big way but that was what he wanted, wasn't it? He'd actively volunteered to be the fall guy.

Rafael paced the room as the evening wore into night, barely seeing anything, aware of the darkness outside getting thicker and denser until the Technicolor tropical landscape outside became shadowy shapes and forms.

Where was she now? He felt haunted by the memory of her face and those green eyes resting on him, seeing deep into him in a way no one else ever had.

He called his PA. He would accelerate his flight back. He needed to leave immediately. There were things to do...no, memories to be contained...and they couldn't be contained here. That done and sorted, Rafael eyed the whisky, reluctantly dismissed the temptation for a top up and instead scooped up his laptop and headed out of the hotel, back to his villa.

Maybe he could leave the thinking behind there. It worked for the length of time it took him to get back to the villa, and only because he had to concentrate on the dark, twisty roads, only sporadically lit, the sort of roads where one small mistake could land his car a little too close to a coconut tree for comfort.

But, the second he was inside his villa—which felt as empty as a wedding venue after all the guests had left and the band had packed up and gone—he sat down in the conservatory and let loose a groan of hurt and despair.

He barely recognised the sound. He leant forward to bury his head in his hands and then, like a swarm of insects released from the safety of a box in which they had been conveniently contained, his thoughts rushed to attack him. He remembered every tender touch, every glance, every smile, every wicked, teasing grin... He could recall how he'd felt when he'd been with her: complete, happy. In no rush to go anywhere, do anything or even think too hard.

She'd reminded him about how they'd talked. He'd responded that *talking* had meant nothing, that it was just a fact that they'd got along, and *getting along* wasn't love.

But he'd done much more than talk to her. He'd opened up. He'd let go of the restraints that had kept him prisoner all his life. He'd confided and shared all those little bits of him he'd become used to keeping to himself and he hadn't even noticed that he'd been doing it.

How could he not have clued in to the obvious? It all added up now: that lazy urge to hold on to what they had; the cold feeling of desperation when he'd thought of her walking away from him; and then, this evening, this sickening horror at a vision of life slipping between his fingers.

Because a life without her in it was no life at all. He'd been so busy polishing the armour he'd spent a lifetime putting in place to protect his heart that he hadn't seen what would have been obvious to an idiot: he'd fallen in love with her.

He couldn't say when or how but he just knew that he had…and now? Now, she'd be busy unravelling what they had built, toughening up and hardening her emotions. She'd be building walls he would never be able to break down, building them with disillusionment and bitterness.

He had to see her. The time between this decision and the flight he had booked, which was just a matter of a handful of hours, felt like a lifetime. If he could have arranged for his private jet to swing by and pick him up like a handy taxi service, he would have, but he still had to pack anyway.

He still had last minute things to do. One of those things was to text her and tell her that he would be coming to see her. He had to know that she would be in, although he would just have gone and waited for as long as it took.

He didn't say why. He simply said that something urgent had come up and that he would have to see her face to face to discuss it. He'd said he would meet her at her house, or she could come to his office—anywhere that suited.

So he was meeting her at his office, and her reply suggested that as far as she was concerned the office was the place for a business discussion. Reading between the lines of her cool, brief response, he got the impression that she had already shut the doors on him and that only the hint that it might be work-oriented had motivated her to agree to see him.

He'd take that.

He couldn't relax. The adrenaline was surging through him and it only began to abate when the plane touched down the following day. He'd asked if she could swing by his office at five-thirty. There would still be people around, of course, but that was okay, because he didn't want her to feel nervous, to feel that there would be just the two of them. If she now hated him, then the last thing he wanted was for her to see an empty office, turn skittish and run away, work talk or no work talk.

Sammy was dabbing her eyes when her mobile pinged and she stared down at Rafael's name on her phone. She'd barely been back in the country and the last person she'd expected to hear from was him. He'd rejected her. She'd said what she had to say, but there hadn't even been a second when he'd considered what she'd told him, not a second when he'd given any thought to the possibility that he might have feelings for her. He'd been appalled. *Love her?* How could she have been foolish enough to think that he might have fallen for her like she'd fallen for him?

The speed of his rejection had said it all.

She'd packed, knowing that he was sitting outside on that veranda with the remains of her specially prepared meal scattered on the table, cruelly lit with the romantic glow of the candles she had taken time to buy and put there. They hadn't even got round to the chocolate fondant she had made.

When had he disappeared off to the hotel? She didn't know, because she'd made sure to stick to her room and pack, only emerging when she knew for certain that he would no longer be in the house. She hadn't cried. The tears had lodged inside her, refusing to come out. They hadn't been able to get past the pain—the pain of her rejected love and the agony of the emptiness that lay ahead, which she would have to fill somehow.

On the flight over, she'd wondered whether she should go to Yorkshire and see her mum immediately so that she could get the whole sorry situation off her chest. She wasn't quite sure what she intended to say but she knew that she would just say whatever it took to make sure her mother didn't get into too much of a state. That would mean plastering a phony, confident smile on her face and launching into some spiel about finding out in the nick of time that she and Rafael weren't suited.

Since she hadn't been able to face the phony smile just yet, she had decided to go to London and stay there for a few days. She knew people there. One of the girls who had come through culinary college with her had her own small flat in Notting Hill, so Sammy had arranged to stay with her for a few days.

'I'll cook,' she'd promised, 'and clean up behind me. I know that's the bit you always hated!'

So, when she'd got Rafael's text, she'd felt the breath leave her in a whoosh. She'd just come back from a very speedy supermarket shop and had been about to sit down, relax and deal with her jet lag.

He wanted to see her. It would be about business, of

course, and she'd been tempted to tell him just to email whatever he wanted to say, but then she'd thought that a series of emails between them would only prolong the misery and keep him alive in her head. Whereas, if she went to see him, spent fifteen minutes hearing whatever he had to say, it would be like lancing a boil—over and done with, only the healing left to endure.

And besides, a little voice had piped up, *you know you want to see him...want to have one last look at that beautiful face and put it in your memory bank so that you can pull it out to gaze at at a later date.*

She had squashed that little voice. She wasn't going to succumb to thinking about him twenty-four-seven even, though she knew that that was exactly what she would probably end up doing. She told herself that, when she saw him, she would make sure to remember the way he had rejected her. She decided that seeing him would give her the sense of closure that she hadn't had when she'd left him out there on the veranda with the warm, tropical breeze and the harmonious sounds of insects, frogs and toads reminding her that there really was no such thing as paradise.

He'd suggested going to Yorkshire but the last thing she wanted was for him to meet her anywhere private. The thought of him in her house had been way too much. That would have left her way too vulnerable. They could meet in his office, surrounded by phones, desks, computers and people working hard making money, and that would be fine.

Still, as she got dressed the following day with a sickening sensation of *déjà vu* in the pit of her stomach, she almost wished that she'd gone for the response for him to email anything he had to say because, whatever he said, there was nothing that couldn't be communicated in writing. Was there?

Rafael could feel the tension building as the time approached to meet her.

Part of him wondered whether she might bail at the last minute, in which case he wasn't entirely sure what he would do. He could hardly pursue her if she really didn't want to lay eyes on him.

Then he wasted some time wondering whether he should meet her in the foyer of the building. Finally, he decided against that because, if the only reason she had agreed to meet him at all was that she thought it was to do with work, then being shown up by one of the receptionists would confirm that. He had tactfully dispatched his PA.

Rafael was a man who was impervious to nerves. Something about having spent his life beating the odds had strengthened his inner core, made him utterly resilient when it came to facing down challenges and making the best of whatever life decided to throw at him.

But right now, drumming his fingers on his desk and resisting the urge to prowl through his office to relieve his tension, he was nervous. He felt vulnerable and hesitant, and for some reason that had made him think of his dad, had made him re-evaluate the black and white vision he had had of him as a man who had lacked the strength to give up on the unattainable.

His father had simply been human, and being human was the very thing Rafael had spent his life trying hard not to be. To be human was to be weak, and being weak was something he had made sure he would never be.

But he was here and he felt *human* for the first time. He hadn't stopped beating himself up for his stubborn blindness in recognising what had been staring him in the face. And yet, how was he to have known that, just when he wasn't expecting it, someone would break down all the barriers he had constructed around himself? His wealth, power and status had made him invincible and, in his head, his iron will had cemented his own formidable belief that the only person who could ever control the direction of his life would be himself. How wrong he'd been.

He stilled when the call came through that Sammy had arrived. He waited, seated behind his desk, counting the seconds until she entered his office. It had only been a matter of hours and yet, as he saw her framed in the door that opened into his PA's office beyond his, Rafael felt as though he was seeing her for the first time.

It felt like being punched in the gut. She was as slight as he remembered, as graceful as a gazelle, and her face was tight and cautious. Her body language screamed discomfort and he rose to his feet and walked towards her.

'Sammy… I wasn't sure whether you would come.'

'You didn't leave me much choice. I'm here because you said you had something to say to me face to face.'

'Yes.'

'Well, go ahead and say it.'

'Come through to my office, please. I can't…say what I want to say with you standing with your back to the door.'

She'd dressed in a prim navy skirt, some workman-like shoes and a white jumper with a thick jacket swamping her. It made him think of her in those sexy summer outfits she had worn, braless and so sexy that she'd always managed to blow his self-control straight out of the water.

He raked his fingers through his hair, shifting uncomfortably, and looked down at his shoes, feeling a bit like a school kid summoned to the principal's office to discuss being caught smoking behind the bike shed. Although, in fairness, he'd faced many a hauling into the principal's office and had never felt like this in any of them.

'I don't intend to stay long, Rafael. Say what you have to say. If I need to sign anything, then I'll do that and leave.'

'Nothing to sign.' He walked back into his office and breathed a sigh of relief when she followed him through to perch on the chair in front of his desk.

'I...' he began. 'I... I see that you got back in one piece.'

'I haven't come here for the chit-chat.'

'I can understand why you're angry with me.'

'I also haven't come here to rake up what's been said between us. That's over and done with and I'm moving on.'

They stared at one another in silence. Lost for words, Rafael cleared his throat and thought that he had seen a million sides of her but never this side—this tough, steely side, closed off and shuttered—not even when she had stormed into his office to see him that very first time.

Just bite the bullet.

'Sammy, I had to see you, had to talk to you. What I have to say could never have been said in an email because I just wouldn't have known how to put it into words.

You're here and I've missed you,' he said quietly in an all-or-nothing impulse. 'I've been a fool.'

'What are you trying to say? I don't understand.'

'And I don't blame you because the last conversation we had involved me telling you that there was no way I could... I could...return your feelings.'

'Rafael, I won't sit here and listen to you say stuff that isn't true!'

'I never lie. Haven't I told you that already?'

'You're also a guy who likes to get what he wants. Do you think that you can say things you believe I want to hear to get me back into bed with you?'

'Please, Sammy, hear me out. We got into a game that had consequences and that game was my idea. A quid pro quo situation was how I thought of it at the time, a favour that carried mutual benefits for both of us. And then...then...the game got a lot more serious than either of us had planned.

'It was selfish of me to get you involved with an ex who was hell-bent on revenge. I knew that, if Clement pulled out of the deal, people's livelihoods would be on the line and I put that ahead of any repercussions that might have happened between us. It never crossed my mind that I couldn't handle the charade. I presented it to you as a deal that would pay off and would cost us nothing because that's what I believed.'

'It's fair to say that the blame for that stupid charade falls on both our shoulders,' Sammy muttered gruffly.

'Then what started as a game became serious. We became lovers.' He watched as colour surged into her cheeks and she lowered her eyes. 'And, like an idiot, I continued thinking that I would continue to have com-

plete control over that situation as well. The truth is that
I have *always* had complete control over my emotions…
that is, until you came along.'

Sammy looked up and their eyes met. Her heart leapt inside her because she could see the blinding sincerity on
his face. Hope began to send shoots through her.

'I'm listening,' she said breathlessly.

'I felt sick when I watched you walk through those
patio doors but I was paralysed. I didn't know what to do.
I told myself that the sick feeling would go, told myself
that I could never return your love because I was inca-
pable of feeling love. I didn't know how to handle what
you'd said and I had no other responses in my repertoire.
I fell back on what I thought was the truth when, in fact,
I'd left that truth behind the second you walked into my
life. I denied feelings I never even recognised because
I'd never had them before.'

'And suddenly you changed in a matter of hours?'
Sammy tried to sound incredulous, but it was difficult,
because she knew that he was being honest, even though
she could scarcely believe it.

'I did. When truth caught up with the lies I'd been telling myself. When the thought of not having you in my
life made me want to cry. I love you, Sammy, and, more
than that I need you, because there's no point to my life
without you in it. I just hope I'm not too late to have you
accept my offer of marriage. Not for show, just for us—
me and you for ever.'

Their eyes met and tangled, just as they had many
times in the past, but this time what Sammy saw was
the heart she'd yearned for in those dark eyes; a heart

this beautiful, strong, proud man was handing to her for safekeeping.

She smiled, slowly at first, and then radiantly and widely, because her own heart was bursting with love.

'Yes,' she murmured, tiptoeing to kiss the side of his mouth and then brushing her finger where her lips had lingered. 'Yes, I think marrying you is just the thing I want to do. This is going to be our fairy tale, Rafael Moreno. And, trust me, it's a fairy tale that's never going to end.'

* * * * *

Did you fall in love with
Emergency Engagement?

*Then why not try these other fabulous stories
by Cathy Williams!*

The Italian's Innocent Cinderella
Unveiled as the Italian's Bride
Bound by Her Baby Revelation
A Wedding Negotiation with Her Boss
Royally Promoted

Available now!

HIS HIDDEN ROYAL HEIRS

LORRAINE HALL

MILLS & BOON

For sisters

CHAPTER ONE

CRISTHIAN STERLING KNEW exactly where he could go and not be recognized. It got easier the older he got, the less he resembled a bewildered, hurting boy who'd just lost his parents—their terrible car accident splashed next to his picture on every paper, magazine, tabloid and so on.

The upper crust set still knew him by sight more often than not, so he preferred to celebrate his successes in more...*middle-class* establishments. Where, typically, no one would realize who he was or that his mother had been a princess and his father had been Hollywood royalty.

Inadvertently, they had both inspired his choice of profession—though their incredible wealth and prestige had passed to him and he didn't *need* to work. His mother had never known quite what to do with her fame, the public's ruthless interest in everything that made up her relationship to his father.

Though he'd only been ten when they'd died, he remembered conversations of "running away." Of disappearing, never to be found.

But his father had continued to make movies, though he'd always put Cristhian and his mother first. His mother, no matter how it had weighed on her, had continued to fulfill her royal duties to her home country of Hisla, even as she'd raised him in a modest home outside the castle walls when they weren't traveling with his father or visiting his American grandparents.

When they'd finally had enough of the paparazzi, of the way his mother's family had constantly been looking for any opportunity to drive his parents apart, they hadn't stood up for themselves. They hadn't taken control of the situation and made it right.

They'd begun to plan their escape from the bright lights of stardom.

And in the process, they'd been involved in a disastrous car crash that had killed them both instantly.

Leaving him behind.

Perhaps if he'd been allowed to stay with his father's parents in America where he'd been staying while his parents tried to find somewhere safe to escape to, he would feel differently about the whole situation these days. But instead he'd been ripped away, into his mother's royal family who didn't want him, but couldn't bear the stories of him being raised by *Americans*.

Cristhian had learned something from that. He was still working what exactly out these twenty-some years later. When his profession—one he'd carved out for himself— involved him being a finder of sorts. Runaways of the royal set, errant wives, those who wished to disappear. He found them, for whomever wanted to pay his exorbitant fee.

Some people called it mercenary. Usually the people he found who weren't happy to be escorted back to what they'd run away from.

But he knew what else awaited them out in that cold, cruel world. When you stepped out of the rules that governed your life, yourself, disaster awaited. There was only one way to deal with the unfairness of the world—it was to face all problems head-on. Running away never amounted to anything but pain. Because these royal types never stopped, never gave up. You had to beat them at their own game or lose.

So Cristhian had built himself a very clear life with very set rules. He'd stood up to the royal family who wanted to control him, and he didn't worry himself with the opinions of others.

Ever.

He studied the drink in front of him, wondered what had made his brain take a trip down *that* memory lane when he should be enjoying a good drink, perhaps a beautiful woman, in celebration of his latest runaway return.

The girl had been *thirteen*. She might not love her life in her tiny kingdom, but thirteen wasn't the age for a countess to try to make a life out there on her own. She would never thank him for his service, but she would not end up dead. He did not need any thanks. He had the satisfaction of a job well done.

He glanced around the bar. There were a lot of corporate types this Friday night. Ties loosened, top buttons undone, blazers discarded. Loud laughter and couples with surreptitious gazes around the bar like they knew they shouldn't be sitting *that* close to their coworker. Portuguese, Spanish and smatterings of English echoed across the large room.

The door opened, letting in a little gust of air, slightly cooler than the over-warm atmosphere in the bar. Cristhian sipped his drink and watched a woman hesitate in the doorway.

She was clearly alone, and for a moment he saw a flash of fear in her expression, in that hesitation. Then the woman seemed to metaphorically straighten her shoulders, push all that fear away with determination to do whatever she came to do. For a moment, he saw a flash of his mother, doing the exact same before facing a royal event.

But he forgot all about his long-lost mother when the woman smiled. Excitement sparkled in her improbably blue eyes. Her short reddish hair swung with her confident strides against her jawbone as she sauntered fully inside. She wore a boxy sort of black dress that didn't show off much of her figure, but it ended mid-thigh and showcased long, mouthwatering legs.

She didn't meet his gaze. She was on a mission, it seemed, heading straight for the bar where he sat. But her gaze was on the bartender.

She leaned forward but didn't say anything at first. The bartender sighed. "What can I get you?"

"Do you have a menu?" She had an interesting accent. Cristhian knew he'd heard it before, but it would take some thought to remind himself what tiny European country it belonged to. Something far north of southern Portugal where they were currently.

The bartender scoffed with an eye roll.

"Allow me to make a suggestion," Cristhian offered, earning the woman's curious gaze. He was half convinced she was wearing some kind of color-correcting contacts. The shade of blue didn't suit her at all.

And yet she was beautiful. Delicate shoulders and a de-termined demeanor. A cupid's-bow mouth and expressive eyebrows that she arched at him now. As if to say *go on, and you had better impress me*.

Cristhian grinned. He *was* impressive in pretty much all things. He didn't consider this conceit so much as a healthy appreciation of facts. "Beirão," he said, turning his attention to the bartender. "Put it on my tab."

The bartender nodded and turned to put the woman's drink together. Cristhian gestured to the empty seat next to him. "Join me."

She narrowed her eyes a little at him. "Typically, that sort of invitation is offered as a *request*, sir."

He didn't so much as flinch. Didn't hide his interest. Why bother? "I'm not typical. *Naturalmente.*"

She laughed. A lyrical sound that was tinged with a little huskiness that intrigued him more than he could remember being intrigued for quite some time. With an elegance that spoke of training—royal training at that—she slid onto the stool next to him.

The hint of royal had him studying her more closely. Her clothes, the haircut, these things were all firmly *not* royal. But Cristhian knew well that facades could be deceiving.

In a corporate bar in Faro? He was letting his work get to him.

The bartender slid her the drink he'd ordered for her, and a refill of Cristhian's own drink. The woman took a tentative sip, and he watched her reaction intently.

"Perfect," she said, then flashed him a dazzling smile. The kind of smile that spelled trouble.

Luckily, Cristhian excelled at trouble. Wrangling it into all the rules he liked to follow.

"So, what brings you to Faro?"

"Work," she said without hesitation. And royals didn't work, he reminded himself. "But I'm done now and headed home tomorrow."

"And where's home?"

This she hesitated over. Which could be chalked up to a woman being careful of what she told a man. "Hamburg," she eventually offered. "For now."

The accent wasn't a perfect match, but the *for now* made him think she wasn't a German native. It all added up, and he was celebrating a job well done, not *working*, so he needed to relax.

Enjoy.

"Are you local?" she asked him, continuing to sip at her drink. Real diamonds winked at her ears. Expensive diamonds.

He tried not to frown at himself. No more work. *Celebrate.* "I'm more of a nomad myself. Though I find myself in Faro often enough."

"A nomad," she said, as if considering. "No home base, then?"

"I have many home bases."

She angled her chin at him, just so. Haughty, but not in a standoffish kind of way. It suited her, this unearned confidence. "With a woman at each?"

His mouth quirked. "Ah, you impinge my character."

She made a waving gesture. "And you don't deny it."

"There is no specific woman in any such home base. I find relationships don't really fit in with my schedule of travel. My work takes up most of my life."

Something about the word *work* had her expression tightening. Some of that easy bemusement melting out of her eyes.

"You look like someone with a home fire burning," he said, hoping to get some of that sparkle back in her gaze.

She shook her head, no amusement. A hint of sadness at the edge of her features instead. "Not the way you mean. But responsibilities, I suppose. *Work.* Calling me home." She took a deep drink, set the glass on the bar. "But not until tomorrow," she said forcefully, staring hard at the bar. "For tonight, I'll enjoy freedom from responsibilities."

"Well, I suppose it's kismet then. I, too, am enjoying my freedom tonight. Freedom is much more fun with some company, don't you think?"

She studied him, some of that amusement returning

to her expression. "I do," she agreed. "Is there anywhere around here with dancing?"

"There's a club right across the street. Rua Noturna." He nodded to the door.

She slid off her stool. "Let's go then."

Zia Rendall had not intended to pick up a man this evening. It wasn't fully out of the scope of her plans. She might have *hoped* she'd meet someone who made her insides hum just from a look, but she'd known how unlikely that would be.

Her week of freedom had been hard-won to say the least. It hadn't just been escaping the palace and Lille—she'd spent most of her adolescence perfecting those things. It had been about getting out *and* flying under the radar for a week.

Luckily her twin sister, Beaugonia, was an expert at so many things, she'd helped. Procured the colored contacts Zia now wore, the dye she'd used in her hair once she'd been free of the palace. Beau had even done the honors and chopped off Zia's hair.

It was Beau's expertise at computers that had gotten Zia fake identification, a flight to Portugal, and a hotel first in Lisbon, then the past few days in Faro.

Zia had left a note for her parents and a promise to return, and Zia knew that and Beau's efforts to smooth over their parents' anger would be the only reasons they wouldn't send armed guards after her.

Not that they hadn't tried, no doubt, but more on the down-low. They would go harder once her week was up. Tomorrow, bright and early, she had to be on a plane back to Lille or things would…implode, no doubt.

So this was it. She hadn't been about to throw herself at just *any* man for the sake of it. Her fun had included being a normal human, walking about without guards. Sleeping,

eating, drinking and doing whatever she fancied, rather
than follow royal protocol and a schedule someone else
had made for her.

It had been like breathing for the first time. She had
lived for herself. While she was still worried about Beau
at home alone with their parents, she hadn't had to think
of how to protect her with every step. For the first time in
her life, a weight she'd grown so accustomed to she had
stopped noticing it had lifted.

And now it was all over. Back to the palace. Back to the
responsibilities she did not want but had to face. For Beau.

Except it wasn't over just yet. She still had tonight.

Walking into that bar and meeting the gaze of *this* man
had made it very easy to determine that a wildly handsome
stranger, and maybe even a night with him, would be the
cherry on top of her last night of freedom.

She had lied to him about some things, but not about
freedom and this being her last day of it. Tomorrow she'd
return to Lille, her role as Princess Zia Asta Alberte Elisa-
beth Rendall and the responsibilities waiting for her.

Like a royal wedding in the spring. Crown Prince Lyon
Traverso was handsome enough, and not *mean*, by any
stretch. But he was aloof, at best. And had plans for his
kingdom that he wanted no help with. She would have no
say as his wife. Her role would essentially be to pop out
princes and princesses until the kingdom was satisfied.

She had no desire to be a broodmare for anyone, let
alone a virtual stranger, but it had certainly not been
her choice, this political merger her father had planned
and inked out. Heir or no, she had no say in her father's
choices. She was promised to Lyon.

She could have refused, she supposed, but her parents
had made it clear if she did not meet her responsibili-

ties, everyone would pay the price. Mostly her twin, who was...*eccentric*.

At least, that's what the palace called it.

This week was the closest thing she was ever going to have to making her own choices, and as much as she hated that, she hated the idea of Beau suffering the slings and arrows of their father more.

Zia didn't want to think about any of it tonight. She wanted to feel freedom in this last night of it. She wanted to drink, to dance.

She wanted the stranger she'd picked up at a bar. Sinfully handsome, too charming for anyone's good. He was impossibly tall, with broad shoulders to match. Dark hair cropped short, dark eyes, wearing all black like some kind of evil spirit. His smile was sin itself. He was no doubt the type to love and leave.

So, perfect. Maybe an evil spirit, but one who would be a lot of fun before she had to spend the rest of her life metaphorically chained to a monarchy and a man she didn't care about in the least.

But she cared about her sister, and—

She wasn't thinking about that tonight. She was thinking about the man dancing with her. His body was a hard wall of heat. His hand on her back felt like a brand, but it was nothing to the way they moved together. Like two interlocking parts.

While lights flashed and music thrummed around them, it felt like they were the only two people in existence. Which was a freedom even greater and more exhilarating than the one she'd found on her own. Because she was still a princess when it was just her. When she was with *him,* she was a nameless woman. Nothing about her title mattered. Nothing about her country or the expectations laid upon her or who she needed to protect. She could just be whoever she was underneath that.

She'd begun to be afraid there was nothing. But this man laughed when she told a joke. He listened when she explained what she liked about Portugal. There was a give-and-take to their conversation, to their dancing. Not just *control*.

In fact, it seemed as if there was no control between either of them at all. Everything that existed here was elemental. Nothing but chemistry and heat and want.

His hand skimmed down her spine, inciting a jolt of desire, a deep, dark craving swirling around inside her, and an arrow of heat straight to her core. She pressed herself even more firmly to him, and his leg skimmed between hers, making the faintest contact with her bare inner thigh.

Her breath came out in a huff she should have done a better job of hiding. Especially when his chuckle was low and rumbled along her exposed neck. She suddenly understood those over-the-top vampire romances her sister loved to read. She'd do anything to feel his mouth on her neck, no matter how reckless or ill-advised.

So she followed all that reckless down the rabbit hole and lifted to her toes to press her mouth to his, here in this crowded club, where she was no one, except a woman who wanted him.

He tasted like danger. It shot through her bloodstream. Stronger than any drink she'd had tonight. Heat and need and the whirling, sparkling joy of doing whatever the hell she wanted.

Royal protocol be damned. *Finally*.

"I have a hotel suite not far from here." His voice was a rasp in her ear. "And a car to get us there."

It was all the invitation she needed. "Let's go."

CHAPTER TWO

CRISTHIAN DID NOT consider himself particularly uptight, despite a life well organized to suit his needs. He enjoyed women, wherever and whenever the opportunity presented itself. He was not choosy.

But he was usually careful. There were ground rules set. *He* was in control, so that nothing messy came from such an encounter. He ordered his life just how he liked it—whether that be business or pleasure. This had always been…easy.

This woman had blasted rules and control all to hell. He had driven too fast, breaking too many laws, with one hand curled in her hair. While her mouth had been pressed in impressively imaginative ways against his neck.

He could not remember a more desperate stumble into any of the many apartments and homes he owned, no needy rush to a hotel room in his many travels. He could not recall a time when the only possible thought in his head was to explore every last inch of her naked body, over and over again. Not since he'd been a teen eager for that first taste of something he only barely understood had he ever felt so out of control.

Control, that tenet to his life, but she seemed too pretty a flame to try to tame. She was brave and impetuous, but with something more careful underneath. Something that spoke to him, as if it needed tending. He had no desire to structure her in some way to suit his needs. He'd rather just…experience something. Without those rules and lines he knew kept him safe.

There was something revelatory in a lack of safety, of control. And the way the minute they stepped inside his hotel suite, she wrapped around him like the tide, pulling him under, into wave after wave until he was drowning in her. Her short hair was silk in his fisted hand, her mouth a fire of need against his.

He pressed her against the door he'd just closed. Unwinding her arms from his neck so he could pull the dress up and off of her.

Her eyes met his, that blue that didn't fit at all. And yet they were still part of that ocean pulling him under. That and the slender, athletic body underneath. Not his usual type, and yet his mouth watered.

Her underthings were silk, terribly expensive, and any alarm bells that rang in the back of his head that she might be more than he bargained for, that she might know who he was despite the fact that they hadn't exchanged names, were completely muffled by the sound she made when he pressed his hand between her legs.

He took his time exploring the contours of her body while she shivered and begged. He slid the straps of her bra down, following the slope of her shoulder with his mouth. She unbuttoned his shirt, pushed it off him.

It was like a battle. Fencing, maybe. Move and countermove. His mouth on her breast. Her hands on his zipper. Her mouth hot, needy, demanding. And yet she submitted to every demand of his own.

She tasted like some brand-new delicacy, felt like some hidden garden that grew things he'd never seen before. He didn't recognize himself or the strange sensations rico-cheting inside him as he devoured her mouth with tongue and teeth.

Her hand fisted over him, gave one slow stroke. "Now," she panted, meeting his gaze. It was an order, and yet... "Please," she added breathlessly.

There was nothing else beyond that *please*. Not a second's thought. Only a need so all-encompassing he'd later wonder if he'd suffered some sort of medical event that had rendered him completely brain-dead.

He lifted her and with quick strides had her laid out on the large, luxurious bed. He rid himself of the rest of his clothes in seconds flat, moved over her, slid home with a pounding desire that blotted everything else out except the slow, slick slide of perfection.

She exploded around him in a rush, so hot and fast it nearly took him out. The word *kismet* seemed to dance around them, like by uttering such a silly pickup line at that bar he had spoken it into existence.

Fate. Destiny. Her.

He didn't even know her name. But that seemed such a shallow thing in the moment. In the panting of her breath, the soft velvet of her skin. The molten give of her.

He rolled her on top of him, and she balanced herself with two hands on his chest. She grinned down at him.

She moved against him, arching that beautiful body. He slid possessive hands down her sides, then urged her to move faster. To chase these things rioting inside him. He toyed with her nipple and her breathing hitched, the graceful pace she'd set fractured.

Into something wild. Frenzied. There was only the sounds of their breathing, interrupted moans and sighs, their bodies moving together in perfect rhythm. She cried out, shuddered over and over again, and still he held on to that tiniest thread of control.

He rolled her under him, slowed it down to take every ounce of pleasure out of every second. Her moan was a shot of adrenaline. That lost look on her face would stay etched into his memory, possibly forever.

When he followed her over that last edge, he couldn't help but feel like they'd both been found.

Zia had to leave. She shouldn't have stayed as long as she did. It was nearly morning. Not only did she have a plane to catch, but this man could never know who she really was. The more time she gave him, the more ammunition she gave him to figure out her secret.

Throughout the course of the evening, he'd looked at her slightly sideways, like he suspected something. But she'd only needed to kiss him, touch him to make that look disappear.

She couldn't risk more, no matter how much she wanted to.

Regret didn't coil inside her like a weight so much as a wistful kind of longing. For a different life, where she could enjoy any kind of intimate relationship without fear all her misdeeds—meant or inadvertent, true or false— could be sold to the press for so much money it would be hard to blame a person for it.

She thought maybe she could live under the weight of the press's scrutiny, but she would not be able to live under the weight of her parents' forever disappointment. She'd already caused them too much grief. It wasn't their fault, any more than it was hers, that they were the king and queen. It was simply the happenstance of the world.

And her world meant responsibility. Because if she

didn't meet it, Beaugonia would suffer. Her parents did not understand Beaugonia. They saw her lack of following their rules as defiance, some act of violence instead of just who Beau was. So true to herself she couldn't pretend. But it wasn't that simple, or Beau wouldn't suffer from the panic attacks that had their parents viewing her as something…inferior.

No, Zia wouldn't let that be Beau's fate. When she was home, her parents focused on her, on the upcoming wedding. On plans for Lille's partnership with Lyon's home country, Divio.

Then it would be Beau's turn for freedom.

So Zia eased out of the warm, soft bed, away from the large, gorgeous man, still fast asleep.

Zia was an expert at sneaking around. Her entire adolescence had been a study in it. The more guards her father had put on her, the sneakier she'd had to be.

The king would be at his wits' end today, worrying if she'd come back at all. Making plans for if she didn't. And all of those plans would be ready to be accomplished the second she broke her promise.

If she didn't make her flight, all hell would break loose.

Zia's time was up. She should be satisfied. Happy she got to do all the things she wanted.

She collected her discarded clothes, then gave *him* a look over her shoulder. He didn't so much as stir. For a moment, she felt the strangest pang. She'd gone into this knowing it was a fling. A one-night stand, and she had no doubt he had done the same. He'd made that clear.

Maybe it had gotten a little muddled in the time in between. When he'd fed her and they'd laughed over steak sandwiches and a bottle of wine. They had not gotten into their personal lives, but they had spoken of places they'd traveled.

He was even more well-traveled than she and could weave entertaining stories of even the most boring museums. He was a fascinating man...even when she knew nothing about him.

So when they'd fallen into his bed again, it had been like they were old friends. When they'd dozed together and turned to each other all over again, she'd had the passing thought of how nice a life like this might be. Not two people fighting for control. Just a kind of...comradery. A partnership. A friendship. With amazing sex thrown in.

Muddled, yes, her feelings were, but the sex was not. It was explosive. Irresistible. An unquenchable hunger, like they were each a dessert they couldn't quite get enough of no matter how they gorged themselves.

But it was over now. There would be no going back. She would be married come spring. Maybe...maybe she could find some semblance of this with her husband, the crown prince.

But Zia doubted it.

Lyon had made it clear that, like her father, he had expectations, roles for her to fill. He was not interested in *her*. He would not ask her opinion on the music in the club or make her a sandwich. Even meeting the prince only twice, she knew this.

But she had also known her whole life, she was not destined for all the *normal* and *simple* she craved. She was a princess. The heir. Her only role was for her country.

No matter how joyous, how right this week, last night had felt.

The future felt like a dead weight in her chest—not a new feeling, but it felt heavier now. Because she'd seen what could be this week. She'd thought that would give her the relief to make it through her responsibilities.

But instead it had given her a taste of joy. Not just *him*, but everything she'd done this week. To walk the streets a nobody. To window-shop without guards, or an assistant having to make the purchases for her. To experience all the normalcies of life, on her own, and not worry about taking a misstep that Beau might be punished for. Because for all she rebelled in the privacy of the castle, she had known her parents would inflict an incredible avalanche of pain if she did it in public.

In this week, she got to make mistakes. She got to be whoever she wanted to be. Rude. Polite. Overzealous. Hysterical.

In absolute *lust* with a complete stranger.

Oh, she knew she was privileged, but her privilege came with a price, and sometimes that price felt so heavy she could scarcely breathe. And still it was the privilege, and her sister back home, that meant she knew she had to follow her responsibilities.

Back to Lille. To a marriage she didn't want. A prison sentence when she wasn't sure what crime she'd ever committed except being born the pretty twin. The elegant twin. The one with natural social graces and whose panic didn't take over at any given moment.

Careful not to sigh, she slid out of the hotel suite, put back together as best she could be. She took a taxi to the airport and flew back home.

Back to being Princess Zia Rendall.

And all the weight that went with that.

CHAPTER THREE

CRISTHIAN HADN'T STOPPED her sneak-away exit. It was best to not share any awkward goodbyes. No matter how often they'd turned into and over each other, they had not shared names. They both knew what it had been.

It had been *irregular*, the conversations they'd had in between the bouts of unbelievable pleasure, but there was no point in dwelling on that.

But dwell on it he did.

For months.

He couldn't seem to eradicate the woman whose name he didn't even know out of his mind. He could have looked for her. Sometimes the memory of one night drove him so crazy, he nearly began a search. He was a finder. It would be easy to do just that.

For *what*? One random woman? Who he knew next to nothing about except that she was well-traveled and gorgeous? That she liked music more than art, gardens more than museums. And what she sounded like when she came apart in his arms.

What was he going to do? Track her down? *Date* her?

It was so ludicrous every time he got to that part in the circular thought process of not being able to forget her, he laughed. And moved on.

For a time.

When a case finally came in, one worthy of his skills and with the kind of payment he preferred, Cristhian took the first plane out to the small country of Lille, nestled in northern Europe.

A job would surely solve this…problem of his. By the end of it, he would forget about some nameless woman and her one night in his bed over six months ago.

But when he was greeted at the airport by a royal guard to the king, Cristhian found himself all too reminded of his mystery woman, because the guard's accent was *exactly* like hers. She had called Hamburg home, but he had a feeling even if she'd been telling the truth about her current home, she was *from* this country.

He was escorted into a blacked-out car and driven to the castle. The country was small and clearly took its traditions very seriously. If not for the people walking streets in jeans and noses pressed to phones, Cristhian might have felt like he was stepping back in time. The architecture was very old, the buildings crowded together, until they reached the center of the capital where a grand square spread out in front of a modest castle. All very old stones and towers and stained glass.

It reminded him of his mother's country. The one that still tried to lure him back from time to time. For a photo op or to stir up stories that made the royal family look good. Luckily, as his mother had been the seventh child of his grandparents, and his aunts and uncles all had multiple children, Cristhian had only a small title, and a few holdings he had negotiated when he had stood up to his aunt, the current queen, and demanded release on his twenty-first birthday.

He had refused to run away. He had fought instead. And

maybe he wasn't as perfectly free of their titles and their legacies as he'd like, but he was *free*.

Somehow, even now, worse than thoughts of those people, were thoughts of the woman he was supposed to forget.

He could picture her here. Walking the street to whatever job she had. Shoulders back, that athletic body carefully hidden away in something boxy. Maybe she was some kind of athlete. *That* would be interesting.

And neither here nor there. Because that had been a nameless night. He would not look for her here. There was no point. He had a job to do.

But if *kismet* stepped in…

The car pulled to a stop in the back of the castle, and Cristhian was led inside, through curving hallways and up elaborate staircases. He was asked to wait in an interior room, and he seated himself on a plush chair, taking in the surroundings. Old, well-preserved wallpaper in deep blues. Dark wood polished to a shine. He vaguely remembered a visit here as a child. Most of the royal visits of his childhood sort of ran together, but this one he remembered because his father was supposed to have been filming somewhere, but he'd left the set to accompany Mother, knowing she hated taking on these royal appearances alone.

She'd been so happy at his surprise arrival. Sometimes Cristhian thought that was the best memory he had of the two of them, when there were so many. But his father's important gesture, and his mother's heartfelt gratitude, had stuck with him in perfect imagery.

It was strange to realize that the memory did not make him as sad as it once had. There was a strange contentment mixed in with the grief. Perhaps their lives had been cut too short, and perhaps they'd had a part in the mistakes that had led them here, but they'd had each other. A love so bright and encompassing they'd both sacrificed for it.

But they'd never sacrificed him, and as Cristhian had navigated the world as an adolescent in high-end circles, he'd realized how very rare that was, and how mixed in all the tragedy he had a little bit of luck on his side.

But none of that was why he was here, so he studied the rest of the room and put the past away.

There was a large royal portrait dominating one wall. Cristhian recognized the current king, and his queen standing next to him. The young girls must be their twin daughters.

Cristhian frowned at the painting. The girls couldn't have been more than ten or so in it, so it was an old painting. But something about them...felt familiar.

An uncomfortable foreboding moved through him, but he didn't have time to analyze it as the king walked in.

Cristhian got to his feet and took the king's outstretched hand. He knew the royal protocol in different countries as he no doubt would if his mother had lived into his adolescence. He considered it a part of his job, but for a strange out-of-body moment he wondered if he'd learned all these silly rules for *her*, because it would have made her proud.

He gave a short bow with the handshake. "King Rendall."

"Cristhian. I haven't seen you since you were a boy." The man slapped him on the shoulder, then gestured to the chair he'd been sitting in.

Cristhian fortified himself for the inevitable comment about his mother. How beautiful she was, how kind, how she was missed. He settled back into the chair knowing all these things were true, but when strangers commented on her he felt a wave of fury that no one had *helped* her.

That she had suffered under all these people who had seen her as a perfect, untouchable princess.

When she'd just been a woman. His mother.

He forced a smile and tried to ignore the ghost that haunted him so often in these royal meetings.

But King Rendall said nothing else about his mother. He handed Cristhian a leather binder with the royal seal of Lille on it. "I have it on good authority you not only help, Cristhian, but you keep secrets."

"All my work is confidential, Your Majesty."

"I am depending on it. This is of the utmost importance to me. None of my own men could accomplish what I need these past few months. We have used every last resource we could. You're my last hope with the most important thing in the world to me."

Cristhian opened the folder and was met with a slick trickle of ice down his spine.

"The princess has run away," King Rendall explained. "It has been months now. Her sister assures us she is alive and well, but she has no other information. I need her found. I need her back."

The princess.

She didn't look the same in this picture. Her hair was a deep, dark brown in this royal portrait. Long and around her shoulders. Her eyes were a mesmerizing green that matched her hair and fair skin. But he would recognize that mouth, the quirk of a smirk underneath that royal smile, anywhere.

Princess Zia Rendall was his mystery woman.

And now he had to track her down.

Zia shivered as she tended the cookstove fire. Outside, polar night was just beginning to lift. It was midafternoon, and the sky was an interesting shade of blue. Her life here on this tiny polar island was always *interesting*.

But it was coming to an end. Not because she wanted it to. She quite enjoyed the cold, the isolation, the stark beauty of it all. But an island like this did not have the facilities for a woman to give birth. So, as she approached her seventh month of pregnancy, she would have to leave.

Maybe she would come back. Maybe she wouldn't. Everything would depend on how well she kept up her new identity throughout the birthing process.

Zia rubbed an absent hand over her belly. She had expected to be *terrified* of becoming a mother. After all, it certainly wasn't planned, but with every month she found herself looking forward to it more and more. To have the space and freedom to take care of her children as she saw fit felt like a gift.

Labor, however, did terrify her. And made her wish for things she couldn't have. Like her sister at her side, or her mother simply because Mother had actually given birth and would know how to calm her down, or even...

Well, it didn't make much sense to think about the man who'd had a hand in this. She didn't know anything about him, and so she was on her own.

The best for all involved. She couldn't imagine her parents' reaction to her pregnancy, especially if they found out the circumstances of *how* it had happened. They certainly wouldn't allow some commoner to have any part in it. No doubt she'd have to hear about hush money again, like when her father had paid a substantial sum to Leopold, the classmate she'd fancied herself in love with, and sneaked out to shed that innocence everyone had told her was so important.

In the aftermath, she wasn't so much heartbroken about

Leopold. She was just heartbroken that nothing in her life could be *normal*. It all had to be palace shenanigans, even something as intimate as a young woman's first time.

So this whole pregnancy was a strange kind of freedom. Running away, for good this time. A new identity. So that the palace didn't have a say in this thing that she still couldn't qualify as a mistake.

She rubbed her hands over the paltry heat the stove gave off. She didn't allow herself to think about how the pregnancy had happened very often. She'd had to focus on the practicalities of everything, and that kept her mind busy.

First, she'd had to accept she was pregnant. Which had not come easily. She'd felt poorly for a good two months before Beau had confronted her about it. In her very pragmatic way, laptop in hand.

Zia, I have searched your symptoms and this combination seems to point toward a pregnancy.

Zia had scoffed at her sister. Then…

You did use protection with that one-night stand, didn't you? Beau had demanded, like she knew anything about sex or one-night stands.

But Zia had been forced to come to a rather startling conclusion.

Some of the time…

Beau had tsked and shaken her head and procured her a pregnancy test without anyone at the palace getting wind of it.

When Zia had seen the positive result, she hadn't had the good sense to feel chastised. For a moment, there'd been the strangest bubble of joy. Like having a connection to that man meant something and wasn't just irresponsible. Like this was her way out when there was *no* way out. Because she could hardly marry Lyon while pregnant with someone else's baby, or anyone else for that matter. An illegitimate child meant her father could not control her life in all the ways he always had.

But slowly she'd come to realize that didn't make it a *good* thing. There were consequences for imploding everyone's lives. And so, to Zia's way of thinking, the only way to deal with this new wrinkle in her life was to run away.

For good this time.

Beau, per usual, was her saving grace. She had figured out everything to allow Zia to start a new life as someone else. She had insisted she could handle the consequences of a life in the palace without Zia there to guard her or act as heir.

Zia had argued. Vehemently. With tears, but Beau had been surprisingly determined. And the only thing that had gotten Zia to let her sister take on the consequences of Zia's own actions was the fact she now had someone besides her sister to protect.

Innocent, helpless babies growing inside her. Who did *not* deserve a life in that castle, being treated like mistakes.

All Zia had had to do was escape then…and she'd proven she was an expert at that. So she'd gotten out, and with Beau's help built this little life under a fake name on a tiny polar island that had mostly been shrouded in polar night for the duration of her pregnancy.

She'd built a small little business designing online exercise programs for people who wanted to do everything at home and only talk to their trainer via email or text—another one of Beau's brilliant ideas. Zia loved it. She even loved life on the polar island, the cozy mystery of polar night. She loved the village and her introverted lifestyle.

Trips to the mainland for her monthly checkups had yielded another surprise.

Twins.

Maybe it should have concerned her. A higher-risk pregnancy, the doctor had explained. But she'd been overjoyed. Just like she'd always had Beau, her babies would always have each other.

She tried to think of things in happy terms only—she was quite positive that was better for the babies growing inside her than anxiety and fear. She refused to consider the *scary*. Like never seeing Beau again outside of a screen. Like being alone, without a partner or a friend to lean on when she needed it. Like the father of these babies never knowing they existed, and being happy that way.

No, only good thoughts were allowed. Her babies would have each other, and they would have her. Maybe she'd failed at protecting Beau, maybe she didn't know how to find the identity of their father, but she'd work so hard to not fail her children. At least not in the ways her own parents had failed her.

She'd learned something from failing Beau. She could never put herself first. That way led to pain.

Which wasn't a very happy thought either, so she focused on making herself a little lunch, ignoring the fact she had to decide where she was going to *have* those babies. Beau had given her two options where she thought she'd be safe from her identity being discovered.

She'd have to chop her hair off again and hope that and the way her body had changed with the pregnancy would throw people off.

She was still surprised news of her disappearance hadn't found any media outlet yet. There were no stories about a canceled wedding. Short missives from Beau came and assured Zia everything at the palace was fine despite it.

Since she had babies to grow, Zia allowed herself to believe that even if it was very unlikely.

Happy, happy thoughts.

Her routine and internal reverie were interrupted by a harsh knock on the door. *Odd.* She had hired someone closer to town to deliver her mail and groceries, but that was only on Tuesdays. This was Thursday.

Maybe something important had come through. *Or maybe…* Fear jostled through her, but that was ridiculous. If her father had found her, sent men to collect her, they wouldn't knock.

Zia edged toward the window next to the door, tried to look out without being seen. There was a man out there. Bundled up in all black, a stocking cap low on his head. Despite the swirling winds, he didn't look the least bit cold.

But there was something familiar in that height, in the way the man stood…in everything. Her whole body seemed to go lax as she recognized the figure on her porch.

It was *him*. Something like joy surged through her. Silly, she knew, and yet there it was. How had he found her? *Why* had he found her? She nearly smiled.

Until his gaze lifted, met hers through the glass, and offered nothing but pure icy fury.

CHAPTER FOUR

CRISTHIAN DID NOT find anger to be a productive emotion. He preferred to diffuse any boiling intensity with whatever suited the moment—a joke, withdrawal, distraction. Fury led to rash decisions as much as fear did.

And what was anger but fear with a target?

His target stood on the other side of that glass.

A *princess*. He knew the kind of games royalty played. He'd been well-versed all his life. The manipulations and maneuverings his mother had gone to great lengths to try to escape. Then, when she'd died instead, he'd been jostled about, isolated from anyone who actually cared, as though he were merely an inanimate object to be possessed or disposed of. A narrative to be protected, not a life to be protected.

Sometimes he thought he was at peace with it.

Sometimes he realized he was not even close.

He watched Zia through the window. She took a deep breath, then disappeared. Before he could find any emotion about that, the doorknob turned, and she opened it. She stood there, framed by the rustic door.

She looked so different—dark hair, green eyes. And yet the same—the slope of her nose, the point of her chin. That regal way she held herself that he'd noted and dismissed in his sexual haze.

Except in the here and now, she seemed softer. More...

Everything inside him dropped out as his gaze lowered. He heard nothing but a high buzzing in his ears. He saw nothing now but a very rounded belly underneath a fuzzy sweater that could not hide it.

A *pregnant* belly.

"You had better come inside," she said in that voice he remembered all too well. Like she was all too used to ordering people around. "It's very cold."

He didn't feel the cold at all. Hadn't, since he'd seen her in that window. And he had no desire to step inside what seemed a cozy enough little cabin out here on this tundra. He wanted to stay rooted to this spot. Or rewind time. *Something*. But he was a man of action.

He had to be.

He stepped inside, let her close the door behind him. It was certainly warmer in here, out of the bitter wind, but he wasn't sure it was warm enough for her...condition. He stared at it now, too many things inside him jostling for space when he'd long ago learned that every feeling, thought, and action had an ordered space within.

She'd jumbled it all up almost seven months ago. Now, again. *Seven months*. "What is this?" he demanded, his voice too rough.

"Perhaps you should tell me why you're here first," she said, with a kind of businesslike demeanor that infuriated him beyond reason.

Fury is just fear with a target.

He wanted to growl at his internal monologue, but he didn't.

"Were you...looking for me?" she asked carefully. There was a neutral look on her face, but he saw something he didn't like in her eyes. A kind of hope.

For a moment, he was rendered perfectly frozen by it. *Hope*. When he had settled *hope* firmly behind him long, long ago. When he'd realized would always be the only person looking out for his own good. When he'd realized he had to take a stand against the forces who wanted him to be nothing more than an anecdote trotted out when they were trying to hide their more sordid truths.

Uncle Gregio found with his pants around his ankles in a young woman's room? Let's run an in-depth story on the poor orphaned child of a princess and an actor, raised benevolently by the grieving family—ha!—left behind. Pictures. Of him. Of his parents' crash. All of it dragged out again.

No, hope was useless, but he had learned it could be a weapon.

It felt like he'd been assaulted. A child. A *child* growing inside this beautiful woman. A *royal* child.

Still, he needed a weapon to fight all this. So he could lie. Get under all her defenses and get all the information he desired in seconds flat with said lie, no doubt. Let her believe in that hope until he'd gotten every answer he needed to know how to move forward, and then do whatever needed to be done to fix…this.

But he'd made promises to himself long ago about what kind of man he wanted to be. What kind of legacy he would leave his parents' memories.

And since he was the only one he trusted to make that legacy, he gave Zia the truth.

"My name is Cristhian Sterling. I was hired by your father to track you down. When he gave me the details of your disappearance early this week, I saw a photograph and this is when I recognized you. He did not mention…" Cristhian waved a hand at her stomach.

"My father's men have been looking for me for months. He hired you *this week*?"

"I am a finder, Zia. I would have found you months ago if he'd come to me."

Something about the word *finder* must have struck her, because she tilted her head and studied him. "Cristhian Sterling. I know that name." Her eyebrows drew together as though she were thinking.

There was some strange relief in her having not known who he was either those months ago. That, if nothing else, the night they had shared had been honest. True.

But a tense, coiling dread at the idea she *knew* anything about him now that she knew his identity wiped away any relief.

"You…you tracked down Lady Lina Sorenson," she said after a while. "A friend of mine. Years ago. We were fourteen."

He immediately remembered the name, because it had been one of the first cases he'd taken on as an official job, on his own, after helping a few of his mother's relatives track down people.

"You saved her, actually," Zia continued. "She was in quite a dire situation."

Cristhian shrugged, remembering all too well how close the young teen had been to being left to the whims of a group of very dangerous gentleman. "This is my job."

Zia inclined a royal nod. "Ah, yes. So you are here to drag me back to my father." She shook her head. "He doesn't know." She rested her hands over her stomach as if to protect the life inside it. She kept her gaze calm and on his. "It's best if he doesn't."

"Does the father know?" he asked, once again gesturing toward her belly. And maybe he knew what her answer would be. Maybe he knew all too well what he'd just walked into.

But he wanted her to say it. In no uncertain terms.

"Cristhian." Her voice was scolding, slightly disdainful. "*You* are the father."

And that complicated *everything*.

Zia still couldn't quite believe this was happening. A name for the man she'd spent the past six months dreaming about. What had brought him here. *Her father*. His job. She knew *of* him, even if she didn't know him, and that she hadn't expected at all.

And still, she found herself wanting to throw her arms around him. He was *here*, and it felt as if…it meant something. Because now he could know, and didn't that change everything?

But she could tell from the look on his face that it meant and changed *nothing*.

"So, you were never planning on telling me," he said, a harsh statement. An indictment, not a question.

She blinked at him. He had been there and knew just how little they knew of each other, so the indictment felt patently unfair. "I did not even know your *name*, where you came from. How was I supposed to tell you?" Of course, he'd found her, but that had been with her father's help. It had been by *accident*.

"You have ample resources, Zia." Her name rolled off his tongue, and in his unique, piecemeal accent of too many different places to count, her whole body lit up in reaction.

She could not allow that to distract her from the important thing here. Protecting her children. Protecting *herself*. Her father had sent him, and she did not consider her father an evil man, exactly.

She just knew that what was best for the kingdom was his only priority, and nothing else ranked against that. Not her well-being, not Beau's. Not their mother's. The kingdom and only the kingdom. She couldn't even blame him for that—he'd been bred from the cradle to think and feel and act that way.

She did not know why she couldn't have absorbed his blind faith in the crown above all else, but she had not been able to. Perhaps only men could be that foolish.

And now this man was here, father of her children or not, as an arm of that crown. And she could not forget that. The crown had never cared about *her*. Only what she kind of tool she could be used as.

"The hotel would have had my name," Cristhian continued. "Someone at the bar, the dancing club. So many avenues would have led you to my name and *me* if you had only tried."

She supposed all of that was true, but it never would have occurred to her, which felt like an insult to her intelligence, she supposed. Or maybe how sheltered she was, no matter how hard she tried to be otherwise. But there was no point in lying, in trying to save face.

If her father had hired him, he knew every unsavory detail of her already.

"None of that ever occurred to me, Cristhian. *I* am not a finder of lost things. I am simply a princess. Not even that anymore. I have left that life behind."

"Unfortunately, you are wrong. You are just another runaway princess who would do best if she were returned to the responsible people in her life. We will leave at once."

She sighed heavily. It had been much nicer when he'd only been a fantasy. When she could make him into the man she wanted. Now he'd ruined it, by being like every other man in her acquaintance. Sure he—or the king who'd supplied him the information—knew everything.

When Cristhian clearly knew nothing. He was being paid by the king. And he hadn't taken this new piece of information into consideration. Because his involvement in her pregnancy changed everything.

"Do you honestly think you can return me to the palace like *this* and escape unscathed? I can only imagine what my father will do now. You're not a commoner, are you? Your mother was…some kind of royalty in her own right, was she not?"

He did not respond immediately to that. Instead looked fully impassive, so she cast back trying to remember the story of him. The finder of royal pedigree. His father had been American. A movie star? Something like that. But his mother… "They call you a prince."

"I am *not* a prince."

"Your mother was a princess." She didn't remember all the details, but after Lina's return, there was much talk about the handsome young man who'd saved her. He had indeed been called a finder. Over the years, she thought perhaps she'd heard other stories, though she'd never paid much attention to them. But he was known, and he *was* royal.

Which was actually a worst-case scenario for the both of them.

"My mother was the youngest of seven princes and princesses of a very, *very* small country," he said, and she could read the reluctance in every word.

But each word was pertinent. "Regardless of her place in line, you would be an heir of something. You must have a title yourself. A *royal* title."

"I have rejected it," he returned, looking so stormy and

disdainful, and yet… She knew royalty well enough, knew his story somewhat. That would have caused a ripple, and she remembered no ripples.

"Formally?" she returned. She even smiled placidly. "Or in your head when it suits you?" Because she knew plenty of lesser royals who wanted to live in both worlds. Who claimed whatever when it suited them.

She could tell by the way he crossed his arms over his chest and firmed his mouth, without saying a thing, that she'd hit the nail on the head. He didn't *wish* to be royalty, but he was, after a fashion. And hadn't cut *all* ties with that.

Which made this even more complicated than it had been. "My father will insist we marry. Perhaps I was meant for greater than minor, unknown royalty, but…" She gave her stomach a little pat. "If you take me back, this will seal both of our futures."

This did not faze Cristhian for even a moment. He lifted a large, muscled shoulder. "Perhaps *I* will insist we marry."

Her mouth dropped open at that. *"What?"*

"I haven't decided yet. This is a shock. I'll have to work through the possibilities."

He couldn't be serious. "We don't know each other. We can't…"

His gaze moved from the top of her head, all the way down to her toes and back up again. Her body throbbed with memories that had kept her warm at night for some time. She now wished she'd eradicated them rather than indulged them many a sleepless night when she'd wished to know his identity. Fantasized about a future that could include the possibility of him in it.

And now he was standing there like a jail sentence. Even if it was one that still made everything inside her buzz with a physical anticipation that did not match her internal, emotional dread.

"We know each other well enough, Princesa," he said, his voice a low scrape against the most sensitive parts of her.

But he was saying marriage was some kind of option. Returning her to her father was an option. She could only stand, mouth dropped open, air struggling to reach her lungs. Was he *insane*?

He made a shooing motion. "Go on then. Pack your things."

"I will not go back to my father," she said through gritted teeth. Her hands curled into fists. She knew she couldn't fight him. Not physically. But the desire to do so coursed through her all the same.

"Not yet. No," he agreed with annoying ease. "We have some decisions of our own to make first, but not here." He looked around her small cabin with clear distaste. "We will go to one of my estates."

"*Estates?* Tell me again you're not royalty, Cristhian."

"I am a self-made man," he returned. Then gave a grand, elegant bow, though his gaze never left hers. "I will not wait, Your Highness. We leave in thirty minutes."

CHAPTER FIVE

SHE TOOK EVERY last one of those thirty minutes, but not one second more. She did not have much, but Cristhian supposed even a runaway princess could only travel with what she could carry. He plucked the bags from her hands and marched them out to his car.

She followed him at a much slower pace. Her gait was careful, one hand placed over the rounded stomach as she stepped around icy patches in the snowy path. He had to fight the urge to cross to her and offer an arm. He prided himself on being polite in all situations, even finding missions, but it would be best for the both of them if he limited any and all physical contact that might be a dangerous reminder.

Especially since he was planning on taking her to his estate just north of Lille. Close enough to returning her, should he decide that be their fate. But also on his own turf, so *he* would be making the decisions.

It would just be the two of them and his very minimal staff. Where they could privately and safely work out some kind of…agreement. Risky, considering his body had not gotten the memo that she was his adversary now. But necessary.

Marriage? He would not be party to any more royal tricks and maneuvers, so a union seemed like the worst-case scenario. And yet he *would* be a part of his child's life. Perhaps he'd never had any driving desire to be a father, but he knew he had wisdom to impart. He would ensure his child received that over any royal brainwashing that would no doubt come from the king.

Zia was young. Perhaps her running away meant she was not fully under her father's thumb, but Cristhian knew how this went. He had watched it play out in his mother's short life. Princesses might try to escape, but they never succeeded. They ran away instead of making a stand.

Case in point.

Moreover, Zia would not be immune from running back to Lille. She would want more for her—their—child, as his mother once had. Birthrights were dug in deep, no matter how stifling a person found the royal life.

Cristhian needed time to think. To plan. To prepare. To rearrange the world to his specifications. In a way his parents had not been able to accomplish.

Because he would not meet their fate, and he would not allow Zia to. There would be no running away, and his child would have their parents. One way or another.

He drove them to the small airport. The sky was dark, and snow had begun to fall. Takeoff would be tricky, but necessary. Once he parked, he gathered Zia's things. He could not stop himself from helping her out of the car, her slender, gloved hand sliding into his offering too many memories that threatened to distract him from his cause.

But Cristhian was stronger than that. He dropped her hand and led her into the terminal of the airport. He found his assistant.

"Is the plane ready?"

"Yes, sir. But we must take off as soon as possible.

Weather is coming in. They're anticipating they'll have to lock everything down before the hour is out."

Cristhian nodded. Then followed as his assistant led them through a maze of hallways and out onto the tarmac. As they approached his plane, he handed the bags to his assistant, who would stow them away in the back of the plane.

With reluctance yet again, Cristhian offered his hand so he could help Zia up the stairs into the plane.

But she hesitated. "This plane is very small."

"An excellent quality for a plane that will land on my private airstrip."

She gave him a look, the same look she'd leveled him with inside the cabin when she'd said, "Tell me again you're not royalty, Cristhian."

But he was not. Perhaps he had an official title in Hisla, but he never used it, and the current queen—his mother's older sister—had no use for him. Nor he for her, so it worked out. Perhaps some of his estates came as an inheritance from his mother, but most of the inherited money that he'd turned into his own fortune had been from his father's movie earnings.

He thought for a moment of his grandparents in the States. His mother's family had kept them out of his childhood as best they could, but as an adult he'd forged a relationship with them. They were elderly now, his grandmother frail, his grandfather stubborn. But they would welcome news of a child.

It almost warmed him.

But there were too many complications to wade through first. Like how he had managed to make his one and only adult mistake with a *princess*.

He helped her up the stairs and gestured her to a seat.

"Take your pick and make yourself comfortable. The flight will be a few hours."

She began to follow instructions, then looked back at him as he began to duck into the cockpit.

"You're flying?" she demanded, her voice going up an octave.

He looked over his shoulder at her, eyebrow raised. "A pilot wasn't in the budget."

She scoffed. "I can only imagine what you charge for your finding services. I imagine your *budget* can include whatever you wish."

He lifted a shoulder and didn't bother to answer. "I would buckle up, Princesa. It looks like we'll be flying around some weather."

The he pushed her existence out of his mind and focused on flying.

The flight had not been smooth. Zia's nerves were shot by the time they, what felt like, skidded to a landing. She had to pry her fingers off the armrests as they were stiff from gripping so hard.

It was not Cristhian who helped her down the stairs of the plane this time, but the man he'd met at the airport. Who offered her a kind, encouraging smile, which certainly was a change of events.

She was led to another car while snow fell at heavier and heavier rates. She had no idea what country they were in, where Cristhian was taking her, and she knew she should be more concerned about that than she was, but what was there to do? He *was* the father. He had a right to some say in this.

She just had to figure out how to make sure he did not somehow have *all* the say. She had to maintain some amount of power and agency here, and she did not know how to do that just yet. She'd never had a chance to learn. Running away had always been the only answer.

She couldn't run from this, any more than she could run from the pregnancy or the fact that Cristhian was the father of her children.

Children. The most important part of all this. She would do anything for them, fight whatever powerful men she had to fight. She would have a say because she would protect them in all things. She would put their needs above all else.

The way her own mother had never stepped in and protected her or Beau. The way her father had never put anyone's needs above his country's.

She smoothed her hands over her belly, gave her children an internal promise she'd do whatever it took. To keep them safe. To keep them happy. She'd find a way.

Cristhian took the wheel of the car, his assistant not getting in with them. Zia felt a little deflated at the loss of the one person who'd offered a glimmer of kindness, but exhaustion was creeping up on her. She'd eaten on the plane, but she had not been able to sleep.

Cristhian drove them over twisting and rolling roads, the snow nearly blinding the whole way. Zia gripped the car door just as tightly as she'd held on to her seat on the airplane. Cristhian drove through it at a slow pace, and still it seemed impossible he knew where the roads were.

The snow began to ease a little. Big flakes still fell, but not at quite the alarming rate. Cristhian slowed at a gate that after a few moments began to slowly open. He drove through it once there was enough space, then over a winding drive that led toward a…

"Cristhian."

"What?"

"This is a *castle*." Perhaps on the smaller side of many of the royal palaces she'd been to in her life, but it was still so clearly built for royalty. Stately stones, towers, intricate windows and cornices. Like a fairy tale with the snow fluttering in huge flakes all around them, and the trees and rolling ground heavy with snow.

Cristhian studied the grand building as if he'd never considered that term before. "Not a castle."

"It has *turrets*."

But he would not be deterred, because of course the man she'd been so physically attracted to she'd forgotten all sense would be the most stubborn man alive.

"Old, yes," he returned. "There's some ancient Scandinavian line to my grandmother's family. But we have never called it a castle. This is Espinas Cottage."

She snorted at the word *cottage*, but he ignored her.

"Very private. Very out of the way. We will have a few days to determine how we will move forward."

"*We* or *you*?"

He shrugged in that arrogant way of his. "Feel free to argue semantics all you like. For now, we should get in out of the cold."

Which meant he thought he was going to be making all the choices. And she was clearly stuck here—in a castle, in the middle of a blizzard, with a man who thought he ran the world.

How familiar, all in all.

And because it was familiar and frustrating, she found those old rebellions swimming around in her as he helped her walk through the snow, up grand *castle* stairs. She wanted to lash out, shock, get a leg up on all that male certainty. Just like she had as a wild, impetuous teenager who'd only ever been cowed by threats against her sister.

Because her parents saw Beau's panic attacks as a weakness, a blight. Not simply a condition to be treated. For years, Zia had done whatever they wanted in the hopes they wouldn't lock Beau away.

But her sister wasn't here. The only one Zia could hurt now was herself. And *him*.

"There is something I forgot to mention," she offered as they stepped into a grand, echoing foyer.

"What's that?" he returned somewhat absently.

"I'm not having your baby, Cristhian."

He sighed heavily, disdain in every second of the sound. "Zia—"

"I am having your *babies*. Twins." And she had the great satisfaction of seeing his mouth go slack for a moment. The total and utter shock she'd put in his expression. Not put together even enough to find that blank look. Just pure, unadulterated shock.

So she smiled at him for the first time since he'd shown up in her life again, and meant that smile.

CHAPTER SIX

ZIA WAS SMUG. That self-satisfied smiled landed in his gut with a twist of fury and want, a dangerous and unfortunate combination. Because he could indulge in neither feeling that plagued him.

Twins. Two babies. It really didn't matter the number, he supposed, but it felt like a blow all the same. She *wanted* it to feel like a blow if that smile of hers was anything to go by.

So he would not react to her words. He would try not to react to her words.

"I will show you to your rooms." He sounded stiff even to his own ears, and this would not do. He could not let her know when her barbs landed. He could not show any weakness. This was too delicate. "You are no doubt exhausted. You certainly look it."

She chuckled, as if this was not an insult. "No doubt," she agreed readily. "Hungry as well."

"I will have the cook make you up a tray."

"Excellent." He led her to the stairs. Maybe the staircase was ornate. Maybe the large, uniquely shaped windows, the soaring apses, the intricate corbels and arcading gave the illusion of great elegance, but the building was a bit squat, all in all. Much of the royal accoutrements had been taken down and away before the cottage had come into his possession.

He kept it and *liked* it because it was off the beaten path. No relatives tried to "drop in" to this cottage far north of their kingdom like they did some of his other estates, usually in some effort to stir up some gossip or hard feelings. No, this was one of the few things passed down from his mother that felt like *his*.

So he would not be irritated that she insisted it had a turret, or that she wanted to keep pushing the point he was royal. It did not matter what *she* thought.

And what of King Rendall?

That was thornier, certainly, and he hadn't worked it all out yet, but he would. Once he got his more…emotional responses under control.

Twins. Not just one child, but two. It didn't really change the situation, and yet he felt changed. Like he had been able to pretend her pregnancy was simply a problem to be solved when it was just one, and now that he knew two children grew inside her they seemed more…real.

He led her up the stairs and to the first set of bedrooms he'd instructed his staff to ready. His rooms were much deeper in the castle—the *cottage*. Far, *far* away from her. He opened the door to her small guest suite.

"The rooms are readied, but my staff here is minimal, and with the snow as it is, we may be stuck that way for a time. You will have to get used to doing things on your own."

She aimed a haughty look at him. One that made him wonder how he hadn't seen *princess* written all over that elegant point of a chin. "I have been taking care of myself in a cabin on a polar island for months now, Cristhian. I am quite certain I can handle it."

"You are a princess. A few runaway attempts do not make you well-versed in roughing it, Princesa."

"I quite agree. I'm not sure spending the next few days in an understaffed castle will be the hardship you're making it out to be, but your point is taken. Though living on my own, under the detection of my father these past few months, has taught me much, I have had many cushions in this life. But with every cushion comes a condition, and sometimes those conditions are…" She trailed off, clearly struggling with a suitable word.

He could think of a few himself, but he kept his mouth resolutely closed. It would not do to relate to her. Whether it be from his own experience or his mother's.

Perhaps they would have to come to work as partners in some way to be parents to their children, but until he decided how that would work, they were adversaries. Until he set up everything exactly as he wanted it.

She never finished her sentence. He led her into the suite—a prettily appointed sitting room. The doors to the bedroom and en suite bathroom were open so she could explore. He could see her bags neatly situated along the wall.

Zia moved around the room, and he knew he should excuse himself. Inform the cook she would need some food. He should leave her, so that he could begin to enact his plans.

But the strangest thing was happening to him. No matter what forward steps he took, he couldn't decide how he wanted to proceed past tonight.

He did not know what to do.

When he was a man who always knew the next step to take. Who made quick, correct decisions in all things. He had learned it was the only way to survive with himself intact. Indecision was poison.

And currently infecting every step he took. Because he did not know what to do about *this*. About *her*.

So he hesitated, when he never hesitated. He didn't leave the room, because if he left he would have to face himself and the fact that he had no idea what his next move should be.

"What were your plans then?"

She turned to study him. "What do you mean?"

"Your plans. For you. For the babies."

Her study never stopped, but after a time she gave a little nod as if deciding to give him the truth. "In the close future, I was making the decision of where to go into labor. The island does not have the facilities for that, so you have to go to the mainland. I had some contenders. How I handled what came next would depend on how well labor went, and if I had been found out."

It was well thought out, but it was hardly the kind of thing someone could do on their own. "You must have had help."

She shrugged. And said nothing.

He had no right to be irritated by her lack of details. This was not important. What was important was what came next. "I will leave you to rest. Someone will bring some food up soon."

"And what will you be off doing?"

"Making arrangements."

"Without me?"

"It seems you have had ample time to make arrangements without *me*. Perhaps it is my turn."

She shook her head. "I am the one carrying them. I will be the one bringing them into the world. You will not shut me out of any decisions made. I will do whatever is in my power, even if it requires involving my father, to ensure that."

He was relieved that she was showing a little temper.

That she was putting up a fight. He could always find his way in a fight.

"I would be careful how you threaten me with your *king*, Your Highness."

"It is not a threat," she replied, not the least bit concerned or chagrined. "It is simply explaining myself. They are my top priority. I will do whatever it takes to protect them. I am their mother."

"And I am their father."

She sighed, something in her expression softening. "I am glad you know that," she said after a moment. Then she crossed to him. Stood in front of him with wide, serious green eyes. "For all the ways we'll no doubt disagree, I *am* glad you know that."

He didn't want to believe her. He wanted to convince himself that she was simply an adept liar. He didn't know very much about her at all. She could be the most deceitful woman on the planet.

But no amount of wanting could make falsehoods a reality. Zia would no doubt lie to him at some point, but this was not a lie.

Perhaps it was a common ground to work from. Perhaps he should be glad of it, for his children's sakes. Perhaps this was some kind of hope to hold on to.

But he knew too well what hoping got a person. Where believing someone might have an interest other than their own at heart might land a person. He had learned that lesson the hard way with his mother's family. First, believing that they'd taken him from his paternal grandparents because they'd *cared*. Then, growing up knowing they didn't, being foolish enough to believe one of his cousins had befriended him out of kindness and honesty.

Instead, all Antonio had ever been doing was keeping

tabs on him, all so his mother—who'd been the newly minted queen at the time—could decide how to best use him and his story for her own gain.

So Cristhian knew better than to trust. Than to believe. Than to *hope*.

Something tried to expand within him, with her standing too close. Memories knocking at the door of his mind. The way that one night had wrapped around him, held him against his will.

Even now. When he should be thinking of *anything* but the way her body might feel under his hands. The way she would taste again, here in his own world—not that fictional one they'd built that night. No, this would be real.

And unacceptable.

But she was looking up at him now as if there was something real to be salvaged, and that was her weapon. One she would no doubt wield against him if he didn't make himself clear. Right here. Right now.

"I could have you in my bed in under five minutes," he said, making certain she would feel his breath dance along her neck. "And you would do whatever I said, whatever I liked."

He saw the tremor move through her, the heat they couldn't ever share again leap into her green eyes. His own body hardened in reaction, but he would not be so easily distracted. No matter how much the potency of whatever arced between them still knocked him off his usually perfectly kept axis.

"But we are here to decide the future, Princesa. Nothing else."

And now it was *his* turn to be smug as he turned on a heel and walked out of her room.

* * *

Zia had slept well in spite of the unusual and unfortunate circumstances. She was getting more and more physically uncomfortable as the days went, but the exhaustion of lugging around two growing babies inside her always took a toll at night.

So after he'd left, no matter how frustrated and confused and worked up she'd been, hungry, too, she'd crawled into the huge, comfortable bed and fallen straight to sleep.

Unfortunately, her dreams had been…vivid. And had been less dreams and more flashes of memory. Dancing with him, the hard, hot wall he'd made. The reckless ride back to his hotel room. The sound he'd made when he'd been over her, inside her. Those dark eyes holding her gaze through it all…and how they'd been the same exact eyes to tell her he could have her in his bed in under five minutes.

So while she awoke feeling better rested, she did not feel settled. Because even awake his words kept replaying in her head like some kind of spell.

I could have you in my bed in under five minutes. And you would do whatever I said, whatever I liked.

In spite of herself, she knew it was true, and she couldn't help but wonder just what he "liked" that might be different than that first night when they'd been strangers and under some kind of spell of their own.

But he'd only said it to put her in her place, she knew. She knew *men*, powerful men. Everything had to be their way. Everything had to be under their, what they considered, clever control. She had watched her father lash out at anyone and everyone with as many cutting remarks as he could hurl when things did not go precisely as he wanted.

So she knew Cristhian's parting shot had been launched

because he did not feel in control. And *that* at least gave her some satisfaction.

He didn't know what to do with her, with this, and it was gratifying because she hadn't known what to do at first, either.

But right now she was too hungry to consider her next steps beyond food. She changed her clothes quickly and then stopped short in the sitting room. A platter with an array of baked goods sat on one of the little tables.

She settled herself in the chair and polished off two before she'd taken more than a breath or two. Immediately, she felt better. She considered a third, and then thought better of it. She drank a glass of water—it was cold as though it had been ice water a time ago, but the ice had melted.

She had no idea what time it was. She couldn't find a clock in these rooms, and her phone had died sometime in the night. She plugged it in, waited for it to boot up, then sent Beau a little text message that she had left the island, that she was fine, and more information would be forthcoming.

Beau wouldn't love that, but it was the best Zia could offer until she knew what the next steps were going to be. Certainly not be carted back to Lille by Cristhian, but if Cristhian's alternatives involved something she didn't think was best for the children, she might be forced to go back to her father and ask for his help.

Her stomach sank, hard and painful at the thought. That eventuality would not be protecting her children, because whatever her father could do for her, for them, it would only be in service to Lille.

Which meant, likely, a marriage to Cristhian either way. Some kind of insulting agreement with his mother's fam-

ily. No choice. Her children treated like little dolls or ro-
bots, unable to have their own feelings or flaws.

Just the thought filled her with the kind of anxiety that
could not be good for her children. These were all ifs and
worst-case scenarios. She shouldn't get too far ahead of
herself. She had to deal with this step by practical step.
Just like she had been since she'd finally made that choice
to disappear.

She wished she could talk to Beau, but they had deemed
phone conversations too dangerous. Too easily tracked
and found. She would have to work this out on her own,
with just the occasional text message from an unmarked
number.

She blew out a breath. She could do it. She'd been
doing it all these months. But first she needed something
more than a pastry. She left her room, followed the hallway to the grand staircase Cristhian had led her up last
night. Downstairs, she poked around in empty rooms until
she found what appeared to be a dining room. Narrow, but
long, a table mimicking the room in the center…

With Cristhian sitting at the head of it. A plate of food in
front of him at one side, a laptop at the other. His dark hair
was a little damp, like he'd just emerged from a shower
not that long ago, and he was dressed casually in a sweater
and soft-looking pants.

Her heart felt as though it tripped over itself in her chest.
She did not know how one man could be so handsome.
She might keep pointing out that he was royalty no mat-
ter how little he liked it, but he didn't look it. He was so
tall and broad, muscular as though he did a lot of labor.
He must have taken after his American father.

No doubt another sore subject. Because she'd remembered belatedly that his parents had died in a very fa-

mous car accident. She had been too young to remember the actual event, but it had still been discussed as she'd been growing up. One of those tragedies people whispered about, hoping if they expressed enough dismay at lives cut too short, it wouldn't happen to them.

It was so strange how all the facets of him were unfurling in the here and now after she'd convinced herself he was just a phantom in her life, never to return. But she hadn't let herself think much about the reality of the babies she would one day hold. She was struck with the thought now. Who would they look like? Would they have his dark eyes, or some mix of her green?

She had wanted to be surprised about the sex, because the truth was it was too much to think about the babies as *people* when he hadn't been in her life.

And now he was…sort of. She had no idea how it would play out, but it made everything feel all the more real.

"Good morning," he said, somewhat absently, without lifting his gaze. As if he'd known she was standing there taking stock all along. "We are well and truly snowed in. We do not anticipate being able to dig out for at least forty-eight hours. I suggest you make yourself comfortable in whatever ways you can, and certainly let the staff know if you require anything." He made a broad gesture. "Sit. Ramon will bring you out a plate."

She wanted to eat, but the need to be contrary was too deep-seated to ignore. "I ate some of the food left for me upstairs."

He nodded. "And now you will sit and eat some protein."

A man with a plate appeared as if on cue. He placed it at the seat next to Cristhian, who gave the man a sharp look that the man ignored.

Zia raised an eyebrow, surprised to read how little Cristhian wanted her to sit next to him written all over his face.

Well, that was enough to get her feet moving and to settle herself into the seat next to him. She flashed a smile at the retreating man, and then her breakfast companion.

He did not react in any way, except to look at his laptop.

Her plate was full of a large omelet, which looked delicious. She'd cut out coffee for the duration of her pregnancy, so she was grateful for the large glasses of juice and water at her plate. Though she wouldn't mind a warm beverage later. The room was warm, but she could practically feel the cold from outside pressing against the walls of the *castle*.

She took a few bites of her breakfast, then studied the man seated next to her. "Have you informed my father you've found me?" She genuinely didn't know what he would have done last night. On the one hand, he seemed fully…himself. The kind of man who would take orders from no one and would do exactly as he pleased.

On the other hand, he took these jobs of finding people, so he must have *some* deference to the people paying him.

There was a slight hesitation from Cristhian. Nothing in his expression changed. He didn't move. But she sensed just the hint of…something. Not discomfort, because the man seemed endlessly comfortable in every situation. But something akin to it.

"I will make my decisions about how to proceed before I report to your father," he said at length. His posture and his delivery stiff.

Interesting. She took another bite of the delicious omelet and watched Cristhian. "And you have yet to make those decisions?"

His expression changed. Hardened ever so slightly.

It was no mystery why she'd allowed herself a nameless night with this man. He was too handsome for anyone's own good. It didn't matter if it was that sly smile and easy flirtations of their first meeting, or that hard, angry demeanor. It *all* did something to her.

Something she was going to have to learn how to control. She had always been a bit…spiteful. Not her best quality, but she didn't like to be told what to do—a problem as a princess who was constantly being told what to do. She hid her contradictory nature better than Beau, but it was still a struggle. When someone told her something she *should*, it automatically made her want to not.

She supposed that was why her father had learned the only way to get through to her was to threaten Beau's future. Spite never held up in the face of protecting her sister from the possibilities her father used like a bludgeon. Private asylums. Medical interventions she certainly didn't need. Anything that made it seem like Beau's hardships were something she should be ashamed of.

Zia wouldn't allow it. Beau claimed she had everything under control at the moment, and Zia had to believe her, but there was still the possibility that how Cristhian handled this with the king would reflect back on what Father did to Beau.

So Zia *should not* want to sleep with Cristhian ever again. She shouldn't be the least bit interested in his bed or what he would want to do in it. His arrogant little quip last night should have cured her of all her lust.

But it decidedly had not.

Until he spoke his next words. "Once my doctor is able to make the trip, we will do a paternity test."

CHAPTER SEVEN

CRISTHIAN HAD BEEN careful not to look too much in Zia's direction since she'd appeared. There was a danger in her beauty, in the way those fluffy sweaters hugged the fascinating bump she'd grown since he'd last seen her.

So he didn't look at her for more than the briefest of seconds, until he'd delivered his current challenge. Her eyes went wide, her mouth a little slack. He'd certainly shocked her. She blinked once, and when she spoke it wasn't with that haughtiness she'd come into the dining room with this morning.

"You brought me here and you don't believe me?" she asked, sounding…younger and more hurt than she had any right to.

He could let her think that he didn't believe her. He *wanted* to let her think that. But every time his mercenary instincts wanted to take over, he was reminded of his parents. Of the way they had worked together—no matter all their outside problems—to ensure he was safe and well.

His parents *had* loved each other, so it was different, but everything he had been able to rise above had been because they had started his life out in a safe, loving place.

He wanted the same for his children, and that meant he could not be cruel to their mother, even when it would be a solid weapon to use to save himself.

But that made every step he took more complicated than he was used to. There was no clear enemy here. For all Zia represented a complicated issue, she was not like his mother's family trying to use him. The paths ahead were all thorny. And he did not doubt his ability to maneuver through them and come out on top. He was just uncomfortable with the time and care it would take to accomplish the perfect, controlled outcome. One that did not leave him open to being used. One that did not result in rash decisions to run away, and the punishments that came from that.

So sometimes he would have to give her the truth. Even when he didn't want to.

"It is not about belief. It is about everything legal that will plague us. Inheritances, trusts, titles." He wanted to blame her for bringing those things to the table, but she was a little too on the nose about all the royal things he disdained…but hadn't formally denounced. That had been the deal he'd struck with his aunt. That had been the condition in getting his freedom, his own life.

Most days, he considered that a great win. Standing up, not running away. It grated that in the face of Zia it felt less a win and more a concession.

His feelings, however, did not matter. Only settling this did. "We will need to have incontrovertible proof that our children are biologically ours in order to move forward."

She swallowed at that, and he had to look away from the way her emotions chased across her face. They had to work together in order to make the world a safe place for their children, but that did not mean he needed to concern himself with her *feelings*.

"I suppose that makes sense. But you said we'd be stuck here for at least forty-eight hours."

"Yes."

"What shall we do in the meantime?"

It wasn't meant to be flirtatious. He could tell by the way her gaze was on her food, the way she didn't offer him any sultry looks. But when he didn't respond right away, when he let the silence settle after her question, she must have realized what it sounded like. Because her cheeks turned a faint shade of pink.

She cleared her throat. "What I mean is, how do you entertain yourself in this large castle? *Alone*." She tacked on the last word forcefully enough he could not quite resist the slight curve of his mouth.

"Did I say I spend a lot of time here *alone*?" he returned, when that's exactly what he did. Of all his estates, this was the one he considered his personal, private sanctuary, when he wanted nothing to do with the world around him.

It was happenstance it was his closest holding to her home country, which was why he'd brought her here. Geography.

She sighed. "I suppose you have a parade of women littered at every spot. Women do love a prince."

He knew she was poking at him, and yet he couldn't stop himself from scowling.

Her smile went sharp, delight in a barb landed. That look shouldn't hit him like a blow, knocking enough sense out of him he remembered all too clearly what she tasted like.

"However," she continued, "unless you have someone locked away in an attic, I believe we—and your minimal staff—are all that are here in the moment. So what do you suggest we do for the next forty-eight hours? Get to know one another?"

"I thought we were *well* acquainted, Zia."

She rolled her eyes. "Perhaps it is worth mentioning that there are many things I shouldn't do in my condition."

He could ignore her meaning. He probably *should* ignore her. But he couldn't help himself. "Is that pointed, Zia?"

Her gaze didn't flutter. She didn't look away from him. She lifted her chin, all royal and dignified. But he had seen her *very* undignified, and that memory served neither of them.

He indulged it all the same.

"Does it need to be pointed, Cristhian?"

He lifted a shoulder. Did his best to embody a casual carelessness he didn't exactly feel at the moment. "What is it you want to know then?"

She rested her chin on her fist as if she took that question very seriously. "Who were you raised by after your parents died?"

He wasn't sure what he expected, but not that, and he did not care for the way it made him feel like he was backed into a corner, in a defensive position. Particularly when it was clear she was curious, not starting some kind of war.

Pretending the answer meant more than it did would no doubt give her ammunition for whatever battles lay ahead, so he spelled it out as nonchalantly as he could manage.

"I bounced around family. They had a lot of it."

"They? Not you?"

"My father's family was interested, but American and less powerful when it came to things like citizenships and titles. My mother's family was not the biggest proponent of her marriage. I was…a problem to be solved more than anything, but an heir of sorts, whether they liked it or not. And a convenient story to trot out when they wanted attention."

"I have found that you do not have to be the result of a disdained marriage to be considered a problem to be solved."

Cristhian studied her as she finished the last bite of

her breakfast. "You are a princess. An heir. What's the problem?"

"I had more interest in playing football than learning protocol. I was much better at sneaking around the rules than following them. I need...ed freedom and fresh air, and there is little of that to be had while growing up a princess. My sister would have been better suited, I think, to some of it, but..." She shrugged her shoulders.

"You are older?" he prompted when she said nothing more. He could have found this information out himself, but in his work he found the stories people told themselves, and then shared, offered more information than facts did.

"No. Beau is actually three minutes older. But since there were two of us, my parents got to choose who would be considered the heir. They held it over our heads like a prize, but neither of us were too eager to win it."

"Then how did you get chosen?"

"I was deemed prettier. Easier to mold. My sister... She has a head for details. She could recite protocol back to you better than even my father. But..." She shook her head, and the smile on her face was found even though she was explaining her own demise. "You cannot threaten or manipulate Beaugonia. She will do as she will. I...did not like the consequences my parents threatened me with, so I learned to pretend better than she did. And so I was chosen."

She leaned forward then, a serious, intent look on her face. When she spoke, it was with a quiet, careful fervor. "If I am returned to my father, he will insist we marry. Since you are royal, we will be named heirs to his throne. Me as queen, you as something. And we will be told to make the same choices with our children. Well, unless one is a boy and one is a girl. Guess who gets chosen then."

He did not like the picture she painted at all, but he also

had infinite confidence that if he did return her to King Rendall, Cristhian would find a way to get what *he* wanted out of the arrangement. She wouldn't sway his opinion of what must be done, of what would be best. So what struck him in the moment was her *unless one is a boy*.

"You do not know the sex of the babies?"

She sat back in her chair, rested her hands over that swell of her stomach. "I wanted to be surprised," she returned, so primly and without meeting his gaze that he knew there was more to that story than she was giving him at the moment.

But he would know it eventually.

"The doctor will tell us. So that we can make the appropriate plans."

She eyed him then, with a disdain he didn't care to admit made him want to fidget.

Unheard of.

"It does not matter their sex. They will not be heirs to anything. I will not imprison my children."

"Come, Princesa, surely you're not so dramatic as to liken *prison* to the privilege and opportunity you were raised with."

"I try to tell myself that. I try to be grateful for all that I have, but, Cristhian, do you have any idea what it's like to know everything you are is a mismatch for the life you are expected to lead? And so the entirety of that life stretching out before you will be nothing but a farce. For someone else. Never yourself."

He didn't scowl at her, though he wanted to. "So many people concerned with themselves, and so little concern for the people who must deal with the fallout of their actions."

The rejoinder didn't seem to land as he'd hope it might. She tilted her head and studied him, as though she could see straight through. When no one saw straight through.

Not even yourself.

He pushed that thought away as she spoke.

"You see, the difference here is, I can acknowledge the great privilege you were brought up with, and still imagine that losing your parents, being bounced around without love, was difficult for you." She stood then, and he couldn't quite take his gaze from the pregnant belly. Where his children grew inside her. *His.*

Children who would not be bounced around. Who would feel love, and not have it ripped away from them by fate.

"I can have empathy for you, no matter the circumstance, Cristhian. I consider that a gift."

He looked up at her then, at those green eyes. And he knew what he must do. "I must thank you for this little speech. It has given me clarity on how we will move forward."

She raised an eyebrow. "Oh?"

"The moment we can get a minister here, we will be married."

Zia wondered if she'd had some kind of cardiac event. She was standing, but she couldn't feel her legs. Her breath didn't come in and out as it should.

"I beg your pardon?" she managed.

"We will marry," he repeated, pushing out of the chair himself. "There is no other way that truly gives our children the childhood I want them to have. Bouncing around is a no go for me, and a life without their mother would also not do."

"What about a life without their father?"

"You should have hidden better if you wished for that."

"Better than an isolated arctic island shrouded by polar

night?" she demanded, facing off with him as if they were in a boxing ring rather than a posh dining room.

He smiled at her then, and she had to wonder what was wrong with her that his smile could still send a shimmer of sparks through her when he was being the most ridiculous man alive.

"Unfortunately for you, Zia, I would have found you anywhere."

Which might have been romantic if he'd been the one looking for her. But no, it had been her father. Cristhian had no doubt forgotten about her the morning she'd disappeared. Hopped in the next bed and so on and so forth for the past seven months.

Which was reason enough to stop this right here, right now. "I will not marry you."

"I did not ask. You said it yourself. Your father will insist we marry should I return you to him. I cannot really be insisted upon, if I do not agree, but in this case, it is the best-case scenario."

"To marry a veritable stranger so we don't have to work out a custody agreement?"

He considered this, or more likely pretended to. Then he shrugged. "Yes."

She shook her head. She had known he wouldn't be reasonable, but she didn't think he'd be this. "This is ridiculous. You clearly haven't thought this through at all."

"On the contrary, I've done nothing but think since I was met with this." He gestured at her stomach. "The options are limited with our complicated backgrounds. We must marry and prepare a united front against all that will come. We are not enemies, Zia. We will work out what is best for the children. Together."

But he didn't say that like some kind of promise of

compromise and reason. He said it like *together* meant her trotting along after him, doing whatever he wished. And that was exactly what she'd escaped.

She wouldn't go back. Her children would be raised to be strong and independent and not victims to other people's whims or power. She knew what it was like. To endure it. To watch other people endure it. She wanted more for them. So much more.

"Perhaps I am not your enemy, Cristhian, but you are turning into mine."

He chuckled at that. *Chuckled.* She wanted to slap him.

"What is it you think a marriage should be that we could not accomplish? If we are both reasonable, we can make all important decisions as a team. We have many estates to choose from. We can be as involved or as not involved in Lille as you wish. It's actually the perfect answer to all your problems."

"Is it?"

"You were all set to marry that duke or what have you?"

She didn't believe for a second he didn't know exactly who she'd been set to marry. "A crown prince," she bit out.

"Ah, of course. Were you desperately in love with him? Did you know each other well? My guess is no if you so willingly went to my bed all those months ago."

She had no argument for that. She had met Lyon Traverso all of twice. And they'd never been alone together. He'd shown about as much interest in her as he'd shown in the salmon that had been served at dinner.

"So, what is the difference?" Cristhian asked, with a kind of patience she didn't trust at all. "Rank?" he asked silkily.

"It has nothing to do with rank." He wanted to paint her some spoiled, ignorant, materialistic princess, and maybe she should let him. Maybe it would take this ridiculous idea of marriage off the table.

"Then what does it have to do with?" he asked, with an innocence so ludicrous she was tempted to chuckle herself.

"It has to do with the fact I have a right to…make my own decisions. To be free of yet another man who wants me to follow along, regardless of my own thoughts or opinions or fears. I knew what I was getting into with the arranged marriage." Protecting her sister if nothing else, but now she had children to protect. "I don't know what I'm getting into with you, Cristhian, and I will not put myself through that simply because *you* think it's the best course of action, when *I* know it's not."

All his casual masks melted off his face in that moment. His mouth got very hard, very serious. His eyes all dark flame and intensity, which reminded her of things it shouldn't when he looked as angry as he had when his gaze had met hers through the window back in her cabin.

But her body couldn't seem to tell the difference between anger and heat. Fury and lust. They seemed all tangled up together low in her belly, in the heaviness of her breasts.

When he stepped closer, she had to internally remind herself to breathe. Not lean in.

"One thing I will make sure of, Zia, regardless of you, is that these children will come first. Your whims are immaterial."

Whims. He really was the most frustrating and infuriating man she could have made this mistake with. "My whims?" She gestured at the castle around them. "What about yours? They seem to be winning."

"*I* am thinking about what's best for the children. *You* keep talking about yourself."

Perhaps that's what it sounded like to him. She couldn't even quite blame him for thinking that was what she meant. Even if it poked at her so that everything seemed to deflate. Exhaustion crept in, tears trying to find purchase in her eyes, though she fought them.

She could explain it to him. What it was like to watch a mother bow and scrape to a father who had all the control. She could tell him what it felt like as a young girl to watch her mother whisper truths, but always, *always* capitulate to her father's orders and mandates. No matter what she told her daughters. She could tell him in no uncertain terms she wanted more for her children. A mother who they could be proud of, who they could trust.

That all the things she desired for herself were really for them. And so much she'd done before this pregnancy had been for Beau, not herself. Because for all Beau's strong personality, her panic attacks left her vulnerable. She'd needed a protector. Zia had the ability to be that. Just like she had the ability, the *requirement* to be her children's staunchest supporter. This was love, above all else, she believed. Sacrificing everything to protect those who needed it.

But he couldn't possibly understand. He wanted her to be the selfish, pampered princess. And so, in his mind, she always would be. So it was with her father, so it was with no doubt every man.

"Well, Cristhian, this *self* you're so disdainful of will have to say *I do* for you to force me into marriage. So unless you have mastered brainwashing or ventriloquism, I think we are at an impasse." And with that, she turned on a heel and left his grand dining room and his fuming expression.

CHAPTER EIGHT

CRISTHIAN DIDN'T FUME for long. He knew how to deal with selfish, childish royalty. Let her throw her tantrums. Let her storm out of every room in this place.

He would come out on top. He'd spent his morning after breakfast lining up a minister to arrive once the roads were passable. He'd had a long call with his lawyer about all the necessary legalities of naming heirs of his own fortune.

They would deal with her family...after a time. Because he still had not determined the right approach to King Rendall. According to Zia, he would want the same thing Cristhian wanted: a marriage. Admittedly, in the privacy of his own head, Cristhian didn't love the idea of wanting the same thing as a king, but it was the only plausible option to give his children the family they deserved.

Zia could worry about *her* freedom, *her* whims, *her* selfish desires all she wanted. *He* would not be swayed. Their children would have the support of two parents, no matter what Cristhian had to threaten to accomplish it. They would have the options of the best of everything. But most of all, they would receive the same foundation Cristhian had received.

Which meant he was in charge. He did not have to convince Zia to follow his way. She would simply follow it or...lose.

What, he did not know yet, but he would use whatever means he wished to protect his children, and their mother, no matter how selfish she might be. And now that he had the practicalities out of the way, and nothing to do but wait for the snow to stop, he called his grandparents.

He decided on a video call, as he wanted to see their faces when they reacted to the news. He'd taught them how to answer one on their phones, but that didn't necessarily mean they would manage. Still, after a few rings, his grandmother's face appeared on his screen.

"Did we do it right?" his grandmother asked, squinting at him.

"If you can hear me."

"Yes, we've got it. Well, now. To what do we owe this out-of-the-blue call?" His grandfather looked older every time Cristhian got on a video call with them. It was a sad mark of time, and yet one his parents had never gotten to enjoy. So Cristhian tried to be grateful for what he had in them.

"I have a bit of announcement. I am to be married."

"Cristhian!" His grandmother clapped her hands together in delight. "We didn't know you were seeing anyone. You haven't even brought her to visit." It was a scolding, but it was wrapped up in love and joy for what his grandmother no doubt thought a happy occasion.

He wouldn't take that idea from them, but he couldn't outright lie about it either. "It is…complicated."

"Ah," his grandfather said in that world wise way of his. "The kind of complicated that will make us greatgrandparents?"

His grandfather had always known how to get right to the point, and even though it twisted something tangled inside him, he smiled. "Yes."

"Oh," his grandmother said, so desperately trying to hide her disappointment with enthusiasm. "Well, aren't we lucky? To have lived this long. You'll bring everyone to meet us, won't you?"

"Of course. Once we are able." His grandparents nodded along, not letting any disdain show through. They never had, no matter what he'd done. "Zia is having twins."

"Twins? Twins! Robert, do we have any twins in the family?"

"My grandmother was a twin!" his grandfather all but shouted, pride in every word.

Cristhian smiled in spite of himself. "Zia is a twin herself."

"That's excellent. She'll know just how to raise them then. Oh, two great-grandbabies. Aren't we lucky?" His grandmother beamed over at Grandfather. Disappointment over the nontraditional circumstances quickly and easily left behind.

Cristhian should feel relieved or warmed by their excitement, but there was a strange kind of discomfort twirling around inside him. He couldn't put his finger on what was causing it, so he just pushed the conversation forward.

"I wanted you to know as it is likely to move forward... quickly. I will keep you updated, of course."

His grandparents nodded, then looked at each other in that way they had that spoke of some internal communication no one else was privy to.

"May we offer some advice?" his grandmother asked gently. Because she was a gentle woman. Too gentle, perhaps, for the world she'd been thrust into. A famous son. The slings and arrows of their daughter-in-law's family in the aftermath of such loss.

And yet she had never taken any of that out on Cristhian himself. He held this as a personal guidepost. These people on the screen in front of him, so unlike the world he lived in, and yet, the exact guide he wanted.

"Of course."

"Your parents loved each other very much," Grandmother said with a heavy wistfulness and a look away from the screen, no doubt at one of the many pictures she kept of his father.

"Yes, I know."

She turned back to the screen. "It was the foundation, and why you're such a good man, despite such…trials."

He could not quite manage the smile he knew his grandmother wanted. He had not set out to be *good*, per se, and the thought she might think it settled in a bit like guilt.

"And your father was a good man for the same reason," Grandfather said firmly. "Love is always the foundation. If you'd take any advice from us, we hope it's that. With love as a foundation, no matter the tragedies life throws at you, you'll find a way to endure."

Cristhian did not want any more tragedies, but he knew his grandparents spoke of their own. One they had weathered, with love.

No, Cristhian didn't care for that advice, but it was… interesting. So he smiled. Chatted some more about people his grandparents knew. He let them tell all their stories from church, the beauty parlor, the grain elevator coffee shop. These things were foreign in Cristhian's life, but his grandparents always made it sound like a world he could step into if he ever needed.

Like the foundation his parents had built him, his grandparents had offered an escape hatch—once he'd been old enough to rid himself of his mother's family's royal shenanigans. He'd never taken it, still didn't want to, but something about it being there…meant something.

He tried not to think about Zia, talking about her royal prison. Perhaps she had not been afforded an escape hatch, but she'd found one, hadn't she? And still, the way he saw it, she cared for her own wants more than their children's needs.

But his grandparents had raised a good man by loving each other. His parents, the same, if he was to be counted a good man. So, Cristhian supposed, that was the answer to his trouble.

Love.

He would simply make Zia fall in love with him. Then all would fall into place. And be well.

After a post-breakfast nap, Zia felt slightly more herself. She still thought Cristhian was a ridiculous ogre, but she was reminded she had the strength and cleverness to out-maneuver her father. What was Cristhian but a slightly different version of that?

She just needed to pace herself. To think. And didn't this blizzard that had them stuck here without doctors or ministers give her just that kind of time?

She considered her phone. A missive to Beau would help her think through her options, but it was still risky. Beau was clever enough to outmaneuver their father and his men, but Cristhian complicated things. He was certainly smarter than Father's men, considering he'd been the only one capable of finding Zia, which meant he might be Beau's match in terms of sneakiness.

If she needed to escape him, too, she would need to do it without putting Beau in the crosshairs of it all. She would need to do it without anyone. She would have to rely on herself.

So, she decided the first step was to explore the castle. Get to know it. She knew better than most that a good escape required an excellent understanding of the landscape you were living in. She did not have the benefit of growing up here to know the nooks and crannies of where to hide and where to bolt.

So that was her first mission.

She left her room, but instead of taking the usual stairs down, she walked deeper into the hallway upstairs.

It wasn't quite like the castle she'd grown up in. The architecture was rather similar, but there were no royal portraits. No cases or walls of heirlooms. Everything was rather bare. But there were grand windows—some with beautiful stained-glass scenes, some floor-to-ceiling looking out over the estate around the castle.

Outside the world was nothing but bright, expansive white. She could almost believe they'd been snowed in here forever. It looked and felt like some kind of fairy tale out there.

Except here she was, trapped with the villain rather than the hero.

She sighed. She shouldn't think of him as either. The truth was, no matter what happened, Cristhian *was* her children's father. And she didn't know enough about him as a person to determine him a villain in that respect.

She didn't consider her own father a villain, either. The idea of him being her adversary really gave him too much credit. He was simply…self-absorbed. He could be cruel, but only when it suited his purposes—his purpose was running a kingdom. She figured all men probably fit that mold, but she wasn't yet sure what purpose Cristhian was acting under.

Since he did not have a kingdom to run, maybe she could find some inner core of reason inside him. Maybe if she got a better sense of *him*, she would know how to handle all this. How to maneuver.

Or how to escape.

She did not know if this castle meant anything to Cristhian when he was a man with *estates*. If it did, perhaps it would give some insight into his character, so she continued her exploration. Poking her head into any and every room. A library, an office that looked unused, a few generic bedrooms that had most of the furniture under coverings.

About halfway down the hall, she found a gorgeous conservatory. She spent the better part of thirty minutes there, enjoying the sunlight and beautiful green in contrast to all the white outside. So far, it was her favorite room.

Of course *her* favorite didn't matter, she reminded herself when she was tempted to curl up in the chair and doze. She was on a mission. So, with reluctance, she left the sunny room and went back into the hallway that now felt chilly in comparison. More covered up, unused rooms greeted her as she made her way around the curve of the hallway.

Once she made it to the almost complete other side of the castle, she found a suite of rooms that she had the sneaking suspicion were Cristhian's. She almost didn't notice it at first, because the decor in the room was as bare as the halls. It could be any guest room, anywhere, but none of the furniture was covered up, and there were little signs of life in the sitting room.

A folded-up newspaper on an end table, a jacket hung on the back of a chair. There was a computer cord coiled on a desk in the corner, missing its laptop.

Perhaps that should have been a sign to stop her perusal—no doubt Cristhian was a private man—but instead she pushed forward. Into a sprawling bedroom. The bed was huge; the windows that looked over yet more snow dominated one wall. There was no art on the walls, just a beautiful wallpaper that reminded Zia of the blue back on the island when polar night had just begun to lift.

She saw nothing personal in the whole expanse of a sleeping area, until her gaze landed on a large dresser. On top, a framed picture. Zia moved closer.

It was a wedding portrait of two outrageously gorgeous people. Then it dawned on her.

His late parents.

Cristhian looked almost exactly like the man she believed to be his father. A movie star, if she recalled correctly. The only real difference she could note from the picture was Cristhian had more of his mother's darker coloring than the blond and blue-eyed star.

Zia still couldn't remember what country his mother was from, but she'd look it up once she was back in her room. Maybe that would be a clue in to him as well. Maybe if she got a better handle on the people who'd made him, she'd have a better handle on *him*.

She snorted, alone in his bedroom, because the idea of handling him was so ridiculous. From that very first moment in the bar, her gaze meeting his, she hadn't been able to handle him or what he brought out in her.

But things were different now. They had to be. She smoothed a hand over her stomach, her babies, dancing around in there as if already jostling for space in whatever rooms they entered. She wanted to give them all the space they deserved. She wanted to give them *everything*.

Which wasn't all that different than what Cristhian had said this morning. Maybe there was some common ground to be found. If they both wanted what was best for their children, there was room for a lot of common ground.

But it wouldn't be in marriage. It couldn't be.

Zia looked at the two happy people in the wedding portrait and wondered if that happiness was real or the illusion of a picture. Did happiness with another person exist? Or did it always sour into what her parents shared?

One person wielding all their power over the other. Then either fighting, or her mother's head bowed acquiescence.

Zia wanted neither for her babies.

On a sigh, she turned and left the room. The only real insight gained from the upstairs was that Cristhian either didn't care about decor, or he didn't care much about or spend much time at this castle, and that he had truly loved his parents.

Zia wondered, perhaps unfairly, if it was easy to love parents who had died before you were even a teenager.

She lumbered downstairs, pressing a hand to her stomach. The more she was on her feet, the heavier she felt most days. When she'd been back at the cabin, she had always had ample sitting time. She should likely take a break from her exploring, but she didn't want to sit with inaction and her thoughts right now. So she pressed on.

But she didn't get far. After skipping the dining room since she'd already been familiarized with that, and then poking her head into what had turned out to be some linen closet of some kind, she came to a room with two grand doors open. It was some kind of sitting room, all dark woods and warm colors, with sunlight dappling the plush carpet. It was the kind of room meant for cozy nights and long, meaningful conversations.

A fire crackled in the hearth, and Cristhian sat in an oversize chair, a newspaper spread out in front of him.

She wanted to step back, not let him see her, but he looked up, those dark eyes meeting hers. She still could not quite prepare herself for the way her body reacted to his gaze taking her in. She wanted to be immune, but it always felt like his hands on her again, and no matter how she felt about him rationally, her body was apparently the least rational part of this whole package.

It would revel in his hands on her again, even in this state. Even with her brain telling her to get it together. And she didn't back away or excuse herself. She stepped deeper into the warm, cozy room.

But then his mouth curved into a welcoming smile, not sharp or flirtatious at all. Just kind. *This* she did not trust at all.

"Come. Sit." He gestured at a table full of food. "Are you hungry?"

She shouldn't join him, she knew, but the room smelled like heaven, and she *was* hungry again. Walking around had worked up an appetite.

There was a large chair that matched his on the other side of the table, so she walked over without saying a word and settled herself in it. There were trays of fruit, cheeses, little pastries, all arranged artfully. There were three pitchers, one filled with water, the other two filled with juices. She shouldn't let herself get used to this kind of luxury. If she was going to find her way in this, she was no doubt going to be back to square one at some point. A small cabin, an isolated island. Just her.

And your babies.

She glanced at Cristhian, who was watching her fill her plate. Was there anywhere she could run away to that he would not find? She had the sinking suspicion the answer was no.

So you will just have to figure out a way to get through to him, Zia.

It felt like an impossible task, but she couldn't believe in impossible. Not when it came to her children. Everything had to be possible, if she just worked hard enough.

But first, she was going to eat her fill. She curled up in the big chair and took bites of everything. "Your cook is exceptional," she said in between pastries.

"Yes, I make a habit of exceptional."

She shouldn't find that charming. It shouldn't make her smile. He was arrogant and ridiculous and that was never a good combination.

"Did you enjoy your tour of the castle?" he asked. Blandly.

But she stopped midchew, because she had not been aware of anyone who might have seen her snooping about. And still he knew. Or was pretending to.

So she pretended she didn't care what he knew. "It was very informative. I cannot decide if you have an aversion to art and any of the touches that might make a *castle* a home, or if this simply isn't a space you spend much time in."

He seemed to consider this by looking around the room they were in. Which, in fairness, had art. Books. Nothing *too* personal, though.

"The cottage was stripped before it came into my possession," he said after a moment. His gaze returned to his newspaper.

"Stripped?" Zia echoed, not quite understanding his meaning.

"I may have royal blood, as you like to point out, but no one in my mother's family is too keen on that truth. They prefer to use me or manipulate me, whatever makes them feel powerful. So while my aunt insisted I keep my title and take on Espinas Cottage, she made sure anything not bolted down was taken back to their royal seats that surely deserved such heirlooms."

He said this without any bitterness. Like it was just a fact and it mattered not at all to him. But it had to matter, didn't it? Not the things themselves, but the fact his own family would treat him as an outsider.

She did not care for being one of her family, of having her whole life defined by how well she upheld the Rendall legacy, but she could not imagine being young and orphaned and then feeling as though she did not belong.

Did he have no emotion about that? Or had the years allowed him to heal from it?

These were things that were dangerous for her to wonder, even more dangerous for her to know. She had to keep her wits about her if she was to ensure her freedom.

Something she struggled to remember when he lowered his paper and met her gaze with his dark one. His mouth subtly curved, the firelight giving his skin a burnished gold look about it. Like he'd be warm and safe to the touch.

Be stronger, Zia.

"Your cabin on that island wasn't exactly full of knick-knacks."

"I ran away in the dead of night. To a polar island with limited resources. If I had access to home decor, I would have certainly bought some. But my focus was on not being detected and keeping these two healthy." She rested her hands on her belly.

His gaze followed them. "What made you choose that island for your escape?" he asked, his gaze remaining on her stomach.

She studied him with suspicion. Why did he care? What

was he trying to get out of her? Would he use her answer against her in some way? File away everything she said so he could follow her inevitable escape?

But he was looking at their children, essentially. Even if he couldn't see them, that was why he was studying her stomach. He was thinking about *children*. And maybe if they could both realize that these two were the most important thing, and the adults in the situation weren't sworn enemies, they could come to some reasonable conclusions and agreements.

She had to believe that. "I saw a video. I liked the idea of polar night. Of being able to hide away in months of darkness while I figured out what to do."

"You did not find this polar night…depressing?"

She smiled a little, even though she shouldn't let her guard down like this. "No. It was…cozy. I like being on my own. Deciding each day what I want to do. It was especially important to be alone to make the decisions I needed to make."

Something in his expression darkened, but he made no scathing remark. His attention went back to his newspaper. But she began to wonder if he was even reading it, or if it was just a prop. If this was all just an act.

"I do not know what you think you're doing, but you're hardly going to butter me up with sweets and change my mind about everything."

His eyebrow rose as he slowly set the newspaper aside and then turned to her. "I do not wish to change your mind. The marriage will go through regardless of how you feel about it."

She could have groaned, but she needed to resist those urges. Take a page out of his book and offer nothing but a calm, impenetrable sense of right.

She leaned forward, as comfortably as she could with her belly right there. She tried to sound calm and rational instead of accusatory. "Let me ask you something, then. Why do you think marriage is the right choice? You clearly have not watched two people make each other miserable at the cost of their children."

"No, I have not. Nor will we."

She wished she could believe it would be that easy. But she had seen too much. "Just because we don't love each other doesn't mean there won't be hard feelings. It certainly doesn't mean there won't be battles of our wills. I would like to avoid such things. Perhaps you don't understand. Perhaps I haven't been clear. I truly did not tell you because I was so focused on…making certain my family did not know that I did not think of how to track you down. It was not my intention to cut you out. If we can find a way to keep my identity unknown, I am happy to share custody in a careful, fair way."

"Perhaps *you* don't understand. We might not love each other now, but this does not mean we can't."

Zia laughed. The sound bubbled up and right out of her.

But Cristhian did not laugh at what had to be a joke as well. He did not smile. He did not wink.

He just sat there, looking at her placidly, as if he was serious.

Clearly he'd lost his mind.

Or she had lost hers.

CHAPTER NINE

THE SHOCK ON Zia's face was enough to make Cristhian smile. Genuinely. It was important she think love was an option if he was going to force that eventuality. It was imperative she thought *him* open to such things.

"Cristhian," she finally managed to say. "You... You can't be serious." But she sounded more...frightened than censuring. Interesting.

"The way I see it, we entered into this as strangers who shared an uncommon amount of chemistry. Hence the children."

She wrinkled her nose. "Yes, hence."

"Perhaps you did not go about it the way you should have, but we can set this aside."

"Oh. *Can* we?"

Again, his smile was genuine. She was entertaining at times, he'd give her that. "It is my understanding that the way people go about falling in love is to get to know each other. We should do this. See if we can't...open ourselves up to something."

She blinked once, as if she was trying to rid herself of the look of horror on her face. It didn't work.

He managed, just barely, not to laugh. "My parents loved each other very much. My father's parents are the same."

"My guess is they did not meet in a bar and have a one-night stand that ended with twins."

"Perhaps not, but my parents met at a party and, by all accounts, were inseparable from that moment. My father's parents were far more scandalous. She was dating his best friend when they met at a church function, and she ditched one man for another." He shook his head.

She tried not to smile. He watched her fight it. But slowly the edges of her mouth curved.

"You love them very much."

He did not care for her having that insight, but it was only the truth. "They are good people. They never cared about titles or money. Their lives are simple—they complain when I try to make it simpler. Because they love their family, not what a person in it might offer them."

She sighed and settled deeper into her chair, studying a piece of fruit before setting it aside. "I love my sister. I've put her in an impossible situation with this, and..." She shook her head and spoke no more on it. Clearly it bothered her deeply.

But clearly she had still put herself over her sister's needs. A pattern for the princess.

He couldn't let his disdain for that show. Disdain did not grow love. Nor did suspicion, and she was clearly still suspicious of him. How did he combat that? It frustrated him that it would take time. Trust did not blossom overnight even in the easiest of situations.

"You say your parents loved each other," she said, picking at the hem on the sweater she wore. "But you were so young when they died." She chewed on her generous bottom lip for a moment before raising her gaze to meet his. "So how do you know they did?"

There was something vulnerable in the question, in her

eyes, and it twisted something inside him, a strange need to protect that flash of something soft underneath all her strength and determination.

All her selfishness, he reminded himself. Because that was the issue with her, and he would not let her beauty, or even the odd flash of vulnerability, distract him from that.

He focused on her question and whether he would offer an answer. He did not often speak of his parents with anyone outside of his grandparents. It had been a topic he refused to engage with when it came to his mother's family, when it came to the odd reporter who still thought his life might make a story, or the random person he encountered who had known his parents.

Zia fit into none of those categories. He could make up a few lies, but trust was not built on outright lies, and worse, he never could quite bring himself to *lie* about his parents. It felt like betrayal.

"It was told to me, of course, how much they loved each other, as I grew up. Both as a positive from my father's parents, and a negative from my mother's family. But…children pick up more than adults think, I believe. Perhaps I did not have the maturity for the words yet, but there were things I witnessed that, looking back, could only have been love."

"Like what?" She looked truly intrigued, and he supposed there was no harm in this. It led her exactly where he wanted her, didn't it? Thinking about love, believing it could happen. And if he shared *his* definition of love, and tried to embody it, she would at least think him in love with her.

"I recall my father turning down roles that did not fit into her royal schedule. He would always laugh it off when the movies he turned down did well. He never made it seem…like a bad thing. It was always clear his family was the most important. Being with *her* was his goal. Movie stardom was almost more like…a hobby."

Cristhian frowned at his own words, and the feelings they dredged up. He had not thought of that in some time. The simple and easy ways his father had made Cristhian and his mother feel like the center of his world. He hadn't fully understood it as a child. But now, a man with a career and adult responsibilities, and the prospect of two children greeting him in a short period of time… It felt all that much more important.

Rare.

He dared not look at Zia with these strange feelings rioting around inside him. That would no doubt confuse things when his goals were clear. Even if the methods were murky.

"To my mother, he and I were the center of her world. Everything else a distraction. She struggled more with the lines there, what with the royal responsibilities her family wanted from her and how much her family disliked my father. But she made it clear time with my father was her goal as well."

So, in the here and now, Cristhian would make sure he made time for Zia. For the upcoming children. She would now take this as a sign of love, or potential love, and he would come out on top.

"I know my father does not love my mother," Zia said, very, very quietly. "I highly doubt he ever did. She was a means to an end. His parents died when he was quite young, and he ascended. He needed a wife. A wife with the right pedigree to become a queen."

"This is often the way of royalty."

"Yes," she agreed. She sighed heavily. "But sometimes,

I think she must love him to behave the way she does. Even if he does not love her, though I cannot fathom why he doesn't when she is everything he asks her to be."

"What way does she behave?" Cristhian asked before he thought better of it. Before he weighed what the answer would mean for his goals of getting Zia to fall in love with him.

"Afraid, I think. Oftentimes she will express agreement with me or my sister. She will act as though she will support us in the face of opposition—my father, his advisers and aides, and then the time comes and she…doesn't. She cowers."

Cristhian had seen an array of royal marriages in his adolescence, but he hadn't seen one like that. He supposed his uncle, the prince to his aunt's queen, had a kind of… cowering air about him. But it had never struck Cristhian as *fearful*.

But he understood that fear better than he liked. Because his mother's family had spent those first few years without his parents making things as scary as possible for a young boy. No stability. No support. He had been made to be afraid by people who only knew how to wield their power that way.

He felt an old anger simmer deep in his gut. There would not be *fear* in his children's lives. "Are you afraid of your father?" he asked Zia, trying to keep the old anger out of his tone.

She considered this, as if it required consideration. He did not like to see that kind of behavior continued or rewarded, and it *was* his business, he told himself. Because how Zia's parents dealt with her would inform how they dealt with *his* children, and he would not allow fear.

"I have never been afraid of him, no, because the things

he cared about were not the things I cared about. But…
with this pregnancy, I do have concerns about the reach
of his power and what it could accomplish if I do not have
full autonomy from it. He will consider these children his,
in a way. Heirs."

Heirs. How Cristhian had come to hate that term in
his life.

"Either way," Zia continued, "his family has never come
above his country," Zia said firmly, as if fear did not matter. "I suppose that is the way of a king, and I shouldn't
blame him for it." She shook her head as if to shake the
words away. "Why are we discussing all this?"

"To get to know each other."

She studied him. "Because all of a sudden you think we
could fall in love and somehow make a marriage work in
a way that would support a family?"

"I realized it would be shortsighted not to be open to
the idea, Zia."

He knew he'd gotten her there because she had no quick
quip of a response. She just watched him with a thoughtful
look on her face. Which was a good place to end things
for this morning.

He rose from his chair, crossed to her. "I have a few
phone meetings I must attend to. I would like it if we could
have tea together this afternoon."

"Oh. Well, I don't have anything better to do, I guess."

"Such a ringing endorsement, Princesa."

Her mouth twitched at the corner. "You're going to
have to help me out of this chair, or I'm going to be stuck
here until teatime."

He offered a hand and helped her up and out of the large
chair. He did not release her, convinced this was the way
toward getting what he wanted.

That was the *only* reason he lifted her hand to his mouth. The only possible impetus for brushing his mouth across her knuckles and watching the faint flush creep up her cheeks.

If he remembered all too well the way he'd made that flush take over her whole body months ago, there was nothing wrong with that. This was all part of his grand pursuit for her love.

That was all.

Zia had gone back to the conservatory for the next few hours. She had not been able to stop herself from dwelling on that strange morning. From his honest answers to hers. From the way her body still reacted to every last thing about him.

Was love really such a crazy idea? When her heart hammered about in her chest just from the way his gaze held hers, his lips barely touching her *hand*.

Love. She didn't really have a clue what love was. She loved her sister, her children-to-be. But that felt elemental. Just immediately and easily part of her. Not something that happened, but something that was.

Nothing about Cristhian felt that simple, that certain. It felt all jumbled and confusing—had before she'd even realized she was pregnant. Because no one had ever made her feel like that, and even when she'd walked away from him that morning all those months ago, she had believed nothing and no one would ever make her feel that way again.

It had been a sort of poetic, really. That *one* night.

Now a million nights stretched out before them with consequences complicating things, and that confused everything.

Even the stories he told of his parents and grandparents loving each other made it sound like love was some immediate thing. She had felt attraction for Cristhian, lust, certainly, and everything she learned about him was interesting.

Were those ingredients to love?

And if they were, was that even something she wanted to consider? It seemed a dangerous element to add between them when they had to put their children first and foremost. Not each other. How could she take care of her children if she was worried about taking care of him?

She ruminated over that for the next few hours. She'd been brought lunch up in the conservatory. She'd enjoyed the plants, read a little, dozed. She'd even risked a text to Beau. Still just to assure her sister things were fine, not to ask for help...yet.

They were stuck in this castle for a few days. Perhaps she should simply...hear Cristhian out. Get to know him. She didn't know how to believe in something like love as some magical answer to this complicated problem, but maybe understanding could lead to...

She blew out a breath, frustrated with her mind turning in the same circles. Because it always came back to the fact that everything she understood about relationships was that one person inevitably came out the victor.

Even with Beau, whom she loved with her whole heart, everything ended up a contest with a winner and a loser. And she always tried to protect Beau from being the loser. A protection born out of necessity—the heir, the...very much not heir.

And now you've left Beau with all that baggage. So who's the victor?

"Ugh," she said aloud, to try to force herself out of the

loop. She couldn't fix what was going on at home, whatever Beau was dealing with, though Beau insisted she was fine.

But Zia could find a way to deal with her current situation. Cristhian. These babies. She had to. That was her responsibility now.

She spent a considerable amount of time having to maneuver herself out of the chair and onto her feet. Sometimes, she had the fleeting thought that she would be quite glad when she wasn't pregnant any longer.

Then she thought about the fact that two babies had to come *out* of her, and she walked that back pretty fast. And did something to forget about the very looming realities creeping up on her.

She went in search of Cristhian since it was nearing their agreed-upon teatime. She hoped there were more pastries. She hadn't been exaggerating about his cook. He was a miracle worker with sugar and butter.

Lucky for her.

She didn't make it all the way downstairs before she ran into Cristhian. He was standing on a landing on the grand staircase, looking out one of the tall, narrow windows. Outside, there were no longer rolls of white. It was just... all white. She couldn't discern anything beyond snow.

More snow. A blizzard.

He glanced at her. "I was on my way to fetch you." He nodded toward the window. "We may be stuck a few more days yet."

She rubbed at her stomach, trying not to worry. "I have an appointment with my doctor in three days."

"My doctor is on his way. This might set her back another day or two, but it should not be impossible to get her here in that time frame." He turned to face her fully now, standing a few stairs above him. He studied her. "Do you have concerns we need taken care of?"

Zia shook her head. "No. So far everything has been right on track. Twins offer more risk, but I have not displayed any risk factors."

"I have not asked. When are they due?"

"My doctor was hoping I would make it to thirty-six weeks without needing any interventions to extend the pregnancy. I will be at thirty-four weeks at my next appointment. So far, so good. A full term would be another six weeks, but that's unlikely. Next month, probably."

Cristhian nodded at this information. Then he offered his arm. "Tea is set up in the dining room."

She hesitated. No matter how she felt about him on an intellectual level, even something as platonic as linking her arm with his was dangerous. He was too...*something*. Even when she wanted to hate him, every touch was charged with electricity. Like he was a current she would always react to.

But something too close to smug appeared on the lines of his face, like he understood her reluctance, so she straightened her shoulders and took the last few stairs to link arms with his.

And it *was* electric, no matter how stiffly she held herself against it. The heat of him, that spicy scent that had haunted her dreams these past few months. No doubt some cologne he wore, but also just *him*.

"Tell me more about your sister," he offered conversationally as they walked down the rest of the staircase.

"Why?"

He shrugged. "I am curious. I have no siblings, and we are to have twins. What is that like?"

"Well, it's hard to explain, since I don't know what it's

not like. In some ways, it was a great gift to always have Beaugonia by my side."

"And in others?"

"When you are a twin, it is a constant comparison. Who is developing faster? Who has a higher intellect? Which one's prettier? Which one's more rebellious?"

"And yet you speak of her as if you are not in competition."

Zia shook her head as he led her into the dining room. Another cornucopia of delightful-looking food—small sandwiches, more pastries, desserts. He certainly knew how to feed a woman if nothing else. "Those were outside forces. Our parents, royal staff, media. *I* never felt in competition to Beau."

"Did she you?"

He helped her into her seat as she considered the question. "I don't think so. Beau is…unique. She has always been more…interior than I am. The outside world doesn't often factor into her decision-making. She has never expressed to me any real competition, but that is the thing about twins. It doesn't matter what the two of you do, the outside world will judge you against each other all the same."

"And so you were chosen as heir. Because, in comparison, you came out on top?"

"Because I could be told what to do," she corrected. It had taken her until just a few years ago to realize this. That it wasn't just luck of the draw that people saw her as more suitable. Maturity had made her realize it was her ability to be manipulated that led her into the life of heir.

But she didn't want him to think that was still the case. As much as she didn't want to let him into every facet of her life, he needed to understand that obedience and ability to be manipulated had been bred into her.

She didn't fall for it anymore. Only when she needed to protect Beau. "I think I was only twelve or thirteen when they informed me of the trajectory of my life. Marry a royal my father would choose. Produce many a child with said royal so that, since I would be acting queen of whatever husband's country, one of my children could be heir to my father's throne *and* this other throne. And so, last year, the crown prince was chosen, and I was told I would marry him. Our countries would be linked in a positive way for both. A familiar pressure was pushed upon me to agree, and I caved to it."

"You speak of an obedience I have yet to see considering both times we have met, you have been running away."

She shook her head. "When I first met you, it wasn't to run away. I had given myself a week to…escape. Briefly. I had a time limit. I just wanted to see what it would be like to make my own decisions, have my own life. I thought it would help. Obviously, I was a bit naive there, and then compounded that naivete with a mistake with you. But at the end of the day, my father had made it very clear to me if I did not do *my* duty, that Beau's life would suffer. So I was going to do my duty."

She poured the tea while he filled both their plates. Small domestic movements that felt strangely…comforting. She supposed because they were stuck here, in this unreal world, where they could get along and nothing outside the walls of the castle had to matter.

But this was very temporary, and she needed to remember that.

"It seems to me your sister is a grown woman who can handle herself if she is as you describe. Why are you so protective?"

"In some ways she is that." She would not let Cristhian

or anyone else in on Beau's issues. Not because she felt as her parents did that Beau's panic attacks were embarrassing and a bad mark on the crown. If anything, she felt the opposite. Beau's issues meant she deserved protecting from *anyone*.

Silence fell after that, as if he expected her to fill it. She didn't. She busied herself with baked goods and tea. When he finally spoke again, it seemed he'd realized she wouldn't speak any more about her sister.

"And what did you do on this week of freedom you took? Besides me, of course."

She laughed in spite of herself. Perhaps she was giving him too much information, too much ammunition. But maybe…maybe she could allow him to fall in love with her, if she believed such things possible. As long as *she* didn't fall in love, didn't have to serve him in that way, that meant she had control of the situation.

Didn't it?

"I shopped alone," she said, thinking back to that glorious week. So glorious she'd let everything go wrong, and even now, couldn't regret it. "I went to a concert and lost myself in the music *I* chose to like. I walked in cities at night, in broad daylight, all on my own. I even found an athletic club and joined a little pickup football game one day. No one treated me any different than anyone else. It was like breathing for the first time."

He didn't say anything right away. He was staring at her intently, an odd expression on his face she couldn't quite parse. Intense, yes, but as if he was trying to puzzle her out, like she was some sort of brain teaser.

"Were you expecting something else?" she asked.

He shook his head, looked down at his plate. "I do not know what I expected."

But he got that look about him. She was beginning to recognize it was usually when he brought up something about royalty. And his mother was a princess. Like her.

"Did your mother ever try to step out of royal life?"

His expression shuttered. "I should like to meet your sister, I think. Perhaps we can get her here for the wedding."

She did not know if he meant to be provoking, or if he was simply so used to always telling people how it would be that he did not consider her feelings on the wedding she hadn't agreed to at all.

"I haven't agreed to marry you, Cristhian," she stated very firmly.

He looked over at her and smiled then, and she should *not* react to that. It shouldn't flutter through her like some heady liquor. He was smiling because he thought what she wanted didn't matter.

And still she throbbed with too many memories of *that* night to name.

"My mistake, Princesa," he said, his voice a low, sultry menace. "More tea?"

CHAPTER TEN

CRISTHIAN FELT AS though he were making some progress. Zia was forthcoming with most information. About her family, her upbringing, what she wanted for the children.

She was a fascinating woman. She had a wide variety of interests, and she talked easily and happily about most of them. When he prodded about her family in an effort to determine the best way to handle them, she presented a strange figure. Obedient, yet driven by an internal need to be herself. Easily manipulated by an authoritarian father, and yet not ignorant or foolish. Most of her purpose, at least as she stated it, was to protect her sister.

If he felt like there were some similarities there, in how she viewed the royal machine in many of the same ways he did, well… He didn't think too deeply on it. Similarities didn't mean anything. Not when he had a situation to control in order to ensure the best outcomes for everyone.

He had not yet figured out how she could talk of her sister so protectively, and yet have abandoned the woman to handle the mess Zia herself had made. He could not quite make sense of the spoiled princess who clearly did as she pleased, and yet, at times, had not. And the more he dug into these seemingly disparate facets of her, the more she took up residence in his mind even when he was not spending time with her.

He was quite sure he could have handled all this, even if it was a tad alarming and unique, if it weren't for the physical undercurrents that still traveled between them.

He knew she was attracted to him still. She could not hide her reaction to him. The issue was that he had his own reaction to her, and he did not care for it. She haunted his dreams, in that same way she had before he'd known she carried his children. As if this huge turn of events had not changed anything at all.

When it *should*.

Still, Cristhian had not lost his head. He had continued to engage her in conversation, in meals together. He had worked on charming her, and he thought he was succeeding as that suspicious look rarely crossed her face anymore. He would have been happy to leave it at just the two of them for a few days more yet, but he could sense she had some concerns about her doctor's appointment, so he had done everything in his considerable power to have the doctor arrive, hiring an entire fleet of people to get the doctor across closed roads and looming snowdrifts.

Though he still felt marriage the best course of action, and certainly something that needed to be acted upon before they approached any signs of her going into labor, making certain all three parties were healthy was paramount to everything else.

Even worrying about getting a clergy member who could marry them to the castle.

The doctor arrived one snowy afternoon, with the fleet he'd hired to get her to the castle safely.

She was a middle-aged woman with a no-nonsense way about her that Cristhian appreciated, and her reputation was one of excellent work and, just as important, working with royals and celebrities and never once letting their secrets wind their way into the press.

Cristhian still had not contacted King Rendall, and since the king's own men had searched for months for Zia with no luck, he figured he still had a few weeks yet before he needed to answer to the man.

He would do so with a clear way forward. This respite wasn't *running away*. It was preparing a battle plan. Just as he had done once as a young man, ready to cut ties with his mother's family. More or less.

"I can do an exam," the doctor explained to him as they walked up the staircase to Zia's room. "But a paternity test will have to wait until we have access to a lab without worrying about the state of the roads."

Cristhian nodded. He had not been lying to Zia about not having any true concerns about paternity, but a child of his, a child of hers... There would need to be legal proof along with protection. So that would be the next step after this.

When they knocked on the door to her suite, Zia answered the door herself. He made the introductions, there was some brief small talk, and then the doctor got to work. She didn't seem to have much in the way of equipment, but she chatted cheerfully while she worked, setting Zia up in her bed, propped up on pillows.

She took vitals, then talked them through the process, explaining her sonogram machine—an incredibly small little device—would transmit the images to her laptop screen, set up on the nightstand next to the doctor. Cristhian was somewhat dubious of the equipment, but once she started...he forgot all about technology.

On the screen, it was black and gray. The gray and white forming different shapes against the black. The doctor held her little machine this way and that on Zia's round stomach. She made considering noises, but Cristhian couldn't begin to imagine what they meant.

Then it was hard to listen to her, because she explained the odd *womp-womp* noise that filled the room was a heartbeat. And then another.

His children's hearts. Beating. The sound echoed inside him like some kind of avalanche.

Eventually, the doctor took the machine off Zia's stomach, and gave Zia permission to get comfortable. She clicked a few keys on her laptop and pulled up one of the sonogram images.

"This is Baby A," she explained, and she outlined the head, an arm, a knee. She did the same with Baby B. She mentioned heart rates and growth patterns, but Cristhian couldn't take it all in once he could fully recognize what she outlined as bodies.

He had seen the physical evidence of them all these days from the size of Zia's stomach. He had been fascinated that two children could be nestled inside her, and still…this was something else entirely.

Hearts beating. Limbs moving. Life. A life he'd had a hand in creating. It swamped him, in a way perhaps he had not allowed himself to fully accept yet.

"You are very lucky, ma'am," the doctor said to Zia. "Everything is just as it should be. I see no risk factors for preterm labor. At this rate, you could make it to thirty-six weeks and perhaps even after. We'll want to keep a close eye on things, of course, but everything is just as it should be."

But Zia wasn't looking at the doctor, and neither was he.

"We can discuss the sex, if you'd like," the doctor continued.

Neither of them looked at the doctor. Neither of them answered her. The doctor cleared her throat, but Cristhian could not take his eyes off the tears in Zia's. The way everything about her shone with some... He did not know. He felt bowled over by *everything*. Like he was no longer the foundation he stood on, survived on.

Like something else had upended him, wrestled his control and strength away. Which was ludicrous, of course, and a thought to be pushed away. Without control, only danger and tragedy lay ahead.

"I'll...give you two a private moment," the doctor said. "Then we can discuss next steps once you're ready."

Cristhian had no idea if the doctor left then. He couldn't have cared less. He couldn't seem to break his gaze from the myriad of Zia's green. The tears that spilled over now, dotting her cheeks like sparkling jewels.

He brushed the tears away. "What is this?" he murmured, something heavy and painful in his chest, and yet it held no candle to the pain the tears brought.

Zia shook her head and sniffled. "I cry every time I hear their heartbeats. Not out of any sadness. It's just so amazing. I don't know how to explain it. They just...are about to exist in this world and I..." Her voice squeaked, and she made a vague kind of gesture.

But she didn't have to explain what she felt. Perhaps he would not shed any tears, but he understood the *overwhelmingness*. It was just...too big, this reality of theirs. Children. *Children*. Coming sooner rather than later. Each their own individual person who would exist and live in this world.

So he took Zia's hand in his, sat next to her on the bed. Trying to find some semblance of the anchor that had once tethered him to earth.

She made a little "oh" noise, then her mouth curved. She squeezed his hand and pulled it to her stomach. She pressed his palm there, right at the side of the swell of their children.

"Do you feel it?" she asked.

But he did not know what he was meant to feel, and not knowing left him perfectly speechless.

He always knew.

Her mouth curved, even with the evidence of the tears still on her cheeks, as though she understood he was at a complete and utter loss. Unacceptable.

But before he could do anything about that, wrestle control of the situation back in place, she pressed his hand into her stomach with more force, and then he felt it…something *ripple* across his hand. If he had been untethered before, this became the anchor to everything.

His child, moving, there underneath her skin. This new version of his life. A new reason for *everything*. A purpose born of the future rather than the past.

And it all centered on Zia. Not just because she carried these babies, but because she was the mitigating factor. She was…

He did not know. Found he did not want to delve too much into these thoughts scrambling around in his mind, only half formed. So he pushed them out of his mind the only way he knew how.

He pressed his mouth to hers. Like he had those months ago. As if he was finding some new answer to an old question. Perhaps she *was* the answer.

Because she kissed him back. Like the moment had bowled her over, too. Rearranged something inside her, when she'd had all these months to carry this new life and grow it inside her and become accustomed to it all.

Everything had changed and yet she tasted the same. A same he shouldn't remember quite as well as he did. Still, for all that *same*, she was different under his hands. Ripe and round and lovely. She sighed into him, like she had found respite after a long journey and this intoxicating feeling was new, strange, heady.

Her arms came around him. All the heat and flame they'd been ignoring for these past few days lighting between them.

Not smart, when he was always smart. Not in control, when he was always in control.

Except when it came to her.

Zia felt as though she were drowning in a storm of too many things. Joy. Fear. Hope and anxiety. Need, want, lust.

And the impossible and irresistible chemistry between them. She had been so sure she could resist it. Avoid it. That his sudden and unwanted appearance in her life, complete with overbearing decisions and control issues, *clearly*, should have taken all of this away.

But no.

It was not as though she had gone about kissing many a man. She'd had her little rebellions, just to prove to her father that he would not have a say in *everything* she did, even if he had a say in the last things she did.

But nothing had ever remotely felt like this. Like she might die if she did not get to experience that night again.

Just once, she thought to herself. It was the heat of the moment. Zia tried to assure herself of this. She just… hadn't had anyone with her for any of these checkups. It was just the emotion that always struck her, but she had someone to pour it into.

But he was different, and she knew it. No matter how little she liked it.

The way he kissed her was like altering all the shaky foundations she'd managed to build since she'd left his bed, since she'd found out she was pregnant, and then that there were *two* babies. She had lovingly placed every floorboard in this brand-new life.

And he'd taken an axe to all of them. Hacked it all to pieces.

In the flame of this kiss she didn't care. Who needed foundations when she had his arms around her and his mouth on her? When his hands smoothed over her stomach as if he sought to protect the little lives she grew?

And then lower, to stoke every fire that had ever existed within her, like they existed just for him.

She wanted him. Again. Even knowing it was a mistake. A temporary madness, really. But who cared in this temporary moment, knowing how good it would feel?

One of the babies rolled, long and hard against her stomach. Against *him*. He startled, pulling back and staring at her stomach in a kind of shock that made her want to laugh.

Not *at* him. Just at everything. And this strange, dizzying joy that came with it all, when she should know better than to believe in someone, in something. But no matter how hard she tried in this life to remind herself everyone else was living in a competition even if she didn't realize it, she didn't want to feel she was at war with *him*.

So when their gazes met, she was smiling in spite of herself. His gaze was hot, fervent. But he did not press his mouth to her again. Carefully, gingerly almost, he released her and got up off the bed. "The doctor is waiting." He said this as though he had some control, but she watched the way he struggled to catch his breath. She saw the wild need in his eyes that couldn't quite leave hers.

But if he could find some kernel of control in all this, so could she. "Yes." The doctor. Sonograms and babies and…all that entailed. She could be in control, too. She could…be just as strong as him. The doctor was waiting because she had more information to impart.

Zia steeled herself to meet his dark, intense gaze. "Would you like to know the sex?" she managed to ask, though her voice sounded a bit strangled.

He didn't say anything at first. He kept staring at her with all that *fire* that had her curling her hands into fists so she did not reach for him.

"I would, yes, if that is acceptable to you." His voice was a rasp, reminding her of too many pieces of that night she'd spent with him. His mouth, his hands, the things he made her feel with just that dark, delicious voice of his.

But this was not that night. So she managed a tiny nod even though it wasn't a question exactly. Still, she thought, maybe with someone by her side, she *was* ready. Or maybe it was just that time was running out, and she had to be ready whether she liked it or not.

He strode out of the bedroom, and within a few minutes was back with the doctor. Whose gaze moved from Cristhian to Zia in a way that had Zia blushing.

Profusely.

"Mr. Sterling has informed me you'd like to know the sex now."

Zia nodded.

"A boy," the doctor said. "And a girl. The girl is currently measuring a bit smaller than baby boy, but this is very common with twins, and so far, not a concern."

A boy. A girl. Zia didn't know why this came as such

a shock. She supposed that because she had a twin sister, she'd just…always imagined them both as girls. Even *knowing* they could be one or two boys, she hadn't been able to visualize that.

Now, with their father standing next to her, she could visualize far too many things. Children with darker features. One that looked like her, and one like him.

This made her want to cry all over again.

"Mr. Sterling? If you'll excuse us? I'd like to have a private discussion with the expectant mother."

Cristhian frowned at the doctor, but then he looked at Zia and some strange emotion she couldn't parse passed over his face. He nodded. "Very well." He gave Zia one last confusing look, and then turned and left the bedroom.

Zia had to force herself to tear her gaze from the door and smile politely at the doctor. "Thank you for braving the roads and such. It has put my mind at ease."

"I'm glad. These last weeks of pregnancy can be stressful, but rest assured, you will be well taken care of. As a physician, I want it to be clear. While I will be staying here throughout the rest of your term, per Mr. Sterling's request, and with his compensation, my duty is to you, ma'am. Your health, and your children's health. You can come to me with any questions, voice any opinion you like. And I will always be honest with my recommendations."

Zia blinked at the woman. While these were all nice things to hear, she supposed she hadn't thought that far ahead. Hadn't considered that Cristhian might hire a doctor who *wouldn't* put her health first.

What a terrible thought. But the doctor kept talking.

"I have worked with many…well-known individuals. The rich and powerful. My record is above reproach. Never once have I been the source of gossip. Nor have I ever let a powerful man have sway over someone's health."

"This is all very comforting to hear, of course," Zia said carefully. "But I… I guess I don't know where it's coming from."

"Intercourse is not off the table," the doctor said matter-of-factly.

Zia nearly choked on nothing but her own saliva. "I'm sorry?"

"You'll want to monitor how you feel. If there's any cramping, bleeding, discomfort after, you would want to avoid it from there on out."

Zia could not stop the hot blush that worked up her cheeks. She had to clear her throat to speak as she wrapped her arms around her stomach. "I wouldn't want to put them at risk."

The doctor shrugged as if this was a very normal conversation, and she supposed it was. For parents who were married or in a relationship. It *was* straightforward for those people, no doubt.

But nothing was straightforward for her and Cristhian. No matter what the doctor said about it.

"We always want a mother to come as close to term as possible, particularly with twins," she said, as though delivering a well-practiced speech. "But you are very healthy, your babies are very healthy. The risks are minimal at this stage. That can always change, but it might not. You have your own wants and needs, ma'am. Those are valid, too. But not a requirement of you, either."

It all made a weird kind of sense now. The doctor was making sure she understood the green light was not because Cristhian was paying her, but because it was a perfectly reasonable option. But she left the caveat in, because no doubt women had been in her position where they had *not* wanted to deal with the advances of the men who were overseeing their health.

"I'm at your service, whenever you need," the doctor said.

Zia managed a nod. "Thank you. I appreciate it. Genuinely."

"I'll leave you then, unless you have more questions?"

Zia shook her head. No. Not questions. Uncertainty, yes. But not questions. The doctor left her alone with her whirling thoughts. She pushed herself up and out of the bed and walked over to one of the windows, looking out into all that white.

The snow had stopped falling again, but still so much had piled up around the castle. It still felt like a fairy-tale world she knew she could not let herself be fooled by.

But she *wanted* to be. Just another day or two. Fooled and foolish. Believing in fairy tales of happily-ever-afters instead of the harsh reality of responsibility and control and protecting those she loved in whatever ways she could.

Beau. Her babies.

End of list.

Cristhian stepped into the bedroom then. He closed the door behind him. And Zia knew there was still a choice to be had here. She did not *have* to give in to her body's desires. She could use her brain, protect her heart that felt so strangely bruised after all of this.

But she didn't.

CHAPTER ELEVEN

ZIA STOOD JUST out of reach, looking like some beautiful statue. A paragon of fertility and female beauty. Regal. Knowing. The light from outside shining on her like some kind of beacon.

For a moment, just a flash, Cristhian could picture himself on his knees worshipping at her very feet.

The problem with love, mi princesa, *is that it is beyond our control. And we are beyond theirs.*

Sometimes he preferred to think of memories as dreams, rather than flashes of his childhood.

But that voice in his head was his father's—American accent and all—and the image of his parents together, while she cried over some royal slight, was real. Stuck in his head. Because once his father had seen him there, he'd beckoned him over. Insisted they go on a picnic. And his mother had stopped crying. They had enjoyed a perfect afternoon.

That happy memory, of that picnic, of his father's love, was the reason he felt this way. It had nothing to do with *her.* He wouldn't allow it. Things were too complicated already.

Weren't they?

Cristhian took a step back before what he realized he was doing. *Retreat? Never.* He lifted his chin, continued to study her. But this did not help. She was some beautiful siren, luring him off course.

"I liked her," Zia said at last. "You made an excellent choice."

"I am glad. She will remain on property until the children are born."

Something flitted through her expression he did not quite recognize, but she put one hand over her stomach in a protective gesture, as if she was afraid of…something.

A sharp, curling need took him over then. It was the only way to explain it. He moved toward her. "You will have the best of everything, Zia." He touched her shoulder, couldn't seem to stop himself, even though he had never been any good at comfort. But he had to do something to assuage that fear. "There is nothing to worry about."

She huffed out a little laugh. "Only a man could say that. There is *so* much to worry about." Still, she put her hand over his on her shoulder and smiled up at him. "But I appreciate the… I know we want the same thing. Two happy, healthy babies."

"Yes." But it felt like she was leaving something out.

He didn't want to think at all about what it might be. Because his children would come first. Before his own happiness. And hers. He would organize their lives so that everything turned out better than his had.

It put them at a crossroads, because he knew she put herself first. She had made that clear to him, and he would not let her do that to his children. His children would never know this conflict between them, though. Cristhian would ensure it.

He wanted Zia, yes. With a need that was blinding him to what was necessary. What was right. Such was her power, but he was a man in control of himself. In control of *everything*.

He could leave.

He *would* leave.

But her hand was on his. Her body so close. That lush mouth of hers tilted up, just within reach. A taste… What was a little taste? It would just keep her thinking love was an option.

Perhaps she would even mistake it for love. He could kiss her and maintain control. Because if she loved him, that would be all the control he needed.

Warning bells sounded in his head. The kind he listened to in his work. Those gut feelings he never took for granted. Because so often they told him where he was making a misstep, warned him he was going down a wrong path.

Today, he ignored them and pressed his mouth to hers. Just another small taste. Not for him, but to fool her. *Her.*

She met his kiss, pressed her palms to his cheeks as she lifted to her toes to get a better angle. Sweet and lovely, with enough bite to send a jolt through his system.

Control. I am in control.

He was sure of it.

"The doctor said it was safe," she whispered against his mouth. He looked down at her, and those siren-green eyes, a myriad of colors he was drowning in.

Because it was a simple sentence, but her expression showed a variety of complexity behind that it.

Safe. Not just safe, but here Zia stood giving him the go-ahead. When it was not *safe* for either of them. It was just like that first and only night. A loss of control. No doubt full of consequences that would echo through them forever.

He knew what consequences did. He knew what happened when he gave up his control.

He kissed her anyway. Deep and hard, pouring months and months of frustration into her. Because how he had *dreamed* of her against his will. How he had *wanted* her and been unable to want anyone or anything else.

She had ruined him somehow, and this felt like control. Like reclaiming...something. So he claimed her mouth. He lifted her shirt off her and let it fall to the ground, claiming her breasts, the stomach where she carried their children.

So perfect, lush and vibrant. He remembered with a ferocity it didn't do to dwell on every inch of her, but she had changed. Become fuller, softer. So he cataloged this new version of her, laying her out on the bed, naked and perfect just for him. He studied her, with his hands, with his mouth. Until she was all but sobbing out his name, writhing there on this large bed.

His. *His.* Because together they created something bigger than themselves. Not just the result of their night together, but this all-encompassing thing that stripped him of his control, his certainty. Stripped him of everything he was.

Because in this moment all he could be was *hers*.

He stripped himself of his own clothes, slid his palms along her inner thighs, opening her for him. He slid into her in one long, slow stroke, the wave of pleasure and *right* sweeping through him like an eruption. As if things had not been right since she'd left his bed that morning, and now they finally could be again.

She cried out, shuddering around him almost immediately. So responsive, always, like they had been designed to bring out a pleasure in each other that no one else could even begin to know.

So he moved, slow and steady, drawing her up that heady peak once more. Watching as the pleasure chased over her gorgeous features. He watched her mouth form his name, and he felt her lose herself once more around him.

He roared out his own release as she held on to him, strong and sure. But it left him feeling none of those things. Fear sneaked in under all the swirling pleasure as she rolled into him, as he pulled her close.

He held her too tight, he knew. This was out of his control. Beyond his rules. He had crossed all his own lines, and he had to get them back into place. The only way to take hold of this situation was to make certain everything happened the way he saw fit.

"You will marry me, Zia."

He shouldn't have said it. He didn't know what had come over him. Just a need to have everything right and in place and her to be…

Mine.

But not that. Not in *that* way. Just in the way that…that they would… That would allow him to make everything right. Make the *world* right.

For his children. That was all.

Zia was amazed that someone could ruin something so thoroughly and so quickly. For a moment, the pleasure and joy of finding what they had had their first night had completely taken her over. There'd been some sliver of hope that something…good and right could come out of all of this.

Then he'd crushed it. While the orgasm still pulsed through her. She wriggled away from his too-tight grip, from that fervent, nearly wild gaze.

Maybe later she could consider what that lack of control on his face meant. Maybe later she could give him some benefit of the doubt. But in the here and now? The only way to protect herself was to lash out.

"So, that's not a question," she said, searching the floor

for her clothes. When she couldn't find them, she jerked a blanket off the bed and wrapped it around her.

He made a sound perilously close to a growl. "It is the appropriate course of action."

"Have you been talking to my father? You sound just like him." Which was possibly only an insult in *her* mind. But one that showed her just how stupid she could be. Leave it to her to be so consumed by a man as obsessed with control as any king.

He pulled on his pants, somehow looking perfectly businesslike and in control while she no doubt looked like a ridiculous potato wrapped in his blanket.

He seared her with a look. "You cannot take me to your bed and oppose marriage."

"I think you'll find that not only *can* I, but I do."

"You are being contrary for the sake of it."

She shook her head, even though a little voice in her head whispered, *Aren't you?* But as contrary as she *could* be, this wasn't about anything like that. Because it wasn't about her. It was about their future, and how she could ensure it was the right one for their children.

"No, Cristhian. I will not go from one controlling ogre to another. I will have some say in my life, and so will my children."

"Our children."

"*Our* means we share. *Our* means there are two people involved. *Our* means you don't just get to…order things and have them be so. *Our* is a compromise."

He held his jaw so tight now it was a wonder he didn't crush his own teeth to dust. Anger simmered in his eyes, but when he spoke, he sounded very calm. Very cool.

"It is interesting that you feel qualified to give lectures

on what *our* means, when everything you demonstrate is that you are only interested in *you*."

It shouldn't hurt. She shouldn't let him fool her into thinking they were more than strangers. A few days of meals and conversations didn't mean you knew someone well enough to…

It didn't matter. Whatever she thought or didn't, he clearly saw her as someone too selfish to understand an *our*. "Is that what you think of me?" she asked, trying to use his calm, cool tone.

He did not answer right away. He stared at her, his entire body seemingly taut like it was ready to explode. But he didn't do that, she'd give him some credit there.

"I was hoping that you would be willing to be reasonable," he said after a long, strained moment of silence.

"You were hoping that good sex would lead me to believe we were in love and should be married immediately." Which nearly made her want to cry. That he'd just been using it as a weapon, not this irresistible need she had felt it was. "What you fail to understand is that I already knew the sex was good, Cristhian. *That* is not the concern." She pointed at the rumpled bed. "This isn't some new experience that was about to change my mind about anything."

His expression went…arrested, almost. Like she'd stabbed him straight through and he was surprised to find it hurt. She didn't know what to think of that, or why it should make her feel small and hurting.

Then he smoothed it all out. Back to in-control, certain Cristhian Sterling who ruled the world. "I will contact your father immediately and inform him that you have been found, and we will be married."

It was absolutely ridiculous that she was shocked. *Hurt*.

She knew better. But somehow…he'd fooled her. "What happened to the possibility of love?"

He eyed her, like she was some…piece of gum stuck to the bottom of his shoe, as if gum would dare. "I thought you could be reasonable. I thought, perhaps, there *was* a possibility that underneath the pampered princess veneer, there was a woman who could see beyond herself to the life she could give her children. Now that I see that I was wrong, we will proceed my way."

She was struggling to breathe normally, to keep the tears that wanted to fall in check. She would be strong. For those children he didn't think she cared about. Because she would not be a doormat. She would not *bend* for him. Because Zia knew, deep and personal, that a mother like that wasn't a good mother at all.

"I won't say yes."

"I won't need you to." And with that, he left her room with quick, certain strides. So fast she couldn't even find the words to argue with him.

He couldn't *force* her to marry him. No matter what he said.

I will call your father.

What had happened? She sank onto the edge of the bed, at a total loss. How had sex turned into this…this? How had thinking they could find some common ground flipped so quickly?

What had she done so wrong?

She shook her head. No, she wouldn't blame herself. Well, not fully. She had made mistakes, yes. She had let her guard down, and then she had let something as foolish as chemistry cloud her good judgment.

Because it *was* good judgment to not want to jump into

marriage. If they married, he would have all the say. Over her, over the children. There would be no compromise.

He could talk about love all he wanted, but she had nothing to offer him. No way to protect a man like him. How could he love what essentially was a useless object to him?

For the first time, she pictured those children. Cristhian ordering them the way her father had ordered her. She would stand up for them, of course, like her mother never had.

But in this new visualization, with actual children, with Cristhian, she almost thought she understood why her mother caved.

Because what was worse? The caving to avoid the explosion, or the explosions themselves? If she fought Cristhian in front of their children, was that really any better for them? She had never witnessed her mother put up a fight, and she'd always thought she wanted to.

But now…with her in the mother role, she wasn't so sure. That wouldn't feel safe to two little children. Angry parents, conflicting parents.

So how did she make this right?

She pulled out her phone with shaky hands.

Beau. I need help…

CHAPTER TWELVE

CRISTHIAN KEPT EXPECTING the fury to fade, but it didn't. It just…flipped. Because as angry as he was at the woman Zia was, the real, enduring anger was at himself.

He'd mishandled everything that day with the doctor. And then spent the next two days allowing her to ignore and avoid him while he arranged all the plans that he knew were right.

He didn't need her to agree to know they were right, and he was hardly going to scrape and beg to get her to see his way of things. Married parents, living together under the same roof: this was what his children deserved, and nothing could change that.

That was why he had used considerable money and influence to get all the roads from airport to castle cleared. That was why he'd flown in staff from his home base estate in Spain. That was why Zia's family was on their way to the cottage and would arrive at any moment.

Tomorrow, they were going to have a royal wedding. No matter *who* approved. Even his bride.

Once that was out of the way, a paternity test situated, they would bring in the lawyers. Everything would be carefully and *legally* outlined. So that neither the king nor his own so-called "family" would have a say in his children's lives.

They would be protected at all costs.

He had given this a lot of thought. More than Zia, clearly. Sure, she had escaped her father for a few months, but then King Rendall had hired *Cristhian* to find her, and while Cristhian might be the best and the most discreet about that sort of thing, there was likely someone else King Rendall could hire who would eventually track her down. And then what? Did she have *any* plans besides running away?

He thought of his parents and convinced himself he didn't know why they were on the forefront of his mind lately. It was simply because he was in the process of becoming a parent himself.

It wasn't about love. It wasn't about their own runaway attempt that had ended so horribly.

Because what Zia didn't understand was that running away would never be the answer. Being under his protection was the only way forward, and there was no point wasting any more time trying to win her over.

Cristhian didn't know why this felt different from his usual decisions. Why he woke up every morning with a strange tension inside him, fingers curled into fists, as if he was constantly fighting in his sleep.

He didn't know why whirling feelings and second thoughts plagued him when he had not allowed something so pointless since he'd been a teenager.

There were no second thoughts here. Control would keep everyone safe and sound.

He'd put his plan into action, so now everyone would see it through. And no one would end up dying on the side of the road.

He pushed that thought away mercilessly. Because this was not about his parents. It was about his present.

He was standing in his office, looking out one of the large windows with a view of the rolling hills of his estate. All covered in a picturesque white, while flurries started again. A snow globe, a postcard, a fairy tale. But even when everything looked beautiful from the outside, it was still messy, uncertain life on the inside.

Which was why Cristhian had to put his stamp of control on what was happening.

When he was informed that the small royal motorcade had pulled up to the cottage, he left his office and went to greet his guests. The minister had been delayed a little, but Cristhian had been assured he would arrive later today.

Cristhian had decided to let Zia continue to hide in her room. She did not know that her parents were coming, he didn't think. Unless she'd had communication with her sister. Possible, but Cristhian did not concern himself with informing her of his plans.

She would be part of them whether she liked it or not, so there was no point having a conversation that would no doubt only end in more conflict.

He was done with conflict.

A staff member opened the large front door, while more staff ushered the royal family inside.

"Your Majesties. Your Highness." He gave a short bow to the three royals who stood on the threshold of his home. "Welcome."

He had not met the queen before, but he could see bits and pieces of Zia in her. The green eyes, the sharp chin. Her expression was one of regal distance, but she gripped her husband's arm so tight the knuckles on her hand were white.

The younger woman who stood behind the king and queen, almost as if she was purposely trying to hide, was

Zia's sister, no doubt. Zia's twin. For twins, they did not look too much alike. Sure, there was a sisterly resemblance in coloring, but he supposed he'd expected something more like imprints of each other. But where Zia was tall, athletic, regal, Beaugonia was smaller, softer. Her eyes were more hazel, but sharp and taking everything in, even as she kept herself as much out of the center as possible.

"I hope you traveled well. It's not a long journey, I know, but my staff can show you to your rooms if you'd like to rest up before dinner."

King Rendall looked down at him with a clearly growing suspicion. "I have come here as a courtesy since you claim to have found my daughter."

"I appreciate such courtesy," Cristhian replied with an easy smile. He gestured at his staff who were bringing in the royal family's belongings. "They will show you the way to your rooms."

"Where is my daughter?" the queen asked. King Rendall looked down at her with a sharp, disapproving glare, but the queen ignored him, keeping her worried gaze on Cristhian.

"She will be meeting us for dinner. We will have much to discuss." Cristhian wanted to make sure he had a moment to sit the king down and explain the entirety of the situation to him before they dealt with this…en masse. He would make it clear to the king that Cristhian did not care what lands he ruled, these children would be Cristhian's responsibility alone.

Cristhian turned his attention to the one person who hadn't spoken yet. He smiled at Beaugonia, but she decidedly did not smile back. "Zia will be most happy to see you, Princess."

And still Zia's sister didn't speak or look upon him any

less suspiciously. No doubt Zia had filled her head with tales. Well, so be it.

He didn't need anyone's approval or acceptance. There would be a wedding. Tomorrow.

He heard a strange noise behind him, looked over his shoulder and saw Zia standing there at the top of the staircase. Her stomach was hidden by the balcony. "Beau." For a moment, there was a flash of true joy on Zia's face. Cristhian felt a strange stabbing pain in the center of his chest.

Not because he wanted to be the source of such joy. How ludicrous. It was because she'd ruined his plans. Yet again.

But he didn't scowl. He didn't chastise her. Simply because it would look poorly in front of the king and queen.

Not because he was mesmerized by that joy on her face as she ran down the stairs and approached her sister. Not because the way they wrapped their arms around each other made him feel...alone. Not because it warmed him to watch them sway in each other's arms like long-lost friends. So much joy between them, Cristhian could almost feel it himself.

He smiled in spite of himself, in hope for a future where his children greeted each other in just the same way.

Certainly not any hopes for himself in there.

The king and queen clearly did not share this joy. The queen's eyes were as wide as saucers. The king looked as though he was ready to call for some beheadings.

Because Zia had ruined that gentle announcement Cristhian had planned.

Oh, well. Cristhian had to force himself to look away from Zia's happiness and turned to face the king. "You see now, sir, why I called you all here. And why a wedding will be happening tomorrow."

* * *

The joy Zia felt at seeing Beau was immediately tempered not just by her parents standing there, but also by Cristhian's heavy-handed proclamation. By the reality of this situation. Because it wasn't Beau coming to save her.

It was Cristhian following through with his…utter ridiculousness.

She didn't know why she'd allowed herself to be fooled by the past two days of quiet, of spending no time with him. She didn't know why she'd been foolish enough to think avoiding him was a punishment to him.

The way it had felt to her. Because she'd missed their conversations, his presence. And she didn't know what to do with that.

Any more than she knew what to do with her father standing there. Looking angry and threatening. Because Cristhian had *brought* him here.

So he wasn't at all concerned with if she was afraid of her father or not, even though he'd asked that question and seemed so…genuinely concerned.

What a fool she was. But she couldn't let herself wilt under the grief of that. She had her babies to protect. From everyone.

"There will be no wedding," Zia said firmly, though maybe all that firmness was undercut by how hard she held on to Beau. "I don't know what he's told you, Father—"

"That is enough, Zia," the king said, speaking over her. "Cristhian and I will discuss this matter in private."

Zia looked at Cristhian then, wondering what the hell he thought he was doing. But his expression was carefully blank. She knew he was controlling, that he thought he knew best. She knew he could be *like* her father, but surely he wouldn't honestly secret off with her father and handle things without her having *any* say?

"Very well," Cristhian said, pointing toward the hallway. "Follow me, sir."

The king stormed after Cristhian and Zia was left with her mother and her sister, a few staff members she didn't recognize. And the sinking sensation that she was drowning. In a world she'd thought she'd escaped.

A young woman among them cleared her throat. "I'd be happy to show the queen and the princess to their suite."

"Beau will stay with me," Zia said, blinking away the tears, the utter disappointment in Cristhian.

"But Mr. Sterling said—"

"The princess will be staying in my suite with me," Zia interrupted, using all her royal training to sound as commanding as Cristhian no doubt did. She smiled at the woman though, trying to sort through all her conflicting feelings.

Because as much as her heart ached, she blamed herself for that. For having some sort of hope when it came to the man she'd somehow...trusted. But why? Why had she trusted him when he'd shown her, over and over again, exactly what he was?

But mixed in with all that disappointment was utter relief. Because Beau was here, and if Beau was here that meant Zia could find a purpose in all this pain. "The three of us will have tea in the conservatory, if someone will bring it up?"

The woman nodded and quickly disappeared.

"Follow me," Zia said to her mother and sister, heading for the stairs.

"Zia. You cannot just...take us to some conservatory

and not address the…the…the issue at hand," her mother sputtered.

"Which is?" Zia asked innocently. Beau made a sound that Zia knew was her coughing to try to cover up a laugh. Because this was familiar ground. Her and Beau against the world. It would be okay. They would find a way to make it okay together.

They linked arms and Zia started up the stairs, but Beau looked back to make sure Mother was following. The queen was not happy, but she was following.

Beau leaned close. "He lives in a castle," she whispered.

"Right? He calls it a cottage. What rot."

Beau laughed again, earning them a sharp look from their mother. It was so familiar Zia almost felt herself relax. She led them both into the conservatory, offering seats. Beau took one immediately, but Mother didn't. She stood at the entrance to the room, shaking her head.

"Zia, I do not understand any of this. What has happened?"

Zia considered different versions of the truth but decided to go with the most simple and straightforward. "Cristhian and I met months ago. During—what did you call it?—my *responsibility vacation* we…hit it off. When I learned I was pregnant a few months after, I did not know how to find him. Or break it to Father. Or anyone, frankly. So I ran away."

"Pregnant," Mother echoed. "By some man you didn't even know."

Mother made it sound like she'd murdered someone in cold blood, and maybe in Mother's world it was all the same. A stain on the monarchy no matter what.

And that was all that mattered, wasn't it?

"I know him now well enough," Zia said, trying to be

gentle about it. How could she blame her mother for being shocked and appalled? Cristhian had dumped this on them with no warning.

"And I suppose in some strange twist of fate, I have Father to thank for that." Was it a thank-you in her current predicament? It didn't feel it. "When Father hired Cristhian to track me down, Cristhian did not know who I was. Until he recognized me. He did not know about the babies until he found me and—"

"Babies? Zia." Mother sat then, all but collapsing into the chair, her hand to her heart. "Twins."

"Yes," Zia agreed. "Twins." She gave Beau a little smile, because especially now she was so grateful her children would have each other.

"My pregnancy was horrible," Mother said, almost to herself. She even placed a hand over her stomach. "I was so sick. So afraid. Constantly on bed rest. It was why we never had more children though your father would have liked a boy."

Zia smiled thinly. Mother had regaled them of tales of her terrible pregnancy, but she tried not to think of that. Or the boy that they all believed would have made their lives better. "Mine has been very uneventful. The doctor tells me all the time how lucky I am that we're all so healthy."

"Yes. Incredibly so." Mother finally looked at her. *Really* looked at her. Her eyes filled. "Zia, darling, why would you keep something like this from me?"

Zia watched her mother fight back the tears, fascinated. Mother cried quite a lot, really. Always in private, of course. The *public* mask of Queen Rendall was impenetrable, emotionless. Grace and detachment above all else.

Zia never confused the two faces her mother wore, they were so intrinsically different. The public, perfect queen the king demanded. And the interior woman so afraid of going against him.

But right now, in this moment, Zia felt confused. She had expected recriminations—no doubt that would come. She had expected her mother's upset...but over the public image. Over the king's reaction.

Not Zia not *telling* her. There were so many things over the years she hadn't shared with her mother.

Namely, for one reason. "How could I tell you? I knew how Father would react. Which meant that would be how you would react as well. So I had to handle things on my own."

"Your own?" Mother scoffed, narrowed her eyes at Beau. "I hardly think so."

But before any more discussion could be had, two staff members entered with trays and quietly and quickly set up the tea for three women, then disappeared. Zia moved forward to pour, but Mother waved her off.

"Well. We must focus on the current situation we are in, not a past that cannot be changed. A small intimate ceremony is necessary for your condition, of course, but there must be *some* royal formality."

Zia watched her mother pour the tea gracefully, while Beau piled her plate high with a little bit of everything food-wise. Zia had been starving, but now her appetite left her.

"Mother. I don't care what Cristhian says, what he thinks he's planning with Father. I will not be marrying him."

"Zia." Mother set the tea pot down with a *clank*. "You're *pregnant*."

"Oh, you don't say."

But Mother was so worked up, she didn't even send

Zia a censuring glance. Or Beau one when she laughed. She stood instead, wringing her hands together. "You must marry. And you'll have to stay out of sight for… Oh, I don't even know how long. No one can know…" She trailed off again, but the wringing hands certainly didn't stop. "Your father…" Again she trailed off.

"Alternatively," Zia replied, trying to maintain her calm and composure. There was really no point in lashing out at her mother. She was simply a vessel for Father's wants and desires. "I will not marry, but I can happily stay out of sight…forever."

"You're the heir," her mother said, so *scandalized* and *horrified* that being an heir might not be something Zia was going to prioritize. Not over her children.

Children. She settled her hand over her stomach. She knew her mother meant well, and yet she had caused harm to both Zia and Beau. Was that the curse of a mother? No matter how hard you tried, you would hurt your children?

Would twenty-some years down the line the two little lives growing inside her look at her and wonder why she'd denied them a legacy? Parents who were married? Or would her loving them be enough?

Because Cristhian had talked about loving his parents, and she was sure he did. Sure they sounded lovely and loving. But sometimes the image of them sounded…too good to be true. Or at least, the story as told from a child, which he had been when he'd lost them.

"I heard this crazy rumor that the king gets to choose whatever heir he likes," Beau said, interrupting Zia's thoughts on motherhood. The doubts that continued to creep up, no matter how certain she was in her choice of action.

Should she marry Cristhian…for them? Would that create a kind of insulated safety? He *was* controlling, but he claimed to want the children to come first. That was certainly not in her parents' vocabulary.

Mother whirled on Beau and shot her a sharp look. "I told your father we should leave you at home."

"What's-his-name insisted I come. He was quite adamant," Beau said, sniffing a sandwich before taking a delicate bite.

Zia stared at her sister, more than surprised by this information. Beau didn't really need to be here, and it *was* highly unlikely either parent had wanted her here. Had Cristhian insisted...for her? "He did?"

Beau looked at her speculatively. "Yes. That's what Father said anyway. He made certain I knew I wasn't wanted on this trip."

Zia sat back in her chair and closed her eyes. Oh, what kind of idiot was she? It didn't matter. Cristhian was trying to force her into a wedding. Any gesture that seemed kind was either by accident or to purposefully get under her defenses.

She couldn't keep falling for that. "Well, we are all here now. And now we must decide how to proceed." She couldn't capitulate to Cristhian now. It would be like capitulating to Father. "Because I will not marry him. No matter what Cristhian says. No matter what *Father* says."

"You were going to marry the crown prince, Zia," Mother pointed out. "How is this different? A step down, of course, but—"

"A step down?" Zia scoffed, then inwardly berated herself for defending Cristhian when she had no reason to. But at least she had *chemistry* with Cristhian. At least they'd had conversations and...well, sex. If she was going to marry anyone...

But she wasn't. "Mother. I appreciate that me not marrying might make things…difficult for Father. But he is the *king*. I'm sure he'll weather the storm, and as Beau said, choose whatever heir he likes in the wake of me abdicating."

The queen just kept shaking her head. "You must marry the father of your children. They must be legitimate. They have kingdoms to inherit, Zia. How can you be so selfish?"

Selfish. Yes, that kept being used against her, and maybe it was fair. She did not know how to deny it. She wanted *some* things for herself. Some agency. Some freedom. Maybe that was just as wrong as her mother bowing and scraping. She genuinely didn't know.

She just knew she could not bow. She could not scrape. For herself, maybe, but first and foremost for her children.

Her children would not suffer. *They* would not be made to bow and scrape. Maybe Cristhian wouldn't expect that of them, but he was currently meeting with a man who would. Who would try everything to have an influence over them if Cristhian did not stand up to him here and now.

She had to protect them, just as she had protected Beau for all these years. It was her responsibility.

"The kingdom *I* am meant to inherit has only ever been a threat and punishment used against me." She met her mother's gaze then. "I will not do the same to my children. Maybe that is a mistake—"

"Maybe?"

"But it is my mistake to make."

Mother shook her head. "You fancy yourself very strong and very modern." Tears were in her eyes again. "You'll stand up to your father, to the world that built you?" She laughed. Bitterly. "They will crush you, Zia. I don't know why I could never teach either of you that bending keeps you from getting crushed."

"Why is bending better than crushed?" Beau asked. And Zia wanted to know the answer, but she also knew it wasn't the time to ask. One of those differences between the two of them. One of those reasons Beau would not be named heir. *Timing* wasn't in her vocabulary.

But Lille *was* modern enough. Father did have the right and law behind him to choose an heir of his own making. Maybe he wouldn't like it, but it did not *have* to be Beau replacing her.

So why did she feel so guilty? Why did bending suddenly seem like it was on the table? Because if she bent... Beau wouldn't suffer. If Cristhian could bend a little to keep her father out of this, perhaps the children wouldn't suffer.

Could she find compromise in a man who seemed to have none?

Mother shook her head, whirled around and exited the room in a huff.

Zia closed her eyes, wishing she could take a nap. Instead, she had to leverage herself up out of this chair. "I should show Mother to her room."

But Beau put a hand over her arm. "She'll find some staff person to do it. Long before we get you out of that chair."

Zia laughed in spite of herself, but Beau continued.

"Because Mother is right. You can't just stand up to them, Zia. We don't have that kind of power. They *will* crush us if we try. So we're going to have to have a plan. We're going to have to escape."

CHAPTER THIRTEEN

CRISTHIAN DIDN'T CARE for the realization that the more time he spent with King Rendall, the less he liked the man. It wasn't just that he was demanding and pompous and, well, *royal* in all those negative ways Cristhian had grown up hating.

It was the way the king spoke of the women in his family. As though they were nothing more than pawns to be moved about a board. Cristhian could picture, all too easily, his mother's family talking the same way about her when she hadn't done what she'd asked, about him when he'd been an orphaned child.

It filled him with a boiling anger he knew he needed to keep control over, but it was a struggle. Another slight he could lay at Zia's feet, once this was all over and they were married.

Settled. Once everything was settled just the way he wanted, the anger, the frustration, this damn uncertainty would go away. Everyone would be safe, and he would be able to relax.

"King Rendall," Cristhian said, after the king had gone on and on about royal weddings and whatnot. "I think you've misunderstood me. You are not in charge here."

The king narrowed his eyes at Cristhian from his seat in an luxurious overstuffed leather chair seated in the corner of Cristhian's office. "It is not customary for *anyone* to address the king in such a manner."

"I am not a subject of your country," Cristhian replied, standing behind his desk. Then smiled and tacked on a *sir*.

The king was clearly not placated. "Do you have proof *you* are the father of these children?"

Cristhian didn't let the insult land. "I will," he responded calmly.

"I suppose your name and pedigree comes with a certain amount of…reach."

Cristhian felt he was holding his own in this ridiculous back-and-forth, but this change of topic was…confusing at best. "Reach?"

"Hisla is a small country."

Cristhian had no great love for his mother's country, but he had to admit it grated to hear the king act as though it was somehow *beneath* him. "As is Lille."

"Indeed. A partnership is what I've been after in securing my heir a husband. Both political and ensuring that the best bloodlines continue." He frowned a little and drummed heavy fingers against Cristhian's desk. "I don't know what I'll do about the crown prince. Beaugonia won't do. I don't suppose you have some princess cousins who might want to marry a crown prince?"

"I couldn't tell you. I have little to no contact with my mother's family, Your Majesty. I intend to keep it that way."

"No, that won't do. You want to marry my daughter, raise these children as you see fit, but you don't understand. It is our responsibility as leaders to consolidate and protect the kind of power that will keep our families safe and profitable until the end of times. Lille and Hisla must come to a kind of…partnership. You'll need to secure agreements with your family."

Cristhian stood there and felt something so strange and out of place he didn't recognize it at first. But eventually, understanding seeped in.

He regretted this. He'd made a mistake. To involve Zia's father, her family. He knew he wasn't wrong about getting married. But he had been wrong about trying to use her own blood as a weapon against her.

Because now, more than ever, he wanted to protect her from...*this*. Power and profits, when a child's future should be about happiness. About peace. Not just *his* children's.

But Zia's.

He had no doubt, even now, Zia and her sister were up there planning rebellions. Escapes. Just as they had planned and enacted Zia's escape to the island. In this moment of King Rendall talking about power and kingdoms, Cristhian was tempted to allow them to do just that. To get away from the man who sat before him.

But if he let Zia run away, the king would find her again. Maybe not right away. Maybe Cristhian could even thwart him, but it would mean a life of constant vigilance for Zia *and* his children. A life, essentially, on the run.

And running away never solved a thing. If anything, it always ended in destruction.

At some point, Zia was going to have to see that he was offering her protection just as much as anything else by marrying her. He was trying to do right by her, even if she didn't see it. He would protect her. He would...

A strange, clutching feeling took residence in his chest. An understanding just out of reach. And an old memory from long ago.

Your family does not have power over you unless you give it to them.

They control everything.

Not me.

Cristhian stood there while King Rendall prattled on, stuck in that memory of his parents. One from not long before they died. He'd been meant to be asleep, but he'd gone to find them for some reason he could not remember now.

They were huddled on the floor of their living room in his grandparents' house in the States, a fire crackling in the hearth. His mother had been crying. She was shaking even now, but his father held her as he always did. And said those words that echoed in his mind, as if his father was reaching out from whatever great beyond and whispering them to him now.

He'd always thought his father's words were simply love talking. Cristhian still thought that, all these years later. His father had loved his mother enough to take on some sort of unearned arrogance that he could face down an entire monarchy.

Now Cristhian was following in those same footsteps.

But it wasn't love on his part. Protecting Zia was about protecting his children. If he didn't like the thought of her under King Rendall's thumb, it was because he hated bullies. Royal bullies especially. It was because he'd watched his mother struggle and did not want that for the mother of his own children. The children would watch, they would see. So it was for them.

He had believed all of that, until this very moment.

He *didn't* love Zia. Couldn't. What was there to love? He barely knew her.

Cristhian watched King Rendall's mouth move and move and move, but he heard nothing the man was blathering on about. The word *love* clattering around inside him like some kind of internal grenade.

He thought her selfish, even if she had described a childhood where at every turn she'd made some sacrifice to protect her sister. She had run away for *herself*, not their children.

He could picture her perfectly in that cozy little cabin on an arctic island. Roughing it, essentially. It was hard to convince himself that had been selfish, exactly. There had been some sacrifice involved.

But for her own gains.

Gains she hadn't attempted until she'd fallen pregnant. Then, very resourcefully, had escaped her royal chains and somehow lived for months on that tiny, isolated island. All those small, meaningful things she'd told him about doing the week she'd been exploring freedom, just to get a taste before taking on a marriage, an inheritance she didn't want, to protect her sister.

And only the appearance of their *children* had changed the course of that. Because she had put them first.

He hadn't wanted to believe that, but he'd seen her face when she'd seen Beaugonia.

That was love. Devotion. Zia was not selfish. Perhaps, if anything, she was a little too self*less*.

He blinked at this realization, at the warmth that seemed to settle over him when she smiled at him, when she let her guard down and *trusted* him. Something he'd broken now, but he'd had there for a few days.

And he heard his father's words once more.

I saw her across the room, and she was the most beautiful thing I'd ever seen. My heart stopped.

After their deaths, Cristhian had watched many videos of his father's interviews. Before and after he'd married his mother. In those first few years after Cristhian had lost them, he'd collected any and every scrap that might keep them alive to him, that might give him hope for a life beyond his mother's family's machinations.

Sometime in his teen years, he'd cut himself off. Realizing he had to focus on his future to escape his present, rather than dwell forever in a past he couldn't get back.

But that interview played in a loop in his head now. Because from that first moment of seeing Zia walk in the door at that bar, he had felt altered. And nothing had been the same since.

My heart stopped.

Something seemed to stop inside him then. Or start. Or break apart. He moved from behind his desk. "Your Majesty," he said firmly, interrupting the king's diatribe. "This is not Lille. And Zia is not your possession. I have my own money, my own power. I do not need your permission. I do not need to follow your orders. Here, you will follow mine. There will be a wedding tomorrow. You can be there, or not. But I will not be agreeing to anything with you or Lille."

King Rendall shoved to his feet. His cheeks turning a mottled shade of red. "Then you will not inherit a dime. And neither will they. Whatever marriage you think you can enact, I will invalidate."

"I don't need your dimes, sir. Your titles. I don't need any of it." He did not say it angrily. It was a simple, easy truth. "Your reach does not extend beyond your country, and we are not *in* your country."

The king *fumed*. For a moment or two, before turning on a heel and storming out of Cristhian's office.

It wasn't over, no, but Cristhian wasn't backing down. Because love or no, nothing changed what he had to do.

Protect Zia and their children at all costs.

"We have to wait until the last possible moment," Beau was saying as they got ready for bed that night. Zia had refused to attend dinner, which was perhaps petty, but she had been exhausted and known she wouldn't be up to dealing with her father *and* Cristhian.

Because already she was having doubts of her rebellion. The more excitedly Beau spoke of escape, the more tired Zia felt. The heavier her stomach seemed. Something inside her ached, and it was hard to think past it.

What kind of life was she making for her children if they ran away? What kind of life was she making for them if she stayed? And where did either option leave Beau?

"If they have time to look for you, then they could stop us," Beau continued, crawling into the huge bed next to Zia. "So we have to create some sort of trick where they *think* they know where we are, but we're on our way. That they don't come looking until the very last minute."

"Beau. Realistically. Where are we going to go? This is not as simple as it was," she said, gesturing at the very large bump under her blanket.

"What about your island? We still have that cabin for another few months."

"Even if I didn't think Cristhian would look there first, I can't go back with this." Maybe she could get by for a week or two, but soon enough the island would insist she return to the mainland until her babies were born.

Beau had her phone in her hand. "I'll come up with something," she said, the screen illuminating her face. No doubt researching all-new lives for them.

But… Zia couldn't dream of an all-new life anymore. She had to deal with the people in this one. Not just her children, but their father. "You can't find a new life for us before tomorrow."

"Before morning," Beau replied firmly. "You're not marrying that incredibly handsome monster."

Zia laughed in spite of herself. Incredibly handsome indeed. But… "He's not a monster, Beau. And…we have to face facts. Not only will I be incredibly recognizable now that Father knows I'm pregnant, I need access to a doctor. I need lots of things, Beau. I can't fly under the radar like I did. I know I said I needed help, but…"

"Zia." Beau turned to her side to give Zia a stern look. "You can't actually be considering marrying him."

But she was. Ever since tea with Mother, she hadn't been able to completely eradicate the idea of…just letting this happen.

"Mother was right. I was ready to marry Lyon. I never expected to marry for love. I never expected to have freedom. I want it for my children, of course, but… How can *I* give it to them? Father is a worst-case scenario. Cristhian isn't as bad as that."

She believed Cristhian at least had the potential to care about their children more than any legacy or *bloodlines*. He'd spoken of loving parents, grandparents. He expected there to be some…taking care of and putting the children first.

That was better than Father.

"He is the children's father, Beau," Zia said, and if it sounded like she was trying to convince herself, well, so be it. "That means something."

"Why?" Beau flopped onto her back. "I'd rather go through the rest of my life without dealing with *our* father."

"Cristhian isn't like him."

"He's forcing you to marry him."

"He…" Well, he *was* doing that, so how could she feel the need to defend him? After that beautiful moment of seeing their children, listening to their heartbeats, coming together again… He'd insisted on marriage. Without any care or concern about her.

He'd brought her parents here against her will. *And insisted Beau come along, too.* He'd once said he'd like to meet Beau because of the picture Zia painted.

Zia closed her eyes. She'd rather just sleep it all away. Wake up and maybe she'd have some new grand understanding of what was going on inside her.

"Zia, do you have feelings for him?" Beau asked carefully.

Zia wanted to deny it. She even opened her eyes and then her mouth, sure she could get the words out. But none came.

He was so very heavy-handed. So certain he knew what was right. Controlling.

And sometimes, she saw flashes of why. A boy who'd lost his parents at a young age, been thrust into someone else's world. He was trying to make his own world where he could never be upended again.

And she'd upended him. The children had upended him. But he hadn't gone to sleep and hoped it would all be better in the morning. He'd made decision after decision. Wrong decisions at times, but wasn't that better than her? Letting everyone else make the decisions for her.

Even when she'd first found out she was pregnant, she'd let Beau take the reins. Beau had planned her escape, essentially, and kept her going.

Cristhian hadn't disowned his soon-to-be children. Hadn't marched her back to Lille and her father, even though that's what he'd been hired to do. No, he'd taken control of that situation by insisting they work together. Put the children first.

Was that really as bad as she was making it out to be?

When he also made her heart hammer in her chest? When there was this physical chemistry that made every rational thought leave her?

Shouldn't she *want* to put the children above herself, like her mother never had? And wouldn't having two parents be better than…a mother who'd run away from their father? A mother who'd had not *one* good example of what being a good parent looked like, when their father had many?

It was enough to make her want to go to Cristhian and the minister right now and say *I do*.

But she was so worried she would become like her own mother. A shell of a person living only for the king. Or, in this case, Cristhian and *his* decisions.

And still… "I suppose I do have some sort of feelings for him," she said after a while, choosing each word carefully. "I'm not sure what they are. They're so jumbled. I'm so angry at him for pushing this marriage nonsense, and yet… I think… He speaks of his parents so…lovingly."

Zia swallowed. Beau was the only one in her whole life she could be fully honest with. Because Beau was honest back. Too blunt about it sometimes, but still. No games. No machinations. *Real*.

"It makes me think he knows what it takes to be a good parent, and that he'll be one. Maybe I need that."

"You'll be a good parent."

Beau said it with such confidence, but Zia had almost none. The closer she got to actually bringing them into the world, the more she worried how she would ever be the kind of mother that inspired the kind of feelings Cristhian had for his own. "How can you be so sure?"

"If you think he will be a good one because he had a good example, by the same logic, you will be a good one because you will know to do the opposite of our bad example."

Zia chuckled in spite of herself. It was impossible to argue with Beau's logic, but… The very simple truth was she did not know the correct course of action beyond what she did *not* want to happen.

Could she run away with Beau, somehow raise two children, free of all the controlling men in her life, and still give everyone what they deserved?

Beau needed freedom, too. She'd been dealing with their parents alone for months now. She deserved her own shot at something besides the palace and overbearing rules.

"We will be together, no matter what I decide. You aren't going back there. I promise you."

Beau was quiet for a long minute. "Zia, the truth of it all is, you care deeply about everyone and try to protect them. Maybe too much sometimes, but it is not like *our* mother. She is not evil, I know, but the only thing she has ever sought to protect is the peace. Sometimes, you need the fight. Sometimes bending *isn't* the answer, even if you get crushed."

Beau's hand found hers under the covers as she continued. "Those babies are lucky to have you as a mother, no matter what you decide. But I think you need to stop making decisions based on what's best for me."

Zia squeezed Beau's hand, turned to her in the dark. "But you can escape. Use my wedding to Cristhian as a diversion." At least that would make it worth something then. "You can take this as *your* freedom."

Beau squeezed her hand back. "You know I can't."

She didn't agree with her sister, but she understood to an extent. Beau never knew when a panic attack might hit, which made it harder to be on her own. Especially if she was trying to hide.

"At some point, you have to face yourself, Zia. Not me.

Not your babies. *You.* Long after your children are born and grown, you'll still be around, and then what? Who will you be when there's no one left to protect?"

The words made Zia teary-eyed. And scared. Facing herself? When she didn't understand herself outside of those hard lines she'd grown up bowing under? When the only role that had ever made any sense to her was to protect her sister?

She swallowed at the lump in her throat. "What if I don't know how?"

Beau's hand squeezed even tighter. "I guess it's time we both figured it out."

CHAPTER FOURTEEN

CRISTHIAN DID NOT sleep well. Too many things working against him. Old memories. New problems. Threats from a king. The look on Zia's face when he'd insisted they marry.

And though that haunted him most of all, or at least tied with his father's words repeating in his head like some kind of ominous guilty conscience, he began to make the arrangements.

Maybe Zia would hate him for eternity, but he would protect her. As his father had once protected his mother. She didn't have to like it or appreciate it for the course of action to be correct.

And if he was concerned that love was clouding his judgment, he set aside for after the wedding. When everything was settled and organized, and he could work through it all and twist it to his specifications. He would not *run away* from anything. He would make sure everything…worked. Everything made sense. *Everything* protected.

He needed to find the king to lay out the consequences of his actions. To explain what would happen, and what wouldn't happen. But the queen had insisted King Rendall was not in their suite, and none of the staff had seen him, so Cristhian searched his own grounds trying not to let frustration take hold.

He was nearing the wing with Zia's set of rooms, and his mood darkened even further at the thought King Rendall was bothering her. No, this would end *now*.

But before he made it to the door to Zia's suite, the king appeared in the hallway, exiting a mostly unused library.

He stopped, gave Cristhian one disgusted look, then stormed up to him. "I will agree to the wedding. Our lawyers will call yours. Once paternity is proven, everything will be sorted from a financial standpoint." His scowl turned into something closer to a sneer. "You and Zia will be free from any responsibility to the kingdom of Lille."

Cristhian could not remember a time in his adulthood when he'd been left as utterly speechless as he was now. He hadn't even made any of the arrangements that would impress upon the king he needed to agree for Zia's sake.

What had happened?

The king stormed away before Cristhian could find his voice. Could find any sense in this strange change of heart. He snorted to himself at the idea of King Rendall having a heart.

But then he heard a strange noise. Almost like a gasp. Strangled breathing? He poked his head into the room and saw a figure huddled in a corner amid covered furniture, arms wrapped around her knees.

Zia's sister. Who was struggling to breathe, clearly. Shaking like a leaf.

No doubt over something the king had done as this was the room he'd come out of all blusteringly angry. Cristhian strode forward.

"What did he do to you?" he demanded.

Beaugonia's body jerked in surprise, and her head came up with a snap. Her eyes were wild with something he could only call panic. But she shook her head, wiping the tears off her cheeks with the sleeve of her shirt, even as her arms shook. "N-n-nothing."

"This is not nothing."

No, it was a very large something that had more of his old memories surfacing from wherever in his psyche he'd packed them away as he'd stepped into adulthood.

All those times he'd simply thought his mother...*emotional*, he supposed, it had been more, hadn't it? More serious. More...this.

Whatever this was.

And every time his mother had behaved in this way, Cristhian had a clear memory of his father sitting next to her, taking her hand in his. He would press a kiss to her forehead, brush a hand over her hair, then tell her a story in low, calming tones. The same kind he had always delivered bedtime stories with.

As Zia's sister sat there, shaking and struggling to breathe easily, Cristhian knew he could not leave her. Even to fetch Zia or a staff member. He swallowed, then lowered himself to the ground next to her.

He wasn't sure how any of this would be received considering she no doubt viewed him as the enemy, but he took her hand anyway. It was cold, shaking. He tried to warm it in his. And when she didn't immediately pull away, or scramble away, or scream, he patted her hand.

He cast back to his memories. His father had always spoken to his mother. Told her stories. Movie stars he'd met. A ridiculous stunt he'd done. Cristhian hadn't realized it at the time, but now he realized it was to take his mother's mind off of whatever was upsetting her.

So Cristhian figured he should do the same, even if he did not know what upset Beaugonia, or anything about her, he knew one thing. She loved her sister.

So he started there.

"I met your sister at a bar." He could see it so clearly, even all these months later. "She walked in, her hair all cut off, dyed a ridiculous attempt at red. She was even wearing colored contacts. The blue eyes didn't look right, I knew that even then. And still, even with all that fake, she swept through me like a storm." He supposed he did not need to be giving the woman *quite* so much truth.

But he thought it was helping. Maybe he was delusional. "She asked the bartender for a menu. The bartender was clearly annoyed, so I offered a suggestion. I bought her the drink. We...talked. Of work responsibilities and freedom."

He had turned that conversation over and over in his head for those months between meeting her and seeing her again. And now he understood why she had been celebrating freedom, and dreading responsibility.

Now he understood in a way he hadn't let himself up until now that this was not the action of a selfish woman. No matter how much easier it would be if he believed that of her.

"Then she invited me to go dancing with her."

"I c-can't p-picture you d-dancing."

"Ah, but I am a fantastic dancer," Cristhian returned, pretending to be offended. "Your sister certainly thought so."

Beaugonia didn't laugh, but her mouth curved a little and some of the shaking seemed to have subsided. Her breathing was coming a little easier, and no more tears tripped over onto her cheeks.

"K-keep going," she said, then she met his gaze. "I w-want to hear it all from your p-point of view."

So he sat there on the floor, and told Zia's twin the entire story—from then to now.

* * *

With Beau nowhere to be found, Zia began to worry. Because her sister was no doubt up to something. Especially considering her parents would not come out of their suite to talk to her. And now she couldn't find Cristhian.

Something was definitely happening. Not even the staff could help her track down Cristhian, which felt so ominous nausea started roiling in her stomach. She had made almost a full circle upstairs when she finally heard a low male voice.

When she came to the open door where the voice was coming from, she looked in and then froze in utter shock.

Cristhian *and* Beau. They sat next to each other. Cristhian held Beau's hand gingerly. He was speaking in calm, low tones.

Beau had clearly had a panic attack, but she was on the other side of it now. Tears had tracked her cheeks, but she was breathing normally. Maybe she was a little shaky, but not the full-blown shakes she got in the midst of it. Her eyes weren't wild or panicked.

And Cristhian sat next to her. Right at her level, *holding her hand*. Zia's heart clutched. Because it looked like he was…comforting her. She could hear him now that she stood in the entrance to the room.

"I told myself I would not track her down after she left. It had only been meant to be that one night," he was saying. Like he was telling a story.

But Zia quickly realized it was *their* story.

"Six months, and I could not stop thinking about her. I told myself all sorts of reasons for why that was."

The same as she had done. So he hadn't forgotten about her the moment she'd left as she'd believed all this time.

Convinced she was just one woman in the midst of many. He'd thought of her. Couldn't stop.

It shouldn't soften her, or she didn't think it should. But he was sitting there on the ground, clearly comforting Beau with this story of *them* in the aftermath of a panic attack. He had not left her to fend for herself, had not called staff in to deal with it. He had clearly not told her to handle herself, as Father so often did.

He'd sat on the floor and held her hand. For what? There was no clear ulterior motive. Just the fact that he might be…good, underneath all that controlling.

"And what do you think the reason was?" Beau asked, but as she looked up at Cristhian, she must have caught a glimpse of Zia, because her chin jerked and her eyes widened.

So Cristhian looked over, too. He did not have the same surprise in his reaction, but he did not answer Beau's question. He got to his feet, then using the hand that had been holding Beau's, helped her up off the floor gently.

He did not seem disgusted or horrified. Zia stood there and saw with her own eyes as he gave Beau's hand a little squeeze before releasing it.

For a moment, Beau stood there looking at Cristhian with a considering expression before she carefully turned to Zia. Beau walked over to her and wrapped her arms around Zia.

"I'm going to go lie down," she whispered into Zia's ear, holding her tight.

Zia wanted to demand to know what was going on, but she knew Beau needed a good, quiet rest after an attack. "I'll come with."

"No. I'd like to be alone for a bit." Beau looked back at Cristhian, then at Zia. She continued to whisper. "Whatever you decide, I want you to know that it's okay. *I'm okay.*"

"Beau…"

But Beau released her and moved into the hallway. Zia wanted nothing more than to follow, but she knew her sister well enough to know that Beau did need the alone time now.

Cristhian approached, and Zia had to turn her attention to him. She had to clear her throat to speak, because she felt very shaken, uncertain. Confused about everything she'd just seen. "I should go after her, but she wanted to be alone."

"She was…very distraught when I came upon her," Cristhian said. Clearly being very careful about words to choose. But he had an expression on his face she didn't recognize. Something very…soft.

There was no point lying, Zia supposed. "She has panic attacks. They're often brought on by…stressful social situations." But there was nothing social going on, except dealing with Cristhian, she supposed. But Beau was usually fine with anyone one-on-one. "I cannot fathom what might have brought this one on."

"Your father was in the room with her before I got here. I do not know what was discussed, but he was angry and she upset."

Zia's expression darkened. "Well, that will do it." She was glad she had a lifetime of learning how to handle her temper and she no longer went tearing into her father after one of his arguments with Beau.

That had always ended badly for Beau in the long run. He'd often made Beau even more a prisoner in the castle after that. Kept Zia from seeing her. Kept anyone from seeing her until Beau could "handle herself."

So Zia had learned to keep her anger internalized. Plan little rebellions. Ones that had no chance of hurting Beau.

And for the past few months, while Beau had been helping her with her own, who had Beau had? No one. Zia couldn't take back protecting her children, but what she *could* do was make decisions in the here and now that did both things.

Zia would get Beau out of this. She looked up at Cristhian…who had been kind in the face of Beau's panic attack. She could tell from the position she'd found them in, from Beau's reaction.

But he was looking at the door, a strange frown on his face. "Panic attacks."

Zia braced herself for an insensitive comment. The ones her parents and their staff had leveled at Beau her whole life. Cristhian had been kind to Beau's face, but there was no way he could understand—

"It was so familiar," he said, as if in a kind of trance. "I think… My mother had them. I simply thought she was crying, but it was like that. The shaking, the struggling to breathe. I never understood. I don't know if *they* did." He said it like he was lost in some old memory.

And was potentially realizing his mother might have been a real and complex person, even if his memories were from a child's perspective of simplifying things. But children knew. They understood the world around them, often better than adults understood, or at least differently.

Cristhian was clearly having a moment of clarity, and she yearned to give him more, if she could. "Do you think they were brought on by her leaving her family?" She certainly wouldn't be having any panic attacks about that, but maybe it was more complicated than she was giving it credit for.

"She never fully left. They wouldn't allow it. Even disapproving of my father, they did not want to lose their control over her completely. So she struggled with the way they treated her. So often they tried to stir up false stories. Infidelities. Abuse. My parents never believed these things, and the media never could seem to make the accusations stick, either. It was all...mind games, but the complications went away if she attended the events they wanted. I always thought her reaction was just the stress. I have always blamed her family for pushing at her, tearing at her, but some small part of me... I have always felt guilty of it, but deep down I blamed her, too. For running instead of standing up to them."

Zia watched him, surprised to find this moment of pure vulnerability. He was coming to some new conclusions and allowing her to be a part of it. She wanted to reach out and comfort him, and she would have held herself back. Even now, she would have held herself back.

But he'd comforted Beau. So she reached out and took his had in hers, as he had done for her sister.

"Sometimes running away is the only option we have. Sometimes, there is no standing up, no matter how much we'd like to."

He looked at her then. Still caught up in his past, but she knew he saw the connection, and because she did, she felt even softer toward him. She had never realized until this moment, and maybe he had not fully either, just how much *running* represented something horrible to him.

"I did not realize that perhaps she was not able to stand up to them," he said, his voice low, strained. "No matter how she tried. And my father tried. To protect her from it, but he couldn't, either. Because it wasn't them. It was her."

She tried to drop his hand. Every time she thought she

glimpsed some human part of him… "People are not to blame for the ways their brains and bodies betray them."

But he squeezed her hand so she could not pull away. And then he held it gently. So gently it seemed wrong to pull her arm away.

"No, that is not how I mean it, Zia. I did… I think. I loved my mother more than anything, but still I blamed her for that. Somewhere. Deep down. Until I saw your sister and understood." He swallowed, as if some deep emotion was clogged there in his throat.

Which in turn made her own throat feel tight. That a man so bent on control could acknowledge that maybe… maybe he was not always right, maybe he didn't *always* understand every little thing.

"No one could protect my mother, and that was wrong. My father tried with all he was, but he couldn't… He wasn't given the time to accomplish this goal," he said, some conviction and strength returning to his voice. "I know you don't want to marry me. I understand you think I will rule your life as your father has. But, Zia, I will protect you. I will protect our children. I will protect Beaugonia and anyone else you'd like me to."

Her heart began to beat double time in her chest. She knew he could lie if he wanted to, but he spoke with a fervency she did not know how to take as anything but truth. The kind of promise she'd never been given before.

"I can make certain we marry, Zia. I can make certain I protect you no matter what. But if you could see my side of things, it will be easier. For everyone. If you can agree, without a fight, without an escape attempt, we can make a world that is better for our children than what we ended up with."

She should be offended that he thought she couldn't say

no, that she couldn't escape, no matter what, but he was talking to something bigger now. Protection.

Of the babies. Of Beau. Of *her*.

These were words and promises she'd wanted. These were words that made everything she needed to do okay. Her babies and Beau free of her father. It should be enough, but...

"Because you hate what royalty did to your mother? Because you could not protect her, and she could not protect you?"

His dark eyes studied her, like he was taking in every line and curve of her face. So much so she thought maybe there would be...some other answer. Maybe she even held her breath hoping for some *more*.

"Yes."

It was less than she wanted from Cristhian, and still more than she'd dared hope for when it came to a future marriage. It was what she'd tried to live her life for. To protect Beau, and then these babies once she'd learned of them. So how could she say no? He was offering her a way out of the walls that had held her and the people she loved captive.

Maybe there would be new walls involved, but in protecting everything she held dear, did it matter? He was offering more than she'd had under her father's thumb, and maybe in that there would be some space for her own say.

"All right." She tried to manage a smile, but couldn't quite get there. "I'll marry you."

CHAPTER FIFTEEN

CRISTHIAN HAD ALREADY made certain all the wedding plans were in place. He had foreseen no circumstance where the wedding would *not* happen. But now that Zia had agreed, he expected to feel an even stronger sense of certainty. He would not have to thwart any escapes or overcome any overzealous nos.

Everything should be fine and settled with her agreement and everyone in the household on the same page.

If anything, as he got word the minister would be arriving shortly, he felt the opposite. As though her saying she would marry him without incident harvested an entire field of doubts inside him.

Which was ridiculous. Marriage was the right course of action. And he would protect her, their children, her sister. Anyone else. From all that the monarchy so carelessly hurt.

That was the legacy his father had left him.

And look how that turned out.

He shook his head. They weren't running away. If anything, they were standing up to the pressures. Just as he had done as a young man, extricating himself from a family who had never cared about anything other than their own reputations.

He was taking that need to run away from her. *For* her. In all the ways he'd been too young to do it for his parents.

He had been a success ever since he'd stepped away from his mother's family. So how could getting Zia away from hers not be a success?

And the king had agreed. Even now, their lawyers were hashing out the details. All necessary agreements would be completed and signed before the small ceremony tonight.

But what had caused the king's change of heart? Something to do with Beaugonia. It had to be. The timing made no sense otherwise. Which was really none of his business.

So he tried to convince himself. Still, the worry, the confusion, the frustration lingered.

If whatever had gone on between the king and Beaugonia hurt Zia…

Eventually, Cristhian could not stand it any longer. He had one of his staff members hunt down Beau and bring her to him. Without Zia.

It took longer than he would have liked. First his lawyers swept in with their concerns and paperwork. Things the king had tried to sneak by them, things they had tried to sneak by the king. But in the end, Cristhian had what he wanted.

A legal guarantee Zia would not be required to fulfill any royal duties she did not wish, that their children would make their own decisions on if they would like titles or not. A small and, to Cristhian's mind, unnecessary inheritance, but he wouldn't fault the king for that.

All would go into place once he and Zia were married, and then all would be just as Cristhian wanted it. Everyone protected as he saw fit. By the law and his own hand.

And still no sense of calm came over him.

When Beaugonia was ushered into his office, he was certain once he dealt with her, he would feel it. She was the last loose thread.

"Good afternoon, Cristhian," she offered cheerfully, though he didn't fully believe the cheer. "It seems you are in desperate need of my company."

"I have an important question to ask you, Your Highness." He walked over to the door, closed and locked it himself. Beaugonia looked at the knob with great suspicion, so Cristhian stayed by the door rather than approach her. It was not his goal to make her uncomfortable.

But he had to know the truth.

"I would like to know what you and your father discussed this morning that had such an…effect on you."

Beau looked him up and down, head cocked to one side. "Too bad."

For a moment, he couldn't speak. When he did, he was alarmed to find his voice had raised an octave. "I beg your pardon."

"I don't want you to know. So you won't. Not yet, anyway." Then she shrugged. As if that was that.

He supposed he finally saw some of the resemblance between the two sisters. Stubbornness in direct opposition to his goals.

"Princess—"

"You saw me through a panic attack, Cristhian. I think you can call me by my name."

It was hard to reconcile this self-possessed woman with the woman from this morning, shaking and struggling to breathe, the one he'd initially met who hid behind her parents and didn't speak. And yet he'd always seen his mother as a whole, complicated woman, hadn't he? Sometimes she was upset, and sometimes she had it all handled. She was not all one thing.

Perhaps none of them were all *one* thing.

"Beaugonia," he said then, keeping his gaze on hers. A

firmness in his tone so she could understand he was serious and would not be deterred. He needed answers. With answers, everything would be sorted. "Your father had a seemingly miraculous change of heart after charging out of that room. I would like to know what caused it, and if it might affect Zia in some way that she is not aware of."

Beau didn't react to this right away. She stood, still and blank-expressioned. Then she turned away from him, walking around his office, poking at books on shelves, papers on his desk. She settled herself at the window, looking out over a world of white.

"Everything I do is for my sister," she said at last. "For the entirety of my life, she has put herself in front of me like a human shield. Because I was different and couldn't be what our parents wanted me to be. Well, I'm old enough, clever enough and aware enough now to deal with all that. Strong enough to be the one shielding Zia this time around, so she can protect those children." She met his gaze then, direct and determined. "I would do anything to keep my parents from having any influence on another generation."

"I may not know your sister as well as you do, but I can assure you, she wouldn't want you to sacrifice yourself for anything."

"No," Beaugonia said with a smile. But it didn't last long. Her mouth curved back into a frown. "But I didn't always want her to protect me at great cost to herself. Helping someone isn't always about *wants*. I suppose that's love, all in all."

Love. Cristhian did not like how this topic kept coming up, how it seemed to root him to the spot. Like an anchor.

Drowning him? It should feel like it was drowning him, against his will. But he had a strange new thought then.

An anchor didn't drown. It tethered. Kept a boat secured to an important shore.

And if love…could be an anchor. If he loved Zia, told her that, would she stay tethered to his very important shore?

What the hell was wrong with him thinking in boat analogies?

But then Beaugonia crossed the room to him. She stopped a few feet away, but he could see Zia stamped all over her. The soft cast of her mouth, the intelligence behind her eyes. All behind a very thin mask of wariness.

But willing to brave the wariness to do what needed to be done, say what needed to be said. Protect who needed protecting.

How could he not respect that?

"I think you might be a good man, Cristhian Sterling. And if you're not, I'll make sure to make you suffer. But for now, I'm entrusting you to protect Zia. And that niece and nephew of mine."

"There is nothing I take more seriously. I could protect you, too. Now, or in the future should you need it."

She smiled. "That is very kind. Zia never mentioned you were such a softy."

He scowled a little at that, and she laughed, reminding him of Zia.

"Should I need it, I'll take you up on that help. But for now, I need you to leave this. To make Zia leave it as well. These are the things I need to do for my sister, with no interference. Please."

Cristhian normally would have left nothing. Not for anyone.

But with *love* rattling around inside him, some unwieldy thing, he could only nod and let Beaugonia go.

* * *

Zia had needed a nap before she was to start getting ready for the wedding. She hadn't slept well last night due to stress, and the aches and pains of pregnancy were really announcing themselves because of it.

It was just the stress of everything. The doubts. The fear she was making a mistake. The fear she was doing what was right, what needed to be done, and it would still somehow turn out all wrong.

The loop of wondering if thinking you knew what the right thing to do was an endless generational curse on your children.

And worse, so much worse, silly little fantasies about somehow…somehow creating a real marriage with Cristhian. Something with chemistry and trust and partnership and…love.

Oh, honestly. Could she be more foolish?

She maneuvered her way up and out of bed. She had to pause once she was standing, breathe deeply a few times through all the anxiety making breathing feel harder than it should. That and two babies squishing up against her lungs making it impossible to take a full breath. Every day it seemed a little bit more impossible that this could go on for *weeks*.

And still she wasn't eager for the alternative. She took a step, a sharp pain lodging itself in her side. Sort of like a cramp after running too hard and long. And certainly too far to the side to be anything involving the children. She'd probably pulled a muscle or something while she was sleeping, or maybe when she'd struggled to get up off the bed.

She took another step and the pain loosened a little, so she went in search of Beau. But as she went from room to room in their suites, she was nowhere to be found. She couldn't find her mother, either, which was odd since they had said they would be ready to help her get ready once she woke up.

She searched the entire upstairs to no avail. The pain in her side pretty much disappeared, until she started going down the stairs. Then it started up again. She stretched her arm up above her head, moved around a bit, and it went away.

Once downstairs, she decided to find Cristhian, see if he knew what was going on. Staff members were scarce. Alejandra had said most of them were in the main ballroom getting it ready for the ceremony. So she went to the rooms Cristhian favored, starting with his office.

He sat behind his desk, frowning over a stack of papers. Zia stood in the entrance, simply watching him for a silent moment.

In a few short hours, she would agree to marry this man. She would commit herself to a life of...controlling behavior. He would do everything *he* thought was right, and she would have no say.

But did it matter if he was doing it to love and protect their children? He had been kind to Beau, when so many people had not been—including their own parents. Should their children struggle with something, he would be kind to them, too.

What more could she really ask for? Love? When the only love she had ever witnessed was the kind that sacrificed self over all else?

She shook her head. She had to find Beau. She had to go through with this, so Beau could escape. She would find a way to make sure Beau got out. With Cristhian's help, she could do it.

He glanced up, as if he'd sensed her there. He got to his feet, something like concern flitting over his face. "Is everything all right?" he asked when she didn't speak.

She moved a little farther into the office, trying to focus on the task at hand. "Have you seen my sister?"

Cristhian looked at her and frowned. "Are you quite all right? You're looking pale."

"Fine. Just tired. But I can't find my mother or Beau. I asked Alejandra to search for them, but it's been quite a while now and she hasn't returned either." The pain seized her side again, and she rubbed at it, taking a few more steps into his office in hopes of soothing it out.

"You couldn't find any of them?"

Zia shook her head. "Mother and Beau are supposed to help me get ready for the ceremony. I don't know where they could be."

Cristhian skirted his desk, but before he moved fully to her or said anything else, one of his staff members entered the room. The man cleared his throat.

"Sir, I am to inform you that the king and queen and the princess have left."

"Left?" Cristhian and Zia echoed at the same time.

"Yes, sir. Just now. I was just told of this and came to relay it immediately."

"Why was I not informed of their plan?" Cristhian demanded, and he seemed *very* convincing in his surprise, so Zia didn't think he was acting.

"I'm very sorry, sir. Apparently they made all of the arrangements themselves. The princess even carried their bags out to the waiting vehicle. No one knew about it until just now, when they were seen driving away."

Zia was utterly speechless, but the man turned to her. Held out an envelope.

"This was left in their rooms with your name on it, ma'am."

Zia took the envelope with nerveless fingers. It was her sister's handwriting on the outside, and on the inside as well.

Zia,

I've got this under control.

Love,

B

It made no sense. Why would Beau go off with Mother and Father? Why would any of this be happening before the wedding that was supposed to make everything all right?

"Cristhian, we have to… We have to go after her." The pain in her side was getting worse, but she tried to ignore it. "I don't know what's going on, but I prom…" She couldn't finish the word. A wave of pain seemed to clamp down on her.

Cristhian was at her side immediately. "Are you in pain? What is it?"

"Just…" But she couldn't quite get the words out. She had to grit her teeth against the wave of tension that seized her body.

"Go get the doctor," he said in harsh tones, and the man quickly disappeared.

"Cristhian." Zia was panting now, though she couldn't understand why. Maybe *she* was having a panic attack. "She can't just leave."

"Once we have you settled, I will see what I can do. But for now, we must have you checked out. Yes?" But he wasn't allowing her a chance to respond, he was just ushering her to a different room. One with a couch.

He eased her onto it. That did help, lying down. Cristhian crouched next to her, brushed some hair off her face in a move so gentle her heart stuttered.

"I promise, I will do what I can, but I think your sister had some plans of her own. I know I can't tell you not to worry about her, but I think she has a better control of whatever situation she's in than you think."

"Her letter. She said she has it under control."

Cristhian nodded, his gaze never leaving hers, his fingers still on her face.

"I believe her. Your parents have their deep, deep faults, Princesa, but they have raised two very capable women."

Zia didn't know why that made her want to cry, but the tears filled her eyes. She didn't let them fall, mostly because the doctor strode in, bag in hand. She went straight for the couch, immediately shooing Cristhian out of the way.

"What has happened, Your Highness?"

Cristhian opened his mouth, but the doctor held up a hand. "In the patient's own words, thank you."

Cristhian clamped his mouth shut, though he looked stormy and angry about it, which almost amused Zia enough to smile.

"My side was hurting," Zia told the doctor. "I thought I'd simply slept on it wrong, but it got worse."

The doctor had her point to where it hurt, asked her more questions about the pain, then enlisted Cristhian to help arrange things so the doctor could do a more in-depth exam.

The doctor made considering noises as she took different vital signs, both from Zia and from the babies, then poked around at this and that. When she was done, and she let Cristhian help Zia into a more comfortable position on the couch, she smiled at both of them.

"Everything is just fine."

The doctor's words sent a wave of relief through her, even though she still worried about Beau. About what her father thought he was doing making them all leave before the wedding even happened.

"I think I was just panicking," Zia said on a whisper.

The doctor shook her head. "Princess, you've begun to dilate, and you're having some very minor contractions. Perhaps panic played a role, but that's not the whole story. You'll want to stay in bed for the next few days. We'll monitor, make sure everything calms down. It should, but stress is to be avoided."

The doctor glanced at Cristhian, then returned her gaze to Zia and smiled. "Rest. Relax. That's the best thing for you right now. Should you have more pain, call me immediately."

Zia managed to nod at the doctor. Everything was fine. *Fine*. She placed her hands over her stomach, felt a tiny little roll against her palm. They were good.

But what about Beau?

"Once the pain is completely gone, move her up to her room," the doctor was telling Cristhian. "She should stay there. All meals brought to her. Supervision when she needs to get up. This is very common, particularly with multiples, but it'll require some more care taken from the day-to-day to make sure she isn't overtaxing herself."

"I will make certain she doesn't."

The doctor nodded. "Either of you, fetch me if you need anything." And then she was gone as quickly as she'd come.

Cristhian stood at the threshold to the room. He didn't say anything, and a long silence stretched out between them. Until Zia couldn't take it any longer.

"I suppose we'll have to postpone the wedding then."

He gave a short little nod. "Of course."

"I didn't mean for…"

"Zia." He sounded pained. "Of course you didn't. Our number one priority is that you and the children are healthy. Weddings can wait."

"But—"

"You need not worry. Doctor's orders. Trust me. I promised you. I will protect you all. Beau included."

She studied him then, and there was something different about him. A softness she had not fully seen in him before—at least before he hid it behind that arrogance and control. She understood that Beau's panic attack had made him realize things about his mother, and she supposed that's why he was offering to be so supportive of her, but…

"Why, Cristhian? I understand the children are yours, but Beau and I are not. You don't owe us your protection."

"I have never been a fan of the word *owe*. It was used against me for many years. What I *owed* my mother's legacy." He shook his head. "But what I discovered in those difficult years is that anyone's life is a tapestry. What might life have been like if my mother's family had included my father's, instead of trying to fight a war? My children will have all the pieces they can of people who will put them first. That includes their mother, and their aunt."

"Aunt," Zia repeated. She'd spent so much of the past few months trying to set up a life for her children, but she admittedly had spent little time thinking of them as…little people in the world, in *her* world. Calling Beau *Aunt*. And Cristhian *Father*.

"Family protects, or it should. So that is what we will do." He took her hand then, clasped it between his two much larger ones. "But I'm discovering there is more, Zia.

Quite unexpectedly, I find myself...being in love with you."

Love. For a moment, she didn't breathe, but even when she reminded herself to, she didn't say anything.

Ever since he'd introduced the idea, what felt like forever ago but was only perhaps a week now, she had been convinced that she would allow him to fall in love with *her*. That this would be best, really. And she would stay perfectly...detached. She would use his love as a kind of safeguard, but she would not allow herself to feel that much, that deeply, so that it ended up affecting her choices when it came to their children.

So she didn't speak. Even with her heart racing in her chest, even with this strange...elation soaring through her. She didn't respond to him.

He could love her, and that would be okay. Best even.

But she would not allow herself to love him.

Ever.

CHAPTER SIXTEEN

AFTER A TIME, Cristhian helped Zia back upstairs to her room. He tucked her into bed, then began to give instructions to staff about how to proceed while she was on bed rest. Including moving some of his things into her suite.

He would be here through the night, and as long as he needed until he felt assured that all would be well. He trusted the doctor, but his brain had not yet taken the doctor's assurances on board.

Perhaps his brain was no longer functioning, since he had told Zia that he was in love with her.

She had very purposely not said it back.

This was fine, perhaps even best. It allowed him to make the right choices. Love did not need to be reciprocal to put things in their place.

He would love her, and their children, and *that* would be the settled, controlled feeling he was searching for.

So he made sure an array of foods were brought up for her to eat, a drink within arm's reach at all times, and he ignored her protests when he settled himself into a chair and insisted he would not leave until she fell asleep.

Once she finally did, he watched her for a time. The slow, steady rise and fall of her breathing. Everything was under control, because he had put everything in perfect place. The doctor on property, quick to drop in and make certain everything was okay.

Perhaps the wedding had not gone according to plan, perhaps nothing with Zia's family had, but he had rolled with every punch.

Perhaps he had not fully thought through love declarations, but what did a few words matter?

His phone began to buzz for what felt like the hundredth time. He finally pulled it out of his pocket and looked at the screen. He had quite a few messages, but he ignored all of them except the one from his grandparents. He moved out of Zia's bedroom and into one of the exterior rooms where he could make a call to them without waking Zia. They had been expecting to video into his wedding, so no doubt they were concerned they'd missed something.

His grandmother's kitchen table appeared on the screen, and Cristhian smiled in spite of himself. "Hello, Grandmother. Your camera is backward."

She muttered something, then got it to turn around so that both his grandparents' faces were on the screen.

"I apologize," he said, surprised at how stiff he sounded. "The ceremony had to be postponed. Zia begun to have some contractions. She is to be on bed rest for the next few days, and then we will reevaluate."

"How frightening for her," Grandmother said, a worried frown crossing her features.

"Indeed."

"And you."

Indeed.

She had been looking pale, pained. So worried about Beaugonia when she should be worrying about herself.

"What can we do, Cristhian?" his grandfather asked gently.

What can we do?

They had always asked that. Even when there was an ocean of impossibility between them, they had always asked what they could do. Not what *he* could do. Not what *he* could offer.

"Nothing." He smiled thinly. "But thank you. The doctor assures us all is well, and that is the most important thing now. The wedding will commence once she's better, and I'll make certain you're able to watch."

"Yes, of course. We'll watch whenever it is. But, dear, are you sure *you're* all right?"

"It has been…a stressful day."

"Tell us," Grandfather urged gently.

For much of his early adulthood, he had sat down and done just that. Dumped everything on his grandparents, and then listened to their advice. Sometimes he'd taken it. Sometimes he hadn't. But either way, he'd never been worried about their censure, and they'd always been there, ready to listen to his next conundrum, no matter the outcome of the last.

For the past few years, he had not leaned on them as much. He was an adult. In charge of his life. He worried about their health, the effect stress or worry would have on them.

But tonight, when they encouraged him to tell, he sat down and did just that. King Rendall. Beaugonia's panic attack and the clarity it gave him. Down to telling Zia he loved her. And her saying nothing back.

"Well, that is *certainly* a stressful day," Grandfather said after a bit.

"It is under control, though," Cristhian said. "Zia has agreed to marry me. Her father has agreed to let her go. All will be well."

His grandparents shared one of their looks.

"You do understand you can't control *life*, Cristhian."

Cristhian didn't have a quick return for that. It wasn't that he thought he was controlling *life*, just that if he organized things a certain way, all would be well. If he got everyone to agree to his way of things, then things would turn out the way they should.

That wasn't *control*. It was just…being in charge, being successful, not letting life knock you out. Because you were protected.

"Once we are married, everything will fall into place. Zia does care for me," Cristhian said, sure he was comforting them…and not himself. Because there was *something* between Zia and him, or they wouldn't be in this predicament.

"Cristhian, you can't *make* anyone love you. You can't perfect all the conditions so they decide to. You can only honor your own feelings and your own needs. While respecting theirs."

Cristhian tried to reject those words, but he'd never been any good at ignoring his grandparents' wisdom. They'd been there, every step they could be. The only solid points in his life along with his parents' memory.

And even that had been rocked by his realizations this morning about panic attacks. About how deep everything with his mother had gone. And now, in this moment, that someday he would not have his grandparents' wisdom to rely on.

Life and time would march on. Both too short, and infinite, all at the same time. Everything he'd been trying to control, since that moment he'd lost his parents, was an exercise in futility.

"You know," Grandmother said after the silence had

stretched on too long. "I said I love you to your grandfather first and he didn't say anything back."

"That is not true!"

"It is absolutely true," Grandmother shot back. "You were so busy playing with that damn dog of yours—"

"Which means I didn't *hear* you, not that I didn't *say it back*."

"I think you heard me."

They bickered like that for a few minutes, shoulder to shoulder, smiling even as they disagreed. About events long gone. And through that time and this time, they had loved each other. Weathered storms and tragedies and challenges, alongside joys.

Cristhian had spent his life with these examples of love. So much so he'd been sure love was the answer.

And he supposed it was. But not just the words. Something bigger. Something deeper. Not love as an agent of *control*, but something far more terrifying.

"Thank you."

"For what?" Grandfather asked, confusion drawing his bushy white brows together.

"For being yourselves. It has been an invaluable part of my life." One that Zia did not have. So, no, he could not control things to ensure her feelings. But what he could do, but what he would do, was give her something she'd never had.

And spread that love and support to their children, no matter where life took them.

They said their I-love-yous and their goodbyes. For a moment Cristhian sat in the darkened room and just listened to his own breathing.

You can't make anyone love you.

Had he thought he could? No, it was more complicated

than that. Perhaps he'd rested too much on the idea that love would be the answer. That if she loved him, he would get what he wanted.

Also simplistic, when his feelings were anything but.

He returned to her bedroom. She was still asleep.

He had received confirmation that the royal family had returned to their castle in Lille. He still did not know what had happened, but he had decided to trust that Beaugonia had it all under control, as she'd claimed.

And for the first time in his life since he'd lost his parents, he had to trust that control was *not* the answer.

Letting go was.

Zia woke up. Her room was dim, the curtains drawn, but she noted there was sunlight creeping around the edges. She glanced at the clock. It was well into the morning. She'd slept a ridiculous amount.

She stretched in the bed, took stock of her body. She did feel better than she had at any point yesterday. More herself, or at least her healthy pregnant self. She yawned and pushed herself into a tentative sitting position, ready for any little twinge that she thought meant she should lie back down.

But none came. She let out a long breath of relief, then studied the dim room around her. She startled a bit when she realized there was a body on the little lounge in the corner. Cristhian. Fast asleep.

So handsome it nearly took her breath away. Had he really said he loved her, or was that some dream she'd had? Or maybe another machination. Could she put that past him?

She watched him sleep, her heart twisting in a million little knots. He had said he *loved* her, and she did not know how to take it for a lie. But *why*? She had finally agreed to marry him; he didn't need to make up stories now.

So why had he said it?

His phone vibrated in his pocket, and this seemed to wake him. He didn't notice her sitting and looking at him as he pulled his phone out of his pocket. He frowned at the screen, poked at it a few times, then shook his head.

When he looked up, he didn't register any surprise that she was sitting there watching him, but something did cross his expression. A kind of resignation. He got to his feet, walked over to the bed.

"Good morning. Did you sleep?"

She nodded.

"Zia…" He sighed, like he was about to deliver bad news. "I want to make something clear before I tell you what's happened."

"What's happened?"

But he ignored her. "We do not need to marry, if you'd rather not. We can live here, or at one of my other estates, and raise the children together. As…friends, I suppose you'd call it. We can find a way. It was wrong of me to think only marriage could accomplish this."

Her mouth dropped open, like all her facial muscles had deserted her in shock. He was admitting he was wrong? Just as she'd finally agreed to marry him, he was saying they didn't have to? *After* he'd said he *loved* her? "Why are you saying this?"

"To be clear, I think marrying would be best. I think you could learn to love me. I think we could build a family, putting our children first. Protecting them. But your sister said something to me that has stuck with me. She did not always appreciate your protection, and yet what she's done was out of love and a gratefulness for that pro-

tection. So that you would take a turn at…living your own
life, I suppose. So I want you to have a chance at that life
that *you* choose. Because I, too, love you."

There was that word again, and she just…didn't know
what to do with it. So she focused on her sister. "What
has she done?"

He handed her his phone and Zia looked at the arti-
cle on the screen. The headline was in big block letters:
Princess Beaugonia Rendall, Newly Minted Heir of Lille,
Weds Crown Prince Lyon Traverso of Divio in Private
Ceremony!

Zia could only stare, reading the headline over and over
again until she finally found her voice. "She can't do that."

"It seems she already has," Cristhian said gently, taking the phone from her hand.

"But how? I don't…" Zia shook her head.

"She set you free."

So why did it feel like she was drowning? Facing down
some unknown future instead of one that was clear. "I
didn't ask to be set free! I am not *free*!" Zia pushed out of
bed, not sure where she thought she was going. "She is
my sister. I love her, and I'm worried for her."

Cristhian stood in her way, then gently nudged her back
onto the bed. Because she was on *bed rest*.

"Sit. Rest."

She did as she was told because those were the doctor's
orders and she would follow them. But…how could she
just lie here while her sister… She shook her head. This
couldn't be true.

"Cristhian. This is why my father agreed to let me go.
She took my place." She looked up at him, on the verge
of tears. And his expression was sympathetic. But he simply nodded.

"Yes, that is what it looks like."

"What am I to do if…?"

At some point, you have to face yourself, Zia. Not me. Not your babies. You.

Beau had said that to her. And now she was forcing Zia to do it. Not just her, but Cristhian, too. It wasn't fair. "Why are you doing this to me?"

He cocked his head, as if he didn't understand the accusation. Maybe *she* didn't understand it either, but it felt better to demand it of him than figure out what was going on inside her.

"I don't think I am doing anything *to* you, Zia. I am giving you a choice."

She stared at him, bowled over by such a sentence. By the realization that swelled through her. "I have never had a choice. Not about anything." It was an exaggeration, she supposed. She had *chosen* to protect Beau. She had *chosen* to have her little week rebellion, then run away for good when she discovered the consequences.

But no one had ever looked at her and told her she did not have to think about consequences. She could just *choose*. And everything would be taken care of regardless of her choice.

"Not long ago, I would have scoffed at that, but I think you're right in a way. I think everything you have done has been in reaction to something. To protect someone. So here we are. With no one left to protect. Because your sister has made her choice, and I have ensured our children's protection. So it might be difficult and uncomfortable, but it is time, Zia. Make a choice for yourself."

She stared at him, completely and utterly lost. Make a choice for *her*? Without thought to anyone else? She didn't… She couldn't…

"You have time, *Princesa*. There is no rush. I thought I knew how it should all go to make it exactly right. I suppose, in a way, I've been searching for exactly right since I lost my parents. I have tried to control you, because I thought it was best. *Right*. But there is no exactly right. None to be had. So we will take whatever time we need to make every next step. Perhaps not all the right ones, but if we put our children first, they will be right enough."

He took her hand, kept saying these words that seemed to tear down all the protections she'd so carefully hung up over the years. They'd started crumbling when Beau had told her to make choices for herself, and now there was nothing left.

He'd taken it all away.

"I have not been the same since you walked into my life, Zia. I thought I could put that into a neat little order, control it all, make it be what I wanted. That is how I am used to dealing with my life being upended."

"*My* life was upended."

"Yes. We both have been forced to face the consequences of our actions. I'm not sure either of us handled it as well as perhaps we should have, but we have not done irreparable damage. We have done our best, and now we'll do better."

"By *not* marrying?"

"By choosing, Zia. On my end, I choose you. I have fallen in love with you. Your strength and protective spirit. Your beauty and your wit. But regardless of my feelings, I think we can raise these children mostly on the same page. And that is what I vow to do, regardless of what you choose for yourself."

"Cristhian…"

"So you take your time. You think on what *you* vow to do. For yourself."

At some point, you have to face yourself, Zia. Not me. Not your babies. You.

Cristhian watched over her for the next few days, barely leaving her side, but he did not push the matter. The doctor gave her the all clear to leave bed rest, but she was cautioned to listen to her body, to watch for signs she needed to rest.

He gave her space then. They ate dinner together, but unless she requested his presence, he stayed away.

And she found it didn't take long at all to miss him. At first, she convinced herself it was just the company she missed. She was lonely.

But Beau called her every day. She wouldn't give too much away about her new life as a married woman, but she didn't seem upset or unhappy. She seemed very much herself.

And still, Zia longed for Cristhian. There was something comforting about his presence. In so many different ways.

"So," Beau drew out, making Zia realize she'd zoned out of their conversation. "I take it you haven't decided what to do about Cristhian."

"I am still living here, aren't I?"

"That's not a decision, Zia. That's staying still hoping someone swoops in and makes the decision for you."

She wasn't hoping for that. She didn't think. "How am I supposed to just *decide* if I love him, or if I could? They are feelings. Not decisions. Not math facts."

"I am learning all sorts of fascinating things about being married to a man I barely know. One of them is this. I do not question whether or not I love Lyon. I *know* I do not."

"It isn't that simple," Zia insisted. How could it be? She

had a relationship with Cristhian. It wasn't just taking on an arranged marriage.

"Hmm," Beau replied.

"It *isn't*. I'm confused because… He says he loves me, Beau, but how could he? Why would he? We only barely know each other. I have nothing to offer him, really. I can't do any protecting, play some role in his life. I am simply the mother of his children."

"Nothing to offer… Zia, it's not a *transaction*."

"No, but…"

"Zia, you don't have to be useful to him for him to love you. You know that, don't you?"

"I don't think…" But she supposed, in a way, she didn't understand why he would claim love when there was nothing she was really giving him, beyond birthing their children.

"It doesn't take Psychology 101 to determine that's a warped thought no doubt brought on by how our parents treated you as heir. I love you regardless of what you've done for me."

"You're my sister."

"Yes, and I happen to think you're smart and funny and delightfully spiteful, when you want to be. I know you'll be as wonderful a mother as you were a sister. So, again, why wouldn't Cristhian love that? You're beautiful, and clearly your chemistry is through the roof. I think these are the things normal people use to determine love."

Zia didn't have the words to answer that. Mostly because she didn't think Beau was *wrong*, per se, just…how could that apply to her? She didn't want to delve into that. "How is Lyon treating you?"

She could practically hear Beau roll her eyes at the topic change.

"Quite well, all in all. You know, I'm glad it's me, Zia. I should like to think that you would be so kind as to use the freedom I helped you accomplish to be happy."

That little remark landed a bit like a slap. "Beau."

"I have to go. Dinner waits for no crown princess and future popper-outer of heirs. I love you, Zia. For who you are. Not what you can do."

"Beau."

But the line went dead, and Zia was forced to face too much of her sister's very smart words. Forced to face too many things she'd been ignoring. Yes, hoping something would come along to force her into a decision.

How utterly ridiculous for a woman who'd once fancied herself strong enough to run away from a powerful monarchy, hide away on a polar island, plan to raise her babies alone. She, who had whined about having no agency, no choice, was now…cowering in a castle? *Waiting*.

Hiding away from a man who said he loved her? Who wanted to *marry* her and raise their children, putting the children first. Not letting monarchies have any say.

Honestly, it was the most foolish thing, she could scarcely believe she'd fallen so far. Not quite sure what she was going to do about it, she marched out of her room and went in search of Cristhian.

She was shocked to find him not far away, in a room across the hall. Inside the room was…baby furniture. Two cribs. A bureau. She recognized all of it, because they were all she'd bookmarked on her phone.

He glanced up at her in the entry.

"I hope you don't mind me taking the liberty. I thought it best we have the furniture at the very least. Beau assured me you would like these items."

Leave it to Beau. "You're quite right," Zia managed though her throat had gone tight.

"I have some mock-ups of designs for decor. Apparently these things are meant to have themes. You can choose one or come up with your own." He walked over to her, held out his phone.

On the screen was a picture of a beautifully done nursery. It was football themed. She swiped through the pictures from there. Every design offered things they had discussed before. Colors and subjects she knew she'd told him she liked.

Because he listened. Because, and maybe she did not fully understand *why*, he must love her. None of this was the act of a man who did not care.

She knew she had feelings for him, but she'd been trying to keep them…safe. Controllable. Because loving someone, trusting someone, had always been so…transactional with her parents. With friends. And she knew she had nothing special to offer Cristhian.

Beau was the only relationship she'd ever had that felt real, and she'd chalked that up to being twins. And maybe, if she was going to be really honest with herself, she'd even turned that into a transaction. Her protecting Beau in order to earn her love.

No, she supposed it didn't take Psychology 101.

"I think I should like to get married," she said.

He stood very still, his eyes even narrowing a bit as he studied her. "Why?"

She wanted to laugh. It was, somehow, the perfect response.

"Cristhian… My whole life I only wanted someone to care about me…as a person. The way you have shown that to our children has always impressed me, but it isn't just that. You… You have taken *my* feelings into account. As though they matter."

"Of course they do."

"You say that as if you didn't spend the first part of our time here demanding what I should do."

"I suppose that's fair." He sighed, took the phone back and shoved it into his pocket before turning to face her. "And they do matter to me, Zia. They always will. I am not perfect. I suppose I have made and will make mistakes, but I will always fix them. Always."

And she knew that he would. Or at least try to. She had compared him to her father when she'd been angry at him, but her father's orders had never come from a place of care. They came from a place of wanting power.

That had never been Cristhian's way. Even when he'd been controlling, it had been…to make things right. A world safe for their family. In a strange way, it was not all that different from the way she'd acted to protect Beau. Because at the end of the day, she and Cristhian wanted the same things.

The same things.

"How about today?"

"Get married? Today?"

She nodded. "I don't want fanfare. I don't want…anything but us. Promising each other. Because that will be all that matters. As we raise these children together, much will change. But we will believe in our promises, and I think that will make everything okay."

He studied her for another moment. "Zia, I want to get married. I love you, but I want you to be certain. To be sure. I will marry you, if that's what you want, but there should be love. I have always trusted my grandparents' advice. And they have always said love is the foundation. We do not need to start with a ceremony. We can—"

"We started the second I laid eyes on you, and something inside me clicked…as if I knew. As if you were made exactly for me. And I have run from a lot in my life, but that certainty was the most confronting and frightening thing of all. Because I couldn't protect myself on it, or martyr myself to it. And so I have spent all these months trying to convince myself I am not worthy of it."

"Zia. You are beyond worthy."

She didn't know if she fully believed that just yet, but she had faith she would. Just as she had faith now that what she felt, what she had felt all along, was exactly this.

"I love you, Cristhian." And more than the past few days of wondering, she felt so certain now. Because he'd cataloged what he loved about her, and she could so easily do the same. "Your…heart. The way you take care. Even when you are being overbearing and ridiculously heavy-handed, it is only because you are trying to do what is right, and I know too well how hard that can be. Now we can try to do right, together. Maybe leaning on each other will make it less hard."

His mouth curved, and his smile was just like it had been at the bar that night. Charming, special, *for her*.

"I shall call the minister at once."

EPILOGUE

THEY WERE, IN FACT, married that day, with only staff members for an audience, and Cristhian's grandparents and Beau on a video call. The twins were born two weeks later, healthy and perfect.

They named their son after the best man Cristhian had ever known. The newly minted Harrison Sterling would be told of his namesake, but encouraged to live his own, best life. They named their daughter after the woman who had helped set them free. Begonia Sterling, Bee to her loved ones, to avoid confusion.

When Bee met her aunt and namesake for the first time, it was obvious the two would be lifelong friends. And that the Sterlings were in for it.

And when the twins were old enough, they all flew to America, to the same house Cristhian's grandparents had lived in since he'd been born. He was able to introduce his wife and children to the people who had given him everything, in a house he'd once visited with his own parents.

Grandma Connie, as she now insisted upon being called, cried as she held each little bundle. Pop couldn't stop marveling at their size, making sure to read to them every night of their visit.

Grandma Connie even let Zia help with dinner preparation. A great honor indeed.

"It is such a lovely home you have," Zia said, as she worked side by side in the small kitchen with his grandmother. She was beautiful and elegant always, a princess through and through. But she looked exactly right in his grandmother's kitchen.

He'd known she would.

"You grew up in a castle, dear," Grandmother said with a gentle scolding. "I'm sure this is nothing compared to that."

"A castle, yes. Not a home. I didn't have a home before Cristhian, before the children. And now I do, and much of that, I can tell, is thanks to you."

If his grandparents hadn't been willing to love her because he did before that, they certainly did now.

Both Zia and his grandmother looked over at where he sat helping his grandfather with a puzzle. And Cristhian knew that for the rest of his life, only the day Zia had married him and the birth of his children would hold a candle to this very moment in this place that meant so much to him.

Because the foundation of everything had started right here. With love. A love that he now got to pass down.

* * * * *

COMING SOON!

We really hope you enjoyed reading this book.
If you're looking for more romance
be sure to head to the shops when
new books are available on

Thursday 24th October

MILLS & BOON

MILLS & BOON ®

Coming next month

HUSBAND FOR THE HOLIDAYS
Dani Collins

In so many ways, this was her dream come true. Could she really complain if it wasn't exactly perfect? "Yes. I will marry you, Konstantin."

"Good." He slid the cool ring onto her finger, then looped his arms behind her.

Eloise's hands were on his lapels, quivering with pleasure at having this right to touch him.

She looked up at him, expecting him to kiss her, but he only caressed the edge of her jaw with his bent finger.

He dipped his head into her throat and nuzzled his lips against her skin.

She gasped and shivered. Her nipples stung and her knees grew weak.

His breath pooled near her ear, fanning the arousal taking hold in her. This was surreal. Too perfect. Like a Christmas miracle. Not that she believed in such things, but maybe it was?

Continue reading
HUSBAND FOR THE HOLIDAYS
Dani Collins

Available next month
millsandboon.co.uk

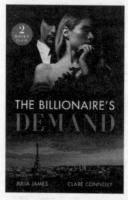
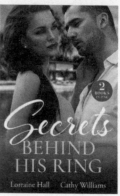

LET'S TALK
Romance

For exclusive extracts, competitions
and special offers, find us online:

f MillsandBoon

X @MillsandBoon

⊙ @MillsandBoonUK

♪ @MillsandBoonUK

Get in touch on 01413 063 232

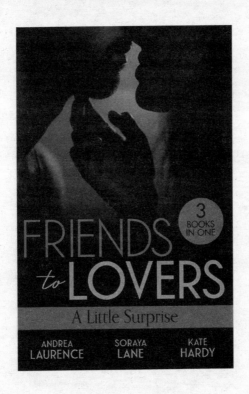

OUT NOW!

Available at
millsandboon.co.uk

MILLS & BOON

MILLS & BOON
A ROMANCE FOR EVERY READER

- **FREE** delivery direct to your door
- **EXCLUSIVE** offers every month
- **SAVE** up to 30% on pre-paid subscriptions

SUBSCRIBE AND SAVE

millsandboon.co.uk/Subscribe